The shining splendor of our Zebra Lovegram logo on the cover of this book reflects the glittering excellence of the story inside. Look for the Zebra Lovegram whenever you buy a historical romance. It's a trademark that guarantees the very best in quality and reading entertainment.

FORBIDDEN DESIRE

"Why are you staring at me?" she finally asked.

"Just wondering if it is as hard for you as it is for me to sit in the same room together without touching?"

She dropped her eyes to the book on her lap.

"Woman, you're incredible. I want you so bad I hurt."

"Then let me ease your pain," she whispered, leveling her gaze with his.

In no time, Will had swept her up in his arms. Bevin was so caught up in the moment she didn't give a second thought to slipping her arms around his neck and leaning against his chest as he climbed the stairs to his room.

He reached his room and nudged the door open with his foot. Bevin gazed up at him. Although the room was nearly dark, there was anticipation in the eyes that gazed back at her. He strode to the bed and set her down on the worn quilt. "I hope you realize that you won't be going anywhere for some time. . . ."

ROMANCE REIGNS
WITH ZEBRA BOOKS!

SILVER ROSE (2275, $3.95)
by Penelope Neri
Fleeing her lecherous boss, Silver Dupres disguised herself as a boy and joined an expedition to chart the wild Colorado River. But with one glance at Jesse Wilder, the explorers' rugged, towering scout, Silver knew she'd have to abandon her protective masquerade or else be consumed by her raging unfulfilled desire!

STARLIT ECSTASY (2134, $3.95)
by Phoebe Conn
Cold-hearted heiress Alicia Caldwell swore that Rafael Ramirez, San Francisco's most successful attorney, would never win her money . . . or her love. But before she could refuse him, she was shamelessly clasped against Rafael's muscular chest and hungrily matching his relentless ardor!

LOVING LIES (2034, $3.95)
by Penelope Neri
When she agreed to wed Joel McCaleb, Seraphina wanted nothing more than to gain her best friend's inheritance. But then she saw the virile stranger . . . and the green-eyed beauty knew she'd never be able to escape the rapture of his kiss and the sweet agony of his caress.

EMERALD FIRE (3193, $4.50)
by Phoebe Conn
When his brother died for loving gorgeous Bianca Antonelli, Evan Sinclair swore to find the killer by seducing the tempress who lured him to his death. But once the blond witch willingly surrendered all he sought, Evan's lust for revenge gave way to the desire for unrestrained rapture.

SEA JEWEL (3013, $4.50)
by Penelope Neri
Hot-tempered Alaric had long planned the humiliation of Freya, the daughter of the most hated foe. He'd make the wench from across the ocean his lowly bedchamber slave—but he never suspected she would become the mistress of his heart, his treasured SEA JEWEL.

Available wherever paperbacks are sold, or order direct from the Publisher. Send cover price plus 50¢ per copy for mailing and handling to Zebra Books, Dept. 3314, 475 Park Avenue South, New York, N.Y. 10016. Residents of New York, New Jersey and Pennsylvania must include sales tax. DO NOT SEND CASH.

MISSOURI FLAME

GWEN CLEARY

ZEBRA BOOKS
KENSINGTON PUBLISHING CORP.

This book is dedicated to my mom and dad.
  I love you . . .

I would like to offer special thanks to Meryl and Jean Price who were always there to help and share their expertise, which added intimate color and life to many of the details I have written about.

Thanks, Meryl and Jean

ZEBRA BOOKS

are published by

Kensington Publishing Corp.
475 Park Avenue South
New York, NY 10016

First printing: February, 1991

Printed in the United States of America

Chapter One

1874
Boston

Despite the pounding of her heart, Bevin O'Dea looked up at the judge and kept her face impassive while he shuffled through the mound of paperwork. If he discovered that she had altered the documents, she would never get away with it. She had to. She had no other choice. Her conscience would not allow her to stand by and accept the court's decision this time simply because the children's parents could not be bothered to make an appearance today.

Judge Spielman took off his spectacles and set them on top of the stack of papers. He studied the children's scrubbed faces. He counted a dozen sitting quietly behind the prim and proper child-welfare worker. Putting the glasses back on, he thumbed through a few more sheets.

Rubbing his jaw, he said, "Miss O'Dea, I must say I am surprised. I expected to see the parents present to swear their agreement with the disposition of these cases. This is highly irregular."

"Yes, your honor, it is. But I believe that everything

is in order."

"I know you are dedicated to your work for the Children's Aid Society, and have made a thorough investigation in these cases. But I find it difficult to believe that not one of these parents could be present before this court today."

Bevin threw a quick glance back at her friend and lawyer. Gregory Danson was sitting stiffly in the last row of the richly paneled courtroom, clutching a briefcase to his chest. From the look on his narrow face, she knew he would not come to her rescue if the judge discovered what she had done. Gregory had advised against it . . . warned her that she would face the court's wrath if found out. She had come this far; she could not back out now. The children deserved a chance in life, and for once she was in the perfect position to provide it.

"Your honor, I think the alternative presented to this court and agreed upon by the children's parents in writing is much more desirable than sending these children to a reformatory or workhouse because their parents failed to appear today. The children are helpless victims—"

"Not from what I read in their files," the judge answered gruffly.

"Sir, if you will only read the letters I have received from people as far away as Ohio, Indiana and Missouri offering to take in children like these," she lied, "I'm certain you will agree that their parents feel they are doing what's best for them by giving me guardianship until I can personally place them with loving families."

"Miss O'Dea, this court is well aware of the newspaper stories singing your praises for the work you've done on behalf of children who are in trouble with the law. And the court has no doubt of the validity of the letters or your concern. It is merely questioning the sagacity of such an undertaking."

While the man in the black robe and Miss O'Dea continued to discuss her plans for them, eight-year-old Johnny Martin's brown eyes glittered with mischief. No one was going to talk to Miss O'Dea that way and get away with it. His gaze shifted around the room. When he was sure no one was looking, he pulled out a wad of paper he kept in his pocket and chewed it into a gooey spitball. Taking careful aim, he lobbed it at the old codger giving Miss O'Dea such a hard time.

The wad hit its mark.

"Children!" Bevin screamed, swinging around to glare at the boy she instinctively knew was guilty. She had warned him to be good while she pleaded their cases. Moving quickly to get the children out of the judge's sight before he ruled against her recommendation, she offered, "I apologize, your honor. They are active youngsters. I think it might be wise if you allow Mr. Danson to take the children out of the courtroom. They have been sitting quietly for some time, sir."

The judge took out a handkerchief and wiped his face. "Yes, this court quite agrees. Mr. Danson, since you have accompanied Miss O'Dea and drew up the papers before this court this morning, I am going to hold you responsible for any mischief that occurs outside this courtroom while these cases are under advisement."

The judge's censuring gaze shifted to the children. "If this court hears of any more attacks while you are under its jurisdiction it will not hesitate to recommend incarceration rather than the solution set before this court today."

"What'd he say?" a scrawny boy of nine whispered to Johnny.

Johnny shrugged. "Who cares. All I know is if that man ain't nice to Miss O'Dea I'll go up there and kick

7

him in the shins next time."

The judge hid a smile at the child's protectiveness of Bevin O'Dea while she hurriedly ushered the children from the courtroom. During the five years that he had known the straitlaced redhead, he had never found her to be in need of protection.

Shaking his head, the judge again perused the children's histories and the charges leveled against them. All the documents Bevin O'Dea had submitted to the court seemed to be in order; she had seen to every legal detail. She was always thorough. It was apparent from the report she had filed that her recommendation might very well be the most expedient way to deal with those children. If anyone could take that lot in hand before they grew up to become hardened criminals, Bevin O'Dea could.

Out in the hallway it did not take Bevin long to ferret out the truth. Johnny admitted throwing the spitball but refused to go back inside the courtroom and apologize. Once she had reprimanded him and felt assured that there would be no further incidents, Bevin left Gregory and the children seated on a bench along the wall outside the door and slipped back into the courtroom to mollify the judge.

William Parrish Shoemaker pondered the wisdom of his decision to accept his inheritance all the way to the courthouse as he walked the two miles across town from his hotel to meet with the attorney and sign the necessary papers. He had been drifting around the country for so long without any responsibility that it seemed almost sacrilegious to become half owner of a plot of land now. Land tied one down, demanded that one set roots and live according to the dictates of the community. Will had been free of those restraints since leaving his stepfather's farm and wasn't sure he wanted to accept them now.

And it didn't make sense.

His stepfather never had considered him any more than excess baggage tied to his mother when the man had married her. Will had been grudgingly taken in to Straub's home and tolerated. Nothing more. Just tolerated . . . barely. Even the man's son by his first marriage had made it clear that Will was not welcome. So why would the old man leave him half the farm after all these years? Will wondered as he crossed the street to the courthouse. To ease a guilty conscience, no doubt.

Sadness banked Will's usual easy smile. Once he had left the farm, he had not gone back to see his mother before she died. It was one of life's regrets he had put in that corner of his mind where he stored the rest of the unhappiness he deemed to put behind him or deny. By accepting the inheritance, Will had made the difficult decision to deal with the past and finally lay it to rest.

Weighted down with old memories, Will trudged up the steps and went inside the courthouse. An attractive clerk sat behind a desk busily answering questions put to her. Will waited his turn, then said, "Mr. Gregory Danson left word for me to meet him here—"

"Oh yes, sir. Mr. Danson told me to expect you. The clerk from his office described you perfectly," she tittered. "Tall, black wavy hair and handsome." When the man did not respond, she sobered and directed, "Mr. Danson is on the second floor observing the proceedings in Judge Spielman's court. The third door to your left at the top of the stairs."

She beamed him a sultry smile. Will had a way with the ladies and seldom missed an opportunity to enjoy their company. But today he had more pressing matters on his mind.

"Thank you."

Will took the stairs two at a time. There was no use delaying it any longer. He already had kept the man waiting six months after receiving word through a cousin that half the farm was his.

Ignoring the passel of children and the harried man trying to keep them under control, Will was about to enter Judge Spielman's court when a raspy voice assailed him.

"You can't go in there now. Miss O'Dea and the judge are deciding the future of these children."

Will looked at the kids. A boy stuck his tongue out at him. Another screwed up his face, then turned back to argue with a little girl. Will was set to turn his attention back to the man when out of the corner of his eye he caught sight of a spitball hurtling his way.

He dodged it.

"Johnny Martin, go pick that paper up and get back to your seat. And I do not want to have to speak to you again."

"I ain't gonna pick nothing up for you," the freckle-faced kid returned.

Will sent the child a piercing look and said menacingly, "Do as the man says and I'll forget what you intended."

Johnny blanched. The big stranger looked like he meant business. Johnny limped over to the wad and retrieved it. "You ain't so tough," he grumbled as he sat back down.

"You aiming to find out, son?" Will said. Seeing the boy's built-up shoe, Will's expression softened.

"I ain't your son. You big dummy," Johnny sneered.

"I apologize for him," Gregory said, sending the glowering boy a silencing look.

"No doubt the judge is deciding which reformatory to send him to," Will said to the man.

"No doubt," Gregory repeated. The stranger was

closer to the truth than he realized. "Miss O'Dea should not be much longer, if you do not mind waiting outside here with us."

"With you . . . maybe. But not with that pack. Don't worry, I won't disturb the proceedings. I need to see Mr. Danson, who left word he would be inside."

"I'm Danson." The man of medium build rose and offered his hand.

"Will Shoemaker. You have some papers for me to sign?"

"Yes. Your stepbrother hired my firm since you have a cousin near Boston, and he knew you two kept in touch. He wants everything legal. Hear you were out prospecting in Colorado Territory."

Despite Danson's expectant gaze, Will did not offer an explanation.

While the two men talked and dumb old Danson had the other man sign some papers, Johnny sat there and sulked. The man had gotten the better of him, and Johnny didn't like it. He was still fuming when the men concluded their business and the giant stranger headed back down the stairs. An idea flickered into his head when he caught sight of a pail and mop at the end of the corridor.

Johnny raised his hand. "Mr. Danson, I got to go."

"Can't you wait?"

"No, sir," he answered urgently, "I can't."

"I can't take all of you."

"I won't get lost. The washroom is just down the hall. You can watch me to the door, if you're afraid I'll try to sneak away."

"I am not afraid," Gregory protested, knowing that the little scamp was testing him. He would be relieved when Bevin returned and took them off his hands. "Go ahead."

Gregory closely watched Johnny half skip and half

11

limp down the hall and disappear into the washroom, and then directed his attention to yet another squabble.

Will stuffed the papers into his coat pocket and smoothed his hair back before he left the courthouse. He was glad it had been so painless. Danson did not question why he had waited so long to claim his inheritance after being notified. If anything, it seemed that the man was so preoccupied with those motley children that all he wanted to do was get Will's signature and be done with it. It was no wonder, Will figured. That unruly horde was enough to rattle a nun. He was thankful he did not have to have any further dealings with such a handful.

Will held the door open for two finely dressed ladies and followed them outside. The day was warm in a cloudless sky. He stopped to look at his watch. He had plenty of time to return to the hotel before he had to check out.

He had not taken four steps before a sudden deluge of soapy water soaked him clean through.

"What the hell!" he sputtered and looked up to see where the cascade had come from.

There, leaning out the second-story window above him was the little monster who had thrown a spitball at him only moments ago.

And the little devil was grinning.

Chapter Two

Bevin breathed a silent sigh of relief. She had to force herself from crying out with joy and throwing her arms around the gruff juror's neck; a proper lady did not behave in such a manner. Judge Spielman had not made it easy, but he approved her recommendations despite the absentee parents. The children were now legally in her care.

"Thank you, your honor," Bevin said.

Judge Spielman cleared his throat. He was not a man of emotion. "No need. I am glad the court could help. Danson told me that this is your last official duty for the Society. He said you are going to Missouri to marry a farmer you have never met."

"I know Benjamin through his letters. He helped me locate my brother Patrick."

"We are all happy you have finally found the brother you have been searching for for so long. But your leaving is going to be a great loss, young lady."

"Thank you, your honor," she said again. "I consider myself to be the fortunate one," she added, then said no more since she feared she might slip and inadvertently unmask her duplicity before the court.

"Do not forget to see that the necessary paperwork is filled out as you place those children."

"I won't neglect my duty."

"Good luck to you, Miss O'Dea. No doubt you will need it in placing that one boy." The judge shook his head at the thought of the crippled child with nerve enough to throw that wad at him. "This court still cannot understand why you are taking that one little girl along; she is hardly more than a baby and could easily be placed locally. She is not like the rest of those street urchins."

"Crissy is Johnny's sister. I would like to keep them together if possible. Unlike the others, they do not have any family."

"Yes, well . . ." His voice trailed off. He struck his gavel against the bench. "This court stands in recess."

Bevin watched the man leave the courtroom. She did it! The judge had not caught her! The children were not going to be locked up and eventually returned to parents either too drunk or worn out to care about them enough to come to the court and attest that they agreed with her recommendations, as was the usual procedure. And Johnny and Crissy no longer would be used by that dreadful man to thieve on the streets for their existence.

Bevin was picking up her notes and packing them away in her case when the children filed into the courtroom, followed by Gregory.

"Oh, Gregory," she said, folding her gloved hands over her heart. "Thank you. We did it!"

Just as quick as she was to express her appreciation, she seemed to forget Gregory's existence and called the children around her to give them the good news. He watched her laugh and hug those grubby street urchins. At twenty-five she was considered an old maid by most and dressed like one. But she had kept to her goal. She had turned down all offers of marriage until she located her brother. She was a hard worker, a loyal friend, and

14

a steadfast supporter of the persecuted. As he quietly retreated from the touching scene, he regretted her leaving and the loss of their friendship.

Will stormed back into the courthouse. As he pounded up the stairs he wasn't sure whether he would demand that the kid's parents pay to have his clothes laundered, or simply grab that ruffian by the seat of the pants and give him a good walloping.

Outside the courtroom he ran into the attorney. "Where are those little monsters?" Will demanded.

Gregory gave Shoemaker a cursory examination and groaned inside. Johnny. Gregory knew he should not have let that child go to the washroom unchaperoned. "Are you all right?"

"Do I look all right?"

At the vehemence in Shoemaker's voice, Gregory stammered, "Well . . . no. Ah—"

"Just tell me where that kid is."

"Inside the courtroom . . . with Miss O'Dea," Gregory croaked and hurried from the man's sight. He wanted no part of the confrontation he knew was coming. Will Shoemaker was furious; he had good reason to be. Bevin was too emotionally involved with Johnny for her own good, and undoubtedly would not listen to anything Shoemaker had to say. Gregory rushed down the stairs. He had no intention of being within earshot when that pair came face-to-face.

The door to the courtroom crashed open with a loud bang, snapping Bevin's attention from the children to the rear of the room.

"May I help you?" she asked the strange man stomping toward her.

Will stopped directly in front of the lady and narrowed his eyes. "Only if you have a paddle."

Johnny ducked behind Bevin's skirts and stood there quietly. The other children giggled and took up positions behind Johnny.

"I beg your pardon," Bevin bristled, thinning her lips into a tight line.

"As you just as well might," Will returned.

He got a good look at the lady the attorney had called Bevin O'Dea. He enjoyed a pretty face and tiny waist. He had always found that a smile brightened the appearance and increased the attraction of even the homeliest female.

But that woman looked like she had been sucking on a lemon!

Her stiff stance caused him to refrain from further comment for a moment and stare at her. Despite his first assessment there was something about her that caught his attention and stopped him cold from grabbing the little hoodlum. She possessed an aura of strength and maturity. Will admired that in a woman; he had little use for young, tittering females.

Bevin lifted her chin to look into brown eyes which sparked fire and a most pleasant face set in stone. The man stood rigid, his broad shoulders squared, his hands balled into fists against lean hips.

And he was soaking wet!

"If you are quite through gawking, I suggest you tell me what your problem seems to be. Other than, of course, that you are in need of a change of clothing."

"Which is exactly why I'm here now, instead of enjoying a pleasant dinner somewhere far away."

"I hardly see how that concerns me."

"It *concerns* you because that brat hiding behind your skirts is responsible for my soggy condition."

Affronted by his selection of terms, she drew herself up to her full height. Even so, she barely reached his shoulders. "I am afraid, mister—"

16

"Shoemaker. Will Shoemaker . . . Miss O'Dea." At her look of shock, he added, "That incompetent attorney you had watching that bunch of ruffians told me who you are."

Bevin glanced back at Johnny; he stood angelically still, his big eyes saucered with innocence. The other children looked to be just as confused by the man as was she. "As I had begun to say, I am afraid that whatever is troubling you, Mr. Shoemaker, has nothing to do with my children. And they are not ruffians!"

"Your children?"

"They are in my care. I am responsible for them."

"Then you can pay to have my clothes laundered, because that devil in sheepskin just dumped a pail of dirty water over my head from a second-story window as I was leaving the building."

"I did not!" Johnny spat as another round of giggles erupted from the other children.

Bevin studied the boy. He could be impetuous and given to pranks. But he would not deliberately drench some total stranger. There was no cause for him to do it.

"I do not know what your motives are for accusing Johnny. But I can assure you that you are mistaken in your identification, if indeed some child is responsible for your condition. So I suggest you seek redress elsewhere."

Will rolled his eyes in defeat. The sourpuss was not about to admit that *her children,* as she called them, were capable of such a deed. Why he had the fleeting thought that under other circumstances he might have been attracted to her, he could not fathom. How wrong could a man be? He admired strength in a woman, not mule-headed stubbornness. And all that one needed was a harness!

Totally exasperated and fighting to keep his temper

17

under control, he grated out, "First the kid throws a spitball at me outside the courtroom, then dumps water over my head after I leave the building. Lady, if you don't know what kind of miniature terror you have on your hands and refuse to listen when someone tries to point it out to you, then you deserve to reap whatever havoc that one sows."

He spun on his heel and sloshed from the room.

Bevin watched the man leave, flinching when he slammed the door. "Johnny, are you sure you know nothing about what happened to Mr. Shoemaker?" she questioned. "And what about the spitball?"

"I threw the spitball. But I wouldn't dump no water on nobody," he said in his most innocent voice, wide-eyed. "You believe me, don't you, Miss O'Dea?"

"Yes, dear. I know you would never do such a thing." She patted Johnny on the head, then directed, "All right, children, we shall wait five minutes to make sure that terrible man is gone and then go back to the Society. As soon as I can make the necessary arrangements we will be leaving Boston."

Sighting Bevin come out of the courthouse, Prudence Truesdale leaped from the bench where she had been instructed to wait and rushed over to Bevin. "Oh, Evvie, Gregory told me the judge made you the children's guardian. You are so clever. I wish I would have thought of writing those letters and—"

"Hush, Prudence!"

Prudence looked around. "I am sorry, Evvie. I suppose I did not think. I wish I were like you. You are so capable and smart."

"Capable, perhaps. But only time will tell if I have been smart."

"Oh, but you are," the petite girl gushed. "You are. I am glad you had me wait outside. I never would have had the nerve to do what you did."

18

"Yes, well, let's get the children back to the Society. Line up in pairs, children."

Prudence proudly took up her position beside Bevin at the front of the line. She was smaller and shorter than Bevin, but always felt that she walked taller when she was around Bevin O'Dea. Bevin made her feel important and useful, and treated her as if she were an equal. Bevin knew she cared about the work they did, and appreciated her for it. When she was with Bevin, Prudence didn't feel like just another empty-headed heiress forced by her parents to volunteer her time so she would appear concerned about how the less fortunate lived.

Prudence thought how she had begged to accompany Bevin to Missouri. At first Bevin had refused, but finally relented after Prudence promised to continue Bevin's work when she returned to Boston.

"Evvie, do you see that man glaring at us from across the street? He came out of the courthouse shortly before you did. He looked to be awfully angry about something. And he was all wet!"

"Yes, I know. That must be Mr. Shoemaker," Bevin said, keeping her nose pointed in the direction of the Society. "Don't stare at him, Prudence. You will only encourage the man. He accused Johnny of dumping a pail of dirty water over his head as he left the building."

"I did not see Johnny do such a thing. And I was waiting right where you instructed."

"I thought as much. Ignore him," Bevin directed. Will Shoemaker was a most unpleasant sort. She was thankful that her fiancé was nothing like Mr. Shoemaker. From Benjamin's letters she knew that he was a man of honor who did not suffer from temper outbursts. She could not abide a man who did, although she could not help from stealing a sideways glance at the big, handsome man leaning stiffly against a lamp

19

pole.

Bevin stepped up the pace. The sooner the arrangements were made and they were on their way, the sooner the children would be settled; the sooner she would be reunited with her brother and begin married life. And she was confident that once they left the big city behind she would never again have to be subjected to men like Will Shoemaker.

Chapter Three

Bevin stood on the platform outside the train's drawing-room car and inhaled the warm fall air. The air smelled fresh and clean, not like the stale air of the city. As the train sped along the tracks, the picturesque hills sprinkled with dark pines seemed to fly by. Taking in the changing landscape, her breast filled with excitement.

She still had trouble believing it. After fifteen years of searching she had finally located her brother and was on her way to Missouri to begin a new life. Before she could continue her musings the door opened and a squeaky, high-pitched voice assailed her.

"Evvie, you must come at once!" implored Prudence, cradling her pale cheeks in tiny hands. "That . . . that awful man has hold of one of the children again."

Bevin stiffened her spine and sucked in a breath. "Well, this time I am not going to stand meekly by and tolerate that man's unconscionable behavior!"

Passing her coworker, Bevin purposefully strode back inside. Her features thinned into a taut line of rising ire as she headed toward the giant of a man stomping down the aisle toward her.

This was the second time this morning, since that horrid person from the courthouse had boarded the train, that he had hold of one of the children in her care. Only this time he had one of her charges by the scruff of the neck! Well, despite the sharp words they had already exchanged twice, she would not permit him to get away with it again!

What kind of man would use undue force against a mere child? Bevin considered. Certainly, only the worst sort would manhandle a young lad. Why that man outweighed the struggling boy by way over twice, more than likely, close to three times. Scrawny arms fought against the muscular strength of a man who towered over the lad straining just to reach the man's rib cage.

The train jarred, slamming Bevin into one of the seats with a jolt. The wind temporarily knocked out of her, she grabbed her midriff with a small, gloved hand and inhaled several times to catch her breath.

She would not remain bested by an iron horse, much less a man the size of one!

Back to her feet, she squared her shoulders encased in a starched white blouse tied high at the neck, straightened her flowered hat, and hastened to put a stop to such an outrage.

Eleven children of assorted shapes and sizes had scrambled from their seats when they sighted one of their own under apparent siege and were bearing down on the duo now standing in the center of the aisle. From the determined looks on their little faces, Bevin knew the situation would become a melee if she did not stop them immediately.

"You children," Bevin announced in an authoritative voice which brooked no dissent, "go back to your seats at once. And do not leave them until I say you may."

The children stopped and turned wide eyes to their guardian.

"Yes, ma'am," they chorused and climbed back into their respective spots.

Ignoring gaping looks and behind-the-hand snickers of her overawed charges and an assortment of bemused passengers, Bevin stepped in between that insufferable man and the boy. She had no intention of shirking her duty regardless of the disparity in size between herself and the big man.

"Do be careful, Evvie," called out Prudence, halting a safe distance from the budding fray. A young girl darted from her seat and Prudence caught her up, restraining the pigtailed child in front of her as if the five-year-old were a shield.

The swirl of her protective instincts wrapping her in a wave of flapping effrontery, Bevin raised her chin to stare into the eyes of the towering male brute.

"If you do not liberate that poor misunderstood waif this moment, Mr. Shoemaker, I am quite prepared to lodge a protest with the conductor this time and seek your removal from the train."

The grubby little urchin tried to twist out of his grip, but Will caught him before he could escape. Will held fast to the fighting youth's arm with an easy grasp of his big callused hand. A slow insolent grin—despite the throbbing in his shin from that *poor, misunderstood waif's* boot—spread to his lips. " 'Fraid I can't do that this time, Miss O'Dea."

Bevin had been ready to outface the man if necessary, but his blatant refusal momentarily took her by surprise. "What do you mean, you can't do that?" she demanded once she had recovered herself.

"Simple. Until this thief-in-miniature returns my property—"

"Your property?" she parroted with an air of registered aspersion at the negative reference to the child.

"As I was saying, until this midget footpad returns my money clip, I intend to keep him in custody." To her huff of disbelief, he added, "And if I don't get it back right quick, ma'am, I may be the one to hail the conductor."

Bevin's hand flew to her throat at yet another grossly heralded accusation. "And by what authority have you become the law, sir?"

Will gave a harsh laugh. "By the authority that this little scamp and his gang of ruffians have been taking turns harassing me since I had the misfortune to be exposed to them at the courthouse back in Boston."

Bevin looked down at the freckle-faced Johnny Martin. Those big, innocent brown eyes stared back at her, silently beseeching her to defend him.

Johnny looked so like her remembrances of her own younger brother Patrick, before he had been swept from the streets of Boston where she and Patrick as children had been forced to live after their immigrant parents' deaths. The thought that her brother may have suffered a similar circumstance gave Bevin added purpose to carry the child's banner.

Her gaze shifted back to the big man, who, to her further chagrin, now had a disgusting smile dazzling his teeth. How dare he stand there so nonchalant as if he were the innocent victim, no less! Well, at least he wasn't losing his temper this time.

"You may summon the conductor then, Mr. Shoemaker. I have no doubt he will know how to deal with such a clearly unmistakable error of poor judgment on your part."

Will had to laugh out loud at her candor. If nothing else, he had to give her credit for her nerve. She was not about to back down.

"Irish, aren't you?"

"What if I am, Mr. Shoemaker?"

"I thought so when I first laid eyes on you back in the courtroom."

Heat rose up her cheeks at his mention of noticing

her. "I suppose my name had nothing to do with your astute powers of observation."

She was trying to rattle him again with that cool exterior. It wasn't going to work any longer. He'd always had an easygoing way about him, and despite how mad she managed to make him, he wasn't going to show it.

He grinned. "I would have recognized a colleen with that flaming red hair and freckled nose anywhere."

The insufferable man was trying to charm her; she would have none it! Yet her cheeks darkened further despite her resolve, and she unconsciously fingered an escaping curl at the nape of her neck. Catching herself, she snapped her hands down to her sides. "My heritage and appearance are none of your concern."

"Guess with all a soft lady such as yourself has got to contend with, that fit of overworked temper of yours can only be considered an unmistakable error of poor judgment on your part, Miss O'Dea," he drawled, beginning to enjoy having the upper hand.

Bevin's entire face turned the color of her hair at his parody of her comment on his observational abilities, and her blue eyes snapped fire. Forcing herself to ignore the urge to make further mention of his incensing remarks, she said with deliberation, "Are you going to release that child immediately or not?"

"Once I get my property back I shall be more than happy to relinquish any claim I have now or in the future to this young precedent for criminal proceedings."

Bevin steamed inside her corset. From the look of the sizable man — his dark features set in an unbending line — Bevin knew she would not be able to disengage the squirming child without help.

"Very well, Mr. Shoemaker, I can see I am not getting anywhere trying to reason with your sense of honor as a gentleman. Therefore, I shall have Miss Truesdale fetch the conductor." Her lips tight, Bevin turned and instructed, "Prudence, hurry along and inform the conductor that we have a most pressing problem here which requires his immediate attention."

Her eyes blinking in beat with her racing heart, Prudence grasped her throat. Uncertain whether to leave Bevin to face the man alone, Prudence hesitated. But at Bevin's silent nod toward the door Prudence set the little girl she had been restraining back in her seat, then spun around and fled into the next car.

"Do not worry, Johnny," Bevin consoled the youngster. "This unfortunate matter shall be cleared up shortly."

Long moments stretched taunt while the threesome waited. Bevin's color continued to heighten under Mr. Shoemaker's open assessment. Yet she kept her angry gaze affixed to his. She would not give him the satisfaction of breaking her line of vision, despite the knot of tension tightening at the back of her neck.

Will returned the lady's icy glare. After the earlier confrontations he'd had with her over those unruly children, he could not afford to let go of the little urchin or he'd never get his money clip back. The sticky-fingered beggar, no doubt, would stash the piece and Will would be out his last twenty dollars. Despite his rising ire he wasn't losing his humor this time, and he could not help but smile to himself; he, too, had been considered quite a handful as a boy.

Will's attention whipped toward the front of the car when the portly conductor, decked out in brass buttons, strutted into the coach, trailed by the retiring, birdlike young lady accompanying Miss O'Dea and her horde.

Liam Halsley tapped the big man on the shoulder, prepared to demand that the passenger let go of the child at once. But when the tall, black-haired man turned full on toward Liam his face lit up and relief and surprise relaxed his features.

"Will Shoemaker? Is it really you?" Liam astounded.

"Yes, Liam."

"By God, folks never thought you'd return."

"Well, I guess they were wrong."

Bevin impatiently listened to the cordial exchange until she could not take any more. She had not called forth the conductor to be ignored while they enjoyed a reunion.

"Sir, I must protest. You were summoned to resolve the difficulty I am having with this unreasonable man."

The men ceased their conversation and looked down at the lady.

"Beg your pardon, ma'am," Liam rasped, having been forced to remember his duty.

"The name is Miss O'Dea."

Liam tipped his hat in more of a gesture of coming to attention for inspection rather than in one of respect. "What can I do for you, *Miss* O'Dea?"

Losing what was left of her patience, Bevin said hotly, "I requested your presence here to demand that . . . that man" — she pointed an accusing finger at Mr. Shoemaker — "relinquish his hold on this poor, innocent child. As you know, I am responsible for these children and I will not . . . I repeat . . . I will *not* tolerate anyone harassing one of them. That man has been harassing us since we had the misfortune to be at the courthouse in Boston at the same time."

"Harassing?" Will choked out, incredulous.

She glared at him. "That is what I said, Mr. Shoemaker." The conductor cleared his throat. "Will, 'fraid I got to ask you to explain what's going on here. It's my job, you know."

"This little terror threw a spitball at me, dumped a pail of water over my head, sent his cronies to bother me, and now has stolen my money clip, Liam. And I'm not letting go of him until he returns it."

"That accusation is totally unwarranted!" croaked Bevin, outraged as much by the devil-may-care expression on that ruffian's handsome face as she was by the conductor's lack of attention to his duty.

"In that case you shouldn't mind having this *innocent child* empty his pockets," Will said, grinning down at the little lady. It gave him a feeling of satisfaction to see her lose her stiff poise. Bevin O'Dea wasn't all ice after all.

Will's momentary inattention to his captive gave Johnny the opportunity he had been waiting for. The slender child wiggled free and swung his foot back to deliver a well-placed blow, but as he angled his body a shiny gold metal piece clattered to the floor.

Johnny made a grab for it; Will was quicker. He reached down and snatched it up before the boy could hide the evidence.

"Give that back! It's mine," cried Johnny, grabbing for the item securing half a dozen bills. "It belonged to my pa. He gived it to me before he went away."

Shock registered on Bevin's face before she quickly composed herself to address the conductor. "Sir, Johnny is an honest child—"

"Hah! Then why did he lie about what he did to me and then steal my money clip?"

"It is your word against Johnny's. And I am rather inclined to believe the boy," she defended him, although her faith in the child had sagged.

Will turned over the antique gold clip. The engraved swirls W.P.S. sparkled in bold letters across the length of the valuable money clip.

Bevin's face fell.

Will cocked a brow at the boy. "Now, unless your name is William Parrish Shoemaker or you have the same initials, you have some explaining to do. What do you have to say for yourself this time?"

"I didn't do it," Johnny wailed and, breaking free,

scurried behind Miss O'Dea's skirts.

"There must be some mistake," Bevin said weakly, still wanting to believe that Johnny was the innocent victim in all this.

"Yeah, the mistake is that that kid seems to make a habit out of hiding behind your skirts whenever he gets into trouble," Will grumbled. Triumph penned a lop-sided grin on his full lips. "Perhaps you will give more consideration to whom¯ you believe next time some-thing like this happens."

"You want to press charges, Will?" the conductor in-quired after sending Bevin an intimidating look.

"We'll let it go this time, Liam. But the little scamp ought to be taken out behind the woodshed and taught a good lesson."

Bevin bristled at the implication.

"Consider yourself fortunate, Miss O'Dea. Mr. Shoemaker is being mighty generous under the circum-stances. You'd be well-advised to keep a closer watch over those children for the rest of the trip. I'll not have further trouble on my train," the conductor warned.

Bevin stung under the conductor's chastisement, and she stiffened. "You needn't worry, sir," she said tone-lessly. She took Johnny Martin by the hand and sent the child a look that bespoke her intention to give the boy a talking to. "There will be no further incidents as long as Mr. Shoemaker does not decide to take matters into his own hands again."

Will raised his palms. "You needn't worry about me, Miss O'Dea. I have no desire to have any further con-tact with your *poor, innocent children.*"

"I suppose it's settled then," Liam offered, glad to be done with the whole affair so he could get back to more important matters.

"Suppose it is." A lazy smile still spreading his lips, Will touched long slender fingers to his broad-brimmed hat. "Ma'am."

Too humiliated, Bevin stiffled a scathing retort and stood watching the man stroll—bigger than life—toward the front of the car. Engaged in companionable conversation with the conductor, Will Shoemaker opened the door to the next car and disappeared after the unsympathetic railway employee.

Chapter Four

The confrontation over and the men gone, Prudence stepped up to Bevin and Johnny, her eyes wide in a pale, diminutive face, which matched the rest of the petite blonde. Picking at her nails, she dropped her gaze and cleared her throat.

"I—I am sorry, Evvie. I should have kept a closer watch over the children."

"No, Pru. They are my responsibility. Henceforth, I shall remain inside the car. I am afraid I was wool-gathering out on the platform longer than I should have been."

"Thank you for being so kind. But I shall not let the children venture into the next car again. I promise."

Bevin patted Prudence's shoulder in a gesture of sympathy. Prudence Truesdale had a good heart and tried ever so hard. Try as she did though, Prudence just could not seem to manage the group of youths, some not that much younger than her own seventeen years. Sometimes Bevin questioned why she had let Prudence talk her into helping place these particular children. Of course she knew it was because she was not returning to Boston, and it was important to Prudence.

Johnny twitched, which recalled Bevin's attention to the mischievous child standing at her side. A frown settled across her brow. "I think it is time you tell me the truth, young man. The whole truth."

Johnny hung his head, but watched her from beneath his long, curly lashes. "Yessum, Miss O'Dea."

"Come. We'll sit over there." She motioned to a seat away from the other children intently watching from the edges of their benches.

Once Bevin and Prudence settled across from the slender child, the other children left their positions in mass and converged on them.

"You gonna tan Johnny's backside for lying all those times?" asked one bright-eyed girl of nine, who had been caught picking a man's pocket to help pay for her no-account father's liquor; therefore, her presence among the group.

"Tara, you and the rest of the children need to return to your seats and wait for Miss Prudence to take you to the washroom, so you can get cleaned up before we reach the next stop."

"But we wanna know what's gonna happen to Johnny," she complained in a whiny, little-girl voice, shuffling her foot back and forth against the floorboards.

Bevin gave the girl one of her daunting looks, which caused the child to shrug her thin shoulders in defeat and lead the others back to their places. Then she turned to Prudence. She should have known when she questioned Prudence that her coworker would not have seen the incident with the water back at the courthouse. Prudence Truesdale was oblivious to most things that went on around her.

"Pru, while I speak with Johnny, please see that the children are squeaky clean before we reach the next town. And be sure to check behind their ears," Bevin instructed as Prudence jumped to her feet. "Last time I looked several of the younger ones had potato patches growing back there."

Prudence suppressed a grin while the children giggled and cupped their ears, exchanging guilty looks with one another. Prudence winked at Bevin before heading toward the two worst offenders. Bevin O'Dea had such an easy way with difficult children and Prudence silently wished that she, too, could deal with them so effortlessly.

Bevin watched Prudence for a moment, then turned back to Johnny. She took both of his sweaty little hands in hers. "Johnny, I know it's been difficult in the past for you, having to take care of your little sister and all. And I know that sometimes you took things that did not belong to you just to survive—"

"I found that dumb old money clip on the floor. I didn't steal it. I didn't!" he burst out, tears cascading down his hollow cheeks. "Besides, how would you know what it's like not having a ma and pa?"

Her heart aching for the poor discarded child, Bevin gathered the boy into her arms and cradled his head against her shoulder. Rocking him, she soothed, "I do know. I do."

Images of the packing crate, which had been her childhood home after her parents' deaths, rose ghostlike before her eyes. Bevin had to blink several times to keep the haunting visions from her mind's eye.

Once the child had calmed, she said, "Johnny, you no longer have to worry about having enough food or a place to sleep. And no one is ever going to force you to steal or lie again; the man who did is in prison now.

"Soon you and your sister will have a mother and father who will take care of you. So I want you to promise me you won't tell any more stories or play any more pranks on people. And you must not find any more property that might belong to someone else either, especially Mr. Shoemaker. All right?"

With an embarrassed shrug that he'd been found out, Johnny wiped his runny nose on his sleeve and sniffled halfheartedly, "Okay. Me and the others'll try."

"Don't forget, I want you to stay away from Mr. Shoemaker," she reiterated.

Johnny nodded, but a calculating glitter in his eyes warned Bevin that she would have to keep watch over him. He had spent too many years on the streets and was not used to accepting society's limits to meekly comply now.

"Run along and join the others with Miss Prudence. We'll be stopping soon, and I want you to look your best."

The train chugged into the pleasant, wood-hued depot promptly at ten fifteen, its whistle alerting the citizenry of Ashland, Ohio, of its arrival. Bevin glanced out the window in time to see Mr. Shoemaker saunter down the ramp, his hands in his jacket pockets, as if he owned the town. The bright sun shone on his black hair, lending it a blue cast; his shadow stretched out close to ten feet away from him, reminding her how he had towered over her own height.

She watched him disappear around the corner of the station. Perhaps the man had decided to remain here and would not be continuing his journey. It certainly would solve one of her problems. She had enough on her mind without having to worry about one of the children accidentally crossing that man's path again.

"We are all ready, Evvie," Prudence said, redirecting Bevin's attention. "New clothes and all."

Bevin looked up. Standing in front of their seats, twelve shining faces beamed back at her. "Hands out. Let's make sure there are no dirty fingernails."

Prudence stood by the eldest child, proud of her efforts as Bevin made her inspection, checking hands and ears. "Good job. Looks like everyone has passed this time," Bevin pronounced.

They waited until the other passengers had left the train, then lined up. Single file they headed toward the courthouse not far from the train station according to their directions.

"Look at all the people waiting for us," Prudence squealed at the milling clusters.

"Yes, the ad we wired to the newspaper from the last town has brought out quite a crowd."

The corners of Prudence's mouth drooped. "You mean that you wired."

"This is a joint effort, Pru. Our success depends on both of us. I only hope that we are finally able to place some of the children."

"Oh, Evvie, you do not have to give me any credit. I am just happy to be here as your assistant. I just wish you were returning to Boston with me."

"I know you do. I've trained you well, though. You'll be able to carry on this important work in my place. You know how long I have searched for my brother."

"Yes, but to accept the proposal of a man you have never met so you can be close to your brother. I'm afraid I find that too adventuresome for me, becoming a wife to someone I don't even know."

"Benjamin is not exactly a stranger. We have corresponded for nearly a year. From his letters I know that he is a good man, kind and honest and forthright. And he helped me locate Patrick. I am most happy and honored to become his wife, and not only so I can be close to my brother."

"What about love?"

"Pru, I do love Benjamin. There are many kinds of love. I love him in a way that in a few years you'll come to understand."

Prudence scratched her head, still unable to comprehend how Bevin could possibly marry a stranger. "Yes, I suppose I shall."

The five-year-old girl whimpered, causing Bevin to put an end to her conversation with Prudence and tuck the child into her arm.

"I'm scared," the little girl cried, looking around for her older brother.

Bevin kneeled down and wiped her tears. "It's okay Crissy. It'll be all right. These caring people are here to give you a family. Won't it be nice to have a home of your own with your own mommy and daddy?"

Crissy rubbed her eyes. Sucking her thumb, she garbled in a tiny voice, "I guess so."

The entourage claimed the steps to the courthouse and lined up. Across the street, Will leaned against the trunk of a gnarled tree watching with fascination as Miss O'Dea personally hovered over each child before introducing them one at a time to the people gathered around them.

"What's going on over there?" Will asked a plain-dressed man, woman and child heading in the direction of the crowd.

"Them's children brung out from back East to be parceled out." The man dug in his pocket and handed Will a crumpled newspaper clipping. "Here. Read it for yourself, mister. We got to hurry. Aim to get my Erastus here a brother to help out with the work on the farm."

"Ah geez, Pa. Can't I have a little sister?" the gangly young boy begged. "Ma and me both want a girl. Please."

Will stared after the family before he read the advertisement. So Miss Bevin O'Dea worked for the Boston Children's Aid Society as a child-welfare worker. And she hoped to place those miniature street hoodlums with poor, unsuspecting farm families. She had a hel-luva lot of nerve, he thought. Then he had to admit that he had admired her strength the first time he saw her.

His attention caught at the whimpering little girl standing on the steps for inspection, and he felt a stab of pity. He had overheard that her only crime was being the sister to that miniature hoodlum. Softening, he thought how it had to be difficult for those kids being picked over like sales merchandise.

He watched for a time, fascinated and disturbed by the way folks so easily went from one frightened child to the next, looking them over as if they were buying a work horse. Then he tucked the wrinkled sheet of paper in his pocket and strolled back toward the train.

"Isn't that Mr. Shoemaker?" Prudence observed, pulling Bevin off to the side.

"So it seems," Bevin answered absently.

Prudence gave a nervous giggle. "He certainly is a handsome man . . . wet or dry."

"I hadn't noticed."

"Of course you hadn't," Prudence said, her voice filled with disbelief.

Bevin puffed out a breath.

"Too bad he is so mean," Prudence added.

"He was angry. That doesn't make him a mean man, Pru. Furthermore, as it turned out, Mr. Shoemaker was telling the truth all along."

"I'm surprised at you, Evvie, defending the man after the way he treated the children."

Bevin shook her head at Prudence's simple logic, then returned her attention to the children. At last two of the older boys were selected. She had begun to think that no one was going to give them a chance. A loud wail captured her attention.

"Prudence, will you see to the paperwork for these

families?" she directed and headed toward the end of the line where the younger ones stood.

"No! I don't wanna go without Johnny," whined Crissy, blinking back tears after being singled out by an interested family.

Not far from his sister, Johnny limped over and joined her.

"You gotta, Crissy," Johnny said bravely and pushed her toward the plain-dressed man, woman and boy.

"Crissy is a fine child," Bevin offered the couple. She took Johnny's hand and pulled him forward. "This is her brother. Johnny is a strong lad and would be a big help wherever needed."

"I'm sure he is, ceptin' that bum foot of his," the man pointed out, heedless of the child's obviously injured feelings. "But we only got enough room out at the farm for one more mouth to feed right now, and the missus and my boy want a girl. Sorry, lady."

Johnny's eyes fell and he shifted his weight, trying to hide the built-up shoe on his left foot behind the other one.

The woman took Crissy's hand. "This is Erastus. He'll be your big brother from now on, Crissy. You'll like being his sister, and we'll give you a good home."

Her chin trembling, Crissy looked back at Johnny. He stood stiff, biting his lower lip. His hands bailed into tight fists at his sides. "I already got a brother. Johnny's my brother," she sobbed and went to stand by her sibling.

Roughly, he gave her a shove. "No, I ain't. Not anymore. Now get."

Still looking forlorn, confused and frightened, Crissy clutched her battered rag doll to her little breast, sucked on her thumb, and allowed herself to be led away.

Johnny raised his head and stared after his little sister while another one of the children was picked and wrested from the group by an older couple. Bevin quietly stood to the left of the brave boy. His eyes never once left the golden-haired girl. He remained stoic except for a gasp, which escaped his lips when the man picked Crissy up and they joined another family ready to leave.

Bevin's heart bled for the unwanted boy. How could fate be so cruel to one so young? It was no wonder he had gotten into trouble. She wanted to reach out to Johnny and share the youngster's pain. Johnny had just made a very difficult and grown-up sacrifice for a child only eight years old: He had loved his little sister enough to let her go so she would have a future.

Bevin sniffled back her own tears at the heartwrenching scene played out for the frightened children forced to endure the meager lot life had dealt them. She thought of her own brother, and wondered if Patrick had been afraid when a family had led him away. She garnered her resolve. She was glad she had lied to the judge. At least these children would not be tucked away in reformatories and workhouses; they would have a chance for a happy life in real homes.

"Johnny, you did a very brave thing," she said quietly once Crissy was out of sight.

"I didn't do nothin'," he snapped.

"Yes, you did. You gave Crissy a chance in life."

"No, I didn't! I was just tired of takin' care of the dumb old, little brat. I hate her. She was in the way. But no more. She won't never bother me no more!"

Tears in her eyes, Bevin bent down to the boy. "Johnny, it's okay to feel sad. Soon you, too, will have a family. And someday you can come back and see how happy Crissy has grown up."

"I don't feel sad. I don't! I hate girls! And I don't want no stupid, old family. And I'll never come back.

Never!" he shouted and darted toward the train despite his limp, his arms flailing, propelling him away from the courthouse steps.

"Pru, see that the rest of the children get back to the train," Bevin called out and rushed after the troubled boy.

Down the tree-lined street Bevin hurried, fearing that Johnny would come to harm. There was no telling what he would do after the trauma he had undergone over losing his sister. She continued to follow after the child, who had rounded a corner and now was out of sight.

Puffing, Bevin picked up her pace. Her fingers splayed against her head keeping her hat pinned in place when a gust of wind threatened to take it up. An ache in her side threatened to halt her efforts to overtake Johnny, but she refused to stop. She had to catch the fleeing boy and offer him comfort.

Rounding the corner at the train station, Bevin suddenly halted. To her utter shock Johnny was standing on the platform, held securely within the big grasp of Will Shoemaker . . . again.

Chapter Five

Bevin's mind recorded disbelief that Mr. Shoemaker would disregard their earlier agreement so soon. Yet his expression did not register annoyance as it had before. No. This time curiosity and concern sparkled in his brown eyes, which held her at bay until Johnny tried unsuccessfully to wrench away from the man.

"Mr. Shoemaker, I thought we had settled the matter of you bothering the children," she said, stepping forward, as she glared into his smiling eyes.

Will dropped his hand. Unperturbed, despite her agitation, an easy smile cupped his mouth. "I believe we have settled the matter several times, Miss O'Dea."

He hesitated, waiting for a response. When she dropped her fists on her hips, he saw that his easygoing brand of humor had been lost. Continuing, he said, "Just doing you a favor, ma'am. The boy was in an awful rush. After noticing the proceedings back at the courthouse a little while ago, I thought he might be carrying a pretty heavy load."

The man's apparent sympathy for the plight of her young charge took Bevin by complete surprise. She had been prepared to launch an attack against Mr. Shoemaker on Johnny's behalf, but the man's seemingly genuine tone denoting compassion for the child's plight suddenly disarmed her.

His face glowed with sincerity. His square jaw was not jutted out in anger as it had been during their previous confrontations; his heavy brows were not furrowed; nor was his generous mouth rigid. With this new knowledge, Bevin experienced a moment of confusion and a feeling too foreign to name. His actions were totally out of character to the way she expected he would react if he encountered the child again.

"Yes, well, I suppose I owe you an apology this time. Thank you, Mr. Shoemaker, I can handle the child now," she said stiffly after she recovered.

"As you please." He shrugged and moved away.

Once Mr. Shoemaker had left her alone with Johnny, Bevin kneeled down and adjusted the boy's collar.

"He didn't harm you, did he?"

"He grabbed me and wouldn't let go until you got here," Johnny said.

"Well, he is gone now. Come along, Johnny, let's get back on the train and wait for the others. I have some nice treats for everyone, and you can help me pass them out."

"I don't want to help," Johnny said tightly, holding back a sob.

Bevin put her arm around his thin shoulders. "You don't have to, Johnny."

"Good!" He jerked free and darted toward the train.

Bevin boarded the train behind the forlorn child, and began setting out sticks of peppermint on each child's seat as she waited until Prudence returned with the other children.

Four youngsters had been placed, which pleased her greatly. It was a successful morning, although Johnny's pain marred her happiness. He was so young to be separated from the only family he had. Despite her determination not to get too wrapped up personally with the children, Bevin acknowledged to herself that she was beginning to forge a special bond with the rejected little waif. What she refused to think about was the strange feeling she had experienced in Mr. Shoemaker's presence when he'd demonstrated that he had a kind, compassionate side.

One by one the children finished filing into the car. Two had tears in their eyes and red noses. One young boy ran to his seat, ignored his candy and stared sullenly out the window. The other four children excitedly babbled, full of tales. Spotting their treat, they rushed to take possession of the sweet.

All accounted for and their new clothes carefully exchanged for everyday wear, the children clustered off to one side of the car to talk among themselves, and offer support to the ones still upset. Only Johnny refused to accept solace from the others. He remained by himself in a far corner, staring blankly at his left foot.

The train jerked, the whistle blew, and along the tracks they moved toward the next stop. Bevin spent time with each child making sure that the ones remaining did not feel rejected, bolstering their hope that they would soon find families.

An hour out of Ashland, Bevin passed around box lunches. After all were done eating, the children were able to spread out for a nap since they had the car all to themselves now.

Once everyone was bedded down, Bevin leaned back in her seat with a sigh.

"Evvie, you look so tired. Why don't you go to the dining car and have a refreshing cup of tea," Prudence advised. "You really work much too hard."

"I should stay with the children.

Prudence's face fell. "I shan't let them out of my sight this time. And besides, there are four less to watch, so you will not have to worry. Really you won't."

43

Bevin pinched the bridge of her nose. A cup of tea did sound inviting, and she had to admit she could use a break. These stops with the children had proved a most trying time. Prudence had managed to get all the remaining children back to the train without incident.

"Perhaps I shall take a few moments, if you are sure." Prudence squeezed Bevin's forearm. "You work so hard and spend too much time worrying about everyone else, Evvie. Of course I am sure."

Bevin rose and massaged the small of her back before checking each child. She would not leave without making sure every child had calmed. They were slumbering soundly, the two younger ones having cried themselves to sleep, despite the brave front they had tried to set forth. It was impossible to believe that they were considered budding criminals. Quietly, she tiptoed from the car and closed the door behind her so as not to awaken them from their dreams.

In the dining car she settled down at a white linen-covered table and ordered tea. Waiting for her order, she watched out the window at the wide landscape. Golden rolling hills stretched from the train, dotted with tidy farmhouses, which gave way to stands of trees before open spaces again reappeared and blended with a brilliant blue sky.

From his seat Will stared solemnly out the window at terrain that increasingly was becoming familiar. His reflection in the window glass outlined a pensive visage. It had been many years since he had passed this way. Maybe it was the ground parted by the plow or the rich, brown soil that triggered the memories, but Will thought about the first time he had traveled this way as an eight-year-old with his mother. For a moment he could see himself in the frightened little street urchins. Will shook his head. That part of his past was best left buried.

Forcing his thoughts to safer territory, Will's mind drifted to Miss Bevin O'Dea. She looked like an over-starched, soon-to-be spinster with that severe hairstyle, those stiff clothes and the demeanor of a rigid school-marm. Yet the lady possessed the fire and passion of an leashed tornado, the way she had stubbornly defended those children.

The thought of passion sent his mind spinning with visions of the prim redhead. And he wondered what she would be like if that passion were unleashed and redirected. *Toward you,* a voice inside him added.

Will's stomach growled, reminding him that he had not eaten dinner. Dragging his concentration from Miss Bevin O'Dea, Will hunted up the dining car.

It was past the noon hour and the tables were near empty by the time Will walked into the car. He headed toward a lone table until he spied Miss O'Dea seated by herself, staring out the window.

He changed course.

Pulling out a chair across from the lady, Will asked, "Mind if I join you?"

Bevin's head snapped up. "Mr. Shoemaker?"

"One 'n the same. May I?"

"If you think halting Johnny's flight earlier has softened my position toward your incomprehensible behavior this morning, Mr. Shoemaker, I fear you are in error coming here."

Despite her stinging words, Will's smile never wavered. "Wouldn't think of it. Just thought that since I'd like a little company perhaps you might as well."

"If you do not mind, I would prefer my solitude, actually."

Will shrugged and touched the brim of his hat. "Ma'am."

Bevin watched him saunter over to another table and take a seat boldly facing her. Their gazes held for a mo-

45

ment until Bevin felt a surge of self-consciousness and dropped her eyes.

She tried to ignore him.

He made it difficult.

Each time she looked up he was staring at her — quite openly, no less. She had come to the dining car to relax for a few moments, but Mr. Shoemaker was making it impossible.

Will watched the ungrateful lady take two more sips of her tea, then rise to leave. She gave him a stiff nod as she passed him, and he turned to watch her.

Her small shoulders were held proud, her posture stiffly erect as her heels clicked from the car. She definitely looked prudish in that dove gray tailored suit. In a few short years she'd undoubtedly become an old spinster, the way she acted. Hardly a woman to catch a man's eye, although Will had to admit that his had already been caught. Pity she was so unapproachable, because he found himself interested in learning more about her work, and what her red hair would look like hanging loose in curls down her back.

Prudence had been dozing until she felt a hand drop on her shoulder. Startled, she jumped to her feet and frantically looked around to see that the children were all right.

"They're fine, Pru," Bevin announced.

A look of extreme guilt freezing her delicate features, Prudence collapsed in her seat and slumped down. She clasped her hands to her mouth to hide a yawn before splaying them out to her sides. "Oh, Evvie, I am sorry. I only dozed off for a moment. Truly."

Bevin shook her head and took up a place across from Prudence. "It's all right."

Prudence breathed a sigh of relief. Then a line penciled between her brows. "You weren't gone very long."

"No. I wasn't," Bevin answered evasively.

"Why not?"

Prudence was not going to allow Bevin a moment's peace until she answered her probing question. "If you must know, Mr. Shoemaker was in the dining car."

"Why should that matter?" Prudence pressed.

"He took a seat at a table near mine and proceeded to stare at me. It was rather unsettling so I left the car."

"You do not suppose he is interested in you, do you?"

"Don't be silly, Pru. I think he just wanted to annoy me after all the trouble we've caused him."

"Funny. He did not seem like the type of man to do such a thing—not after stating he wanted to keep his distance from all of us," she said dreamily.

"No," Bevin admitted with a sigh, "he certainly didn't seem like that type of man. My goodness, Pru, you aren't mooning over the man, are you?"

"No. Not really. He is too old for me. Why he must be at least thirty." A sheepish grin across her face, she added, "He is awfully handsome, though."

Bevin laughed at Prudence's conception of old. If Mr. Shoemaker was indeed thirty that would make him only five years older than Bevin's twenty-five years.

Bevin and Prudence spent the remainder of the afternoon doting on the children. They played a variety of games, taking the children's minds off their earlier loss. Bevin talked individually with each child, and helped them understand and accept what fate had in store for them, reassuring them that everything would be all right.

When the train stopped at another town, the children begged and pleaded not to have to go through another inspection today. Relenting, Bevin decided not to subject the youngsters to a second ordeal.

"Pru, you stay with the children while I go explain to

47

the people at the station that there will be no children available this trip."

Bevin left them on the train and disembarked to find more people waiting than she had anticipated. She scanned the cluster of unsmiling faces. Mr. Shoemaker stood at the back of the crowd, listening to her as she attempted to satisfy a few of the more vocal men, who were upset at having driven all the way to town only to be disappointed.

"I am sorry. But I am certain you can understand how difficult it is on these boys and girls."

"Look you, me and the misses've wasted a whole dadblamed day away from our place to come to town to get us a youngun' to work the farm. Those beggars should be grateful that folks like us is willing to give their kind a chance. Now go on and get those lazy brats, and line them up so we can choose us our pick."

Horror over the man's complete disregard for the children's welfare overtook Bevin. The man had totally ignored her efforts to politely explain, and the crowd seemed to be growing more agitated. Since the crowd was unwilling to be reasonable, Bevin hesitated to answer as she scanned the angry faces, trying to decide the best way to proceed, when her gaze caught with Mr. Shoemaker's.

Will had originally intended to get off the train and stretch his legs while they were at the station. But the hostility of those people grated on his sense of gallantry. Bevin O'Dea was stubborn and could be a pain in the backside, but she did not deserve the farmer's wrath. And for the first time, she looked as if she could use some help. Ignoring a voice within that warned him to leave the lady to her own devices, he pushed through the crowd.

"The lady told you, mister, that you'd have to wait until another time. 'Course, if that doesn't satisfy you,

you can always hire on a man to do what you got in mind for one of those poor kids."

"And who are you?" the farmer demanded.

"I'm the one who you will have to answer to if you don't decide to leave without causing any more trouble," Will said menacingly.

Will Shoemaker stood over a head taller than the farmer, and outweighed him by a good twenty-five pounds. So the disgruntled man and his prune-faced wife only grunted their disgust before the man sneered, "See if one of them ads brings folks around here running next time you have a bunch of misfits you want to unload."

The pair shoved through the crowd, leaving Bevin to mollify the remaining cluster before she was finally left standing alone on the platform with Mr. Shoemaker.

"I think I owe you a debt of gratitude, Mr. Shoemaker," she said, admiring the way he had stepped in and handled the farmer. "And I admit I was wrong back in Boston. Johnny finally confessed that he did indeed dump water on you. I hope you will accept my apologies for that and the money clip."

"Accepted. But only if you agree to join me in the dining car for supper," Will heard himself say before he realized what he was doing. What was he thinking of? He'd never given Miss O'Dea's kind of woman much more than a passing thought before this morning. And besides, he was almost broke.

"I am afraid I have an obligation to the children. Unless, of course, you'd like to dine with eight rather rambunctious youngsters," she said as a graceful way of turning down his invitation. It would not be proper to take supper with the man, particularly since she was an engaged lady.

Will held up his hands. "No thanks."

The train's whistle, signaling that it would be pulling

49

out soon, put an end to what could have developed into an awkward moment if Will'd had to explain that he had a hard time being around children—even good ones—after his boyhood friend died in a drowning accident years ago.

"I think we'd best get back on board before we're left behind," Will suggested. He took Miss O'Dea by the elbow and ushered her toward the train.

Now that they no longer seemed to be adversaries, Will found himself wondering what the rest of the trip would hold in store.

Chapter Six

Supper proved to be everything Bevin had predicted and more. The children were rambunctious; their table manners left a lot to be desired; and to make matters worse, Johnny took aim at one of the boys with a spoonful of potatoes; he ducked and the white mass landed on Will Shoemaker's — he had the misfortune to be seated nearby — black jacket. The gooey mass dropped off his chest and plopped onto his lap.

Johnny's eyes glittered and he edged closer to Miss O'Dea confident that she'd protect him from the big man Johnny saw as a growing adversary.

Will sent the little hoodlum a look of warning but quietly wiped the potatoes from his person and returned his attention to his meal. Miss O'Dea had been speaking to another of the unruly children and completely missed the little devil's foray.

At first Will had intended to seek redress, but he didn't want her to think he had incited the boy after Will had made peace with the lady. And he had overheard that the kid had been pretty upset being separated from his little sister. In the future, Will decided, he'd make sure the horde was no where near the dining car or any other facility he was tempted to haunt.

"Miss O'Dea, Johnny's being bad," Tara tattled in a

51

singsong little girl voice. "I saw him."

"What?" Bevin's eyes widened.

"He throwed taters on that man." Tara pointed to Mr. Shoemaker.

"Did not!" Johnny retorted.

"Did too!"

"Did not!"

"Yes, you did. Just ask him, Miss O'Dea," the little girl urged, a smugness mirroring her round face.

Bevin looked askance at Mr. Shoemaker. He cocked a brow at her, an unreadable glint in his dark eyes, a half smile on his lips. Despite herself, Bevin shyly smiled back. She wondered if Benjamin would be as handsome.

Putting such outrageous thoughts aside, Bevin watched him wipe a napkin across his mouth before leaving the table. She noticed the dark stain next to his lapel as he passed and wondered why the man had not approached her, if indeed Johnny were guilty. Just then two other children got into an argument over a slice of bread, drawing Bevin's attention from Mr. Shoemaker to settling the dispute.

"Why didn't you ask him?" Tara whined, pouting that Johnny got away with it.

"Tara, if Mr. Shoemaker wanted to take issue with anything I have no doubt the man would not have hesitated. Now, finish your supper."

Smarting under Johnny's muffled laugh, Tara wrinkled her nose at him, stuffed a mound of potatoes into her mouth, then stuck out her tongue.

Bevin squeezed Tara's arm in silent warning, which caused the little girl to glumly return her attention to her own plate. Bevin finished her supper and waited for the other children at the table to clean their plates before she turned to Prudence.

"Pru, are the children at your table finished?" Bevin

asked, interrupting the young woman, who was busily visiting with a couple near her.

The two youngest children looked as if they had been in a food fight. Their faces were smudged with gravy and bits of meat, and vegetable clung in strings down their hair. They had wiped their hands down the front of them.

"Oh, my," Prudence gasped. "What did you two do to yourselves?" She looked up at Bevin's silent stare of disapproval. "Oh, Evvie, I am sorry. I only stopped for a moment to speak with the Morses."

The middle-aged couple nodded. Embarrassment for the young lady caused them to glance away.

"Pru, you really must learn to keep a closer eye on the children."

"Yes. Yes, I shall. Truly."

"Let's get those two cleaned up and back to their seats. It's nearly time to get the younger ones scrubbed and ready for bed. They have another busy day ahead of them tomorrow."

Thoroughly daunted, Prudence wiped the worst of supper off the little ones' faces and hands before trailing meekly after Bevin.

Will half reclined in his seat with a book, trying to concentrate, but disturbing thoughts continued to plague his mind. It had been years since he had been home. Home. He almost laughed out loud. He had never had a true home. His father had died before he was born, and his stepfather had been a dour farmer who had not let him forget he was excess baggage included when the man had married Will's mother.

Will pondered over how he had steadfastly remained on the farm until the war. After the war he had returned East to visit a distant cousin before drifting about the country and mining for gold in Colorado Territory—until now.

He still could not understand why the old man had left half the farm to him. It made no sense. The old man had a son from his first marriage. Will sighed, thinking about his stepbrother. By all reason, the farm should have been left entirely to him.

Will leaned his head back against the seat and closed his eyes. At first he'd deigned to ignore his stepbrother's missive, considering the way it was written—like a summons. But curiosity and an inner desire to heal the rift between them had drawn him back.

To this day he could visualize his mother instructing him to be tolerant of his stepfather in spite of the backbreaking work he'd had to endure.

"You'll grow up the better for it, William," his haggard mother had consoled, sitting on the edge of the narrow bed in Will's cold attic room.

"He's not much better to you, Ma," Will had complained bitterly. "He makes you work hard too."

"Joseph is a good man. It is just his way. He never learned to show his feelings." She mussed his thick black hair before sweeping it back off his forehead. "He comes from the old country and believes one should work hard and suffer in silence. We were lucky, son. He gave us a fine home; we have enough food on the table, a roof over our heads, and in his own way he cares for us very deeply, I know he does."

Will had not believed his mother then, and now he still had difficulty accepting what she had said, although he remembered that at times his mother had laughed and seemed happy despite the simple life of toil they'd led.

It was long after midnight when the smell of smoke wrenched Will from reminiscing. Will's gaze darted about the car. The other passengers appeared to be sleeping. Concerned that one of the men might have fallen asleep while smoking, Will left his seat to investigate.

Will's nose lead him toward the washroom, where the strong odor of cheap cigars seeped underneath the door. He knocked on the door. A high-pitched cough was all that issued in return. Suspicious, Will jiggled the knob.

It was locked.

"Who's in there?" he said in a command.

"No one," came the muffled reply.

"You better open this door . . . immediately, or I'll break it down."

At the click of the latch, Will entered the tiny room. On the floor next to the washstand sat that hoodlum-in-miniature, Johnny Martin, and a young friend. Will narrowed his eyes and crossed his arms over his chest. Johnny was holding a cheap cigar. The pair obviously had been smoking. Guilty, green-fringed faces stared back at Will.

"What do you have to say for yourself this time?" Will demanded of Johnny. The second boy's eyes saucered, and he scrambled from the room before Will could catch him.

"Oh, no, you don't!" Will grabbed Johnny by the seat of the pants and confiscated the cigar as the child tried to follow his companion from the scene.

"Let me go!" Johnny railed.

"Earlier you throw potatoes at me and now this. Aren't you a little young to be smoking?"

"Ah, heck, I been smoking for a couple years already. And I didn't mean to hit you with them potatoes. I was aiming at that dumb old Burt. He ducked and I got you instead."

At the child's reply, Will couldn't help himself; he let out a hearty laugh and released the boy.

Johnny promptly shrunk back into a far corner. "It's true," he insisted.

"Oh, I believe you this time, although I'm not sure why. As far as smoking, I used to puff a bit myself when I was your age, only I used a corncob pipe."

"Where'd you get a pipe?" Johnny questioned, brightening at the thought of a real pipe.

"I made it myself. And I have to say, it probably tasted and surely smelled a helluva lot better than this cheap cigar." Will took a look at the smoldering butt and promptly ground it out under his heel.

"Golly, will you show me how to make a pipe?"

"Maybe someday," Will replied, knowing shortly the boy would be placed with a family, and he'd never see the child again. Not wishing to explore the topic further, Will reached down and picked up the butt. "Which unsuspecting passenger did you steal this from?"

"I didn't steal it." Johnny tried to escape again, but Will blocked his way.

"Well, until you tell me how you came by it you are not leaving."

Ten-year-old Timothy, his heart thrumming, raced directly to Bevin's side. Panting, he shook her. "Miss O'Dea. Miss O'Dea, you gotta wake up and come right away. He's got Johnny again and he looks awful mean!"

"What? Who?" Bevin asked, rousing from a deep, fitful sleep.

"Hurry. You gotta come." Timothy tugged on Bevin's wrist. "He could hurt Johnny before you get there!"

Bevin grabbed the boy by the shoulders and looked right into his frightened eyes. "Calm down, Timothy, and tell me what this is all about?" She glanced at her watch. It was midnight. "What are you doing up at this hour?"

Terror gleamed across his face until it was replaced by a flicker of something Bevin could not quite decipher. "Me and Johnny we was in the washroom when that man—Mr. Shoemaker—pounded on the door, then came in and yelled at us. Come—on. We gotta get to Johnny before he kills him."

"No one is going to be killed," Bevin explained to the distraught youngster.

Bevin wanted to question Timothy further. There was something about his story that didn't make sense. But the urgency in his voice warned her that she'd best not tarry any longer. Quickly Bevin alerted a sleepy Prudence to take a head count and make sure no one else was up while Bevin got to the bottom of this latest episode involving Johnny.

With a quickened pace, Bevin let Timothy lead her by the hand into the next car to the washroom. Without knocking, Bevin opened the door and stepped inside.

To her horror, Mr. Shoemaker had Johnny cornered.

"Mr. Shoemaker, what is the meaning of this?" she demanded, astounded. Her life and those of the children seemed to be inexplicably entangled with that of the coal-haired man since their first meeting, despite their recent truce.

"Seems Johnny, here, and I ended up in the same washroom by accident. It's nothing for you to be concerned about."

Will had intended to inform Miss O'Dea what the pair had been up to, but the defeated look on Johnny's face caused Will to palm the cigar he had confiscated from the child.

Shock registered on Bevin's face. "Nothing to be concerned about? Timothy comes to me half scared out of his wits and you say you ended up in the same washroom by accident?" Unconvinced, she turned to

57

Johnny. "Johnny, would you like to tell me about it?"

Johnny's eyes shifted from Miss O'Dea to Mr. Shoemaker and back again. He could not believe that the man had not told on him after everything he had done to him. He could not understand what the big man was up to. People did not do things without a reason.

To Johnny's way of thinking, people were not to be trusted, for they had brought little more than pain and suffering into his young life. He studied the two adults again and decided that Mr. Shoemaker probably wanted his help to get close to Miss O'Dea. After all, Johnny'd seen the way the man had stared at her, and he'd watched them back at the train station enjoying each other's company.

"I got nothing to tell, Miss O'Dea. Me and Timothy was in the washroom, that's all."

"That's all?" she probed, doubting the simple tale.

"Yeah. Timothy didn't want to go alone so I went with him. He was afraid to pass *him*." Johnny pointed an accusing finger at Mr. Shoemaker.

"Why didn't you use the washroom in our car?"

Johnny's mouth dropped, which caused Will to intercede despite the kid's efforts to put the blame in his lap.

"It's really nothing, Miss O'Dea. The door was stuck and I heard them call out for help. I'm 'fraid I frightened Timothy when I entered. While he went to get you, Johnny told me that they came to this washroom because they didn't want to disturb you or the other children."

Bevin listened but had a difficult time believing the pair. The scent of stale tobacco permeated the small cubicle and clung to Johnny's clothing. She glanced at Timothy. He was nervously chewing the cuticle on his bitten nails. She knew that if she pressed the pale child he would tell the truth. She opened her mouth to interrogate him, then let her questions drop.

58

It was probably the first time in Johnny's life that he had a man to stand up for him. So Bevin decided to accept the story despite the obvious fabrication. Maybe the incident could serve to help Johnny start learning to put faith in someone. The boy was so mistrustful that some good just had to come out of their misadventure.

Her estimation of Mr. Shoemaker's worth grew. The man had taken the boy's side, although this time Bevin was certain Johnny had been up to something.

"I see," she said, cocking a brow to let Mr. Shoemaker know that while she would not inquire further, she did not, for a moment, believe him. "Well, since everything seems to be settled, come along boys, it's long past time you two were asleep.

"Oh, and Mr. Shoemaker, I do hope that in the future you will not indulge in such a nasty habit in front of the children again," she said, looking down at the cigar butt in his hand.

"You needn't worry, Miss O'Dea. I'd planned to give up the habit anyway."

Bevin turned and left with Timothy by the hand, giving Johnny a moment alone with Mr. Shoemaker.

"Why'd you lie for me?" Johnny asked, his eyes narrowed with cynicism.

"No reason for you to be getting into any more trouble as long as I don't catch you smoking again. And that includes stealing anything else or playing pranks on people. Understand?" Will said easily, expecting the deed he'd done for the boy to put a stop to what had seemed to be an undeclared war between man and child.

"You think you did me a favor, huh?"

"I'd say so."

"Well, it ain't gonna work. I don't know what you're up to, but if you're thinking to get close to Miss O'Dea by covering up for me, you're gonna find out otherwise," Johnny snapped and ran from the washroom.

Dumbfounded by the vehemence in the boy's voice after he'd tried to help, Will stood before the mirror and stared at his reflection. Whatever gave that runt such a crazy idea that he was interested in Miss Bevin O'Dea?

The notion caused Will to stop and think before blotting the thought from his mind. He was leaving the train soon and would never see the lady again.

Chapter Seven

Bevin was drained from last night, leaving her feeling as if she had not slept a wink. But looking after children was a twenty-four-hour job. Certainly different from her work at the Society. There she put in her shift — lingering on many occasions — and went home to continue her search for her brother. Not so now. Despite everything, though, Bevin would not trade a moment of the toil. Just watching the faces of the children glow when they were placed made it all worthwhile.

After seeing to all the needs of her charges, Bevin allowed Prudence to convince her to steal a few minutes for herself in the dining car before the next stop. Those few moments were a luxury, and Bevin needed the fortification.

Once Bevin took a seat at an empty table and ordered, she closed her eyes with a sigh. Solitude. No little hands tugging at her, no little voices arguing or crying, no crises.

"Morning."

Bevin's eyes snapped open at the intrusion of the deep male voice into her thoughts. She looked up to see Mr. Shoemaker smiling down at her. This time, instead of asking, he pulled out the chair across from her and sat down. He ordered coffee, then waited for Bevin to speak.

"Mr. Shoemaker, while I appreciate your help with the children last night, please do not think it gives you license to intrude without invitation."

"My, my, how soon we forget," he returned unperturbed, shook out the linen napkin, and placed it in his lap. "I seem to recall you allowing me *license to intrude* on your behalf yesterday and with your charges last night."

"Y-yes," she admitted hesitantly. "I believe I already thanked you. Johnny can be headstrong at times."

"Most children can."

The waiter delivered the coffee and left. Will took a sip of the strong liquid, studying her face over the rim of the cup.

"Thought you might like some adult company after spending so much time with those little hoodlums."

"I have Miss Truesdale for adult company. I am not on this train to spend time socializing." She cocked her brow. "I have a job to do, which includes *those little hoodlums,* as you refer to them, Mr. Shoemaker."

"No offense meant, really."

Disbelief chilled her voice. "No, of course not."

Will pulled his jacket up around his neck and shivered to make his point. "It's a tad cold in here this morning, wouldn't you say?"

"I would say, it would not be if you joined someone more favorably inclined toward your company." Mr. Shoemaker stood, but Bevin reached out and placed a gloved hand on his arm. Perhaps it would not be improper if they shared a meal as long as they were not alone in the dining car, which was crowded. "Please, do forgive me. I am not usually so rude. I know you meant no offense. And I do appreciate your making an effort to answer the children's call for help, despite your personal opinion of them."

She motioned to the chair he had vacated. "Please.

Actually, I would enjoy some adult company this morning after all."

That easy smile reappeared across Will's lips and he sat back down.

She leaned forward in her seat. "What really did happen last night?"

"Just a couple of little boys being boys," Will offered evasively, shielding the children from what he was sure would be a good scolding if she found out that they had been experimenting with tobacco.

"That is all well and good, Mr. Shoemaker. But the children are expected to be well-behaved and act accordingly."

"No doubt a lady such as yourself has always observed proper decorum, and therefore expects as much of others as well."

Bevin smiled weakly, thinking of her own childhood. Proper decorum. The words conjured up memories of a large packing crate behind a fine restaurant. The crate was lined inside with week-old newspapers for warmth against the bitter cold winters in Boston.

"You look as if you are a thousand miles away," he said, interrupting Bevin's remembrances.

"What?"

"I said a lady such as yourself has always undoubtedly observed proper decorum."

"A lady such as myself, Mr. Shoemaker?"

"Sure. A society miss out to do her good deed by saving a bunch of kids from becoming criminals before you go back home, marry some rich man, and settle into your tidy little life."

She tented her slender fingers. "I see. You think I am performing the necessary charity work required of wealthy society matrons and their daughters?"

Will picked a toothpick from the table and chewed on the wooden end. "Pretty good assessment, I'd say."

"Well, for your information, Mr. Shoemaker, I have a personal interest in working for the Children's Aid Society," Bevin blurted out before she could collect herself.

Will furrowed his brows. "A personal interest?"

Bevin studied the linen napkin in her lap, twisting it between her fingers.

"Miss O'Dea?"

"Yes? Oh. I was thinking about my own childhood, I fear." Bevin stared right into his eyes. There was a gentle, curious light glistening in the dark centers.

"The silver spoon set?"

"Hardly, Mr. Shoemaker. I also grew up on the same streets as those children, if you must know. And I will not be returning to Boston to wed some wealthy gentleman. I am en route to become the wife of an honest, hardworking farmer."

Shock registered on Mr. Shoemaker's face, causing the pain of Bevin's past to swell in her chest.

"Now, if you will excuse me. I should be getting back to the children."

"Aren't you going to finish your meal?"

"No. It seems I've had quite enough."

Unwilling to subject herself to further questioning, she quickly rose to her feet and hurried back toward the children, ignoring the man's baritone voice calling out her name.

Bevin strode back to the children's car and plunked down in her seat, staring blankly out the window. Haunting visions of the bony, half-starved child she had been, forced to beg for food floated before her in ghostly images. She could see the rags she and her brother had worn for clothing; the newspaper they'd stuffed into their sorry shoes; the suffering of many others like them all around her.

She was so upset reliving those dreadful years and

then so easily having blurted out her carefully guarded past to a total stranger that she didn't hear the heavy footfalls coming up behind her.

"Ooaf!" Will hit the floor.

A loud thud followed by an undefined oath caused Bevin to swing around. Mr. Shoemaker was sprawled out in the aisle, a dark glower on his face. She shot a glance at Johnny in the seat nearby. Johnny's eyes darted up, and he began a sudden serious study of the ceiling.

Prudence leaped forward to offer her help.

"Prudence, one of the children will aid Mr. Shoemaker," Bevin announced.

Prudence blushed scarlet over her impulsiveness and settled back into her chair.

"Johnny, help Mr. Shoemaker to his feet," Bevin directed, frowning at the boy.

"Yessum, Miss O'Dea," Johnny answered innocently and left his seat to render assistance.

Johnny took a grip around Mr. Shoemaker's arm, his eyes glittering mischief at the big, fallen man. "Guess you mustta tripped."

Will glared silently back at the boy. Tripped indeed. The pint-size hoodlum! "Yeah, tripped," Will grumbled, knowing full well that the midget beggar had Miss O'Dea hoodwinked. His back to the ladies, Will whispered, "You and I'll discuss my *mishap* later — in private, kid."

"No need to thank me, sir," Johnny said brightly for Miss O'Dea's benefit. Johnny smiled to himself. He knew that Mr. Shoemaker literally simmered in his collar under the look of approval Miss O'Dea gave him as he returned to his seat. That would show the big man! For good measure, Johnny made sure Miss O'Dea wasn't looking, then stuck his tongue out at Mr. Shoemaker. He was not through with the man yet!

Will brushed off his trousers and jacket and continued about his business. No sawed-off runt was going to keep him from pursuing the lady if he had a mind to.

Bevin shifted uneasily before Mr. Shoemaker. Noticing that Prudence had edged forward in her seat ready to hang on every word the man uttered, Bevin suggested, "Pru, why don't you see that the children are ready for the next stop."

Prudence's gaze shifted from the big, handsome man to Bevin. Her fingers itched to feel the coarse texture of his black hair. Mr. Shoemaker had followed Bevin and now stood expectantly waiting to speak with her. Prudence cast him a longing look; she wished that men were attracted to her instead of to Bevin.

"If you think I should," Prudence answered.

"Yes, I think it would be an excellent idea."

After the Truesdale girl had shepherded the children toward the washroom, Will joined Miss O'Dea. He didn't totally understand it himself—why he'd needed to follow her from the dining car—but when she had told him that she'd grown up on the streets of Boston, she had pricked more than a passing interest.

He had thought her a prudish heiress on her way to spinsterhood; a woman who saw it her civic duty to find homes for a few young thugs. Her sudden confession had completely taken him by surprise, and he'd found he desired to learn more about the lady despite the code which he had lived by for the last nine years.

From the time he had left his stepfather's home, he had made it a practice to bed only women who made men's pleasure their business. Life proved much less complicated that way.

"Mr. Shoemaker, unless you want something specific, I need to help Prudence with the children."

"Dine with me tonight," he said rashly.

"I thought I made it perfectly clear, I am engaged to

66

be married. I hardly think it would appear proper."

"We were sitting together a short while ago. I don't think you'll be committing an impropriety by sharing a little food across the table from me — not if I promise to stay on my own side and keep the table between us at all times." He smiled, then as an afterthought added, "I'll even keep my hands on the table at all times if it would make you more comfortable."

At her tightening lips, he said, "Miss O'Dea, I don't have an ulterior motive. As I said earlier, I'd simply enjoy some company. And I'd really like to hear more about the work you do. Who knows, could be I might know of a few farmers who could use some extra help."

"Well, as long as you are interested in helping the children, perhaps there would not be any harm in it."

"Good. Six o'clock in the dining car." Without waiting for a response Will tipped his hat and sauntered toward the rear of the coach.

Bevin turned and watched him, wondering why she had accepted such an invitation, yet intrigued by the man just the same.

At the station, the children were ushered onto the platform and toward another courthouse. Anxiously, the eight little children tugged at their stiff new clothing. In front of the building, they lined up again. Johnny slid his left foot behind the other one in an attempt to hide his deformity. He stood impressively, his little chest puffed out, trying hard to smile.

Bevin crossed her fingers and said a prayer that someone would realize Johnny's worth and give the child a chance.

For a half hour she watched a dozen straight-faced farmers head their way and begin to size up the children as if they were cattle.

67

"Open your mouth, girl," ordered a lanky man with teeth crossed like his eyes.

Tara sent Bevin a frightened look, fighting back tears as the man pinched her cheeks.

Bevin stepped over and put a comforting arm around the little girl's thin shoulders. Then she pushed the man's arm away.

"Sir, you aren't purchasing an animal," Bevin said.

"Look, little girlie, before I'm gonna take one them castoffs in, I want to be sure the girl ain't gonna cost me nothing."

Bevin's hand flew to her throat, scandalized by the cold, unfeeling way the children were treated at this stop.

"Perhaps you'd be well-advised to go buy yourself a draft animal and quit wasting your time here," Will growled, stepping forward.

"Hummph! People's doing these younguns a favor to take 'em in." He swung his arm out to indicate Johnny. "Why look at those puny, broken bodies. You're trying to palm off a bunch of misfits on good honest folk. No one's gonna want no cripple."

"Since that's the way you look at things, take your *favors* elsewhere, mister," Will warned.

The man slitted his eyes at Bevin and Will; he moved off, muttering to himself.

"Prudence, I think it would be a good idea if you helped the children back on the train," suggested Bevin, unwilling to subject them to further cruelties.

A plump, matronly woman with a fringed scarf tied over her head stepped up. "Wait, miss. Mr. Muhlberg and me, we would be mighty pleased to take those two into our home." She pointed out the oldest two. "We ain't got no children of our own and we would do right by them."

"Ya, we would," the brawny man with the heavy

accent seconded.

The couple's genuine honesty caused Bevin to warm toward them.

"Would you like to be our little children? Ya?" she asked and held out her hands.

"This lady seems awfully nice," urged Bevin, dropping a hand lightly on the nearest boy's shoulder. "Would you like to be their sons?"

"Think so," came the whispers in unison. Prudence immediately stopped her efforts to tend to the rest of the children and turned to dig in her bag for the necessary paperwork.

"I'll take the rest of the children back on board the train while you and Miss Truesdale make the final arrangements," Will offered, getting caught up in the emotion of the proceedings.

"Why, thank you, Mr. Shoemaker." Bevin was grateful for the man's generosity.

"He is just chock-full of surprises, isn't he?" Prudence gushed as she finished gathering the forms together.

Bevin ignored Prudence, completed the paperwork and gave the boys one last hug. She waited until the lads were out of sight before heading for the telegraph office to wire Benjamin.

Five children left; three more had been placed today. Another two days and Bevin would be at her destination. She hoped all the children would be placed by then. If not, Bevin was sure Benjamin would take them. He had such a good heart; she knew it from his letters. And there was Mr. Shoemaker's offer. He had mentioned the possibility of knowing people who might be interested in the children.

The telegram sent, Bevin rejoined the remaining children, her thoughts consumed by the upcoming meal with Mr. Shoemaker. Her spirits were suddenly buoyed and a strange quickening filled her chest. Indigestion, she chided herself. That and the tension she'd experienced at the station were the culprits for the tightening in her breast. There was no other explanation.

Chapter Eight

By the time Bevin joined Mr. Shoemaker the sun had set, giving way to the engulfing darkness outside the train. The other diners had long ago finished their meals and returned to their accommodations. Alone in the finely outfitted coach, Mr. Shoemaker sat bent over the table reading. She could not help but notice the hint of muscles straining underneath the somber coat he wore.

"I apologize for being so tardy," Bevin said as he jumped up and pulled out a chair.

His smile never wavered. "Made the anticipation all the greater."

"You are much too kind, Mr. Shoemaker." Behind the bright smile she flashed him, disappointment lurked. She had hoped he would have grown tired of waiting and left, for she was not convinced it was proper to be dining with a man whom she had to admit she found handsome.

"Please, call me Will. I think we can dispense with such stiff formality after our late-night foray last night, don't you? And, if I may, I'd like to call you Bevin."

The sheepish grin crossing his lips made Bevin think how innocently boyish he appeared, and disarmed momentary thoughts of protest over the concept of improper intimacy that use of given names implied.

She dropped her eyes, thinking how others might perceive her if, particularly, Benjamin should learn that she had allowed some strange man from the train to use such familiarity.

Will sensed her misgivings.

"You needn't worry that I'll seek further liberties. One of us shall be leaving the train soon and we'll never see each other again. Until that time, don't you think it would be more pleasant if we made an attempt to get on rather than fight it?" he suggested.

"Well, I suppose there really isn't any harm in it," she relented, despite a voice within her boding trouble.

"Good . . . Bevin it is then. I took the liberty of ordering, and told the waiter to serve the food once you arrived; I hope you don't mind."

"You are used to taking charge, it appears."

"Seems we're two of a kind."

"Only I happen to like children . . . Will."

He only smiled at her observation, refraining from comment.

The food was served and they began to eat.

"Tell me. You said earlier that you grew up on the streets. You give the impression of a rich, only child."

"I'm afraid you have just described Prudence Truesdale, my coworker. I worked for a wealthy family as a maid and spent years learning proper decorum until I was able to secure a position at the Society."

"I wondered why she seemed so helpless."

"You can't blame Prudence. I'm sure it was equally as difficult growing up in a family with such high expectations for their daughter. It has been hard for her living in a family like hers; their accomplishments tend to overshadow the poor girl. Sometimes I think that's why Prudence wanted to come along on this trip so badly — to escape all their demands that she donate time to her mother's charitable endeavors, then marry some young swain of her parents' choice. Prudence still believes in romantic love and happy endings, you see."

"And you don't?" he asked, noting how adeptly she had transferred the topic away from herself.

"Certainly not in the sense of a white knight on a charger. I know better."

The harsh tone in her voice gave Will pause. Life obviously had been difficult for her. "Then what do you believe in?"

"Compatibility, companionship, security."

"Can't he be tall, dark and handsome and ride a white horse as well?"

Bevin cast him a look of disdain. "There is no room in my world for such nonsense — not after my first, foolish crush on the son of the family for which I worked. I discovered — almost too late — that I had been little more than a light diversion to him until he married someone from his own station in life. It was a hard lesson, but one which taught me the value of making appropriate choices in life."

"You never know. That white knight could still come along and sweep you off your feet."

"Those are foolish childhood fantasies. I believe that what is on the inside of a person is more important than outside trappings, don't you?"

"Never spent much time looking on the inside," Will admitted.

"You may be well advised to try it sometime."

Will shrugged. "Some day maybe I'll make a point of it." He took a drink of coffee, set the cup down and leaned forward with his elbows on the table. "I'm still interested in hearing more about you."

"There really isn't that much else to tell. My little brother and I came to this country with my parents to start a better life, but my parents died before they left

73

Ellis Island."

"So you looked after your brother?"

"Of course."

"There wasn't anyone else who'd give you a home?"

"The others were as destitute as we were. One kind couple helped us get off the island by claiming us as their own. After that we made our way to Boston on our own." She lifted her chin proudly. "Furthermore, I do not believe in taking charity."

"So you and your brother work for the Children's Aid Society now, I suppose."

"I do. My brother was sent out West our second winter in Boston."

"Not you?"

"No. Patrick was picked off the streets while I was out looking for food, if you must know." Tears threatened to form in her eyes, but she fought them back; she would not let this man see her weakness. "I tried to find him, but was too late. He had been put on a train, very much like this one, before I could locate him."

Her voice caught and she paused to take a sip of water before continuing. "I was determined to make it on my own. Patrick was only six years old. I was ten. Not long after I lost Patrick I got a job and determined to educate myself and then find him someday."

Will could not help but be impressed as the story of Bevin's early life and struggles to survive on Boston's streets unfolded. "Looks like you've managed quite well."

"Indeed I have. Working for the Society gave me the opportunity to search for Patrick and help troubled children. And now I will soon be rejoining my brother and marry a very fine man."

"The farmer?"

"Yes. His correspondence helped me locate my brother."

74

"You met your fiancé through your efforts to locate your brother?"

She ignored his apparent surprise. "Yes, my inquiries about Patrick were answered by my intended. And no, I have not actually met the man." At Will's look of incredulity, Bevin clarified, "From his letters I know all I need to know about him. He is honest, kind, loyal and dependable."

"Sounds like the salt of the earth to me," Will mumbled.

Bevin stiffened and her face tightened, which caused Will to add, "Please, it is only my humor. People tell me I need to temper it. I'm sure your fiancé is a veritable pillar of society."

She gasped.

"Forgive me, I couldn't help myself."

Bevin frowned then relaxed her features. She had the distinct feeling he had not meant his last comment to be kind either. But his assessment of her Benjamin was not important anyway. Henceforth, she wouldn't mention Benjamin anymore. She had already divulged much more than intended and was surprised that Will Shoemaker had so easily induced her to talk about herself.

"And you, Will? Are you also one of society's pillars?"

Will laughed at her wit. "You are quick. I'll give you that. Most ladies would have continued to stew."

A more serious note filled his voice. "I'm not sure where I'd fit into society's scheme of things. I suppose I've been drifting through life for the last nine years. But that's about to come to an end. When my stepfather died he made me part owner of the farm where I grew up. I'm going back there to rejoin my stepbrother. So I'd say that gives us something in common. We're both about to be reunited with kin."

"Yes, I guess we are." Bevin smiled weakly, wondering why he had seemed careful not to mention the farm as home, and had been cautious not to divulge much about his early life.

For over an hour Bevin questioned Will about his life, learning little more than he had grown up on a pleasant farm and left after the war with little direction in life — other than to see the world. He was more generous in detailing his life from that point. She was fascinated by his exploits, warmed by his anecdotes, and drawn to him by the ease with which both their stories as adults seemed to tumble out so companionably.

The next two days were much the same. Stops at small towns saw three more children placed. Will hovered in the background to make sure there would not be any repeat of those near disasters of a few days ago. The adoptions had gone smoothly and Bevin had been overjoyed.

Bevin came to look forward to breakfast and supper with Will. They grew relaxed and comfortable in each other's company. A companionable bond formed as they discussed many topics, fought over differing points of view, and laughed together over the children's antics.

With only two children left, Bevin felt free to linger after meals. But while Will spent hours recanting his adventures, he was evasive when she asked about his youth. She had to admit she was curious about his childhood, yet she hadn't shared any more about Benjamin with Will except when she seemed to shock him by saying that in time she'd come to love him as was a wife's duty, she was sure of it.

Although they hadn't discussed their final destinations, Will was relieved the journey was nearing an end and he would be leaving the train and Miss Bevin O'Dea. He had begun to enjoy her company too much; he looked forward too much to spending time with her.

He wasn't the marrying kind and Will knew that a lady such as Bevin O'Dea would never settle for anything less; she didn't deserve anything less.

Will had the dining stewards set out a special table complete with flowers and candles. Despite the relief he felt to get away from Bevin before he no longer could, Will wanted their farewell dinner to be special. He had not told her he would be leaving. Good-byes had always been difficult for him. He had been careful, making it a point not to learn where she would be, since he did not totally trust himself to stay away from her. But for some reason this last night had to be memorable.

Will's back was to the door, facing away from the car Bevin was in, when he heard Bevin's voice. He swung around to greet her.

Bevin noticed the wide smile on his face fade as she, Prudence, and the two remaining children approached.

"Is everything all right?" Bevin asked, bewildered at the dour look shadowing his face.

"Yes. Fine. It's just that I had hoped you and I—"

"Oh." Prudence choked. "If you want I shall take the children back."

"Nonsense," Bevin said. "We want you here. Don't we, Will?"

Will shot Johnny a look clearly warning him he better be on his best behavior. Sly brown eyes smiled back at Will. No matter how hard Will had tried, he had not been able to befriend the little hoodlum. Instead, Will had sat on a tack, found the pant leg of his favorite trousers shortened to calf length, and endured an assortment of other pranks. If Bevin had not seemed to dote on that juvenile delinquent, Will would have enjoyed stringing the little monster up by his mischievous thumbs; for Bevin's sake Will remained silent.

Supper began without incident and was nearly through when Tara dropped her dessert down the front of her and let out a wail. "I ruined my bestest dress!"

In the next moment Tara scurried toward the wash-room in tears, Bevin and Prudence hurrying after her.

Left alone at the table with Johnny, Will was not fooled for an instant. The two youngsters had put their heads together and planned it.

"All right, Johnny, what's going on?"

"I don't know what you mean."

"I think you do. Why did you get everyone away from the table? Whatever it is you have to say, kid, out with it."

A sly grin slanted the youngster's mouth. "Leave Miss O'Dea alone."

"Are you threatening me now?" Will scratched his head, trying hard not to laugh at the miniature bully's tactics. If Will was not about to leave the train, he would have taken the kid over his knee.

Johnny screwed up his face. "What if I am?"

"I suppose I should be worried," Will said with a serious expression, forcing back a smile.

"Yeah."

"Jealous, huh?"

"Naw," Johnny lied. "She's a lady and's gonna get married. And you're not gonna ruin nothin' for her."

"Look, kid, let's get something straight. I have no intention of ruining anything for Miss O'Dea. And no runt is going to tell me whom I can or cannot see. As long as we have this chance to talk privately, you better knock off the pranks or I'm going to forget you're just a kid."

"Oh, yeah?" Johnny challenged. Out of the corner of his eyes he caught sight of Miss O'Dea returning. The man was not going to leave, so Johnny made a quick decision. He would prove to Miss O'Dea that Mr. Shoemaker was not good enough to waste her time on him.

78

Not letting a minute slip by, Johnny leaped up and sent hot coffee spilling into Will's lap.

"Aargh!" Will yelped, straightened up and grabbed Johnny's collar.

"Will Shoemaker! What are you doing?" demanded Bevin.

"I was just showing Johnny how during the war a soldier had me by the neck."

Johnny's mouth dropped open as he listened to the man cover for him again despite their conversation and all the things Johnny had done to him. It gave the boy pause and something to think about as he postured into an air of innocence.

"Will, I don't think it is such a good idea to be telling Johnny war stories. It could give him nightmares."

Give the kid nightmares, Will thought. The kid was a nightmare!

"I don't think the boy and I will have reason to be discussing the topic again," Will said, knowing he would be leaving the train soon and glad Bevin had seemed to forget about his offer of asking the farmers he knew to take in the little devil.

"Remember your offer for the children?" Bevin said, sitting back down.

Will rolled his eyes. He was not going to get off the hook after all. "Where's your assistant?"

"Prudence took Tara back to the car. The little girl was pretty upset about ruining her dress."

Bevin wrapped up her dessert and handed it to Johnny. "Take this back to Tara. It should make her feel better."

"Do I have to? I wanna stay here with you."

Bevin ruffled his mop of brown hair. "Yes, dear. You have to."

"Yessum, Miss O'Dea." When Miss O'Dea wasn't looking, Johnny stuck out his tongue at Mr. Shoe-

79

maker, grabbed the dessert and scurried off.

Once they were alone, she said, "If you've had a change of heart about the children I won't press you. I know Johnny is a handful. But I believe he just needs a family to care for him."

A keeper, don't you mean, Will thought. "No, no," Will said despite his inner feelings. "I'll send off a couple of telegrams tomorrow."

Bevin clasped Will's hands. "Thank you."

For long moments they remained with their hands touching, their eyes silently delving until Bevin haltingly withdrew her fingers and dropped them into her lap.

"Sorry," she said awkwardly.

"No need to be," Will rasped, his heart pounding madly inside his chest.

Bevin wet her suddenly dry lips with her tongue and quickly returned her attention to her empty plate. What had gotten into her? And worse yet, why had their brief contact caused such an unsettling sensation in her breast?

Long after Will had returned to his seat and the rest of the passengers in the car had retired, Will sat staring out the window. He hated good-byes. Always had. That was the reason he'd left the farm nine years ago without saying any. He would be happy to be away from that little terror, but he could not say the same for Bevin.

She had such a bright outlook on life concerning the children, such beautiful dancing blue eyes that they brought to mind a brilliant bluebird. She was a lovely bluebird and every time he saw one from now on he'd think of the spritely Irish lady. Pity her own personal goals were not as hopeful as they were for the children. She should be marrying someone for more than companionship, compatibility and security.

The thought of a lovely bluebird with its wings

clipped saddened him. Shaking himself out of such a dismal vein, he forced himself to think of her request. Tomorrow he would wire the Kruegers. Then he would write their address down and give it to Bevin before he left the train and Miss Bevin O'Dea behind forever.

Chapter Nine

The morning sun lay cold on the ground when Bevin stepped from the train at the station in Bowling Green. Overhead on a branch of a nearby hickory tree three bluebirds twittered, fluttering their wings against a clear sky. The birds drew her attention, reminding her of the strange twinkle in Will's eyes when he had explained that the bright bluebird was Missouri's state bird.

Dragging her attention back to the present, Bevin scanned the area. Only a few farmers had come to town in the cooling, fall weather in answer to the ad she had placed. No matter, thought Bevin. There were only two children left and she was confident that Will would come through for her. If not, surely Benjamin would take in the children.

"What's wrong with the boy?" a sturdy-carved, young man of medium size asked.

By the cut of his clothing, Bevin knew he was a farmer. The man's tone was not censuring, more bluntly inquisitive. By his stance Bevin could tell that the man had an interest in Johnny.

Johnny's mouth thinned, and he tried to hide his foot behind the other one. Instantly Johnny took a dislike to the man and made a mental note that if he ever saw the mean man again he would get even with him.

Bevin studied the stranger for a moment. At first she had intended to put him in his place for his rude observation of the child. But there was no malice in his expression. He had a pleasant face; a strong-set jaw and tight mouth. Wisps of light brown hair hung down to his thin brows. His gray eyes spoke for the stoic man in silent phrases, conveying more than Bevin was sure he used to verbally express himself. Overall, she found she liked him despite the crushing question.

"There's nothing wrong with this child that love and a little patience would not cure," she said, pulling Johnny to her side to return the stranger's piercing assessment.

He crossed heavily muscled arms over his chest. "And you have a lot of that, I suppose."

"I beg your pardon?"

Taking a wrinkled wire from his jacket pocket, the man stepped closer to Bevin. "You are Miss Bevin O'Dea?"

With hesitant suspicion she answered, "Yes."

The stern expression melted and a smile illuminated his face, which Bevin guessed was an all too infrequent gesture.

He held out a hand. "I am Benjamin Straub."

"Oh, how do you do, Mr. Straub," Bevin said awkwardly and placed her hand in his. His skin was warm and rough from years of hard labor. His touch did not cause her to want to shrink away, nor did it illicit the least bit of excitement in her breast either.

"You look surprised. I hope I am not a disappointment to you."

"Oh, dear, no. I just did not expect you to be here, since we've arrived several hours earlier than I wired you we would," Bevin quickly explained.

"I was looking so forward to your arrival that I de-

83

cided to take care of some business here in town early. I heard at the mercantile that there was an early train coming through the station today. So I came to have a look-see. When I saw you I knew you had to be Bevin O'Dea."

Recovering herself, Bevin beamed. "I am so glad you did, Mr. Straub."

The shadow of a frown crossed his face before he dismissed the subject with a wave of his hand. "Since we are engaged, and if you do not think it too forward of me, do you suppose you might consider calling me Benjamin, and allow me to refer to you as Bevin?"

"Yes, yes, of course . . . Benjamin." She hesitated a moment, then asked, "Patrick did not, per chance, accompany you, did he? I am anxious to see him."

"No, he didn't. But don't worry, you'll see him very soon; I know how long you have been waiting to be reunited with your brother."

She let out a nervous giggle of disappointment. She wanted to ask this man a thousand more questions about her brother but decided she must be patient. Instead, she turned toward Prudence. "Pru, do come here, won't you? I have someone I want you to meet. This is Benjamin. Benjamin Straub . . . my fiancé. Benjamin, this is Prudence Truesdale, my coworker and very dear friend."

Shock registered on Prudence's face over Benjamin Straub's sudden appearance at the train. Prudence had expected to be able to travel to the farm with Bevin before she was forced to return to Boston. Knowing that would be out of the question now, Prudence's spirits began to sink.

Prudence despaired of returning to her parents' big, empty house. Bevin O'Dea was the first real friend Prudence had ever had. She had been reared by a bevy of tutors and servants paid by her absent parents to tend all her needs except the most important: love, acceptance and support.

Bevin was the only one who had ever cared enough about Prudence to offer unconditional friendship and guidance. Bevin set limits and made demands on Prudence, and when she failed Bevin offered instruction and support which finally brought Prudence to believe that she did, indeed, have a place in life. But now directly in front of her stood the man who was going to sweep Bevin from Prudence's life, and the thought saddened the young girl.

With a droopy mouth, Prudence stepped forward, Tara in hand. In her excitement Prudence released Tara and the youngster moved to Johnny's side.

"It-it is nice to meet you, Mr. Straub."

"Pru, you do not have to look so forlorn."

"I am not what you expected?" Benjamin boldly asked Bevin, surprising her at his candor.

"No. I mean yes." Bevin's face flushed. "Of course, you are what I expected . . . and more. I think Pru was hoping to forestall her return East a little longer."

"That is a relief." He looked into those pure blue eyes and immediately fell in love.

Benjamin had originally chosen Bevin O'Dea to spend the rest of his life with because her letters had displayed more sincerity and family commitment than he had ever seen in a woman before. He knew she possessed the qualities he had been looking for in the wife who was going to work beside him. Now he was certain he had made the right choice. Together they would build the farm for the children he would leave it to someday.

Feeling particularly charitable due to the wisdom of his choice, Benjamin offered, "My home is not large, but if you are interested, Miss Truesdale, we would be honored if you stayed with us until the wedding, wouldn't we, Bevin?"

Prudence clasped her hands together, her eyes wide. "Please, do call me Prudence. And do you truly mean it?"

"Oh, yes, Pru. That would be wonderful," agreed Bevin, her heart filled with Benjamin's generosity.

"What about us?" interjected Johnny, holding Tara's hand.

At that moment Will rounded the corner. Absently folding a slip of paper he began to speak before assessing the scene before him. "Bevin, I have that address . . . for . . . you—"

"William?" Benjamin said, astonishment thick around each syllable. "I did not think you would come."

"Ben, what are you doing here?"

"Came to fetch my bride-to-be," Benjamin said without emotion, moving to Bevin's side.

"*Your* bride-to-be?" Will responded, his startled gaze spiking to Bevin. He had hoped to leave the train before she did. He swallowed an unexplainable lump clogging his throat; his life was more entwined with Miss Bevin O'Dea's than ever.

Bevin stood as if in a trance. Benjamin was the stepbrother Will had mentioned. A lump formed in her throat and threatened to shut off her air. Rapid-fire her mind did a replay over what she had told Will about Benjamin. Remembering what she had said about love, Bevin sent Will an imploring look.

Benjamin furrowed his brows at Will. "Yes, Bevin is going to become my wife. Do you know the lady?"

"We traveled on the same train. The lady and I had several occasions to speak about the children she has been escorting."

Benjamin looked over Tara and Johnny. Acceptance of William's explanation reflected in his gray eyes. "Yes, I can see where you might."

Another few awkward moments ensued as Johnny opened his mouth to protest. But a nod from Bevin effectively silenced the boy and the moment passed.

"What address were you talking about, William?" Benjamin questioned. Benjamin knew he could not keep his suspicion from his eyes. William had always had an eye for the ladies and Benjamin was going to make sure that William did not have any ideas about Bevin. But of course, he need not worry. Miss Bevin O'Dea was a most respectable lady; she was above reproach and certainly would not fall prey to William's advances as had so many of the town's girls before William had left Bowling Green.

While Benjamin could not entirely fault William for all his amorous escapades, there was no way Benjamin was going to let William think about sullying Miss Bevin's reputation. No. Benjamin's wife would be pure and loyal to him—only to him. Miss Bevin O'Dea possessed those qualities.

"I thought before I left you'd finally agreed to call me Will."

"All right . . . Will," Benjamin grudgingly acknowledged. He had never believed in shortening one's God-given name or addressing others in any other way than by using proper given names. He had grown up by that rule and felt it should be adhered to. His father had been a strict, dour man who commanded respect and Benjamin expected to receive the same due now that he owned the farm—or at least half of it. "Now, what address were you talking about?"

"Well, Ben," Will began purposely, knowing that his stepbrother preferred Benjamin. "I told Miss O'Dea that if she couldn't place the children by the time she reached her destination that I might know of someone who might take them. I was thinking of the Kruegers, but perhaps you'd have room out at the farm."

Bevin quietly watched the two stepbrothers, wondering why Benjamin had not been Will's first choice for someone to take the children. And she wondered at the incredible turn her life had taken: discovering that Will and Benjamin were stepbrothers.

Benjamin glowered darkly as Johnny and Tara jumped at the idea. "Can we? Can we?" Johnny begged, excited at the prospects of remaining near Miss O'Dea. He hid the thoughts of retribution he expected to exact from Benjamin Straub for the comments the man had made about his foot. Secretly, he was glad he would get his chance to make sure that that man would be good to Miss O'Dea—even though he did not like the man.

"Please," whined Tara, eyes saucered. "That'd mean Johnny and me could stay together and be brother and sister."

A look of pain crossed Johnny's face, causing Tara to amend, "I'm sorry, Johnny. I know nobody can take Crissy's place."

"I don't care about Crissy. I don't care!" he wailed and ran behind a nearby wagon.

Benjamin watched the children's high jinks in horror. If he did, indeed, take that pair in, they would have a few lessons to learn if they were going to live under his roof.

Benjamin immediately noted a fault in Bevin: she had a soft heart where those two children were concerned. She would have to learn how to deal effectively with such obvious ploys to get their own way. Children should be taught young that hard, honest work made good citizens, and idle hands were the devil's helpers. From the assessment he had made of the two children, it was obvious to Benjamin that caring for them was going to be no easy task.

Bevin looked imploringly at Benjamin. "They are

good children. While I cannot expect such generosity and I would not, it would be the Christian thing to offer them temporary shelter. And I know they would be a big help."

Bevin dropped her eyes and waited, reminding herself that henceforth she must remember to seek his counsel; she was no longer a woman alone who could speak her mind freely. She had others to consider now, and she wanted to be a good wife to Benjamin.

Benjamin sent William a sour look. William had always managed to get him involved in situations that were none of his concern. As children William brought home all sorts of homeless animals. Even that mangy old mutt, Sourdough, that lived under the house, had been one of William's good deeds. If Benjamin had had his way, he would have shot the flea-riddled beast and been done with it. Life on the farm was hard and there was no room for misplaced sentiment.

Benjamin glanced at Bevin's expectant face. Her demeanor was appropriately docile, but he could tell she silently prayed he would relent. Before Benjamin realized what he was saying, he blurted out, "All right. They can stay with us until we find a permanent placement for them."

"Oh, thank you, Benjamin." Bevin stepped up and threw her arms around his neck. She felt him stiffen. Shame over her bold public display of affection caused her to drop her hands to her sides. "Forgive me."

Benjamin looked around to check if any of his neighbors had been privy to Bevin's sudden neglect of proper decorum. No one seemed to be paying them any heed, so Benjamin relaxed.

"There is nothing to forgive, Bevin. I am happy that I can be of help."

"Big sacrifice," grumbled Johnny from behind the wagon.

89

"What did you say, dear?" Bevin asked Johnny.

Johnny looked from side to side. "Just that me and Tara is happy as mice."

"So am I, Johnny. So am I."

Will stood silently off to the side watching Bevin offer her misplaced thanks. Something akin to jealousy reared up inside him. He and Benjamin had always had a healthy sibling rivalry as children; a voice inside Will warned that a serious competition could very well erupt and create a deeper chasm between Benjamin and himself if he remained. The thought caused Will to admit that he was drawn to Bevin O'Dea more than he'd realized, and it would be difficult to stand by and watch her go to another man.

As the moments passed Will argued with himself. Bevin was his stepbrother's intended. Will had only known the lady but a few short days. While they had shared many insightful conversations after such a dubious beginning, their relationship was really nothing more than a curious budding friendship due to the close physical proximity train travel required.

For an instant Will considered getting back on the train and traveling as far away as the mighty engine would take him. But he had run for enough years. It was time to stop. Furthermore, he told himself, the lady had clearly just demonstrated her preference for Benjamin.

Shortly, Will knew he would discover some pretty face in town or on one of the neighboring farms and forget all about the redhead with the sparkling blue eyes. A bluebird chirped overhead, drawing Will's attention. He was reminded that the vibrant bird was the color of Bevin's eyes. Bluebird. Yes, that's what she was — a beautiful bluebird about to get her wings clipped and be caged by his rigid stepbrother. Well, it was none of his business, Will chided himself.

Bevin left Benjamin's side and retrieved Johnny from behind the wagon while Benjamin collected the baggage from the train and loaded it in the wagon he had driven into town. Once Benjamin was satisfied that everything was secured in the wagon, he helped the ladies up onto the seat and took a position a respectable distance from his bride-to-be.

"Johnny and Tara, you children hop in back," Bevin directed. Dutifully they complied and sat on the edge of the wagon, their feet dangling.

"Aren't you going to join us, Mr. Shoemaker?" Bevin asked Will when he continued to stand where he was, his hands in his pockets.

The return to formality grated on Will but he forced a smile and said, "I wouldn't miss my stepbrother's wedding for the world. Wait up while I get my bag."

"No rush," said Benjamin. "I've got business at the mercantile. We won't be leaving Bowling Green until after dinner."

"*You're* eating in town?" Will said.

"Yes" came the curt reply.

"Shouldn't we be?" questioned Bevin, who could not comprehend Will's attitude.

"Ben's never been much for eating out, is all," Will replied.

Benjamin glowered when Bevin said, "Won't you join us?"

"No, he won't," Benjamin interceded and turned to Will. "We'll meet you *after* dinner."

"Fine," Will said, surprised that his thrifty stepbrother was remaining in town for a meal.

"We'll pick you up on the corner of Main and Court in front of the courthouse at one sharp."

"The courthouse seems a fitting place," Will said, glancing at Bevin.

Bevin pinched her lips and remained silent, remembering that the courthouse was where she had first met Will. That meeting recounted Will's fiery temper in comparison to Benjamin's apparent restraint. The men had grown up together, yet they seemed to be quite opposite in temperament.

Benjamin smiled indulgently. "I am sure you must be tired from the long journey and would enjoy some refreshment before heading out to the farm."

"You are most considerate. Actually, we would appreciate a substantial meal; the children haven't eaten since early this morning." She turned her gaze on Will. "We shall see you after dinner, Mr. Shoemaker."

Will tipped his hat and turned from the cloying domestic scene of Bevin and the children in the wagon with his stepbrother. Without further hesitation, Will headed for the nearest saloon.

Chapter Ten

Gretchen Krueger hugged her shawl around her sturdy form against the crisp day and trudged behind her ma toward the mercantile. Her ma had promised her new material for a dress to wear to the upcoming Calico Ball and Gretchen intended to have it. She had worked hard all summer long doing a man's chores on the family's farm; it was time she reaped some of the rewards. She glanced over her ma's shoulder in time to spy Benjamin Straub helping two strange women from his wagon.

Gretchen's face fell as her ma stopped and swung around to whisper, "There is Benjamin, dear. Why don't you go join him?"

"He seems to be busy, don't you think, Ma?" Gretchen sniffed.

"Nonsense. You'll never catch that man if you wait for him to come to you. I've told you over and over again how I got your pa's attention, and it wasn't by waiting for him to discover that I existed and come running after me," Bertha Krueger lectured, fondly remembering all the machinations she'd gone through before Asa married her.

"I suppose I would like to know what Benjamin is doing with those strangers."

"Well, then, what're you standing here for?"

Gretchen gave her ma a conspiratorial grin and started for Benjamin, her head bobbing atop a jaunty pose.

"Wait, dear. Let me have a good look at you." Bertha smoothed the escaping strands of Gretchen's blond hair back behind her dainty ears. "There. That is much better. And don't forget to stand up straight. No man wants a wife who slouches."

"Yes, Ma."

Gretchen drew her lips into a feigned smile and approached the wagon. "Hello, Benjamin," she said shyly, locking her red-rough hands behind her back.

"Gretchen. How are you?"

"Fine, now that most of the harvest is in. Ma and me are in town shopping. I thought I'd sew up a new dress to wear to the upcoming social." Gretchen's eyes studied the two women as she spoke. She dismissed the birdlike woman as too awkward and unsure by the way she carried herself to be a threat. The redhead stood straight, her shoulders proud, her entire appearance denoting confidence.

"Gretchen, I don't believe you have met my bride-to-be, Miss Bevin O'Dea," Benjamin said. "And her friend, Miss Prudence Truesdale. Bevin, Prudence, this is Gretchen Krueger. Gretchen lives with her family on a neighboring farm."

Gretchen clasped her hand to her chest at the news, and forgot all about asking after the coincidence that the woman shared a common last name with Patrick. "Your bride-to-be?"

"Yes."

"But she is Irish," Gretchen blurted out before thinking.

"Yes. And proud of it," Bevin interceded, keeping her voice light in order to defuse what could become a difficult situation. "How do you do?"

Ignoring the girl's apparent displeasure, Bevin offered her hand in a gesture of friendship, but the Krueger girl stood staring, her mouth agape.

"Gretchen, aren't you going to congratulate us?" prodded Benjamin.

"Oh. Yes . . . yes, sure. Congratulations," Gretchen returned weakly. "Please, forgive me. I didn't mean to be rude. It is just that . . . that folks expected Benjamin to marry someone from around here who shares his proud heritage, not some outsider."

"Gretchen," Benjamin warned.

"I meant—"

"It's all right, Benjamin. I'm sure Gretchen was merely expressing her surprise," Bevin said, wondering why Benjamin had kept his intentions to marry her to himself.

"Thank you, Miss O'Dea. You were quite right. I am afraid I was surprised to learn that Benjamin had chosen a woman who already has children. I know how important having his own family is to Benjamin," Gretchen said.

Johnny glared up at the one called Gretchen. She was not being very nice to Miss O'Dea, and Johnny could not understand why Miss O'Dea did not just tell the big meany off and be done with it. 'Course if it was up to him, he'd send Benjamin Straub and Gretchen Krueger both off. Grown-ups were supposed to know so much, but it was obvious to Johnny that Miss O'Dea was making a big mistake. That dumb, old Benjamin Straub was not good enough to spit on her boots.

Bevin gathered the children into the protective circle of her arms. Johnny pouted; Tara stood wide-eyed.

"Although I wish I could claim Johnny and Tara as my own, I'm afraid Miss Truesdale and I are only their guardians until they are placed in permanent homes."

Gretchen had hoped that the children would become a problem between Benjamin and Bevin O'Dea. Gretchen knew that having his own children was one of Benjamin's top priorities, and the way that woman hung onto those scrawny children would surely lead to difficulties between them. She would have seen to that.

"You hope to place these two on nearby farms?" Gretchen asked, needing to learn if using the two children might still be a possibility.

"As a matter of fact," Bevin unfolded the slip of paper Will had given her and quickly reread the information scribbled there, "Mr. Will Shoemaker wrote your parents' names down as a possible placement for the children." Bevin handed Gretchen a copy of the ad she had placed in the local newspapers to reinforce her story since the Krueger girl looked to be skeptical.

"Will Shoemaker?"

"He's back," Benjamin grumbled.

"Here?" Gretchen asked, astounded. She remembered her parents talking about the circumstances surrounding the man's departure from Bowling Green when she was only ten years old.

"Yes, Gretchen. He came in on the train this morning."

"The same train as Miss O'Dea?"

"Yeah," supplied Johnny. "So what?"

Gretchen clasped her palms to her cheeks. "Oh, my."

An awkward silence ensued until Benjamin broke it. "I have business to tend to and Bevin has only just arrived, so if you will excuse us, Gretchen?"

Knowing how important it was to become an accepted member of the community of which Gretchen was a part, Bevin suggested, "Please. I do hope you will come out to the farm for a visit soon. There is so much I would like to learn about the town, and I'm sure you would be a big help if you do not mind."

Her features pinched around eyes reflecting the coldness of disappointment, Gretchen grated, "Of course not. I look forward to seeing more of you. And you, too, Miss Truesdale."

"Yes, I can tell you do," Prudence snipped, but dropped her eyes at Bevin's look. Surprised by her own sudden display of forcefulness, Prudence meekly stepped back.

"After I get Bevin settled in I will bring her by so you can introduce her to the ladies in the grange," Benjamin said.

"The grange?" questioned Bevin, her interest piqued.

"I'm sure you have a thousand questions about the community and farm life, and all the obligations that you'll have as my wife, Bevin, but there is no need to concern yourself with any of it yet. Once I get you settled, I'll start your education."

Bevin nodded her acceptance despite the stab of resentment she felt by the words *your education* and the questions circulating in her mind. She must learn to adjust to the accepted ways of her new home — even if it meant tempering her curiosity. She would make Benjamin a good wife he would always be proud of, she silently vowed.

Gretchen stood stiff with horror as Benjamin dismissed her and blithely escorted those two interlopers into the mercantile. She simmered inside with disappointment and anger. She had waited for Benjamin for years, discouraging all other suitors because she was certain that she would become Mrs. Benjamin Straub. Now out of nowhere that . . . *that Irishwoman* arrives with plans to lead her Benjamin to the altar — seemingly without effort.

"My dear, who were those women?" questioned Bertha Krueger, adjusting her blouse front across her heavy bosom as she joined her daughter.

Her ma's voice intruding into her murderous thoughts, Gretchen glanced down at the advertisement Bevin O'Dea had given her. "They are from the Children's Aid Society in Boston and hope to place those two children in permanent homes."

"Oh, those two darling children need homes?" She felt a surge of excitement. "Just like my Patrick years ago."

"Yes," Gretchen replied, thinking only of Benjamin. "And undoubtedly they hope to place two more with you and Pa."

Bertha cocked her head, considering the benefits of having a couple of extra pairs of hands around the farm. Then her vision fastened on the boy's limp. Asa would never agree to take in a child who could not carry his weight.

Bertha gave voice to her thoughts. "Those two ladies must be special indeed to devote their time to seeing that children find families."

Gretchen settled a look of disgust on her ma. "The redhead is Benjamin's bride-to-be."

Bertha's hands flew to her temples. "Goodness gracious! Benjamin never even hinted at his intentions to import a bride."

Temporarily at a loss for words, the two women stood side by side as silent minutes ticked off the clock.

Remembering herself all of a sudden, Bertha uttered, "How dreadful for you, dear. But it may be a blessing in disguise. Benjamin thinks more of you as family, I'm afraid. I've hated watching you pine away for him all these years. There are plenty of young men in town who would be more than willing to become your beau — men who you would not have to pursue."

"Well, I have no intention of just pining any longer."

"Benjamin has made his choice," Bertha ventured,

still puzzled.

"He isn't married yet. And who knows? With a little help he might just up and change his mind."

Bertha's weathered face paled. "You're not thinking of taking my advice on how to catch a husband now, are you?"

"I'm long past the thinking stage, Ma. Let's go home. I've got some plans to make."

"But what about the material for your new dress?" Bertha protested, wishing that she hadn't told her daughter how she had finally gotten her husband to the altar by allowing Asa rein to his amorous appetites.

"Later. I'll worry about a new dress later."

Gretchen took her ma's arm and ushered the aging woman along the walk at a fast clip. The girl's mind was whirring so fast with possible scenarios that she failed to notice the man standing directly in front of her path.

"Oh!" Gretchen squealed as she smashed into the tall stranger.

Startled by the impact, Will circled his arms around the young girl in a natural reaction. He looked down at the stunned blonde. There was a vague familiarity about her.

"Have we met before?" Will asked, then noticed the elder woman. "Mrs. Krueger."

Confusion held Bertha's expression. "Do I know you?"

Will released Gretchen, who had remained, seemingly content, in his arms. "You used to run me out of your kitchen with a broom after I snatched a handful of your freshly baked cookies."

Bertha scrutinized the ebony-haired man closer. "Well, landsakes, I can't believe my eyes. You're Mary's boy. Little Willie Shoemaker! 'Course, you're not so little anymore. And you know very well, I used to let you get away with those cookies."

"It's Will now. Please."

"Little Willie Shoemaker," she repeated, musing over times past. Her brows joined as a thought overtook her. "Folks never thought you'd return, the way you left the farm 'n all."

"Guess they were mistaken."

"They sure were." Bertha tittered. "When did you get back into town?"

"I just arrived on the train this morning."

"Well, glory be. Won't Asa be surprised to see you again."

"Ma, aren't you going to introduce me?" Gretchen whined, thinking how the man had given Bevin O'Dea her parents' names as a possible placement for those two children. It had annoyed her at first, but the more she thought about it, she realized it might have a wide range of possibilities.

"Will, you remember Gretchen, don't you, son?"

Will surveyed the sturdy-built, young woman. She had nicely rounded proportions. She no longer resembled the scrawny little nuisance in pigtails he recalled. The Kruegers had always doted on the girl since she'd been their only child to survive infancy. They had always welcomed Will into their home when he ran away from Joseph Straub. Asa Krueger had longed for a son after they lost three male babies shortly after birth, and treated Will like the son he had never been able to have.

"I remember Will," Gretchen said, blushing for the man's benefit. "Have you come home to stay?" she asked.

"Gretchen, that's no kind of a question to ask a man who has just returned," Bertha chided.

"I apologize, Will."

"No need. It was an honest question. Fact is, Mrs. Krueger, I'm not sure what my plans are yet."

"Have you heard that Joseph passed on?" Bertha

asked.

"Yes. Benjamin got a letter to me. Seems the old man left me half the farm in his will."

"It's about time he done something for you," Bertha said without thinking, then fastened a hand over her mouth to cover her embarrassment.

At the tightening of Will's face, Bertha quickly amended, "Forgive an old woman, Will. I didn't mean to be carrying on the way I done."

"Think nothing of it. There's nothing to forgive."

Gretchen stood taking in the whole scene. Will Shoemaker was back after a long absence; Benjamin had taken a fiancée who had arrived on the same train as Will Shoemaker. She mulled it over in her mind for a moment. That meant that they had been traveling together. Perhaps he could tell her more about the Irishwoman.

"Oh, Will, it's near dinnertime. How would you like to join Ma and me at the restaurant? We are going to have something to eat before we head back home."

"We are?" Bertha said, confused by the sudden change in her daughter. At Gretchen's glare, Bertha amended, "Oh, yes, we are. Please, join us, son. I want to hear where you've been keeping yourself."

"And I'd love to hear all about your train trip. I've never been on one, you know," Gretchen gushed.

Bertha's head snapped up at the way Gretchen was acting. The girl only had eyes for Benjamin since she turned fourteen and now here she was turning her wiles on Will Shoemaker.

Remembering her own plan to make Asa jealous and then let him have his way with her years ago, Bertha started to worry. If Gretchen had in mind a similar scheme or thought to use Will Shoemaker to try to make Benjamin Straub notice her, Gretchen was toying with wildfire.

101

Bertha continued to fret as they headed toward the restaurant. Trying to pit those stepbrothers against each other could end up bringing everyone involved a whole lot more grief than Gretchen realized.

Chapter Eleven

Bevin browsed about the mercantile while Benjamin carried out his business with a group of six men seated around a potbelly stove set in the middle of the store. She strolled along one side of the spacious room stacked with a variety of household items, can goods and open barrels filled with flour and grains. Then she moved to the other side, which held an assortment of cloth, ready-made clothing and other necessities. Four worn straight-back chairs stood under the picture window in front of the shop, three of which were occupied by matronly ladies in worn calico.

Bevin looked up to catch sight of the women watching her. She smiled. She started in their direction when a loud crash stopped her. She whirled around to see Johnny, sitting in the midst of a mountain of spilled flour. The white dust covered the child from head to toe and surrounded him.

"What in tarnation?" cried Benjamin from across the room. Horror replaced the proud grin he had worn a minute ago after he had announced his intentions to be married.

That boy again!

The proprietor rushed toward the disaster, waving his apron in distress in an effort to fan out the choking white powder which hung in the air. "What are ya doing in here unaccompanied?" The man yanked the boy up by the arm, sending a white cloud about the store again.

Johnny squealed and kicked at the man.

"Why, ya little varmint. I'll teach ya t' show better respect for your elders."

"Sir, he is just a boy," Bevin said, coming to Johnny's rescue.

"That does not excuse what he did," said Benjamin, joining the fray. He surveyed the mess. That kid had only been in town a short time and he was already causing a stir. Benjamin wished that those two children had been placed. But since they had not been and were Bevin's charges he had to assume responsibility for them. Benjamin Straub did not shirk his responsibilities.

"Oscar, charge the cost of the flour to my account."

Reluctantly, the proprietor let the child go. "It ain't gonna be cheap, ya know. Ya ought t' jist let me charge his pa."

Brushing the child off, Bevin snapped up at the unthinking man, "Johnny doesn't have a father."

Oscar stiffened. "That right, Benjamin?"

" 'Fraid so." Benjamin scratched his ear. "Oscar, I want you to meet Miss Bevin O'Dea, my bride-to-be."

"How do, Miss. Benjamin was just tellin' us 'bout ya. What ya got t' do with this lad?"

"I brought him with me from Boston," she answered proudly.

"Miss Bevin is an angel of mercy of sorts, Oscar. She has been placing children like Johnny with farm families between here and Boston. He and the girl back there"—he motioned to Tara—"are the only ones left."

"No one's gonna want a boy like that one," the proprietor observed.

Bevin stiffened and pulled the boy to her. Anger turned her cheeks red, and she had to bite her lip to keep from retorting with something stronger than, "Johnny will make any family proud."

A murmur buzzed around the room, and shuttered eyes assessed and categorized Bevin and the boy. Bevin felt like a specimen under glass and shifted her stance.

"Evvie," Prudence stepped up, Tara in hand, "perhaps it would be best if Tara and I waited outside for you."

"No, it is all ri—"

"Yes, Prudence, I think that would be an excellent idea. And take Johnny with you, too," Benjamin advised, dismissing Prudence and the children before Bevin had the opportunity to finish her sentence.

Prudence looked to Bevin for direction. When Bevin pinched her lips but said nothing, Prudence grabbed the two children by the hands and quickly left the mercantile.

Although Bevin was most displeased that Benjamin had not taken it upon himself to be Johnny's champion, she reminded herself that Benjamin had offered to pay for the damages. She could not expect any more from a man she had just met.

In time she was certain that Benjamin would come to care for the children as much as did she. Until then, she would have to be patient. After all, Benjamin had not been around children much; his letters had said as much. That was it. It would take time for Benjamin to adjust.

Bevin stood in the store and allowed Benjamin to introduce her to the other patrons. If Bevin had expected to be accepted with open arms, she found she had been sadly mistaken. The residents were coolly cordial, but it was painfully evident that they considered Bevin an outsider.

Once outside, Bevin let out a sigh. "I do not believe those people liked me."

"Nonsense," Benjamin returned. "They don't know you personally yet. Once they do, they won't be able to help themselves. You do need to keep a closer eye on the boy, though."

"Yes, Benjamin, I shall," Bevin said dutifully after suppressing the urge to defend Johnny.

"Good. Why don't we get something to eat before I show you your new home?"

"That would be nice. I know the children are hungry."

"While I load my order, perhaps you could help Prudence clean Johnny up so he'll be presentable."

"Yes, of course."

Bevin walked over to the hitching post and joined Prudence and the children.

"I am sorry, Evvie. I should have been watching Johnny closer."

"It was an accident," sniffled Johnny. "I didn't mean to dump that stupid old flour over. Really I didn't."

Bevin took a handkerchief from her skirt pocket and wiped the white smudges from his cheeks. "I know you didn't, Johnny. But from now on you must try to be more careful. Benjamin has been kind enough to offer to let all of us stay out at the farm, so we must remember to respect the way he does things."

Johnny dropped his head. "Yessum, ma'am. Can I help Benjamin put the boxes in the wagon?"

"I think that would be a real good idea."

Once Bevin finished tidying Johnny up, he ran over to Benjamin. "Can I help?"

Benjamin glanced down at the boy's foot. "No, boy. The boxes are too heavy for you. Another time maybe."

Johnny blanched. "No, they ain't."

Benjamin was not used to having his orders questioned. He gave the boy a look meant to squelch any further discussion on the topic. "You heard me."

"Yessum." Defeated, Johnny shuffled back to Bevin. "He don't need no help."

Bevin patted his shoulder. "There will be lots to do out at the farm."

"Yeah," the boy grumbled. "But he"—Johnny pointed an accusing finger—"probably won't let me do nothing."

"Why wouldn't Benjamin let you help?"

" 'Cause he's like ever'body else. He thinks I'm nothing but a cripple."

"That's not true."

Johnny pouted. "Yes, it is."

Bevin wiped patches of flour she had missed before from the boy's face and hands. She raised his chin with her crooked index finger. "Well, then, we'll prove him wrong."

Johnny brightened. "You really think so?"

"I know so."

Benjamin loaded the last bag and joined Bevin. "Ready?"

"Yes."

Benjamin offered his arm. Escorting his attractive bride-to-be with Prudence and the children trailing behind, Benjamin held the door open while they entered the restaurant and took a seat near the window.

Sitting across the room, Gretchen watched Benjamin and that woman with keen interest. She should be the one with Benjamin. She had been the one who had stepped in and taken care of the house after the old man died. She had gone over to the Straub farm regularly and cooked and cleaned for almost a year. Then that woman shows up to usurp her position.

"Gretchen, are you all right?" Will asked, intruding into her thoughts.

"Yes, I'm fine. You were saying that you arrived on

107

the train this morning. Wasn't Benjamin's soon-to-be wife on the same train?" she asked with girlish innocence.

Will had not missed the way Gretchen had been staring at Benjamin. The girl was a little too transparent with her feelings.

"Yes."

"Benjamin's already told us that, dear," Bertha interjected, unaware what her daughter was up to.

Gretchen screwed up her face at her ma's interference. She was hoping the man would volunteer information. He had not. She was going to have to work for it.

"Do you know Miss O'Dea?" Gretchen probed.

"Only slightly. 'Fraid there isn't much I can tell you." Will had no intention of getting involved in what he perceived as a disgruntled young woman hoping to glean what she could from him.

"Oh." Disappointment felled her lips.

"Is there something specific you're looking to find out?"

"It isn't important. I was merely making conversation."

Surrounded by an uneasy silence, they placed their orders. Unable to endure it any longer, Bertha chattered, "Will, tell us what you been up to after you left."

"Well, ma'am, there's not much to tell. I've spent a lot of time drifting and seeing the country. Worked at a mill for a while, then bronc busting, and finally mining out in Colorado Territory."

"But you came in on the train from back East, didn't you?" Bertha puzzled.

"Yes. I made a trip to Boston to visit kin. That's when Benjamin's letter caught up with me, and I headed back here."

"You must have many exciting tales to tell," pushed

108

Gretchen.

Will shrugged. "Not so many."

Closed-mouth man, Gretchen silently grated.

For the remainder of the meal not much conversation was exchanged. When Bertha told how much work there continued to be out at the farm, Will brought up the subject of the children needing homes.

"I saw those two darling children. And I know you gave Asa's and my names to Benjamin's pretty little wife-to-be. But you know that the decisions regarding the farm are Asa's. You'll have to speak with him."

"As soon as I get settled I'll bring them over."

"Oh, no. Don't do that," Bertha said, flustered. "I mean . . . you should talk to Asa first." Ashamed, Bertha dropped her eyes.

Realizing that Mrs. Krueger must be aware of Johnny's handicap, Will said, "Those two kids are such good workers Benjamin will probably want to keep them at the farm before I have a chance to talk to Asa."

Her cheeks burning with shame, Bertha gave Will a grateful nod. "Thank you, Will, for saving a foolish old lady from herself."

"Think nothing of it," Will said. Out of the corner of his eye he noticed Bevin rise to leave with Benjamin. "Looks as if I'd best be heading out before I miss my ride out to the farm."

Will rose as Benjamin ushered Bevin toward their table. "Mrs. Krueger, I'd like you to meet Miss Bevin O'Dea, my bride-to-be," Benjamin proudly said.

Bertha smiled brightly while Gretchen sulked as introductions were completed and they left the restaurant.

"Gretchen, dear, you really must try to be more pleasant to Benjamin's future wife," Bertha suggested when they were left alone.

"I don't know why. Miss Bevin O'Dea will never fit

109

into this town and our way of life."

"She will if people give her a chance. Especially if you take her under your wing, introduce her to folks, and help her adjust as Benjamin wants you to do."

Her elbows on the table, Gretchen rested her chin on the palm of her hands. "And what if I don't?"

Bertha ignored the girl's surliness. "O'Dea? Why that was Patrick's last name when he came to us," she said, just now connecting the names.

Gretchen's head popped off her hands, her eyes bright. "It sounded familiar when Benjamin introduced us. So she's the sister Patrick has refused to talk to anyone about."

Seated on the wagon between the two stepbrothers, Bevin could feel the tension despite the seemingly relaxed position the pair maintained. There was no love lost between them. That was evident from the bits and pieces of conversation they had exchanged, and from her conversations with Will on the train.

The wagon rocked and bumped through town, down Ashley Road then turned and passed the brick courthouse, reminding Bevin of all the similar structures she had taken the children to to find homes. The weathervane pivoted south, southeast in answer to the breeze that had come up to further chill the day.

Bevin enjoyed a glimpse of the town as they passed through it. It was a thriving town with a half-dozen stores, blacksmith shop, druggist, milliners and dress shop. She noticed at least eight windows lettered with attorney-at-law signs in bold print. Bowling Green was not Boston, but it looked to be a pleasant, wholesome town in which to raise a family.

Bevin glanced back over her shoulder to make sure the children were bundled up. Prudence sat between

Johnny and Tara, her feet dangling as merrily as the children's among the dust swirls kicked up by the wagon wheels.

Once the trees and shops gave way to open space, Bevin turned to Benjamin and asked, "How far from town do you live?"

" 'Bout ten miles. The farm is only two miles from the granddaddy of rivers, the Mississippi."

"Is it a very big farm?"

" 'Bout one hundred 'n fifty acres more or less. Average size."

"A farm that large could undoubtedly use extra help," she ventured, hoping Benjamin would take the subtle hint about the children. In his letters Benjamin had never written much about his land other than to say that it provided him with an adequate living.

"I've always managed," was all he said in response.

Feeling discouraged, Bevin turned her attention to the landscape. The gently rolling prairie waved golden grasses and wildflowers in the breeze. A neat framed farmhouse stood alone among open fields.

For the rest of the trip all remained quiet, absorbed in their own thoughts. It was nearly five o'clock when Benjamin turned the team off the road and up a long gravel drive. At the end of the drive was a two-story house crafted from walnut logs eight inches in diameter. The sloping roof was covered with shingles, peaking near a chimney which ran up the outside of the house. Running along the length of the house was a covered porch, and Bevin could envision herself sitting on the swing sipping lemonade as she and Benjamin watched their children play in the yard. But when she tried to focus on Benjamin's face, Will's face materialized before her. She blinked to erase the vision, but each time she tried to conjure up Benjamin, Will kept intruding into her mind.

111

"Bevin. Bevin. We're here. We're home." Benjamin stood to the side of the wagon, his arms raised to help her down.

Snapped out of her reverie, Bevin allowed Benjamin to lift her down. "I love your home, Benjamin."

"Soon it will be our home," Benjamin crooned.

"Hope it isn't going to be too crowded with all of us living there," intruded Will, a lopsided grin on his face.

"Not for long," Benjamin grumbled.

"Yeah," Johnny whispered, his eyes glittering with mischief.

Bevin was too wrapped up in the welcoming simplicity of the house and outbuildings to pay any attention to the budding friction. A warmth spread through her. Benjamin and the farm offered the kind of life she had always dreamed of while living on the streets.

This was her home now—where she belonged. Soon she would be reunited with Patrick. Benjamin was sure to come to love the children as much as she did. It was a cozy picture Bevin was painting for herself. She and Benjamin. A family. Her brother. The two children. The farm. Her own home. All she had to do was make herself truly believe that everything was just the way she had envisioned it.

Chapter Twelve

Leaving the children out in the yard, the adults went in the house. The white house consisted of an attic room, three bedrooms, a kitchen, dining room and parlor. Somehow Bevin managed to conceal her burgeoning excitement during the tour despite the pleasure gripping her. It was perfect!

Cozy was the appropriate term for the house. Overstuffed, worn furniture. Braided rag rugs. Homemade tables. There was nothing pretentious about Benjamin's way of life. He obviously did not believe in squandering his money. Yet everything to make the life she had always hoped for was here.

"Bevin, why don't you and Prudence go into the parlor and make yourselves at home while Benjamin and I bring in your bags and fetch wood for the stove," Will suggested. "You ladies have had a pretty busy day and must be exhausted from the long trip."

Bevin looked to Benjamin. If he had other plans he was not voicing them. "It has been a tiring trip. Prudence and I could use a few moments."

"Then it's settled. Come on, Ben."

"Soon as I change my clothes," Benjamin grated, not understanding the ladies' need to rest. There was little time to sit back on the farm. There were always chores to be done, Sunday being the only day in which he condoned the slightest idleness—but not for himself. Benjamin was accustomed to working seven days a week as his wife would also be expected to do. He made a mental note to make sure that Bevin understood that after he gave her a few days to adjust.

"We can change in the barn. Don't you always keep an extra set of work clothes out there?" Will set forth.

Benjamin grunted his assent and frowned, but followed Will from the house while Bevin and Prudence went into the parlor and settled onto the sofa.

"It is a pleasant little house, is it not?" Prudence said, thinking about her own elegant home. Somehow, though, there was more love inside these walls than there ever had been within the mansion in which she had grown up.

"Yes, it is." Bevin looked down and studied the flowered fabric for a moment before returning her gaze to Prudence. "Pru, what do you think of Benjamin?" Bevin asked, not sure why she was looking to her young companion for reassurance.

"He seems quite nice and capable too. A real upstanding member of the community."

"Yes, that he is. Respected too."

"Is he all that you expected?"

"All and more."

"As his wife you will have a lot to live up to," Prudence said. While she found Benjamin a gentleman, she worried that he was the kind of man who might have trouble allowing someone like Bevin the freedom to be herself. Bevin was not a meek follower and Prudence was surprised that Bevin had held her tongue earlier today. Bevin was used to taking charge, and Prudence could not help but wonder whether Bevin would be able to temper her own personality to fit Benjamin's.

"I realize that, and I am prepared to accept the challenge."

"Challenge? Isn't that a funny way to talk about love and marriage?"

"Pru, marriage presents many challenges in life. Each one requires that a husband and wife have enough love for one another to overcome all that life puts in their way. I'm sure that Benjamin and I will be compatible enough to compliment each other and make a good marriage."

"If you say so." Prudence wanted to ask why Bevin had seemed to skirt the topic of love where she and Benjamin were concerned, but Prudence did not want to mar Bevin's joy with her surroundings on her first day here. "What about the children? Shall I take them with me when I return to Boston?"

"Of course not!" A conspiratorial grin captured Bevin's lips.

"But they . . . they almost seem to annoy him," Prudence blurted out, then slapped a hand to her lips.

"Nonsense! Benjamin loves children. He wrote as much in his letters, and told me how much he wants a family."

"Yes, but was he referring to his own children, and not someone else's?"

"I'm sure that in time Benjamin will come to care as deeply for Johnny and Tara as I do."

"Evvie, I hope you are right. . . ."

Out behind the barn Benjamin had changed into his work clothes and began placing log after log into

115

Will's arms.

"Never thought you'd return," Benjamin said coolly.

"Then why did you write that letter informing me of my inheritance?"

"It was my responsibility."

"Good old Benjamin. Always the responsible one," Will commented as Benjamin heaved yet another log onto the growing stack.

"I consider honor and responsibility a virtue. Pity you never developed more of it."

"You always had more than enough for both of us," Will answered, unaffected by the blot Benjamin applied to Will's character.

"Pity my pa was never able to instill those standards of morality in you before you took off."

"I didn't exactly take off," Will corrected, determined not to let Benjamin push him into another fight as he'd done so often when they were children.

"What would you call leaving Pa and me in the middle of harvest time, like you did?"

"If you'll recall it wasn't exactly my idea. Your father told me to get out so often that I finally obliged him."

"Taking the money that Pa had saved for you, I might add."

Will blanched but quickly recovered himself. "It was owed to me—wages due."

"Many believe otherwise."

"Look, that was nine years ago. I don't intend to stay long, so can't we try'n live peaceably under the same roof while I'm here?"

"Of course we can—that is as long as you don't get any ideas about Bevin."

"She's your fiancée, not mine."

"Just don't go getting any notions in your head to

116

the contrary. She is a lady and I don't want her subjected needlessly to any unwanted advances."

"Quit worrying. I have no plans to force any *unwanted* attentions on your lady," Will said, feeling a strange unsettled sensation at the implication of Bevin being Benjamin's personal property. Then Will almost had to laugh—not a word was mentioned about Prudence.

Benjamin stacked another log onto Will's load. "Go dump those in the woodbox in the kitchen while I chop enough for tomorrow. I intend to spend the entire day showing Bevin the farm."

Once Will disappeared around the corner of the barn, Benjamin brought the ax down and split the logs with all the pent-up feelings he had experienced this day. When he had answered Bevin O'Dea's letter he had never dreamed that their correspondence would develop into anything more than mutual respect. Even after he had become fond of the lady through her letters and had proposed, he had not imagined that such a vision of loveliness would appear at the station to greet him. Benjamin sighed. For the first time in his life he found himself in love, and then his stepbrother had to show up and blight his happiness.

Damn William Shoemaker all the way back to hell!

By the time Will returned with Johnny in tow, Benjamin had a neat pile of wood split and ready to be hauled to the house.

"There's the wood I want you to take to the kitchen like I showed you," Will instructed Johnny.

"Really?" the boy asked excitedly, then grew serious as he noticed Benjamin Straub's dark expression. "Is it okay, Mr. Straub?"

Will patted the child on his thin shoulder. "Of

course it is," he answered for Benjamin.

"Go ahead, boy," Benjamin said gruffly, conceding defeat but looking concerned as the child gathered up an armful and limped off toward the house with his heavy burden.

"You shouldn't have interfered between me and the boy," Benjamin grated.

"Someone had to. You're treating him like a total invalid. He isn't. Can't you see that he's trying to please you? He needs—no, desires—to be treated like a normal child, which he is."

"Not with that foot, he isn't," insisted Benjamin.

"Yes, Ben, he is! And you had better start treating him that way or you're going to lose the best thing to ever happen to you."

"Am I to presume that you are referring to Miss Bevin O'Dea?"

"That's exactly who I'm referring to."

Benjamin glared at William, wondering why William seemed to have developed such an interest in his bride-to-be and her charges. Memories of all the girls William had been involved with before he left Bowling Green caused Benjamin to feel protective toward Bevin. The sooner he settled the issue of the farm and sent William on his way, the better!

Will stared back at Benjamin. Benjamin had always been so narrow-minded and stiffly principled to a fault. Even as a child Benjamin had been rigid in his thinking, and for the lady's sake Will hoped that Benjamin would come to relax with Bevin's influence or he would destroy her spirit and their chances for a happy marriage.

Benjamin was the first to break eye contact. He swung the ax into a big log, wedging it into the dry bark. "We'd best get one thing straight between us from the outset: Miss Bevin O'Dea is off limits to you."

"I think we just had this conversation."

"Just don't try to interfere in our lives."

Will opened his mouth to retort but Benjamin raised a palm to stop him. "No. Don't bother. I won't hear another word on the subject. Now, if you'll leave me alone; I have work to do."

Will shrugged. "Since you obviously don't want any help, I'll be inside."

Left alone, Benjamin picked up a milking pail, hung a stool on his arm, and headed toward his four milch cows. The old barn had always been his special place where he went to sort through things. There was something relaxing, cleansing about being alone in the big old building, surrounded by the smell of hay and leather from the harnesses.

When Benjamin had been a small child he had often retreated into a big, weathered structure in his mind where he curled up with his head on his knees and thought through his troubles. He had clung to his fantasy until he confided in his pa once and the old man had scoffed at the foolishness of it. Wanting to please the man, Benjamin forced himself to substitute the family barn for his make-believe one.

His hands began a rhythmic squeezing as he milked the cow. Flexing his fingers around the soft teats helped release pent-up emotions, and Benjamin pulled until the bucket started to fill with the white liquid.

"Damn you, William Shoemaker." He increased his efforts. "Why did you have to come back now?"

A loud crash snapped his attention to the cut wood.

Johnny stood, a horrified expression on his freck-

119

led face, staring at the wood, which now spread out at his feet in total disarray.

"What are you doing, boy?" Benjamin demanded more harshly than he had intended.

"I-I didn't mean to knock the wood over," Johnny blurted out, his face paled around brown eyes as big as supper plates. "It just sorta fell."

"Don't try to take so much at one time from now on," Benjamin advised a little more evenly.

"Yes, sir."

The boy continued to stand there like a stalk of corn out in the field.

"What are you waiting for? Get to it," Benjamin snapped just like his pa had at him.

Johnny's eyes grew to twice their size and he scrambled to hurry through the chore. He had thought Mr. Straub a meany before, and now his dislike grew into fear. He stumbled as he left the barn with his load, looked back to see if the man was watching him, and let out a relieved sigh that his awkwardness had gone unobserved before disappearing into the twilight.

Benjamin finished the chores and stayed out in the barn, forgoing supper, until all lights in the house had been extinguished. Then, removing his heavy work boots at the back stoop, he quietly crept to his room only to discover his stepbrother spread out on his side of the bed.

"What are you doing in my bedroom?"

"The bedrooms are occupied and Bevin put Johnny in the attic room," Will said, thinking how he had spent his youth there. "Thought you might have decided to sleep in the barn tonight," Will added, turning over to face Benjamin.

"Humph. Tomorrow we'll double up those children." Benjamin shed his clothes. "Move over."

"You missed a good supper tonight. That lady of yours sure can cook."

Benjamin rolled over on his side away from his annoying stepbrother.

"I had hoped you might've outgrown the silent treatment. Aren't you going to talk to me?"

"Nothing to talk about."

"Only a lifetime of friction between us," came back Will, unable to let it drop this time as he had in the past in response to Benjamin's cold shoulder. "Chrissakes, Ben, aren't you ever going to let go of the past?"

"Nothing to let go of."

Frustrated, Will punched the pillow and closed his eyes. Sleep did not come for hours. Over and over in Will's head all the angry battles he'd had with Benjamin replayed as if they had just happened. All the pain Will had caused his mother, who had valiantly tried to keep peace, haunted him. He had left the farm without saying good-bye; left everything and everyone behind. Oh, there were times over the years that he had meant to write to his mother and explain, but somehow he'd never gotten around to it, and then it was too late; she had passed away.

It wasn't too late yet, Bevin pondered, lying in bed. Doubts assailed her. She still could change her mind. She would not be Mrs. Benjamin Straub until the parson pronounced them man and wife.

She shook her head from side to side. She was merely experiencing prewedding doubts. That was it. All women went through the same thing, didn't they?

She reminded herself what a good man Benjamin

was; what a lovely, secure home she would have; she would be near her brother. What more could any woman ask? Nothing. Nothing more. Although when she closed her eyes and tried to envision Benjamin, it was Will Shoemaker's image that continued to haunt her.

Chapter Thirteen

The sun glistened into the bedroom through a break in the blue calico curtains, warming Bevin's face and gently awakening her. She yawned and sat up. Prudence was still fast asleep next to her in the bed they shared. Careful not to disturb the girl, Bevin crept from her warm haven. The bare floor was cold and she hurried to the braided rug in front of the washstand to begin her morning ritual.

By the time she made her way to the kitchen Will and Benjamin were seated at the table drinking coffee. She scanned the warm room. Canning jars filled with newly put-up pickles lined the cupboard. The open shelves held an assortment of containers and tins, displaying colorful fruits and vegetables. Flour and sugar were nestled neatly in the bins underneath the shelves. Pots and pans stacked high along the ledges over the stove showed years of service by their blackened bottoms. Cutlery and utensils stood to the right next to cups, plates and an odd number of tumblers. Each item presented to her line of vision sat in what Bevin presumed to be its precise place. This was the kitchen of a meticulous man. No doubt about that.

"Good morning. Sleep well?" Benjamin asked.

"Yes, thank you." Bevin paused, expecting Will to

offer some kind of greeting. He did not. He sat studying her. Determined not to let the man make her feel self-conscious, Bevin offered Will a cheery smile and said, "Good morning, Mr. Shoemaker."

"Mornin'," he grunted and directed his attention back to his cup.

Benjamin rose and pulled out a straight-back chair. He was dressed in practical work clothes: a plaid shirt tucked neatly into stained dungarees which covered the tops of his heavy boots. Bevin noticed his big rough hands. Her gaze lifted to his head. Not a strand of hair stood out of place.

Bevin sat down and watched Will silently reach for another cup, set it before her and poured the steaming brew. His attire could only be described as more haphazard. His white shirt was creased with the wrinkles one left when in a hurry with the iron. His trousers looked to belong to one less fussy, for while they were clean, the cuffs were uneven.

"You slept late," Benjamin observed.

She took a fortifying sip. "Late? Why it isn't even six o'clock yet."

"Living out in the country is different from the soft city life. We get up early on the farm," Benjamin advised, hoping he would not have to further her education on the topic.

The reference to the soft city life annoyed Bevin, but she hadn't told Benjamin everything about her past. So she had to be patient.

"Ben's a slave driver. You'll get used to it," Will put in without humor.

Benjamin glowered at the inference when he noticed Bevin's slight smile "There is nothing wrong with good, clean living, William. You could take a lesson from it," Benjamin said sourly.

Bevin eased the tension when she said, "I normally rise quite early, actually. Some believe it is the best time of the day."

Benjamin reached over to squeeze Bevin's hand for her support, but thought better of it and pulled his hand back to drop it in his lap. She was a lady and he must honor her. There would be no public displays of affection until after they were married — and even then Benjamin believed affection should only be shown in private.

"Bevin, I want to show you the farm today. I've taken care of the chores so we'll have the whole day to spend together," Benjamin said.

"I look forward to it." Expecting that Will would also want to see the farm, she glanced at Will.

"Well, I have business in town. So if you two will excuse me?" Will picked up his cup and set it on the drain board.

"There must be many changes since you saw the farm last, Mr. Shoemaker. Wouldn't you like to join us?" Bevin asked.

"No. He would not," Benjamin stated flatly, taking Bevin by surprise at the vehemence in his voice.

She was aware of the tension between the two stepsiblings and knew a portion of the story, but she had not been ready for the extent of ill feelings the two men seemed to have for each other.

"I'll get breakfast, then get the children ready," Bevin said, wanting to be away from the stress enveloping the kitchen.

"We've already eaten. Prudence can watch those two today. I want us to have some time to get to know each other," Benjamin announced.

Bevin was disappointed but agreed. She had hoped to introduce the idea of keeping the children permanently. But, of course, Benjamin was right. They did need time to become acquainted.

"Grab some bread and jam from the table while I hitch up the team," Benjamin ordered and headed for the door. He stopped and took an assessing look back at Bevin. "You will need to change that dress before we leave; it's not sturdy enough to wear around a farm. Neither are those shoes."

Bevin held out the blue striped skirt. "I fear this is all I have."

"Tomorrow's Saturday. We'll make a trip into town and get you properly outfitted."

Bevin smarted from the remark that her wearing apparel was not proper, but she withheld comment.

"You'll have her looking like a farmer's wife in short order," snipped Will.

"That is what she is going to be," retorted Benjamin before turning in disgust from Will.

Benjamin snatched his jacket from the hook to the left of the door and shrugged into it. The door slammed behind him and an instant later he stuck his head back in the door, causing a puff of cold, crisp air to rush into the room.

"Pack us a picnic lunch; we'll be gone all day."

Not waiting for a reply, Benjamin gave the door a hard shove and disappeared.

Bevin realized she must have been wearing tight lips because Will observed, "Don't let Ben get to you. He's just used to doing things his way. Set in his ways you might say."

Her brows darted toward her hairline. "Benjamin is *not getting to me* as you put it, Mr. Shoemaker," she shot back curtly, not about to discuss her growing fears. "But you might profit from your own advice."

Will gave her a jaunty salute. "Sorry. Guess I forgot

126

my place. But you needn't worry anymore, Miss O'Dea—"

"Good!" she cut in. "Because my relationship with Benjamin is no concern of yours."

"You must be concerned about it, since you have seen fit to return to calling me Mr. Shoemaker."

"I never should have given in to such improper familiarity," she retorted.

"Yes, ma'am." Will shrugged, and emulating Benjamin secured his jacket from the hook and left the kitchen.

Outside in the cold, Will turned his collar up, slammed his hands in his pockets and headed for the barn. His breath was plainly visible as he huffed across the yard. Irritating woman! Hell, she wasn't about to listen to anything he said.

He made a stop at the outhouse, then continued toward the barn. He ought to ride into town, get on the first train pulling out of the station and never look back. The thought caused him to glance back over his shoulder toward the house. Despite his anger, he was drawn to Bevin O'Dea, and knew he could no more leave right now than he could stop himself from thinking about her.

He followed Benjamin's path to the barn where neither spoke to the other as each pulled tack from the walls and prepared to go their separate ways.

Bevin had hoped Prudence would be awake before she left so she could advise the girl to keep a close watch on the children. These first few days on the farm were important for the children, and Bevin wanted them to make a good impression on Benjamin. As providence would have it, Prudence slept on, forcing Bevin to leave a sketchy note. The girl had been so worn out, Bevin did not have the heart to wake her.

She went and checked on the children; they slumbered peacefully. She grabbed her coat from the tree in the hall, picked up the picnic basket from the kitchen table, and left the house. Standing on the porch, she prayed Prudence would have the presence of mind to see to it that Johnny did not get into any trouble.

The farm was everything Benjamin had described in his letters and more. Benjamin opened up and spoke in loving volumes about his land. It was more than he had written in all his letters or said to her since she had arrived.

Bevin marveled at the outbuildings: the farmyard, the barn, the pigpen with its muddied population, the corncrib and other structures she could not remember the names of. She delighted over the garden plot with its neat rows, weedless to a fault. Every shrub lining the house showed a well-tended face. The gnarled old tree to the side of the house stood with pride, an old swing hanging from its limbs.

"Come, let me help you up on the seat of the wagon. I want to drive you out into the fields," Benjamin said.

It seemed as if he knew each golden stem personally, each stalk's story was written indelibly in his mind. Every grain of rich soil had its place, every hill, field and pasture its purpose in the scheme of his life.

He pulled up on the reins, stopping near an orchard bursting with late fruit.

"Pa and I planted those trees." He made a sweeping gesture of the orchard. "In the next couple of weeks I'll

128

get the harvest in and see it shipped north. Helps provide a little extra cash."

"There are a lot of apples on the trees," she observed.

"Not as many as during a good year," he corrected her. "Fruit's late this year, and the apples are smaller."

"Well, they look beautiful to me," she said.

"You'll learn in time."

She forced a weak smile. "Yes, I suppose I shall."

They spent hours in the work wagon surveying every inch of the one hundred and fifty-acre farm. Way past dinnertime Benjamin reined in the team of his beloved mules beneath a grove of hickory trees.

"Forgive me, Bevin, I was so caught up in showing you the farm that I completely forgot to stop for dinner."

"It doesn't matter. I've so enjoyed seeing it, and this is such a delightful spot that I am glad we waited."

"But it does matter. Dinner should be taken promptly at noon. A farm run with precision is a farm run well," he said with conviction, offering Bevin a further glimpse inside the man that was Benjamin Straub.

"Yes, I am sure it is. You appear to be a man who believes in order."

"Does it bother you?"

"No. I admire you for it." She placed a gloved hand on his arm but he pulled away.

At her look of confusion, Benjamin explained, "Forgive me, Bevin. You see, until we are married touching you would be wrong."

"Wrong?"

"Not that I don't want to," he forced himself to admit and blushed. "I do. I mean I am, after all, human. But you are a fine lady. I would not want to forget myself."

"Yes, Benjamin, you are a man of strong principles."

Bevin dropped her eyes, thinking about her years on the streets and having to steal food just to survive. She had not told Benjamin much about her past other than it had been a difficult time for her and her brother. She wondered if he would think her the fine lady if he knew all she'd had to do to keep body and soul together.

They spread a checkered cloth underneath the umbrella of spreading limbs and set out a fine meal. For over an hour they shared companionable conversation a respectable distance from each other. Benjamin was a good listener and an adroit observer, asking and answering her questions with all due finesse, but always prudent to keep within the limits of proper etiquette.

Bevin's fears eased as the afternoon passed and she found Benjamin Straub a man who would be dedicated and true to his word. In his way, he was a kind and gentle man; a good provider, who would offer a constant in her life; a virtuous, hard-working individual with standing in the community. She would not make a mistake by marrying this man as she had troubled over last night. No. Benjamin was the right choice. She was certain of it now.

As they picked up the picnic, Bevin gathered her resolve. "Benjamin?"

His head snapped up. "Yes?"

"Shouldn't we set a wedding date?"

Benjamin's heart swelled with relief. For a brief while last night and this morning he thought he had noticed an attraction between Bevin and William, and had almost been afraid to hope that the wedding would come off without first having to bar his stepbrother from the property. But after spending the day with Bevin, Benjamin was reassured. It had been a good idea to get her away from the house for the day, even though he would have to work doubly hard on his chores tomorrow.

"On Sunday I'll introduce you to the parson. We'll find out when he can come out to the farm and perform the nuptials."

"Yes, that would be nice." She wondered why they wouldn't be married in church.

A smile of disappointment caused her lips to droop at the corners. There was no excitement in his voice, just matter-of-fact acceptance of the way things were done.

She seemed to be changing already, and she was troubled over her blind acceptance. In an effort not to lose her hard-won independence, she said, "Why aren't we going to be married in a church?"

"You are of a different religious faith. I figured there would be less conflict if we were wed at the farm. Later we can decide how to handle the situation," he said and kept his face impassive.

Behind his bland expression, Benjamin had already decided how to *handle* the situation. As his wife, it would be Bevin's duty to obey her husband and follow his dictates.

"Benjamin?"

He stopped half way to the wagon, his arms filled with their picnic supplies.

"I would like to see my brother as soon as possible."

"Patrick? He'll be at church Sunday. You can see him there."

Bevin had five hundred questions to ask about Patrick. She held her tongue. The finality of his answer had not left room for further questions. She reminded herself that she would have to be patient. Benjamin was a man of abiding endurance. They would make a good match. She had endured much in her life. She could wait another day or two to see her brother, although she could not deny the bubbling anticipation at the thought of seeing Patrick again.

On the drive back to the farm Bevin watched the sturdy mules' rumps sway as they dutifully pulled their burden along the dusty road marked with ruts and rocks. She listened to Benjamin explain how the mule was Missouri's finest contribution to agriculture before the advent of machinery pushed the animals aside. She could not help but be impressed by his devotion to the creatures.

The farmhouse rose white in a flat sea of golden stubble as they neared it. Bevin had to admit that she already loved the unadorned place. There was a no-nonsense aura about Benjamin's farm, and the only thing Bevin decided was lacking was the joyful sounds of children, which she intended to remedy with Johnny and Tara — as soon as she could find the right time to approach Benjamin.

Chapter Fourteen

With drawn lips Will watched Benjamin and Bevin leave the farm before leading his horse from the barn. The sooner he paid a visit to the lawyer in town and settled the issue of the farm, the better. He'd leave immediately after the wedding, he told himself halfheartedly.

"What ya doin'?" Johnny asked, skipping up to Will to see what kind of a prank he could pull on the man.

"Saddling a horse."

"Why?"

Will looked back over his shoulder to see the tousled child rocking back and forth on his heels, watching him with wide eyes.

"So I can ride it."

"Can't you ride him otherwise?"

"You sure ask a lot of questions, runt."

"How else is a fella gonna find out. And I ain't no runt."

At that instant Johnny spotted a gray striped cat peeping out from behind a sawhorse strung with a worn saddle. He made a beeline for the furry critter.

"Wouldn't go trying to get too close to that cat if I were you."

Johnny stopped, a questioning look across his

young face when he looked back. Skeptically, he asked, "Why not?"

"That one's a barn cat. Wild and mean. You could get hurt if you get too close."

Johnny looked unconvinced. "I like animals. I had me a black one back home in Boston." He paused and his face saddened and crinkled. "Before me and . . . and my sister was caught stealing. That's wrong, I was the one doin' the stealing, not C—Crissy."

Turning his attention away from the painful memories, Johnny ignored Will's warning and crept up on the cat. The furry critter promptly hissed, swung a paw at the startled child and scampered away.

Will watched how carefully the boy had approached the cat. He was reminded of himself at Johnny's age. Will had desperately tried to claim one of those mangy critters as his own when he first arrived with his mother. He had been an intruder, an outsider never fully accepted by the other children; lonely by the exclusion and so desperate to have a friend—an animal friend—that he had pursued the farm animals until a young pup had adopted him on the way home from school one day. Johnny's yelp snapped Will's attention back to the present.

Johnny yanked his bloodied hand back, and valiantly fought back tears.

Will had meant to be gone but could not resist the child's plight.

"Come here." When the child hesitated Will urged, "Quit worrying. Just thought you might like a ride, is all."

Johnny immediately forgot about the scratch and the cat, and stepped forward. Maybe the big man wasn't so bad after all.

"Really? You mean it?"

Will cupped his hands. "Yeah. Come on, I'll give you a boost up."

"You're not gonna leave me once I get up there, are ya?"

"Don't give me ideas."

The boy flinched, causing Will to want to bite his tongue. Bevin had told Will that Johnny had been abandoned and did not need a reminder of those years.

"No. I'm not going to leave you," Will amended.

"Sure?"

"Yeah, runt, I'm sure. Up you go."

Johnny sat rigid, his knuckles white, he was hanging onto the pommel so tight. Will walked the animal around the yard slowly until the boy relaxed. Then Will casually dropped his hold on the bridle but kept close, directing the horse and rider into the corral. Johnny took to the saddle and soon was riding around the fenced enclosure like he had been born on the back of the gentle nag.

Tara joined them, and Will soon found himself lifting the excited little girl up behind Johnny. The children delighted in their newfound skill and for hours they whooped and hollered like cavalry officers in pursuit of Indians. To the children's chagrin, their latest pastime was interrupted by Prudence's call for them to come in for dinner.

Gulping the sorry meal Miss Prudence had prepared, Johnny begged until Will good-naturedly conceded defeat and took the pair back out to the corral for another round of rides.

The horse seemed to take it all in stride, and despite his inexperience and the tragedy of his childhood, Will found their childish exuberance infectious. Soon the yard filled with laughter and drifted to the house, capturing Prudence's attention.

Prudence stood at the door, wiping her hands on the crisp white apron she'd found hanging on a hook near the back door. Mr. Shoemaker amazed her. She would have sworn the man disliked children, yet there he was patiently entertaining Johnny and Tara and enjoying every minute of it. A smile on her face, she went back inside to try and clean the burnt pots and pans charred from her culinary efforts.

"Whoa, Cupcake. Ride's over." Will helped the reluctant children off and they scampered away.

"Thank you, Mr. Shoemaker," Johnny hollered. "Guess you ain't so awful after all."

Will had to laugh to himself at the open candidness the boy possessed. Children could be so painfully honest. He patted the ginger-colored horse's withers, mounted and pointed the animal's nose toward town.

"Oh, Mr. Shoemaker," Prudence called, still standing on the porch. "Won't you join us for dessert before you leave?"

Will was about to decline, but the rumble issued from his stomach gave him pause. Surely she couldn't have ruined dessert like she had dinner. "Thank you, I will."

Will remained and visited longer than intended. The food could hardly be considered passable; Prudence could not be called a cook; her cake was dry, burnt and barely recognizable. But the childish glee substituted for the other lacking ingredients.

His stomach complaining from the meal he had graciously forced himself to eat, Will said his good-byes and headed again toward town.

Not five hundred feet from the house, Will caught sight of Bevin and Benjamin. Despite his better judgment, curiosity won out and he wheeled the horse around.

Quietly damning himself for his inability to stay clear of the returning pair, Will pulled up alongside the wagon, and said, "Didn't expect you to return before dark. If I had a lady such as Miss O'Dea out I wouldn't've brung her back till I had to."

"You never did have a sense of responsibility," Benjamin said sourly as he slapped the reins over the team's rumps and spurred the wagon on toward the house without further exchange.

Bevin looked back at Will, left in the center of the road staring after her and Benjamin before returning her attention to Benjamin. "Benjamin, wouldn't it be nice if you and Mr. Shoemaker made some attempt to work out your differences?"

Benjamin's face was chiseled in stone. "I know you mean well, but your efforts are misplaced at best. William Shoemaker has been nothing but trouble from the first day he set foot on this farm."

"He was only a boy then." She defended Will, unable to totally comprehend the unrelenting animosity the two seemed to have for each other.

"Yes, and boys grow into men. Only William never developed a sense of honor a man should possess."

"I see," she answered. But truth was she did not *see* at all. William Shoemaker had proved himself to be most honorable. He possessed more compassion than the man himself probably realized; despite a difficult beginning, he had been a gentleman; he had an easy way about him which some might misconstrue. But William Shoemaker definitely was in possession of a sense of honor.

By the time they reached the yard, there was a terrible commotion coming from underneath the porch. Yelps and screams issued from the crack in the wooden flooring. Scuffling and scraping sounds followed more screeching, and puffs of dust swirled from the small opening to the side of the steps.

At the sight of a worn sole of a shoe stuffed with paper protruding from the opening, Bevin leaped from the wagon, not waiting for Benjamin to help her alight. "Oh dear, Johnny! Benjamin you must do something."

Benjamin noted the size of the shoe, waving about in a frantic dance, and groaned. No one had been under the house since William had hid out there as a child. Benjamin had forgotten about all the nocturnal creatures that took up residence under the house when the weather turned cold—not to mention the never-ending assortment of creepy crawlers Benjamin detested.

Benjamin stomped over to the opening and bent down on one knee. "Come out of there before I take my belt off and tan your hide," he warned, remembering the words his pa had spoken more than twenty years ago.

"Spoken like a true Straub," Will grated, joining the frantic scene.

Benjamin looked up, his eyes shining with malevolence. "I shall take that as a compliment. Thought you were on your way to town."

Will shrugged. "Had been until I heard the ruckus."

An angry flush to his face, Benjamin commanded, "The least you can do is get down off that horse and help get that little brat out from under there before he breaks something, and I'm forced to summon the doctor due to some dumb stunt."

When Will did not move as swiftly as Benjamin thought the situation warranted, he snapped, "What's the matter? Have you forgotten your own escapades under the house?"

Standing helplessly by, her palms pressed against her cheeks in horror, Bevin wailed, "Can't you two set aside your differences long enough to rescue Johnny before he gets hurt or worse?"

Will narrowed his eyes and left unsaid a stinging retort. Instead he got off the horse, handed the reins to Tara, startling Bevin, and managed to grab hold of Johnny's foot.

Fighting and wrestling with the kicking, uncooperative child, Will spilled into the dirt before he was able to dislodge Johnny from his position underneath the house. Much to everyone's amazement out came Johnny, grasping a mangy, liver-colored dog by the tail.

His face smudged, his clothes filthy and torn, Johnny turned in triumph. "I got him."

"You got what?" Bevin choked out at the sight.

"Thought that dog had died long ago," grated Benjamin, eyeing the mutt.

"My God . . . Sourdough," Will said as the rib-thin old dog crawled meekly to Will and licked his hand.

Tears welled up in Will's eyes at the remembrance of his faithful, childhood companion. The dog must be over fifteen years old if he was a day. A quick assessment thinned Will's lips. "You're responsible for the dog's condition, aren't you?" Will hissed at Benjamin, stroking the dog's filthy coat.

"You're the one who left that scraggly beast behind. I'd say his condition is your responsibility," Benjamin returned.

"Can I keep him?" Johnny begged amid the accusations and indictments.

"I should say not!" Benjamin said flatly. "I should have shot him long ago," he added for William's benefit, giving no thought to the boy's reaction.

"No!" Johnny screamed and ringed his arms around the passive critter's neck to hug him close.

"Don't worry, Johnny, Ben is just trying to rile me, is all," put in Will, silently daring Benjamin to say or do otherwise.

"Of course he is, dear," Bevin soothed, hoping to put an end to the growing animosity between Benjamin and Will.

Noticing the way Bevin had taken the side of William and the boy, Benjamin decided now was not the time to insist that the dog be put out of its misery. Benjamin had never been mean to an animal in his life. It was just that he had been raised on a farm. On a farm an animal was just that—an animal. It was a food supply or used for work, never a pet to be coddled. If it didn't carry its load there was no point in wasting valuable food and money on it.

"Can I keep him?" Johnny asked again. "Please. He won't be no bother. Me 'n Tara'll care for him. He won't cost nothin'. I'll share my food with him so you won't have to put no extra out for him. Please?"

Benjamin's gaze shifted between Bevin and the boy. Defeated. He had been defeated by an old mangy dog. "Just until you go to live in your permanent home," Benjamin relented. "I've got milking to do." He turned and headed toward the house before he lost his temper.

Johnny shot Bevin an imploring look, prompting her to rush after Benjamin.

"Wouldn't bother if I were you, Miss O'Dea," Will called out, halting her. "Ben needs time to cool down. 'Fraid he doesn't take kindly to being bested, especially in front of his intended."

His words stopped any thought she had of continuing after Benjamin. "I really should speak with him."

"Wait till after supper. He'll be in a more receptive mood then. That is, if you do the cooking." At Prudence's downcast countenance, Will added, "No offense meant, Miss Prudence."

"I am sorry. I never had much of a chance to ply my hand at cooking before." Prudence dropped her head.

Bevin wrapped a protective arm around Prudence's slumped shoulders. "Don't pay any attention to Mr. Shoemaker, Pru. You can help me."

"Thank you, Evvie."

"Don't you think you could force yourself to call me Will again? After all, I did save the mutt for the runt over there."

Bevin thought it over for a moment, decided there would be no harm in it, and stiffly nodded her agreement, but not without sending him a nettled look. "Very well . . . Will. And do make every attempt to remember that Johnny is a child, not a runt."

Will fixed her a lopsided grin. "Guess I shouldn't complain. One out of two ain't half bad." At her huff, he winked and sauntered toward the barn.

Bevin watched Will walk from her with a swarm of emotion buzzing about her. He was such a gentle man underneath that devil-may-care exterior. The way he had stroked the old dog came to mind. She had not missed the tears in the man's eyes when he had first seen the animal. Despite how irritating he could be, he had displayed feelings of compassion and deep caring for all God's creatures.

Milking pail in hand, Benjamin passed the two women returning to the kitchen. He had donned his well-worn work clothes and jacket. His heavy boots thumped toward the door; his face set in cold, hard lines.

"Benjamin," Bevin said before she could stop herself. "I would like to have a few words with you."

Prudence moved off and tried to appear invisible. She knew what Bevin wanted to talk about, and feared Benjamin Straub's answer would not be all that Bevin expected to hear.

"Can't it wait? I've got milking to do, and stock to feed. Been out all day, you know."

"It's about Johnny and Tara," she persisted.

Benjamin pinched the bridge of his nose. "I saw Bertha Krueger out in the field early this morning and she mentioned she got a glimpse of the girl in town. Bertha expressed an interest. I think the Kruegers will give Tara a fine home."

"Yes, I suppose they will," she mumbled absently and felt dismissed as she watched him disappear without waiting for her to finish what she had desperately wanted to talk to him about.

Disappointed, Bevin set about preparing supper. Now that Tara would probably be placed, Bevin was determined to broach the subject of Johnny and clarify the boy's future living arrangements once and for all.

Chapter Fifteen

It was past dusk by the time Benjamin trudged into the kitchen. Without a word he set the pail down and shrugged out of his jacket.

Bevin took the heavy jacket from him and, as she hung it on the hook, she noticed Benjamin leaving the room.

"Supper's ready."

"I'll be right there," he threw over his shoulder.

Benjamin went to his room, peeled off his work clothes and washed up at the bowl on the dresser. He usually washed up in the kitchen, but tonight he took special pains to look his best. He had important things to discuss with Bevin.

Supper was a nerve-wracking affair. Benjamin watched in horror at the way the children grabbed for the food, slurped their soup and talked with full mouths. He was horrified at Bevin's tolerance of such slovenly manners. Prudence seemed to ignore the scene, and had not looked up once since she filled her plate. Will wore an amused grin, further grating on Benjamin's nerves. Benjamin found supper more than he could endure, and excused himself before Bevin served dessert.

"What's wrong with him?" Johnny asked, stuffing a

heaping spoonful of potatoes into his mouth.

Bevin sighed, casting a frown at the child. "I can't imagine."

"I'd watch it if I were you, runt. Ben just might decide to let you eat with the hogs from now on." Not giving Bevin time to retort to such an outrageous notion, Will also excused himself and left the house.

Bevin watched the children's manners improve markedly with Will and Benjamin absent from the table until she was certain the children had planned to drive Benjamin away.

"Pru, would you do the dishes tonight? The children and I have a few things we need to straighten out."

Prudence nodded and began to clear the table, glad she was not the one who had to talk to the children.

Bevin led the children into the parlor and sat them down across from her. Sitting straight, her arms crossed over her chest, Bevin took a deep breath.

"All right. I think it's time for an explanation."

Johnny frowned. Tara studied her feet.

"We didn't do nothing," Johnny finally said.

"No? Just drive Benjamin from his own table."

"I don't know what you mean," Johnny insisted.

"The way you two were eating, you should have been served out in the pigpen," Bevin stated flatly, losing her patience. "I know you both have better manners than that. Benjamin was kind enough to take all of us in, and from now on I expect you to remember that."

She lectured them a little longer. She wanted Benjamin to want to keep Johnny. Gingerly she explained that if they continued to forget themselves they would not find a place in Benjamin's heart.

Johnny screwed up his face. "All right. I get the picture. If he don't like us we don't get to stay, right?"

Bevin had not meant to be quite so blunt. The boy

144

was perceptive beyond his years.

"I think that if Benjamin comes to love you as much as I do everything could work out to make everyone happy."

"Adults never just say what they mean straight out," Johnny grumped. "They always say one thing, then do something else. They're all the same."

"No, honey. People are not all he same," Bevin tried to explain.

Johnny sent Bevin a disbelieving look, then jumped to his feet. "Come on, Tara, let's go see if we can catch us one of them barn cats."

Bevin shook her head and called out, "Don't stay outside too long; it's almost your bedtime. And please try to get along with Benjamin."

"We never had to go to bed early when we lived back home in Boston," Johnny snickered.

"Boston is not your home any longer; besides, tomorrow we are going to go shopping in town."

"That's girl stuff."

Tara's eyes brightened at the thought. "Shopping? Come on, Johnny, we better hurry. I want to get to bed on time."

"Ugh! Girls!" he moaned as Tara dragged him from the house.

Outside in the yard, Johnny stopped to look around.

"Where we going? I thought we were going to the barn?" Tara whined.

"That dumb old Mr. Straub's in there. 'Sides, we're gonna go get Sourdough and sneak him into our room since we gotta share now."

"I don't think that's a good idea. We could get in trouble for that," she advised.

"So what. Come on."

* * *

Bevin returned to the kitchen and helped Prudence finish the last of the dishes. Bevin explained her talk with the children, and her doubts that the children had taken any of it to heart. Prudence seemed to grow uncomfortable and hurried through the chore. She untied her apron, yawned and announced she was going to turn in.

"Won't you stay up and keep me company?" Bevin prodded.

"This farm life has worn me out. I shall see you in the morning."

Covering her disappointment, Bevin said, "Good night, Pru."

Lonesome for company, Bevin wrapped a shawl around her shoulders and headed outside to spend some time with Benjamin. She was not more than three steps from the house when she met Benjamin returning.

"You feel a little better now?" she asked.

"Huh? Oh, yes."

"I'm sorry about the children's manners. I don't know what got into them. They really do know better."

"Yes, well, I'm sure they do."

"Benjamin, could we walk awhile?

He studied her for a moment. The light against her back glowed around her, illuminating her red hair. She was a petite little thing; hardly looked strong enough to work a butter churn. Of course, he knew she possessed an inner strength equalled by few. In time she would adjust to the routine required by life on a farm, he reassured himself.

"It's getting late. Maybe tomorrow night. I've a lot to do in the morning before we go to town."

Bevin hid her disappointment behind a smile. "Yes, of course."

Benjamin held the door open. "You coming in?"

"I think I'll go sit on the porch swing for a while and get a little air before I turn in."

"Very well. Just don't stay out too late; it's starting to get cold. Good night, Bevin."

"Good night, Benjamin."

Will rode to town and headed for the nearest saloon. What he needed was a diversion. He tied his horse to the hitching post and sauntered through the swinging doors of the Happy Horse Saloon.

The interior of the saloon was cluttered with a dozen round tables and an assortment of patrons. Two drunks with their heads flat against a table snored softly. Gamblers sat engaged in a lively game of poker. The mustached piano player tinkled the keys, and three women dressed in red satin leaned against the piano, giving a rowdy concert in voices better suited for hog calling. The booze flowed freely and smoke stung Will's eyes.

Will stepped up to the bar and ordered three fingers of whiskey. A sour-faced bartender obliged without comment. Will took a swallow and made a face.

Swinging her hips, a heavily rouged woman sauntered over to Will. "What's the matter, honey? Ain't that thar firewater good enough for you?"

"It suits," Will returned, looking the painted woman up and down.

"You could order us up a bottle of champagne. We could go somewhere more private to share it, if you know what I mean."

"How much?"

A seductive grin, which danced from her lips to her eyes, gleamed when she told him what she charged.

" 'Fraid I don't have your price. Guess you'll have to

look for some other customer to buy a bottle of watered-down swill."

The woman cocked her brow, unaffected. "Your loss, honey. I always give my best to good-lookin' fellers like you."

Another one of the saloon gals was heading his way as the first one stopped her. "Don't bother, sweetie, he ain't got no money." Then she looked Will over again. "Pity. We could've had us a real good time. When you get some money, come back, honey. I never forget a nice butt." She gave him a sly wink. "We'll have us a fine time."

"I'll remember."

Will watched the two go up to another man who had just come in and hand him the same line. Smiling to himself, Will turned back to his drink. Two months ago he would have followed the first one up to her room and worried about coming up with the cash to pay for her services afterward. He had never been in the habit of missing out on a willing professional. Tonight he had come to town to drown out feelings for a certain Irish lady. No matter how hard he had tried to get the images of Bevin O'Dea out of his mind, her sparkling blue eyes haunted him.

Will remained at the bar for over an hour. He turned down the offer to join a game; the stakes were too rich for his blood. Two more high-stepping women approached him, and both times he refused them. He had to laugh to himself. He had just set a record for foolishly missed opportunities with four mighty handsome women.

His trip to town did not serve its purpose, as the lady from the Children's Aid Society continued to enter his mind. He decided he might as well return to the farm before he drank too much, passed out, and was forced to spend the night in jail. Will finished his drink and returned to his horse to head back to the farm.

By the time Will rode up the drive the moon hung high in the sky illuminating the white farmhouse. Bevin sat alone on the porch swing, her elbows resting on her knees. She made a fetching sight in the shadows. Will's better judgment warned him that he should put the horse away and give her a wide berth. He knew he should enter the house through the back door and avoid her.

Despite his intention to keep his distance, his feet carried him toward the front of the house where Bevin sat alone on the swing.

"Bevin?"

Will's deep voice snapped Bevin out of her reverie, and her head bobbed up to see him standing over her.

"Yes?"

"You okay?"

"I'm fine."

"What're you doing up so late?" he asked.

"Just getting a little air before I turn in."

"Mind if I join you for a few minutes?"

She swung out her arm to indicate a place next to her on the swing.

"Thanks." He folded his large frame next to her small one. "What do you think of the farm now that you've had the grand tour?"

Bevin noticed the hint of sarcasm in his voice, and that he did not ask her what she thought of Benjamin.

"It's a wonderful place," she enthused, hugging herself.

"Yeah, I suppose it is."

She did not miss the doubt in his voice. "Benjamin spent the whole day showing me around. I think my favorite spot is that grove of hickory trees by the stream. I can picture Johnny there trying to catch tadpoles next summer."

It was once one of Will's favorite places too — before the accident. Now it brought back haunting memories. "You've become pretty fond of that boy, haven't you?"

"He is a special child."

"I hope you can convince Benjamin of that."

Bevin sucked in a breath. So Will, too, had noticed Benjamin's apparent distance with the boy. She turned to study his silhouette. He was a handsome man with his full mouth, slight upturned nose, strong jawline, and thick black hair.

"Benjamin will come to love Johnny too. I'm sure of it. Perhaps if you tried to understand Benjamin, you would come to realize what a good man he is."

Will shrugged. "I know what kind of man he is."

Bevin wrapped her shawl around her and rose. "I'm sorry there is trouble between you and Benjamin. But I have no intention of sitting here and listening to you talk about him like that."

Will grabbed her arm to stop her. At her look of shock he loosened his hand.

"Bevin, please, stay. I promise I won't say another unkind word about Ben."

She relaxed her stance at the sincerity of his plea. She settled back next to him, careful to remain a respectable distance. The heat of his leg next to hers had disturbed her, and she had to make a conscious effort to remember she was engaged to Benjamin and soon would be his wife.

"Perhaps for a few more minutes. I shouldn't be out too late. Benjamin is taking us into town tomorrow to purchase clothing more appropriate for farm life."

Will was glad she had decided to remain out here with him. For moments they sat together in companionable silence. Will wondered how his relationship

150

with this lady had evolved into the warm feelings he had for her. He felt a pang that she had to be the one marrying his stepbrother.

"Mind if I tag along tomorrow?" he finally asked. "There are a few things I need to pick up."

"Of course not. Does that mean you have decided to stay for a while?" she asked hopefully.

Despite himself, Will placed his fingers over hers. "Would you like me to?"

Awkwardly, Bevin removed her hand, but the feeling of his touch remained soft and warm and thought provoking. She mulled over his question and decided that the topic was much too dangerous to consider, let alone give a voice.

"At supper Johnny told me how you let him and Tara ride Cupcake. Seems he's beginning to take quite a liking to you. He does not take to people easily, you know. I hope he accepts Benjamin soon. For a little boy, Johnny has been through a lot."

Will frowned into the darkness. She had completely skirted his question. Somehow she managed to shift the topic away from them. Will did not want to talk about the children; he wanted to hear more about Bevin.

"I'm sure Johnny'll take to Ben. Ben and I don't see eye to eye often, but in his defense I have to say that Ben will do right by the boy."

It was a major concession on Will's part, to defend Benjamin. Maybe the years apart had softened Will more than he had realized. It was food for thought.

"I know he will. I also know that even though Benjamin is a man of few words, he has a lot to give. He wants the same things I do."

"And that is?"

"Marriage. Children. Security."

"You still haven't mentioned love."

151

Bevin stiffened. She'd had practically the same conversation earlier with Prudence. Why did they have to think that love was so important? There were other considerations which made for a life of contentment, and love was not at the top of her list.

"Benjamin and I have that," she defended, knowing full well Will saw through her hasty retort.

"Then Ben is a lucky man, indeed."

Will's answer caught her off balance, and she swallowed hard to keep from asking him exactly what he meant by that. At a loss for suitable words, Bevin dropped her eyes, glad that in the muted light from the parlor Will could not see the blush she knew ran up her cheeks.

For long moments the tension seemed to surround them. Will could feel its burgeoning grasp until he was overcome by an urge to kiss her. Against his better judgment, Will leaned over, gently cupped her chin to lift her face to his and tenderly pressed his lips to hers.

Will's kiss was so sweet, so tentative and gentle that Bevin was totally disarmed. Instead of pulling away, she reveled in the warm texture of the undemanding kiss.

Will longed to pull her to him and deepen the kiss, but she was about to become another man's bride. With reluctance, he broke apart.

"I had no right to do that."

"N-no, you didn't."

"I can't apologize because I'm not sorry, Bevin."

Her senses reeling with unnamed emotions she dared not explore, for fear of what she might discover, Bevin pulled her shawl up close around her neck, jumped to her feet and ran into the house.

Chapter Sixteen

Benjamin awoke early to get the chores done so he could take Bevin into town without fretting that he was leaving the farm untended. He considered making more than one trip a week to town excessive. He had taken care of his business when he had picked Bevin up at the station. He reminded himself again that he must be patient; she needed time to adjust to the routine of the farm. And she needed sturdy clothing.

He dressed quietly, not to disturb William now in the next room. Benjamin had been awake last night and heard his stepbrother follow Bevin down the hall and whisper good night to her at her door. Anger had raged inside him. He cursed himself for sending that letter to William and informing him of his inheritance. His first inclination had been to toss William out on his heels. His conscience would not let him; it would not have been the right thing.

Benjamin Straub always did the right thing.

Down in the kitchen, he lit the lantern. He took his heavy work jacket off the hook and shrugged into it. Hanging the lantern on his arm, he picked up his pail and headed out to milk the cows. The cold, crisp air surrounded him, and his breath came out in icy, white puffs. Winter was just around the corner. A smile came to his lips at the picture in his mind of Bevin sitting in a rocker across from him in front of a crackling fire. Looking to that time, he adjusted the stool beside one of the cows and began to pull rhythmically at the teats.

Bevin heard Benjamin pass her room and slipped from her bed. She did not want a repeat of yesterday morning when Benjamin had accused her of sleeping in late, and she hoped to have breakfast ready before Will came down. A warmth rushed through her at the thought of Will's kiss last night, and she had to fight against the feeling. Forcing Will from her mind, she dressed in her plain blue cotton. It was the sturdiest dress she owned. Surely Benjamin would have to approve, although seeking a man's approval was quite foreign to her.

Halfway down the hall, she stopped to check on the children. She pulled the blanket back up around Tara's neck. She turned to Johnny. He had snuck the dog into the house. The boy lay entwined with the big, liver-colored dog; one arm wrapped around the animal's neck, the other one snugly rested on the wiry coat. The dog lay on its back, four huge paws in the air, watching her with big sad eyes.

Bevin hadn't the heart to turn the dog out; it was the first time she had seen the boy take so strongly to anything. She would just make sure the animal was put outside before Benjamin caught it in the house.

She went to the kitchen, loaded wood from the box into the stove, and started the fire. While waiting for the stove to heat up she slipped into the coat hanging on the hook near the door and went to join Benjamin.

She slipped inside the barn door and stood watching Benjamin. He was at home here; it was obvious the way he crooned to his animals.

"Okay, Millie, be patient a little longer. We're almost done." He squirted a half dozen more pulls into the pail, then patted the cow's rump. "Good girl."

He moved to the next cow, adjusted his position and curled his fingers around its teats.

Fascinated, Bevin moved forward tentatively. "Good morning, Benjamin."

Annoyed that his routine had been disturbed, Benjamin ground out, "Morning," then tempered his tone. "You should be inside getting breakfast. A man needs a hearty meal waiting for him to give him the energy to do what needs to be done each day."

Bevin's face fell at his apparent annoyance, and she flashed him a hurt pose. "I've already started heating up the stove. Will you be long?"

"No," was all he said.

She turned and ran back toward the house. Benjamin cursed himself. He had to remember she needed time. He was a man of few words; she would have to understand that.

When Bevin came back into the kitchen, Will was sitting at the table. He had set up the coffeepot, and it was perking on the hot stove, filling the room with an inviting aroma.

"You're up early this morning. Benjamin should be pleased."

As Bevin hung up her coat, she bit her lip to keep it from trembling. Last night's kiss now made her feel that she was caught between two men; one she was engaged to be married to, and the other whom she found herself drawn toward. She bit down harder to keep from confessing the feelings of uncertainty about her life with Benjamin on the farm.

There were a few moments of awkward silence before Bevin pulled herself together.

"I'm sure Benjamin will be most pleased when he comes in and finds breakfast on the table."

Will's head snapped up at the strange sound to her voice.

"Something wrong?"

Bevin forced herself to brighten, then turned from Will's probing gaze. "No. No, of course not. Why do you ask?" she asked, lifting the lid to add another log to the stove.

"You looked distracted. Not what one would expect a woman to look like after visiting her intended out in the barn, is all."

The keenness of his observation caused Bevin to flinch and drop the heavy iron lid.

"Ouch!" she yelped and sucked on her finger.

Will was to his feet and at her side instantly. "Here, let me see."

He drew her hand from her lips and examined her finger. "Looks like you're going to get a blister."

For a long moment their eyes held each other, Bevin's hand clasped in Will's. Unspoken longing lingering between them. The heat warming her spine from his touch was nearly more excruciating than the burn.

"It's nothing. I must learn to be more careful."

"Best get that hand submerged in the water basin while I get some grease to spread on it. It'll ease the pain."

"Please. Sit back down."

"Don't be silly. I've had many occasions to tend the wounded. It's the least I can do for my future stepsister-in-law."

Bevin ignored the hint of sarcasm in his voice and allowed his tender ministrations.

Will Shoemaker had a gentle touch. And Bevin had to remind herself that Benjamin, too, would be as equally attentive had he been here. A small voice in her mind asked, *Would be?*

"How soon do you and Ben plan to be married?"

Before Will could get an answer, Johnny and Sourdough skidded into the room.

"Sourdough, you mangy mutt. You shouldn't be in here." Will scratched the dog behind the ears, hiding his disappointment that the moment had passed and Bevin took the opportunity to ignore his question. "Runt, you'd best get the old fellow outside."

"And do not bring him in again," Bevin instructed, thankful for the child's appearance, which broke the tension. "After you've put Sourdough out, go wake Tara up and get washed up for breakfast. We will be going into town this morning."

"Do I have to go?" Johnny complained.

"Yes," Will interceded. "You heard Miss O'Dea, get going."

Johnny screwed up his face and reluctantly followed directions.

Bevin was surprised watching Johnny follow Will's direction. The boy was so oppositional, and rarely yielded to instruction without a fight. It gave her something more to think about.

"He's sure taken to that mutt," Will commented. He wished the kid had not interrupted them, but since he had Will decided to ease her discomfort and keep the conversation neutral.

"Yes, he has. I looked in on Johnny earlier and he was curled around the dog, sleeping peacefully. Johnny usually thrashes about in his sleep. It was the first time since Johnny came to the Society that he has slept through the night without nightmares summoning one of the workers to his side," Bevin chattered on as her heart began to return to a normal beat.

"Animals can often reach troubled kids where adults fail; Johnny and Sourdough seem to share a sort of

157

communion with each other."

"That's an interesting notion. They do seem to have an understanding."

"Yeah, the kid tried to adopt one of the barn cats before he discovered Sourdough under the house."

"Sourdough was your dog, wasn't he?"

"Yeah. I found him half-starved along the road as a pup."

"I'm glad Johnny found that dog too."

"So am I," concurred Will, once again drawing a parallel between the troubled boy and himself as a child. "Better tell the kid to keep that dog outside, though. It's a sin to a farmer to bring a dog in the house. Ben'll be furious if he catches it in here," Will warned.

"I shall consider myself forewarned," she said, not fully appreciating the gravity of Will's advice.

"You need help with breakfast?" he offered, changing the subject.

"I think I can manage. But thank you for offering."

"You might find I'm really quite handy to have around."

"No doubt," she said and turned away from the sparkle in his eyes.

Bevin scooped a glob of lard from the tin and put potatoes into a heavy iron skillet. The fat sizzled. She gave the raw-fries a stir, then fixed Will and herself a cup of coffee, and joined Will at the table.

"I've never seen Johnny mind anyone without total warfare before. You have a way with the boy," she observed. "You will make a good father someday." The moment the words tumbled out she wished she could have recanted them.

Will shifted uncomfortably before holding up his hands. "Not me."

Bevin noticed his unease and wondered what could

158

have caused him to behave that way. She took a sip of coffee, then said, "You don't like children?"

"It's not that." He thought of redirecting her attention, but for some reason said, "Being around children has been difficult for me since I was fourteen years old and the Lutherby boy drowned at the creek. Those bitter memories of that tragedy have haunted me for over fifteen years. So it's easier to stay away from all children."

"Because they remind you of that day?"

"Yeah."

"Who knows, perhaps you and Johnny will be able to help each other."

By the time Benjamin came in for breakfast, everyone was seated and waiting for him. They ate in tension-filled silence after Benjamin gave the children daunting looks, which could have stopped the most stouthearted from uttering a word. It was a dismal meal devoid of the conversations Bevin so enjoyed during mealtime at the boardinghouse she had lived in in Boston.

Once the meal was over, Bevin excused the children to get their coats. She scurried around to be ready on time, leaving instructions with Prudence, who was resting in their room, and had declined her invitation to accompany them into town. Bevin quickly cleared the table and put the dishes in the pan to soak before getting her heavy coat and meeting Benjamin out in front of the house.

To Benjamin's dismay, the children hopped into the buggy he had hitched up and waiting. He had not realized when she told the children to bundle up good that she had meant for them to accompany him and Bevin to town.

159

"Get out of there," he bellowed.

"Benjamin, I told them they could come along with us."

Benjamin scowled and looked to Will, leaning against a post, for support. Benjamin had wanted to show off his bride-to-be in town without the children tagging along to get into trouble, which he had no doubt they would do.

It was not forthcoming.

"Oh, all right," he huffed. "Get in the back seat."

It was a small concession and it made Bevin smile. Her smile faded when she found herself sandwiched on the front seat in between Will and Benjamin. They were two such different men. Benjamin was set in his ways: dependable and loyal, possessing an unwavering sense of how things should be done. Will was a man of mystery with a past which had seemed to come home to haunt him since they had arrived at the farm. And yet, the children had taken to him despite the difficult beginning at the courthouse and on the train, and he had compassion and a gentle touch.

All the way into town the children barraged Benjamin with questions about the farm and the animals. They bubbled over about their developing equestrian talents and begged to help out with the animals. Benjamin only grunted and laid the whip to the mules' rumps.

In town Benjamin directed the team to the mercantile. After receiving strict instructions on proper behavior inside the store, the children walked, tight-lipped, behind Benjamin and Bevin. Will lagged behind, surrounded by memories.

"Sit down over there until we are ready to leave," Benjamin directed the children, pointing to the row of empty chairs by the front window.

"I don't like him," Johnny grumbled and went with

160

Tara to the chairs.

Benjamin ushered Bevin over to Oscar Lutherby, the proprietor. Bevin recalled the name Lutherby as belonging to the boy whom Will had told her had drowned at the creek. It brought to mind further questions she managed to suppress.

"Morning, Benjamin. Miss O'Dea. What brings you back into town so soon?"

"We've come in to get Bevin outfitted, Oscar. She needs some sensible clothes."

Oscar Lutherby looked Bevin over. She was a pretty bit. Didn't look like she'd be sturdy enough to be a farmer's wife, though. Pity Benjamin hadn't chosen Gretchen Krueger instead of some lady who wore her Sunday best on Saturday, and probably didn't know that the other farmers' wives wouldn't take to a fancy outsider.

"Got some good, ready-made dresses on the rack."

"We need shoes, too, Oscar."

"On the shelf." As he directed Bevin toward the shelf, his vision caught on Will. "Shoemaker? What are you doing back in town?" he grated out.

Determined to face his past, Will sauntered over and joined the men. "Came to collect my inheritance and bury the past."

Unforgiving, Oscar mumbled "The wife and I *buried* the future that day at the creek" before moving off.

Three men, seated around the potbelly stove, whispered among themselves while Bevin's heart went out to Will and she attempted to ignore them. She picked through the assortment of plain cotton dresses and work shoes. Bevin also attempted to ignore the rude remarks about her attire made by the dowdy women who took seats next to the children along the front of the store to watch.

Bevin had been proud of her efforts to dress fash-

161

ionably, and found the pathetic selection hard to accept. "Remember you are no longer in Boston, Bevin," she mumbled to herself, causing more whispers to float about the store.

She finally picked out two simple calicos and pair of heavy shoes. She took them to the counter, and motioned to the children to join her.

In front of the proprietor, she asked, "Benjamin, Johnny and Tara could use shoes too."

"Got a new shipment of youngun's boots in a couple of days ago," Oscar announced.

"How much?" muttered Benjamin, feeling trapped into putting out good money for two children who would soon go to other families.

"Work boots run a dollar fifty to two fifty for the boy—that is if I got anything to fit that foot of his. The girl, I'll charge you a dollar and a quarter, seein' as how you're buyin' them for castoffs, which by the look of the boy, won't be carryin' his weight 'round the farm."

"Mr. Lutherby, Johnny is a good helper, isn't he, Benjamin?" Bevin insisted.

Benjamin remained silent.

Disappointment gripped her and she began to understand part of the reason why Will must have left town years ago. The proprietor was not merely outspoken; he was cruel. And Benjamin had done nothing to defend Johnny.

Johnny tried to hide his foot. A month ago he would have dumped one of those barrels over out of spite. He looked up at Miss O'Dea. She had been too good to him to cause her any grief.

"I don't need no new shoes!" Johnny cried. He tried to dart from the store, but Benjamin caught him by the arm.

"Mind your manners, boy, or you won't be getting

162

new shoes." Johnny settled down and stood, stiff, next to a glowering Benjamin. "That's better. Now get over to the shelf and let Bevin get you fitted proper."

"Come on, runt, I'll show you what I used to wear," Will finally interceded, unable to stand still and listen to anymore.

To Benjamin's chagrin, he heard Bevin thank William and go with him and the children to a far corner away from prying eyes.

It took some time, but finally she was satisfied that they were able to find a pair that, with a little padding stuffed inside, would meet Johnny's needs. Bevin made a mental note to thank Will for his suggestion that he see to having the sole of Johnny's left shoe built up to further make the shoe workable. She took the shoes to the counter and added them to her purchases. While Bevin escorted the children outside, and Will took the shoes to the cobbler's, Benjamin paid the bill.

"When did that stepbrother of yours get back in town?" Oscar questioned harshly.

"He came in on the same train as Bevin."

"Never thought that one would return," Oscar spat out.

"Neither did anyone else in town."

"Has a lot of nerve to be showing his face in here after all these years. Particularly after the way he let my Matthew drown."

Benjamin heaved a sigh. "Oscar, that was a long time ago."

"Don't make it hurt no less. If he had been doin' his duty instead of tryin' to kiss the Frankfurt girl in the bushes, he'd of seen that Matthew was in trouble. And you know he never should of been shirking his work in the first place. Why, he shouldn't of been no where near that muddy swimmin' hole, let alone lettin' the younger boys near it."

163

"Look, Oscar, the whole town knows how you feel. It was an accident," Benjamin emphasized, defending William. He, too, had wanted to go swimming that day. If his pa hadn't caught him, Benjamin might have been the one at the swimming hole instead of William. Benjamin had secretly carried a share of guilt for that tragic day, for Benjamin, too, had been in on the plan to play hooky from chores.

An idea suddenly came to Benjamin. "Oscar, you said you could use help in the store. I know no one is ever going to take Matthew's place. But since your business is growing, and since I just happen to be playing host to a couple extra pair of hands right now, what if you take the boy, Johnny, in?"

In an attempt to disarm the dark scowl spreading across the proprietor's face, Benjamin added, "You won't have to worry about buying the kid no new shoes, he comes already equipped with a new pair."

"You hain't goin' to palm off no cripple on me, Benjamin Straub. And I doubt that any other family in the area is goin' to take that one in either."

"No harm in trying, Oscar." Benjamin shrugged and went out to join Bevin and the children.

On the sidewalk, Benjamin caught sight of Bevin speaking to Bertha and Asa Krueger. They seemed to be looking Tara over. Benjamin hung back and waited, hoping the couple would agree to take the child. The couple had taken Bevin's brother in years ago. It would be a blessing if they took both children, but Benjamin didn't hold out much hope for them taking Johnny. No. That one would probably have to be sent back to Boston with Prudence Truesdale when she returned. All Benjamin had to do was somehow figure out a way to separate his bride-to-be from the little beggar without too much of a scene, since Bevin seemed to be so fond of that boy.

Chapter Seventeen

Bertha looked pleadingly into Asa's face, leathered from years behind a plow. "Oh, Asa, Tara would be so much help to me. You know Gretchen is marrying age and one of these days'll be going to live with her husband's people. Look at her." Bertha turned Tara around so Asa could have a good look at the child. "She's the picture of health. She'll be perfect."

Asa rubbed his chin. "Well, if she's what you really want, honey, I suppose we can give her a try."

Johnny stood behind Bevin. His lip trembled and he dug his fingers in his palms. He was losing another friend.

"I'll wait in the buggy," Johnny announced abruptly and started to scurry away.

"Ain't you gonna say good-bye, Johnny?" Tara called out, her eyes wide in disbelief over the sudden turn of events.

He stopped and threw back over his shoulder, "What for?"

" 'Cause I'm gonna miss you, that's what for."

Her heart hurting for the little boy, Bevin interceded. "Johnny, Tara won't be far away. The Kruegers live on the farm next to Benjamin's. You'll get to see her. Often."

"Yeah. Sure." He didn't wait any longer. He climbed into the buggy and turned his face away.

"Couldn't you take Johnny too?" Tara begged, tears flooding her imploring eyes.

"No, girl, we couldn't. Farm work's hard on a body, and we hain't got room for no one what hain't goin' to pull his weight," Asa stated flatly.

Tara hung her head, defeated, as Benjamin joined them. When he learned the Kruegers had consented to take the girl, he congratulated the couple on their choice. He handed the child the shoes he'd bought.

"You're getting a good deal, Asa. You won't be having to buy shoes for the girl any time soon," he added in an attempt at levity.

"Don't be expectin' me to pay you for them, Benjamin," Asa Krueger said.

"Don't worry, Asa, I don't. I'm grateful to you for taking the girl in."

"It hain't no favor." The farmer looked down at Tara. "She'll be working for her keep."

Bevin hugged Tara and promised to bring Johnny over to see her soon. Her heart swelled with pain and joy while she stood next to Benjamin and watched another child being led away. It was at that moment she vowed to herself that she would see Johnny happily settled in with a family before she married Benjamin. Preferably, she determined, with her and Benjamin.

Bertha spoke to her husband and hurried back to Bevin.

"My dear, I nearly forgot in all the excitement. Benjamin said you were asking after Patrick, so I told him you were out at Benjamin's place, anxious to see him. I expected him to want to rush right over to see you, him not seeing his sister for so many years. He said he had chores to do. We have the hard wheat to get in,

166

you know. He'll be at church tomorrow; you'll see him there." At Bevin's stung look, Bertha continued. "Don't fret none. He's a fine young man. Turned out right well, he did. He just needs a little time to absorb having kin again, is all."

Bevin's stomach riled with anticipation. Weakly, she answered, "I'm sure that's all it is."

"We'll see you in church tomorrow. If it hain't too much trouble, would you mind bringin' Tara's things with you?"

"I shall be happy to."

"Thank you," Bertha said and hurried off.

"Come along, Bevin, we need to collect William and be getting back. I got chores that need doing."

By the time they returned to the farm, there wasn't much daylight left. Benjamin convinced Will to help out with the chores around the barn and, to Bevin's relief, they included Johnny. The child needed something to take his mind off another loss and rejection this day.

Bevin stood and watched them from the window. While Will took off his jacket and began to chop more wood for the stove, Johnny waited to carry the wood. Benjamin was busy slopping the hogs. It was such a domestic scene which held her enthralled. So different from life in the city, and Bevin found she truly liked being away from the hustle-bustle life of Boston despite the adjustments she would have to make.

"Bevin, I thought I heard you return," Prudence said, joining her at the window.

"Oh, Pru, I didn't hear you come in. Just look at them. It makes my heart swell so to see my two men working together."

"Funny you should say that."

Bevin furrowed her brow. "Why?"

"The only two I see working together are Johnny and Will."

Bevin's breath caught and she swung around to glare at Prudence. "You know what I meant, Pru."

"Do I, Evvie?"

"Of course you do. I was talking about Johnny and Benjamin."

"Naturally you were. Where's Tara?" Prudence asked, realizing the little girl was no where in sight, and changing the topic for Bevin's sake.

"The Kruegers took her. They happened to be in town, and we ran into them outside the mercantile. Bertha Krueger fell in love with Tara and convinced her husband that she would be a good addition to their family. They raised Patrick, you know. So I'm sure Tara will have a good home. Oh, Pru, it is going to be so perfect. Tara will be living on the next farm, so Johnny will have a friend nearby."

"Then you have spoken to Benjamin about keeping Johnny?"

Bevin fidgeted. "Not exactly. But I know that he will want to keep Johnny as much as I do. We best get supper started. I don't want to keep them waiting when they come in after working so hard."

Holding her tongue despite worry that Bevin was getting too deeply enmeshed in her own fantasy world that Benjamin would accept Johnny, Prudence followed Bevin into the kitchen. They donned aprons and got busy chopping potatoes and carrots. Bevin cut generous portions of ham steaks and laid them in the big iron skillet.

Johnny brought in an armload of wood. He dropped it in the wood box, then handed Bevin a piece at a time so she could fire up the stove.

"You are a big help, young man."

Johnny's eyes lit up. "Really? Will is letting me carry the wood again."

"You mean Mr. Shoemaker?"

"He said I could call him Will. Not like that old, dumb Mr. Straub who hollers at me all the time."

"Johnny, it is not nice to talk about Benjamin that way."

Johnny scrunched up his nose. "Well, he's not nice."

"Go get another load, and don't you let me hear you talk that way about Benjamin again, you hear? Then get washed up, supper will be ready soon."

Johnny gave a half nod and rushed from the house.

Prudence dumped the carrots into a pot and carried it to the stove. "Funny how children take to some people and not to others. I wonder—"

"He'll take to Benjamin," Bevin snapped effectively, cutting Prudence off. Even as the words left her lips, she questioned whether what she had said was true.

The men came in and washed up. Bevin watched the two standing next to each other. Benjamin was deeply bronzed; his face weathered from years under the sun. His arms were heavily muscled despite his medium build. Will was a bigger man, broad shoulders and equally muscled, only he was not so tan. The hardness which confirmed Benjamin's features was missing from Will's. Bevin shook her head to snap her mind out of the mental comparison of the two step-brothers.

Sitting around the kitchen table, supper was a livelier meal with Prudence's questions about their trip into town. The girl babbled on her awe of the farm. She had never seen animals mate before and blushed profusely when she mentioned seeing the barnyard animals openly engaged in such activities. Johnny snickered, Will laughed, and Benjamin shifted uneasily at

169

such talk forbidden in mixed company.

"Can I watch sometime?" Johnny asked.

"That's enough of that kind of talk. I'll have no more of it at my table. Let's get this meal over with," Benjamin grated.

Daunted, Bevin finished her supper without the same joy with which she had started it. There were so many adjustments to make.

After supper the women cleaned the kitchen and settled in the parlor to read while Benjamin went back out to the barn, and Will sat across from Bevin, openly watching her. Johnny sat on the floor and waited his chance to sneak outside to give Sourdough the ham scraps he had stolen from the table.

It was not more than a half hour before Prudence rose and yawned. "I'm for bed."

Bevin looked up from her book. "Take Johnny up with you, will you?" She turned to the boy. "It's time you turn in."

"Do I have to?"

"Yes, you do, son," Will said, startling Bevin's gaze to him. "No more back talk. Get going."

Johnny's lips drooping, he said, "Yes, sir," and allowed Miss Prudence to escort him up the stairs.

"You handle the boy with a firm but gentle hand. He responds well to that," Bevin announced once they were alone.

Instinctively knowing that the boy would probably sneak out of his room and collect Sourdough, Will said, "He's just a kid."

"I want to thank you for helping out with Johnny's shoes today; it was kind of Benjamin to provide them."

Will stared at the woman. She seemed to be rationalizing Benjamin's behavior. "Ben knows his duty, Bevin. You will always be able to count on Benjamin to provide."

"Yes, I know I shall. I am most fortunate."

He looked deeply into her eyes, unable to stop himself. "So is Ben."

His observation nearly unnerved her as she was rising and Benjamin joined them.

"Surely you are not going to bed yet?" Benjamin asked, disappointment in his voice that they would not get much time together now that all the chores were done.

"No, I'll be right back. I want to make sure Johnny is tucked in bed."

"He's old enough to tuck himself in," put in Benjamin. "My pa never let my ma tuck me in bed at Johnny's age."

"Let her play mother if it's important to her," Will argued.

"Soon she will have her own family," Benjamin retorted. "I don't want Bevin coddling the boy before he leaves. It'll only put the wrong kind of ideas about life into the child's head."

"Making sure the child is okay is not putting the wrong kind of ideas into Johnny's head. But if you feel that strongly about it, I'll check on him when I go up," Bevin relented, feeling frustrated.

"If you'll excuse me, I think this is my cue to leave you two alone," Will said and promptly left. He stopped in the doorway and looked back at the domestic scene before him, almost wishing it were he in there with Bevin instead of Benjamin. But Will had nothing to offer a lady like Bevin O'Dea. He shook his head; it was only a fleeting fancy.

Left alone with Bevin in the parlor, Benjamin moved to sit closer to his bride-to-be. He had already decided there was no need to discuss the Martin boy further; the child would be gone soon and the issue settled without further strife.

Bevin sat quietly, wondering if Benjamin would take her hand and kiss her. She desperately longed for Benjamin to embrace her and wipe away remembrances of Will's kiss with his own. She needed reassurance that Benjamin could obliterate the persistent thoughts of Will Shoemaker, which had begun creeping into her mind too frequently. She longed to be reminded that she had made the best choice.

When it became apparent that Benjamin planned to keep a respectable distance, her heart sank. She wanted to go into his arms and prove her thoughts about Will were foolish, but Bevin remained where she was, a book in her lap.

"I understand there is a school not far from the farm," she finally said, breaking the awkward silence.

" 'Bout five miles south of here."

"I'd like to enroll Johnny. I think it would be good for him to get some formal education and be with other children, don't you think?"

Benjamin's head snapped up. "Learning is a social frill to be added only after a family's material needs for survival are met," he stated flatly. "He should learn how to do a good day's work first. Then maybe some family might be more inclined to take him in despite that foot of his."

"But, Benjamin, while he is with us—"

Benjamin held up a silencing hand. "Bevin, I know you have taken a liking to the boy. But you must remember that he is only here temporarily."

Bevin stiffened her spine. She was not about to back down on something as important as education.

"Johnny can learn about work from you after school. Learning to read for a young man is a vital skill today." At Benjamin's scowl, she added, "From my letters you must remember how hard I worked to educate myself. I want no less for the boy."

For over an hour Bevin poured out the story of her own childhood, filling in all the blanks she had left out of her letters. She wanted Benjamin to know exactly what he was getting in a wife. And she wanted him to understand why she felt it was so important to have Johnny attend school.

Benjamin listened attentively. It was one of his strengths. Folks had always said they could come to him if they needed a good ear. He had not made it a practice to hand out advice freely, which also pleased folks. Benjamin knew most folks made up their own minds, just as he himself did. He could hear the determination in Bevin's voice, see the set to her jaw. He realized that granting her this one concession could very well cause her to think of keeping the boy.

"Bevin, your past doesn't matter to me. It's our future together that's important. If you stop and consider what's best for the boy, you'll realize that if he can work the farm a family'd be more likely to take him and then be happy to send him to school. I've got to finish getting the winter wheat crop in. After that, if he's still here we'll think about school."

Although Benjamin did not relent to her wishes, he had just taken the first step toward letting Johnny stay; Bevin was certain of it. Hearing only what she wanted to hear, she forgot herself and jumped to her feet. Knocking the book in her lap to the floor, she rushed to Benjamin. She threw her arms around his neck and hugged him.

"Oh, Benjamin, thank you. You won't regret it. I promise."

Their eyes met and held, and the beckoning

strength of her was more than Benjamin could endure. He inhaled the sweet fragrance of her. Despite his belief in keeping his distance until after they were married, he reveled in the feel of her smooth hands. His rough thumbs rubbed her palms until he could no longer endure his restraint.

His hands trembling, he cupped her face and drew her to him. Slowly, ever so gently he brushed his lips against hers before he released her and edged a safe distance away.

"Bevin, I'm sorry. I don't know what came over me. I would never dishonor you before we're married."

"No, Benjamin, I am glad we shared a kiss," she said shyly.

Shock registered on his face. "You are?"

"Yes, a lady engaged to be married enjoys being courted. Now I think I must go up to bed though. Good night, Benjamin. I'll see you in the morning."

Before Benjamin could explore this puzzling development further, Bevin had disappeared up the stairs. For the longest time Benjamin remained in the parlor, thinking. He had never courted a lady before. Bevin seemed to enjoy his kiss; she certainly had not shrunk away from him. Perhaps a kiss or two before they were wed would not be so wrong after all. Or would it?

Humming to himself, Benjamin made his way up the stairs to his room, a new spring in his step.

Chapter Eighteen

For the second night in a row Bevin laid in bed unable to sleep. First Will had kissed her on the porch swing the night before, then tonight Benjamin had kissed her in the parlor. Two brothers. No, stepbrothers. They had reminded her of that fact often enough. Both so different, yet in their own ways alike. Both had kissed her. Benjamin had apologized; Will had not. She could feel their kisses, and despite herself had to admit that it was Will's kiss that had stirred her.

Bevin turned over, bunched the feather pillow and clenched her fists around it. Why did it have to be Will that awakened her desire? He was wrong for her—all wrong. Benjamin offered a home, security, and a way of life for which she had always yearned. Will Shoemaker owned half the farm, but he had openly admitted he was no farmer and had no intention of staying. Nor had he voiced any more than a passing interest in her. She was merely an available female to Will Shoemaker. To Benjamin she was the woman with whom he had chosen to spend the rest of his life. He would honor her by sharing his life with her. Will, she surmised, would probably steal a few moments of passion and then move on.

Prudence stirred, interrupting Bevin's silent debate over the stepbrothers' merits. Time. There was still time to get Will out of her mind before she married Benjamin. Consciously Bevin vowed to do just that before she fell into a fitful sleep.

Bevin was still asleep when Prudence shook her shoulder. "Evvie, wake up. We need to get breakfast and get ready for church."

Bevin was a bundle of nerves by the time she pinned on her frilly hat, straightened her most fashionable emerald striped dress, and let Benjamin help her into the buggy. He offered Prudence a hand up and went around to climb in beside Bevin. Johnny sat in back tugging at his stiff collar. Will had declined Benjamin's urgings to cleanse his soul in church and remained behind.

Will watched the buggy rumble down the drive. He had no desire to make an unwanted appearance in church and listen to those hypocrites whisper behind their hands about him. He had endured too many years of that as a child. Instead he stuffed his hands in his pockets and headed toward the barn to saddle a horse; he needed a good morning's ride to be alone with his God, and he needed to visit his mother's grave.

Bevin could hardly contain her excitement and anticipation at finally seeing her brother again when the white steeple of the church came into view, even though she felt a twinge at attending a church of another faith. She looked over at Benjamin; he sat rigidly next to her, his attention focused on the reins. She squeezed Prudence's hand. Prudence cast her a sympathetic smile.

"Oh, Evvie, I am ever so happy for you. You have

176

waited such a long time for this day."

"What do you think Patrick is like?" Bevin asked for the hundredth time since she had learned Patrick's whereabouts.

"He's a farmer," Benjamin stated flatly. "Don't expect him to fall all over you with excitement." At Bevin's bewildered expression, Benjamin elaborated. "Farmers don't get overly excited. It doesn't mean they don't feel. It's just that folks around here accept life and do what they have to do on a day-to-day basis."

"Of course."

The buggy stopped outside the picket fence surrounding the little church. Bevin counted twelve other carriages before she recognized the one belonging to the Kruegers. She had so hoped that they would have arrived before Patrick so she could speak with him prior to the service. Now she knew she would have to wait.

"You missing the service again, Karl Mueller?" Benjamin said to the spindly youngster.

"Somebody's got to watch the horses so they don't spook in case there's a storm."

At Bevin's bemused expression, Benjamin said, "It is tradition that one of the children remain outside the church and tend the animals since storms are known to come up suddenly and stampede them."

"Can I help out sometime?" asked Johnny, excited about the possibility of spending more time around horses.

Karl frowned at the outsider. "That's my job."

"Seems to me you could use some of the Lord's counsel." Benjamin looked down at Johnny's expectant face. "You think you could handle the job, boy?"

Johnny clasped his hands together. "Yes, sir!"

"No!" Karl protested, glaring at the intruder.

"You get inside, Karl Mueller," Benjamin instructed.

Karl's face screwed up and he leaned close to Johnny. "You dumb, old cripple."

Johnny blanched, but stood his position as he watched the Mueller boy drag himself inside the church.

Bevin patted Johnny on the shoulder. "Benjamin has given you a big job. I know you can do it."

"Yes, ma'am," Johnny said importantly.

Leaving Johnny behind, Bevin took Benjamin's arm, her heart swelling with pride that Benjamin indeed was softening.

"Thank you, Benjamin. It means a lot to Johnny to be given a chance."

"Not much chance of bad weather today," Benjamin grunted.

Inside Benjamin led Bevin and Prudence to his regular pew. Bevin took a seat beside Benjamin with Prudence on the end. Although she tried to focus her attention on the parson's announcements, Bevin could not help herself. She took every opportunity to glance around at the other members of the congregation, hoping for a glimpse of Patrick.

When they rose to sing, Bevin's eyes came to rest on the Kruegers and she sang out a flat note as her breath caught. A muscular, reddish blond-haired man sat next to Bertha Krueger; it had to be Patrick.

The sermon on *loving thy brother* seemed to last an eternity, but was aptly appropriate, considering the way Benjamin and Will felt toward each other, and her upcoming reunion.

As they filed from the church after the service, Bevin felt self-conscious at the plain-dressed farmers' wives who whispered about her trying to outdo plain hard-working folks. She tried to ignore the censuring

178

remarks, but she so wanted to become an accepted member of the community — Benjamin's neighbors and friends.

Benjamin introduced Bevin and Prudence to Parson Pryor. The man's gift of gab threatened to drive Bevin beyond herself, she was so anxious to be reunited with Patrick. Despite her desire to rush over to Patrick, Bevin mulled about the churchyard with Benjamin and the parson. She was introduced to the clusters of worshippers, politely answering all questions and accepting congratulations on her good fortune to be Benjamin's intended.

Unable to endure another syllable, Bevin interrupted, "Parson Pryor, if you will excuse me, I must speak with my brother. Prudence, would you go see how Johnny is getting along?"

"Yes. Yes, of course. It was nice meeting you, Parson Pryor," Prudence said shyly. Turning to Bevin, she whispered, "If that is your brother over there by the Kruegers' carriage, he certainly is a big handsome man." Not waiting for a response, Prudence hurried off to follow Bevin's directive, her heart fluttering each time she glanced in Patrick O'Dea's direction.

"I enjoyed the sermon and meeting all of you," Bevin mumbled to the latest group to surround her before finally disengaging herself. Without offering further explanation, she left them staring after her.

"Her brother?" a balding man inquired, tenting knobby fingers.

"Patrick O'Dea. They were separated as children. As all of you know by now, Bevin and I have been corresponding for some time; I helped her locate her brother."

"Yes. Indeed. Your intended. I'd say she does look a bit frail for farm life, Benjamin," the parson remarked to heads bobbing in agreement among the group.

"She's stronger than she looks. I'm sure she'll make a good wife once things settle down."

Benjamin and Parson Pryor spoke a few more minutes to the group, then drifted off toward the fence to watch the reunion from a respectable distance.

"Speaking of making a wife, Benjamin. When do you plan on getting married?"

"The sooner the better. Why don't you come out to the farm for supper Tuesday night, Gus, and we'll discuss it then."

Being a single man who had dedicated his life to serving the Lord, Gus Pryor never turned down an invitation to share a meal with one of his flock.

"I think that's a good idea. People are beginning to whisper about you keeping her out there at the farm."

Benjamin bristled at the implication. He had to admit he had sinned in his heart—had even been so bold as to kiss her. But he never would wrong the lady, and it galled him that folks could think such thoughts.

"You know Bevin's coworker is staying out at the farm with us, as well as the little boy she hasn't been able to place, and my stepbrother, William."

"Ah, yes, Will Shoemaker. I heard he's back in town. Where is the man? I didn't see him among the congregation."

"You know William. He's always had his own way of doing things."

"So he has," commented the parson dryly, letting his gaze shift to the reunion between brother and sister just outside the fence.

Bevin approached the tall, reddish blond-haired man standing alone by the Kruegers' buggy with his back to her. Her heart pounded and her hands shook.

"P-Patrick?"

He turned toward her, his blue eyes unreadable. "Yes."

She tentatively reached out a gloved hand and placed it on his arm. "Is it really you?"

He pulled his arm back, his handsome Irish face void of emotion. "I am Patrick O'Dea Krueger. I heard you are staying out at Benjamin Straub's farm."

"Benjamin and I are engaged to be married, if you aren't aware. Won't it be nice? We will be together again."

"Don't you think it's a little late for that?"

Disappointment swept over her face, but she fought to recover herself. At the Children's Aid Society she had worked with families that had been separated and then reunited, and was aware of the hurt and pain, the frustrations, the misunderstandings, and the anger that those years of separation could foster.

Despite her training and experience, Bevin stood still, hurt and not knowing what to say. Silently, she breathed a sigh of relief when they were joined by the Kruegers and Benjamin.

"My, but a body certainly can tell you two are kin; you are the spitting image of each other," Bertha observed.

More awkward moments ensued as the beginnings of conversations withered for lack of response from Patrick until Bevin suggested, "If it is acceptable to everyone perhaps Patrick and I might have a better chance to talk and become reacquainted if we went for a drive."

"I have chores," Patrick protested stiffly.

"It's not every day a brother and sister get back together; I'll take care of your work today," Asa offered. "But me and the missus need the buggy. You know the family often spends Sunday afternoons over at Bertha's uncle's place."

Noticing the look of disappointment on Bevin's face, Benjamin forced himself to offer, "They can take my buggy, if you don't mind dropping me and the others off at my place, Asa."

"No trouble at all."

"Thank you, Mr. Krueger," Bevin said.

"Weren't nothing, little lady. Kin's important." Asa shot Patrick a knowing look.

"And thank you, Benjamin, for making it possible for Patrick and I to have a chance to talk." Bevin laid a gloved hand on Benjamin's arm and gave him a gentle squeeze of gratitude. Her estimation of Benjamin surged despite his look of discomfiture over her touch.

Gretchen had been silent, but now a wide grin spread over her lips. "I think that's a good idea, Pa."

"Hush, girl," Bertha snapped. "Get yourself into the buggy. It's time we head home."

"Yes, Ma. You coming, Benjamin?"

"I'll see you back at the farm later, Bevin," Benjamin said before Gretchen linked her arm with his and asked him to help her into the buggy.

"You two take all the time you need," Bertha advised, then she and Asa boarded the buggy. Asa snapped the reins across the rumps of the team and directed the buggy toward Benjamin's buggy to pick up Tara, the birdlike lady and the cripple standing with her. Pity the boy had that bum foot, thought Asa. He could have used another boy on the farm. Patrick had been a godsend all those years ago. And Asa knew that soon Patrick would be wanting to

182

marry and get a farm of his own.

"Are we going to stand here, or go for that ride?" Bevin ventured once they were left alone, fearing he might refuse. "We're becoming quite a spectacle standing here."

"You are the outsider here. It's you they are staring at."

Bevin was stung but hid her hurt. "Yes, I suppose that's true. But will you at least hear me out? I have waited a long time to be with you again, and I have come a long way. Don't we owe that much to each other?"

Patrick gave an impatient huff. "All right, let's get this over with." He motioned for her to lead the way to Benjamin's buggy.

Bevin hurried past curious clusters, having to wait but once while Patrick exchanged friendly greetings with several young girls near his own age. She was disappointed he did not introduce her, but that only made her more determined than ever to work through their troubles. Reaching the buggy, Bevin let Patrick help her onto the seat and waited impatiently while he climbed up and took up a position next to her.

Chapter Nineteen

The sun shone brightly despite the dismal atmosphere surrounding Bevin and Patrick as he turned the buggy north and headed away from town. It was a glorious autumn day. The leaves were beginning to turn in a burst of fall colors, and only a few scattered puffs of clouds rode high in an unusually blue sky.

Unable to endure Patrick's silence for more than a couple of miles, Bevin asked, "Were the Kruegers good to you?"

Patrick broke the straightforward gaze he had maintained since they'd left town and shot her a daunting look. "They are the *only* family I have known."

"I am your family, Patrick. At least if you'll let me be again. We were very close once, remember?"

He gave her a quelling frown, not answering, and returned his attention to the road.

Discouraged but not defeated, Bevin let out a sigh of resignation and decided to wait until they came to a pleasant spot to attempt further conversation. Then she'd ask him to stop so she could have his undivided attention.

They traveled for some time before they came upon the familiar shaded clearing she had picnicked with Benjamin near where the creek formed a delightful pond sprinkled with groupings of boulders, and with a frayed rope dangling from a thick branch overhanging the pond.

"There!" Bevin pointed. "Over there! It's the perfect place to stop and talk."

Patrick reined in the horses and turned to look at Bevin, his features set in stone. "What makes you think I have anything to say to you?"

"Maybe you don't, but I have a lot to say to you. So, please, at least drive over by that tree so we can sit in the shade while I talk."

"All right. But I don't have all day."

"Fair enough."

Bevin smiled to herself as he pulled the coach over to the trees, tied the horses, and helped her down. It was a small concession, but a start nonetheless. Regardless of how her brother felt about her, he was a gentleman; the Kruegers had done a good job. He grabbed a blanket from behind the seat and spread it out at the base of a huge tree near the pond.

"What are you waiting for?" he grumbled when she did not immediately take a place on the blanket.

"Nothing." She sat down and spread her skirts out around her. Patrick remained standing, his back to her. "Please, join me."

He swung around, rubbing his jaw in annoyance. "Look, don't know why we're here. I have nothing to say. There is nothing that can be said. You let those people—strangers—take me away and put me on a train. Never once in all those years did you try to find out what had happened to me."

"I didn't try to find out what had happened to you?" she cried, incredulous that he could believe such a thing. "My God, Patrick, I was only ten years old when they took you. You have no idea how hard

185

I did try to find out what happened to you . . ."

Will was sitting on the other side of the pond, staring into the deep reflecting waters and trying to come to terms with his past. This was where Matthew Lutherby had drowned, and Will needed to put that dreadful accident behind him once and for all. At the sound of voices he was drawn from his own musings. His ears perked up. It was Bevin. He recognized the pain in her voice and moved behind a tree to eavesdrop.

"If you tried so hard to find me, then why weren't you taken and put on one of those damned trains too?" Patrick demanded.

"Because I bribed old lady Finnian to do the asking for me. Do you remember her, the old woman who lived down the alley from us?"

Patrick ran shaking fingers through his heavy reddish-blond waves. "But all those years. It took me years to give up hope and finally accept the Kruegers as my family. It took me years to become a part of this community. Years, Bevin. Years. Now you show up and disrupt everything. Your being here is only going to dredge up all the old hurt and pain, and set others to asking questions all over again. Why don't you just get back on the first train going East and forget you ever had a brother so I can live my life?

"But—"

"No! Try to understand, *I do not want you here.* . . ."

Tears ran down Bevin's cheeks as she listened to what turned into an embittered tirade and indictment against her. When she'd first joined him in the churchyard, she realized that he was hurt, but she'd never imagined the extent to which that pain had festered inside him, transforming him into the angry young man who now stood glowering over her.

"Patrick, please, sit down. I know we can work out

186

our problems if you will only give me half a chance."
His features seemed to soften for an instant, causing
Bevin to add, "You know that Benjamin has asked
me to marry him. I said yes so we could be together
again; so I could be near you. We shall both become
a part of this community. . . ."

So that was the real reason Bevin had accepted
Benjamin's proposal without ever meeting him, and
why she was trying so hard to fit into a way of life so
completely foreign to her, thought Will. The exchange between brother and sister grew softer and
when Will moved closer so he could hear, he stepped
on a twig. It snapped, causing Bevin and Patrick's
heads to swing around in Will's direction.

"Who's there?" Patrick called out.

Will stepped into sight and strolled toward them.

"You! What are *you* doing here?" Bevin said.

At the recognition in Bevin's voice, Patrick sputtered, "Who is he?" His level of irritation was growing by the moment.

"The name's Will Shoemaker. I'm Benjamin's stepbrother."

Patrick swung on Bevin. "What did you do, bring
me out here and have him waiting behind a tree just
in case you couldn't handle the situation by yourself,
Miss O'Dea?"

Oh, Dear Lord, he was denying her, Bevin
thought in total agony. "No. I didn't know Will would
be here. You must believe me." Bevin settled an-
guished eyes on Will. "Would you please leave? Your
presence is only making things worse."

"That your horse over there?" Patrick asked, first
noticing the animal tied nearby.

"It belongs to Benjamin."

"Since the buggy also belongs to Benjamin, you
can drive it and Straub's intended back to the man."

Patrick walked purposely toward the horse and tossed back over his shoulder, "I'll bring the horse back later, although I oughtta let Gretchen, she seems to spend enough time over at Straub's."

"Patrick, please—"

Will grabbed Bevin's arm to keep her from following after her brother. "Let him go, Bevin."

"But—"

"No. He needs time."

Bevin stood trembling and watched Patrick swing easily up into the saddle. Without a backward glance, he laid his heels into the horse's flanks and was gone.

Overwrought with the emotion of such abject rejection, Bevin crumpled to the blanket and began to sob. Will knelt down beside her and gathered her into his arms.

"Bevin, I'm sorry if my presence made your troubles with your brother worse."

She swallowed another sob. "I had hoped he would be as happy to see me as I was to finally see him. I never dreamed he would hold me responsible for being sent West all those years ago, let alone keep his anger inside him like he has done."

He rocked her while he stroked her hair. "It's all right to let your feelings out, Bevin. Don't try to hold them in. Cry it out if you need to."

His compassion released a floodgate inside Bevin and she broke into heart-wrenching sobs. "Oh, Will, I had so hoped he would be happy that we are together again."

Will tightened his arms around her and cradled her against his chest while she cried. He lay his cheek against her hair. His heart ached for Bevin, for he understood—all too well—what her brother was going through inside. Reaching out to Patrick was not going to be easy, not after so many years.

Will brushed back a loose tendril that curled in front of her ear. "Patrick will come around. Don't worry. He'll soon realize what a special sister he has and put the past behind him where it belongs."

Bevin sniffled. "If I didn't love him so much it wouldn't hurt so bad."

"I know, baby. I know."

For the first time in years, Bevin felt unsure of herself, and in need of someone to lean on. She pulled back, drew a hankie out of her skirt pocket and blew her nose. Dabbing at her watery eyes, she studied the man next to her. Benjamin should have been sitting here speaking words of consolation — not Will. Benjamin should have been holding her — not Will. Benjamin was her fiancé — not Will. The realization was sobering, and only served to add to the confusion and anguish she was experiencing.

"I'm sorry if my presence ruined things with Patrick for you."

"I don't think whether you were here or not would have made any difference," she said sadly. "Why were you out here?"

"That boy I told you about drowned here. I thought that coming back here might help me lay my guilt feelings to rest. It's the first time I've been back here since that terrible day."

"Did it help?"

"Yes, in a way it helped put things in order for me. I realize now that I couldn't have saved the boy. He must have hit his head after swinging into the pond."

She squeezed his arm. "I'm sorry, Will. It must be terribly difficult for you."

"Don't worry about me. I'll be fine. I know your troubles with Patrick aren't the same as what hap-

189

pened to me, but perhaps getting away and having time to think everything through will change his mind."

"I wish that were true," she said. Will was in the midst of trying to deal with his own past and yet he was consoling her.

"Patrick's just young. He doesn't realize what a treasure he has in you. When he gets to know you like I have, he'll come around and curse the time he's wasted."

A brief, weighty silence enveloped them. Bevin noticed the strange glimmer in Will's eyes. "Treasure?"

Will fidgeted uneasily. She was his stepbrother's fiancée; the woman Benjamin loved and planned to marry. He knew he had no right to say the words standing on the edge of his tongue. "Yes, Benjamin is a very lucky man," he said instead.

She dropped her eyes, knowing a blush crept up her face. "Thank you. I'm the fortunate one. Benjamin will be a good provider."

"Did you really only accept Benjamin's proposal to be near your brother?" Will heard himself ask.

"What gave you that idea?"

"I overheard you tell your brother that's why you accepted Benjamin's proposal."

"Umm . . . I . . . ah . . . you must have misunderstood," she stammered.

"Did I, Bevin? Did I really misunderstand?" he pressed.

Again an awkward silence settled over them until Bevin pulled herself together enough to answer, "Yes, you did. Benjamin and I are going to be married and I am going to be a good wife to him."

"Knowing you, Bevin, there is no doubt in my mind that you will make a fine wife to whomever you marry."

"Thank you. You are being very kind."

"Kindness has nothing to do with it."

"Well, thank you just the same."

She was filled with a growing uneasiness after what he had just said. She had come to Bowling Green to be reunited with her brother and marry Benjamin Straub, not to sit under a tree, alone, unchaperoned, with a man for whom she had to admit she was discovering a developing attraction; a man whose perceptions were all too keen; a man who seemed to be developing an attraction for her as well.

"If nothing more, I hope we can be friends."

"If nothing more?" she repeated in a bare whisper.

Will inhaled a deep breath of frustration. He had not come to the pond to lay bare his feelings for Miss Bevin O'Dea.

Bevin was knotting up inside. "I should be getting back. I don't want Benjamin to worry."

"No, we certainly don't want to worry Benjamin."

Will's lips were a breath away from Bevin's. He had brushed her cheek with his mouth while she cried and he could taste the salt from her tears. He inhaled deeply; she smelled the way a woman was supposed to smell, not like the paid-for whores with whom he had spent his time. The need to touch her again overwhelmed him and he reached out to run the back of his hand down her moistened cheek and wiped away the tracks of her tears.

"Benjamin will worry when I do not return," Bevin said feebly. She was staring into those hynoptizing brown depths, and could feel herself getting lost.

"No, we don't want him to worry," Will breathed. With his thumb he wiped her cheek and she nuzzled her face against him.

Will had held himself in check the last time he had kissed her. Now her vulnerability and need for his

191

strength released a floodgate of pent-up emotions, and he cupped her face.

"You are quite a lady, Miss Bevin O'Dea."

Slowly, he drew her to him and kissed her. As their kiss deepened an agonized pleasure overtook her and she tried to pull back.

"No, Bevin, don't deny your feelings. Let them flow," Will whispered in a husky voice.

His lips captured hers this time in a searing kiss. She felt his big hands hot on her face, holding her to him. His tongue traced the outline of her mouth until she opened it for him, and he plunged in. His tongue seduced her with its rhythm of love, spilling a flood of pleasure so intense throughout her body that she surrendered to her desire.

The fire of his fingers left her face and blazed a trail down her neck, over her shoulders and down her back to grasp her to him. Ever so gently, he pulled her with him until she lay on the blanket looking up into heated brown eyes ablaze with desire.

"Will, we can't. I—"

He pressed a finger to her lips. "Hush, Bevin. Let yourself go. Let yourself feel what we both know has been growing between us."

Her eyes heavy-lidded with overwhelming emotion, Bevin whimpered. She reached up and entwined her fingers through his hair.

"Oh, God, I've been wanting this," he groaned. "Needing this."

Bevin tilted her head back as his lips made a bold descent from her mouth, down the velvety column of her neck. She felt his warm breath and moist lips linger on her neck while flaming fingers of fire worked the buttons on her dress. The sun through the trees warmed her bared breasts as the insides of his thumbs circled the peaking nipples.

She experienced a flood of moist heat between her thighs at the onslaught of his mouth covering the puckering coral centers. He nipped and suckled while his fingers kneaded and pushed the voluptuous breasts together around his cheeks. Bevin cried out and begin to strain against the length of him as he ignited a need in her woman's core. She could feel his arousal pressing hard against her lower belly.

A hand left her breast and suddenly she felt the roughened fingers gliding up her thigh, pushing up her skirts until he cupped the moistened mound through her thin undergarment. He stroked along the indentation and then suddenly pushed inside the fabric to stroke her swollen, wet lips. When he began to apply pressure, Bevin clamped her thighs together.

Will raised his head and lightly nipped at her lips. "Open to me, love."

Gasping for breath, Bevin panted, "We mustn't."

"We must. Don't stop me," he said huskily. "It's right. Right for both of us."

Before they lost the enchantment driving them forward, he began peeling away her layers of clothing. Bevin was helpless to put a stop to the fiery ball of passion hurtling them toward that ultimate climax. With the rapid thudding of her heart resounding in her head and blocking out thoughts of further protest, she watched her clothes tossed aside to join his on the edge of the blanket.

Bevin moaned and brought her hand up to cover her nakedness.

Taking her fingers in his, Will whispered, "No, my love. Let me feast on all of you for a moment; you are so beautiful."

He kissed each finger. Then he bent to run his hands up the inner smoothness of her thighs, spreading them as he made his ascent. He opened the lips guarding her woman's passion and began to rub the swelling nub. Bevin gasped and writhed against his hand. Her movements became more violent and she bucked, out of control, as he worked faster and faster. Her honeyed liquid spread over his fingers, hot, wet and ready for him.

She cried out when spasm after spasm overtook her.

Hearing her pleading cries, Will rose up between her thighs and positioned his hardness at her throbbing entrance. Slowly, he lowered himself into her, raining kisses over her glistening face. She gazed up at him and Will tasted that moment of triumph he saw in her eyes, signaling to him through dilated pupils that she was about to become his.

"I'll try not to hurt you," he whispered into her mouth before pressing his lips against hers to muffle her cry as he broke through her virgin's barrier.

Bevin moaned, but then began to arch against his powerful body. She wrapped her arms around him and gasped as he plunged into her, deeper and harder, faster and faster, until their movements were completely out of control. Grinding and pressing, Bevin reached the ultimate pinnacle and cried out. The strength of her contractions caused Will to lose what was left of his restraint, and he spilled his seed into her.

Once they had calmed and their breathing returned to normal, Will rolled off her. He moved to her side and stroked the perspiration from her flesh.

Her sensibilities returning with cold realization of what they had just done, Bevin bolted upright and grabbed for her clothing.

"What have we done?" she said miserably. "Oh, Dear Lord, what have we done?" She began to sob quietly. "What have I done to Benjamin?"

Will reached out for her.

"No! Don't touch me!" What had just become of her neat little life? she thought frantically. "We have sinned!"

He grabbed her hands and held them together. "Stop it, Bevin. We have not sinned. You are a woman and I am a man. We needed each other. It was right for us. We made love."

She stared mutely at him. Her emotions were too raw; her feelings too jumbled. Yes, she had needed him. She had been a willing participant. Oh, but, precious Lord, she was promised to another man.

Forcing herself to calm, she said mechanically, "We must get dressed and get back. I don't want Benjamin to worry about me."

Once dressed, Will helped Bevin fold the blanket. He assisted her into the buggy, stowed the blanket on the floor behind the seat, and took up a position next to her. She edged away from him, causing him to curse himself for letting his feelings get out of hand.

"Bevin, if it will make you feel any better, I'm sorry. I hadn't meant to let things get so out of hand."

"Out of hand?"

"You needn't worry. I won't try to come between you and Benjamin, if that's what you want."

"If that's what I want?" she repeated woodenly.

"No one need ever know," he added to salve the crestfallen expression on her face.

"We'll know, Will. We'll always know."

"I can't change what happened. And even if I could, I'm not sure I would. And yes, we'll always know," Will finally said softly, admitting to himself that he cared. "But no one else has to."

As they headed back to the farm, Bevin's feelings were more confused than ever. She cried inside for her loss of innocence. But not because she regretted her actions; truth be known, she wasn't sure she did. It was because her innocence belonged to the man who was to become her husband; it was supposed to be a special gift given only in love, and she had given it away too freely.

Her heart ached for her brother, and she prayed she could help him resolve his feelings of abandonment. And her heart ached for Johnny; he deserved a loving home.

The buggy jolted, throwing her nearer to Will. Bevin's swirling thoughts shifted back to him and what had just happened between them. She was here to marry Benjamin and be close to her brother. She had had her life all mapped out, neatly designed. And now nothing was settled in her mind.

She had suddenly become irretrievably entangled in an already complex mixture of relationships which existed among her loved ones: Will, Benjamin, Patrick and Johnny. Benjamin and Will already had enough problems to settle without her coming between them. Her brother was hurting, as was Johnny.

Somehow this terrible muddle had to be resolved before it led to tragedy.

Chapter Twenty

By the time Will and Bevin drove up to the farm-house, Benjamin was pacing back and forth the length of the porch, his arms crossed, his fingers tapping impatiently on his upper arms; his expression displaying a deep displeasure.

"Oh, dear, he'll know," Bevin fretted, noticing Benjamin. Her plan of being reunited with her brother and marrying Benjamin was crumbling right before her very eyes. She felt as if her self-assurance was deserting her. Her carefully designed future was doubtful.

"You have nothing to worry about," Will reassured her.

"But he'll know."

"Not if you don't tell him."

She cleared her dry throat. "But when I left Benjamin I was with Patrick, and now I am returning with you; I know how Benjamin seems to feel about you, and he'll know what's happened between us."

"Patrick left you, remember? Furthermore, Benjamin's problem with me has nothing to do with you. So quit worrying. He'll only know if you give it away," he counseled calmly.

Inside Will felt anything but calm and for an instant thought of claiming her by right of possession. But he had nothing to offer a woman like Bevin. Jesus Christ! What had gotten into him? He never should have touched her.

Bevin smiled weakly, but was not convinced that her arriving on the same train as Will, and Benjamin's feelings about his step-sibling had not spurred the simmering emotions that Benjamin had begun to display the day after her arrival; emotions that Bevin did not want to be a part of for causing an eruption between the two men if Benjamin found out she had made love with Will.

"Well, it's about time," Benjamin said, stepping off the porch and walking up to the buggy. His tone made it clear he was not at all pleased. "Patrick returned the horse you took, *Will* . . . hours ago."

"Did he say anything?" Bevin questioned, desperate to cover her own troubled emotions.

"Just that your little scheme to have Will waiting out there to provide reinforcements didn't work." Benjamin's eyes flashed at Will. "Are you conspiring behind my back, stepbrother?"

"Benjamin, please," Bevin implored. "Will had nothing to do with Patrick and me. Will just happened to be where Patrick and I stopped to talk."

"It's true, Ben." To Benjamin's look of disbelief, Will added, "I went down to the old swimming hole to think."

"You went back to where Matthew Lutherby drowned? You haven't gone there since the accident," Benjamin said with suspicion.

"Well, I decided that maybe it was time I did go back there. But I think you are getting off the subject. Bevin, here"—Will squeezed her arm—"has had a jarring experience this morning and needs your support, not empty, unwarranted accusations."

Bevin felt a sudden rush of warmth at Will's touch. Yes, she had had a jarring experience this morning, but it didn't have anything to do with her brother.

Benjamin contemplated the pair. He had not missed Will touching his bride-to-be. Bevin had not drawn away, and Benjamin did not like the look that had transpired between them. He would have to talk with Bevin and make sure she understood that he expected his wife not to allow another man to touch her.

"I am quite sure that Bevin is capable of accepting disappointments and dealing with them without your interference. If Patrick is having a hard time accepting Bevin as his sister, it is because the Kruegers have been his family for most of his life."

Bevin blanched at his unthinking comment. She hurt enough inside from Patrick calling the Kruegers his family without Benjamin rubbing salt on recently reopened wounds. But at least what he'd said drew her attention away from her own moral dilemma.

"Come inside. We have been waiting dinner for you, Bevin," Benjamin said. "Prudence was kind enough to take over your responsibilities in the kitchen. You know how important it is to maintain proper order in life."

"If she doesn't, I'm sure you will leave no stone unturned until she does," Will muttered. Listening to Benjamin, Will knew his stepbrother would not waste time clipping the lovely bluebird's wings once he married her. He forced himself to remember that unless Bevin made the choice, he had no right to interfere between Benjamin and his intended despite what they'd shared down by the creek.

Benjamin harumphed, swung around, and went

into the house, leaving Bevin with another disappointment today. She had so hoped Benjamin would understand and support her in the problems she was having with her brother. He had not. Will had defended her: first with Patrick earlier and now with Benjamin. And it was with Will that she had made love.

A moment later Benjamin opened the door and stuck his head back out. "You two coming in so you don't delay dinner any longer than you already have?"

Bevin held back comment. She looked from one stepbrother to the other; she was struck by the contrast between the two and felt a sudden pull in both directions, doubt assailing her decision to come to Bowling Green at all.

She let out a sigh, then held her skirt hem up, mounted the steps, and went into the house. Now was not the time to attempt to sort out the latest developments in her life.

Will shook his head in disgust at Benjamin's self-serving behavior. Benjamin had been a bachelor too long and needed to learn more about how to handle the fairer sex. Well, it was none of his concern to intrude if not asked, Will decided, and followed Bevin inside.

When Bevin entered the kitchen Prudence clasped her hands and surged toward her. "How did it go with Patrick? I saw him when he returned Benjamin's horse earlier. Oh, Bevin he has got to be one of the most attractive men I have ever met. And he smiled at me," she gushed, unmindful that she and Bevin were not alone in the room.

"Patrick and I have some issues to work out, Prudence," Bevin answered awkwardly.

"It must have been most difficult for you, Evvie. Your cheeks are rather flushed."

Bevin's horrified look caused Prudence to slap her palms to her own cheeks, realizing that Benjamin and Will had been listening to them. "Oh, my. Of course it was difficult."

To put an end to the pall which had fallen over the house since she and Will had returned, Bevin said, "Thank you for fixing dinner, Pru." She lifted a lid and forced a smile. "Everything looks and smells great," Bevin announced, despite the assorted burnt pots cluttering the work counter, and the pungent odor of cremated beans.

Prudence blushed with pleasure. "I've been watching you, and remembered how you went about preparing the food. So the credit really belongs to you, Evvie."

"Nonsense. You deserve all the accolades."

Realizing something was out of place, Bevin looked around. "Where's Johnny?"

"He was here a few minutes ago," Prudence said, frantically searching the kitchen. Bevin had entrusted Johnny to her care; she just could not let Bevin down again as she had during the train trip. "He must have just stepped out the back door. Please, do not wait dinner any longer, I shall go fetch him and be right back."

"Hurry up about it. We have waited too long already," Benjamin grumbled. He pulled out a chair for Bevin, and then took his rightful place at the head of the table. Ignoring Bevin's worried expression, he reached for the platter of meat and speared two slices. Passing the platter to her, he said, "Eat. You need the nourishment. You look a little drawn, and could stand to gain a little weight."

Prudence rushed out the back door. On the back steps, she stopped, horrified. Johnny stood in the middle of the pigpen, bucket in hand, surrounded by a half-dozen oinking piglets and one old sow which looked as if it was about ready to give birth. His Sunday clothing looked as if he had been wallowing in the mud with the hogs.

"Johnny Martin! Come over here this instant!" Prudence snapped, anguish filling her voice.

Johnny jumped, dropping the bucket. He shuffled over to Miss Prudence. "I was just helping out," he defended himself.

Prudence began brushing off his clothes as best she could. "How are we ever going to explain the way you look?"

"Golly, nobody should get mad. I was just helping," he repeated, unable to understand what the big to-do was about.

"Hurry and go wash your face and hands at the pump."

Choking down her dread once Johnny returned and held out his hands for inspection, Prudence ushered the boy into the kitchen, careful to keep him behind her. If she was lucky everyone would be too busy eating, and she could get Johnny seated and tuck a cloth napkin at his throat to hide the dirty blotches patterning his shirt.

Will looked up when they entered. His eyes did a quick assessment of the boy. Prudence held her breath expecting Will to give them away. Instead he winked and engaged Benjamin in conversation, drawing his attention away from Prudence and her filthy charge. She felt a rush of gratitude toward Will Shoemaker and decided that the man was okay after all.

Prudence was about to see her plan succeed when Benjamin unexpectedly glanced up. She froze.

Benjamin had started to take another bite of the worst pan-fried potatoes he had ever tasted when he caught a sniff of the distinct odor of pigpen the same time he noticed Johnny's dirty Sunday shirt.

"What the devil were you doing out there, boy?"

Bevin's head snapped up at the harshness in Benjamin's voice.

"Slopping the hogs the way I seen you do it. I was just trying to help out," Johnny said with pride.

"He was just being a boy, Ben," Will said. "Sit down, Johnny. We wouldn't want you to miss out on Miss Prudence's cooking."

Bevin smiled to herself at Will's humor. Prudence quickly took a seat, confident the tense moment would pass without further incident. Johnny hesitated for a moment, then slid out a chair.

"What do you think you're doing now?" Benjamin demanded.

"He is joining us at the table," Bevin answered for the boy.

"Not looking like that, he isn't."

Bevin bit back a retort. Benjamin was right; Johnny was a dreadful sight. "Johnny, hurry to your room and get cleaned up so you don't miss dinner."

"I think going to his room is an excellent idea." Benjamin turned cold eyes on Johnny. "You can stay there and do without dinner. That should learn you to take better care of your clothes. Clothes cost money."

"Pigs don't get in no trouble for getting muddy," Johnny complained.

"Pigs, boy, are a lot cleaner than you are. They wallow in the mud to protect their skin; people wear clothes—clean clothes—when they come to the table. Now git."

Bevin had forced herself to be tolerant of the rigid way Benjamin did things but his idea of discipline this time was more than she could accept. "No! Johnny is not going to go without eating."

Benjamin's mouth tightened into a straight line. "The boy needs to learn that clothes don't come cheap. On a farm you have to work hard for everything you've got."

"Since you insist the boy be sent to his room, why not send him with a tray?" Will suggested. "The child needs nourishment if he is going to grow enough to be able to do the back-breaking work you're talking about."

Johnny stood trembling, close to tears; his little hands wrapped around the back of the chair so tight that his knuckles were white.

Before Benjamin could mount another argument, Bevin flew out of her seat and started dishing up a generous portion of food for Johnny. "It will be all right, Johnny. Run along now. I will bring your dinner to you in a minute."

"Boy, next time you get the notion to go into the pigpen, collect the corncobs and stack them up by the rest. They make good kindling for the cookstove," Benjamin gritted out.

After Johnny had scrambled from the kitchen, Benjamin said in defense, "I'm doing it for his own good. You shouldn't coddle the boy. He'll never learn what it means to take responsibility if you do."

"I don't think that making sure that the child doesn't go hungry is coddling him. Johnny is already troubled, if you will remember. He has already gone hungry enough in his young life."

Benjamin glanced around the table; no one said a word. Prudence was intently studying her plate; Will had that disgusting I-told-you-so expression on his face. He had lived a moral life, Benjamin chaffed. Although he did not believe that Johnny would suffer much from missing one meal, he did not want Bevin to think him less than honorable.

"Bevin, I realize the boy had a difficult life on the streets, but you must remember that when he goes to live with his permanent family he is going to have to adjust to the way his new parents do things. And that will include punishment from time to time until he learns the ways of folks around here."

"Benjamin, I know you are only doing what you believe right, and were taught as a child. And you mean well. Johnny just needs time to adjust." Even as she spoke in support of Benjamin, as a proper wife she would do, Bevin wondered if her own brother had suffered through similar disciplinary measures. The reflection caused her to gain further insight into the troubles she was now experiencing with Patrick.

Will stood up, snapping Bevin's attention back to the present. "Here, Bevin, give me the plate. I'll take it to the boy."

"Thank you." She handed the plate to Will. "That's very thoughtful of you."

To Will's retreating back, Benjamin said, "I want to talk to you later, William."

"I have a few things to say to you as well, Ben."

Bevin choked and turned her attention to her plate. But she worried that Will would tell Benjamin what they'd done.

Prudence hurriedly finished her meal, set her dishes on the drain board, and announced, "If you two will excuse me, I have a letter to write in my room."

Once left alone with Benjamin, Bevin said, "I realize you felt justified by sending Johnny to his room for ruining his good Sunday clothing. But, Benjamin, that boy doesn't know any better. He has lived on the streets for over three years."

"Then it is time he learn the proper way of doing things."

"Yes, I agree. But don't you think sometimes a gentle hand and a little understanding will work just as well? I think if we explain what needs to be done, Johnny will learn just as quickly and be a happy child, not one who builds up inner resentments," she said, again thinking in terms of her own brother.

"What I think is that my pa was strict and I turned out fine. The boy is going to have to learn to adjust to the family who finally takes him. But if it will make you happy I'll try to go easier on him."

"Thank you, Benjamin." Buoyed by Benjamin's concession, Bevin blurted out, "I know that this probably isn't the best time to broach the subject, but I have been hoping that perhaps we might give Johnny a permanent home here with us."

Chapter Twenty-one

A look of disbelief dropped over Benjamin's face, and the kitchen suddenly became deathly quiet. Bevin waited long minutes, her eyes locked with Benjamin's before he broke the silence.

Benjamin set his fork down, took the napkin from his lap and dabbed at the corners of his mouth. "Let me see, you are asking me to keep the boy, is that rightly so?"

Bevin's spine straightened. What had come over her? She certainly hadn't meant to add to her list of troubles today. She took a deep breath and announced, "I want *us* to keep Johnny, Benjamin."

He thought he knew Bevin from her letters. He thought she wanted the same things in life he wanted: a family and a prosperous farm to leave to his sons. *His* sons. As he studied her, he had to admit he wanted her, and he convinced himself that in time she would make him proud. Taking in a boy who probably could not carry his own weight was not part of the careful plan he had laid out for his life, but Benjamin was in love. He rubbed his lips in consideration.

"The boy has only been here a few days." Her lips tightened, causing Benjamin to amend, "I'm not saying yes, but I'm not saying no. Farm life is hard work. It takes a strong back. You know, when an animal on the farm is born not right, it's either destroyed or doesn't survive."

"You cannot compare Johnny to an animal."

"No, but if he hopes to stay on he's got to pull his weight."

"He will." She jumped up and threw her arms around him. "Oh, thank you, Benjamin. You won't regret your decision."

At the moment that Benjamin decided to give Johnny a chance, Bevin made her own secret decision: She would never tell Benjamin what had happened between Will and herself down at the creek. Will had said no one would know if she didn't tell, and she made up her mind to take the secret to her grave. Despite the fluttering in her heart when she thought about those moments with Will Shoemaker, she simply would avoid him until he settled the inheritance with Benjamin and left.

Benjamin hesitantly allowed himself to slip an arm about her waist before he realized how improper it was. The feel of her soft roundness heated his blood, and he instinctively knew this woman would win more battles with him than a wife should. Slowly, he withdrew and she returned to her seat across from him.

"There is nothing to thank me for yet."

"Yes, there is."

"Oh?"

"For being you," she said. He blushed, which caused Bevin to smile. Benjamin, too, needed a little time to adjust. He already had made a big concession by giving Johnny the opportunity to prove himself. Admittedly, she had begun to have doubts about accepting Benjamin's proposal even before she let

Will take advantage of her during such a vulnerable moment in her life—that's all that had happened, she rationalized, Will had taken advantage of her momentary vulnerability—but now she was certain she had made the right choice after all.

"I invited the parson over for supper Tuesday," Benjamin announced. "The man's a bachelor and looks forward to eating a good meal, so I hope you'll do the cooking."

Bevin smiled when she looked down at Prudence's efforts. "Don't worry, I'll put on my best."

"The parson thinks we should set a wedding date," he mentioned without emotion in between cleaning up the last few bites of beef on his plate. One did not waste food. "What do you think?"

She had made a decision, so why did Benjamin's question make her feel uneasy? "I think as soon as Johnny and I get settled in it would be a good idea."

As soon as she and Johnny got settled in? She was determined to keep that boy. "Yes, well, I think the sooner we are married the better for all concerned," he said, then changed the topic. "Oh, by the way, Sunday afternoons around here we spend either paying social calls on neighbors or kinfolk or receiving them. I talked the Kruegers into staying home and letting us pay a call on them today. It'll give you some more time with that brother of yours."

He stood up without giving Bevin a chance to comment and added, "I'll put a fresh team in harness. Be ready."

Bevin was scurrying around the kitchen, straightening up when the sound of Will's deep voice startled her and caused her to drop a cup. It shattered. Ignoring him, she kneeled down to pick up the pieces.

"I said Johnny is fine."

She looked up at him. From her position on the

floor he seemed even taller and bigger looming over her. Her vision caught at the top of his thighs and she quickly dropped her eyes, her pulse hammering double time.

"Bevin, you don't have to act ashamed at what we shared."

"I am not ashamed. You took advantage of my vulnerability."

"Your *vulnerability?*" Her stinging rebuke got his dander up. "I'll have you know that you are the least *vulnerable* woman I have ever met. Although you seemed to have forgotten that fact since moving in under Benjamin's roof."

"That is not true. I am the same person I have always been," she defended herself, but his comment made her stop and think.

"Are you?"

"Of course. And for your information we did not *share* anything. It was a mistake."

"It was no mistake, lady. We shared something special that you will never share with my rigid stepbrother," he said before he could stop himself.

Of all the smug, arrogant men, the first-place winner was standing over her this moment!

She certainly was not going to give him the appearance that she was genuflecting before that aggravating man! She rose to her full height and faced him squarely. "A lot you know."

Will searched her angry face. A smile spread across his lips. "One thing I do know is Benjamin Straub. I grew up with him, remember? Oh, he'll provide you with your precious security—"

"Yes, and he is good and honest and reliable."

"Sounds like my favorite plow horse. They make great workers, but I wouldn't want to bed one."

"How dare you!"

"Easy, because everything I said is true and by now you must know it too. He is opinionated, set in his ways and totally unyielding."

"That's not true. He just agreed to give Johnny a chance," she cried.

"Now I understand."

"Understand what?"

"You're getting exactly what you wanted: You're near your brother and will have Johnny too. And as a bonus you get a good, solid roof over your head."

"That is not true." But it was. In an effort to deny the truth of his words, she said, "Benjamin makes me feel loved."

"Oh, lady, you don't know what love is if you think the way Benjamin is treating you is love."

"Maybe you don't know how he treats me when we are alone," she retorted. "He knows how to make me feel like a fulfilled woman."

Will stared at her in disbelief. She was implying that she and Benjamin had been intimate. For some reason the very thought of Bevin sharing herself with another man infuriated Will and he said, "He'll never, never make you feel the way you felt with me!"

"You give yourself more credit than deserved."

"Maybe . . . maybe not, but you can quit trying to rationalize what occurred between us because it won't work."

"What won't work?" Benjamin asked, coming in at the end of the conversation.

Bevin shot wide eyes at Benjamin.

My God, Will thought, the scrapper he had met back at the courthouse in Boston was speechless; Benjamin was already changing her. Although she rankled him, it would be a crime to break her spirit. "I was just telling Bevin that trying to piece that broken cup back together won't work."

She blinked. "I'm sorry about the cup, Benjamin."

Benjamin took the broken china pieces from her hands. It was his favorite cup, the one he only used on Sundays. Swallowing back the urge to chastise her for her carelessness, he said, "Don't worry about it, we have others."

Grateful that Benjamin hadn't heard the whole exchange between herself and Will, Bevin quickly said, "Just give me a few minutes to freshen up and I'll be ready."

Her angry exchange with Will made her stop at the doorway to look back at the two men. Despite defending Benjamin, she had to admit that Will was right about Benjamin being rigid. Was Will right about Benjamin not being able to make her feel the way he had? Although she would never admit it to Will, she had been worrying about that very thing since they had left the creek.

Before she had experienced such fiery feelings with Will, Bevin had believed that the physical side of marriage was not important. After all, wasn't she about to get what she had wanted all along—exactly what Will had said: her brother, Johnny and a secure home? Was that enough now? Maybe she should find out if Benjamin could make her feel the way Will had. It sure would show him! She was engaged to wed Benjamin. Surely Benjamin would not consider it improper if they shared themselves before the ceremony. It certainly would prove Will Shoemaker wrong and even wipe him from her mind in the process.

She studied both men a minute longer. Will made her heart flutter. Benjamin elicited no reaction at all. Why was it that Will had to be the one who caused unmentionable sensations to bubble inside her? Surely if she and Benjamin shared that same intimate experience it would blot Will from her consciousness forever, wouldn't it? Well, there was only one way to find out. But could she do it? She suddenly realized that if she were ever going to be truly happy with Benjamin she would have to get Will off her mind.

Benjamin waited patiently until he and Will were alone, then turned on Will. "As long as you are under my roof I won't have you interfering with the way I do things, you hear?"

"Interfering?"

"Yes, with Bevin and Johnny."

"Speaking of Johnny, I understand you have decided to take him in after all."

"So she told you already."

"Yes, and she's quite pleased too."

"Well, did she also tell you it is only for a trial period? And don't try to change the subject, I won't have you interfering in our lives."

"Maybe you need someone interfering, as you put it, if you think you are eventually going to put Johnny out from under this roof while Bevin stands idly by. She cares deeply for that child." And you, you fool, whether you admit it or not, care deeply for Bevin.

"And maybe you should think about finding another roof over your head."

"Have you forgotten that this is half my roof? So for the time being I guess we're all going to be one happy little family, Ben."

Benjamin was starting to lose his temper.

"I'm warning you. Stay away from Bevin. She is my betrothed and soon to become my bride."

"Considering your view of life, I do hope you have

213

noticed that your betrothed is not going to be the good little farmer's wife you expect her to be."

"And just what do you mean by that?" Benjamin snapped.

"She's a pretty independent lady, used to making her own decisions; she's not going to give that up overnight to walk meekly in your shadow."

Benjamin glared at Will. "For someone who never gave women a second thought before, you seem to be awfully concerned about how I plan to treat my wife. Aren't you being rather transparent, William?"

"Transparent?"

Benjamin's hands bailed into fists of frustration. "Let me simply repeat what I just said: Stay away from my future wife or you will regret it this time."

"What will Will regret this time?" Bevin said, returning to the kitchen with Prudence and Johnny in tow.

Benjamin looked from Will to Bevin and back again before he answered, "That Will has decided he might not be with us very long after all."

Benjamin watched Bevin's eyes go wide and Will's mouth tighten. It was just as he had suspected: Will was attempting to take his sweet, innocent Bevin away from him. He wasn't surprised that Will would try something so underhanded, but he was momentarily taken back by Bevin's reaction.

"Is that so, Will?" Bevin questioned after recovering herself. His leaving would solve her problem of having to stay away from the man. She had planned to avoid him, but could not deny the catch in her heart when Benjamin had announced that Will would be walking out of her life.

She is calling him Will, Benjamin suddenly realized, recalling that she had referred to him earlier as Will. "How long have you been calling my dear stepbrother by his given name, Bevin?"

"Not long. I thought there would be no harm in it since we are all together under the same roof. Is there a problem, Benjamin?" Bevin asked, startled by the restrained anger in his voice. Benjamin was an intelligent man; she would have to be careful not to make any more slips.

Before Benjamin could answer, Will interceded. "In answer to your question before Benjamin interrupted, Bevin, I actually haven't decided what my plans are yet."

Prudence could feel the tension fill the room and stepped forward. "Benjamin, Bevin told Johnny and me the good news. I am so happy you have decided to let him stay."

Bevin looked at how animated Prudence was being. The girl normally was oblivious to what went on around her. She, too, must have noted the tension. Benjamin looked annoyed. After all he did say Johnny's staying was just a trial. She did not want the boy to hear Benjamin repeat it. She grasped Johnny's upper arm and leaned toward him.

"What do you say to Benjamin, Johnny?"

Johnny frowned and tugged on his lips until Bevin was forced to pull his fingers away from his mouth. He heaved a sigh, and said rotely, "Thank you, Mr. Straub."

Bevin beamed, making Benjamin grunt, "I suppose if you're staying you might as well call me Benjamin, since everyone seems to be on a first-name basis around here now." He cleared his throat in an effort to swallow what he really would have liked to say: *No, Johnny, you may not call me Benjamin because it is disrespectful of your elders. And, Bevin, please don't call Will by his given name.*

"Well, we best get going," Benjamin advised.

"Where are you off to?" Will questioned.

Benjamin was halfway out the door when he stopped and turned back to Will. "It's Sunday afternoon, if you have forgotten the custom around here. I'm taking the ladies and boy to pay a social call on our neighbors."

"You still hitching up the pair of grays on Sundays for social calls?"

Benjamin ignored Will.

"Well, since I'm half owner of this farm and living here now, I suppose it's my responsibility to tag along."

"It's not necessary."

Will smiled. "Oh, but I insist."

As they climbed into the buggy, Bevin was not sure whether she was relieved that Will wasn't leaving or upset that he was going to continue to stay on and spend Sunday afternoon with them at the Kruegers' farm.

Chapter Twenty-two

The Kruegers' clapboard farmhouse was cluttered with Bertha's handiwork, Bevin noticed as she ushered them inside. They took up positions around the kitchen table sharing coffee and conversation. Tara had taken Johnny outside to show him around.

More than ever after her argument with Will, Bevin was aware of how reticent she was becoming around Benjamin. She had remained quiet while Benjamin explained the new arrangement with Johnny and his intention to set a wedding date when the parson came for supper Tuesday. Bevin noticed Gretchen's shock and Patrick's accusing grunt, as well as Will's bland expression at Benjamin's announcement.

Bevin also watched the interactions between Asa and Bertha. The older woman frequently looked in Asa's direction, silently seeking his approval. Was that the point Will had been trying to make about the relationship she could expect with Benjamin? The realization was sobering.

"Patrick, how about showing me all the changes on the farm since I left?" Will suggested.

Patrick glared at the man who had dared to intercede down by the creek. "Asa should be the one to tell you about the place."

"Go along, boy," Asa said. "Don't ya see we got company?"

Patrick shoved his chair back nearly knocking it over as he rose. "Yes, sir."

Without a backward glance, he pushed through the back door followed by Will. At the edge of the garden he stopped. "This is the family garden," he said curtly. "Over there is the barn, and—"

"And, I know, the family buggy, the fence and the chicken coup. Come off it, Patrick. Aren't you a little too old to be acting like a spoiled little boy?" Will said. "I've had just about enough of it. You hurt your sister earlier today by not giving her a chance, and I think it's about time you stop and think."

"Oh, I've thought, all right. I thought about nothing but Bevin coming to get me for three years before I gave up. What's it to you anyway?"

"Maybe I'm interested because you have a chip on your shoulder very much like the one I had when I left the Straub farm at your age." Patrick started to protest, but Will held up a hand. "Let me finish. Then if you still insist on acting like a dumb steer, I'll leave you be."

Patrick crossed his arms over his chest, his mouth tight. "Okay, I'm listening."

"I guess that's a start. Why don't we go sit over there." Will motioned to a rickety bench leaning against the back of the barn. Each sitting at opposite ends, Will noticed that despite his rigid pose there was the gleam of interest in Patrick's cold, blue eyes.

"I was here when you left; you must not remember me," Patrick snarled out.

"You were that snot-nosed kid who always hid out

in the barn when anyone came around."

"Well, I remember you too. I heard all the stories about you from Bertha and Asa," Patrick sneered.

"Yeah, I'm sure you did. But did you hear about what it was like growing up in somebody else's house, being treated like an outsider, and knowing you always would be?"

"Even though the Kruegers have always treated me good, I've lived it, mister. I know all about not being kin."

"Well, so do I. I know all about the pain that rips at your gut; the way it stays inside and festers and grows until you want to lash out at whoever is in your path."

"I heard how you took old man Straub's money when you left."

"Straub worked me from dawn to dusk like a work horse. He owed it to me. Promised it. I only took what rightly belonged to me. If you don't learn to get ahold of that anger inside you, you could end up heading down the same road I did. It's a dead end, Patrick."

"Humph!"

"The Kruegers aren't like old man Straub; they're good folk. And you have a sister who has searched for you since you were taken from her. From what I've learned about you, you have roots in this community. For someone as respected around these parts as much as I hear tell you are, you're acting like the south end of a northbound jackass."

Patrick colored to his hairline and jumped to his feet. "I don't have to sit here and listen to you."

Will blocked his retreat. "You do unless you want to be laid up for a week."

219

"Why are you doing this?" Patrick demanded. When he did not get an immediate response, a sly grin spread across his lips. "You're sweet on my sister, aren't you?"

Bevin being the only one able to crack through Will's veneer in years, Will showed no emotion. "Looks as if maybe I'm gettin' through to you after all."

Confusion dropped over Patrick's face. He hadn't expected an unperturbed grin from the big man in response. "You aren't getting nothing through to me."

"But I am. You've finally acknowledged that Bevin is your sister."

"I'm not gonna stand around here and listen to any more from you."

Patrick tried to shoulder past Will. Will grabbed the angry young man.

The fight was on.

Will outweighed Patrick, but years behind the plow and pitching hay had built Patrick's strength. As the pair tousled on the ground, it soon became apparent that although Will had been drifting around the country, he had kept in top shape.

Will's fist slammed into Patrick's eye, knocking him back against the barn. Panting, Patrick picked up a bench and smashed it into Will, who was advancing on the pigheaded youth. Will fell back against the ground and Patrick flew at him, shouting curses. Will threw him off and jumped to his feet.

Bending over and resting his hands on his knees, Will gasped out, "You had enough yet?"

"No!" Patrick bellowed and tackled Will.

The two men were a tangled ball of flying arms and legs when Johnny and Tara heard the commotion and came running. At the sight, Tara stopped, slapped her hands over her ears and screamed. Johnny turned and fled back toward the house.

Johnny burst inside the kitchen. Conversation ceased and all eyes turned on the wild-eyed child.

"What are you doing coming inside the house without wiping your feet first, boy?" Benjamin barked out. That kid had a lot to learn.

Ignoring Benjamin's disapproving glower, Johnny limped over to Bevin's side and grabbed her arm. "You gotta come! You gotta! He's gonna get hurt!"

"Who is going to get hurt?" Bevin urged.

"Hurry! Please!" Johnny pulled Bevin out of her seat.

"Now wait just a minute, boy. You have some explaining to do first," Benjamin said flatly.

Asa left his chair. "I think we best go find out what's goin' on outside," he said.

With Johnny tugging on Bevin's arm, trailed by the others, they hurried out toward the back of the barn.

"Oh, Dear Lord, stop!" Bevin screamed at the sight of her brother and Will beating each other. She looked back toward the others for help. Asa had turned around and was stomping back toward the house. Prudence stood behind the others, horrified. Bertha had pulled Tara to her, and Gretchen stood by with her palms covering her mouth. Benjamin was shaking his head.

"Do something, Benjamin. You must stop them!"

Benjamin abhorred violence, but secretly hoped William would get the shit kicked out of him. Then Bevin would turn on William and he'd be forced to leave.

221

"Benjamin," she implored.

"They are letting off steam. If it gets any worse I'll intercede."

"If it gets any worse!" she cried. Out of her mind with worry, Bevin ran to the railing and grabbed the nearest thing available: a frayed rope. Doubling it, she fastened a firm grip around the heavy cord as she rushed to the fracas.

"Please, come back with me, Bevin," Prudence shrieked.

"Bevin, no!" Benjamin hollered.

Ignoring Benjamin's orders for her to stay out of it, and Prudence's frantic entreaties, Bevin started lashing out at the two men. She had only gotten in three good licks when a flailing leg swung out and knocked her off her feet.

"Ohh!" She scrambled to her knees and almost instantly received a wild blow, sending her back into the dust.

"Chrissake!" Benjamin exasperated and ran to retrieve his bride-to-be. "Women should never involve themselves in disputes between men," he grumbled. He was almost to the prone lady when a shot blasted out.

The loud burst from Asa's shotgun immediately put an end to the ruckus. The two men stopped, and everyone's heads snapped in Asa's direction.

"That's enough of that!" Asa yelled. "Shame on you, Patrick, using the Lord's day to brawl."

Patrick immediately hung his head.

Taking Asa's lead, Benjamin moved to stand in between William and Bevin. "And you, William, I am kind enough to allow you to accompany us and this is how you repay my generosity." He settled a frown on Bevin. "As for you, young woman, I certainly would expect better from a lady of your quality."

"Benjamin, unless you'd like to end up missing a couple of teeth, I'd suggest you close your mouth," Will warned. "Try helping Prudence with your intended instead of acting like the injured party around here."

Benjamin nudged Prudence aside. He hesitantly dropped an arm around Bevin's shoulders and helped her back to her feet. "Come along, we must get you presentable again. They didn't hurt you, did they?"

Bevin's left cheek throbbed and she feared it would bruise. She was seething at Benjamin's callousness and too furious to chance retorting to his chastisement and transparent concern.

Bevin halted Benjamin's efforts to remove her from the scene. "Patrick, are you going to be all right?"

"Couple of scrapes, is all," he mumbled through a swelling jaw.

"And Will, are you okay?"

"Fine."

"I think you should come along . . . now!" Benjamin insisted.

Bevin continued to hold to her ground. "Children, run along. Everything's fine now. And thank you for coming to get me, Johnny." She waited until the two children grumbled about being dismissed because the grown-ups wanted to talk and ambled away. Once they were out of sight, Bevin snapped, "I want to know what started this."

The two men involved looked at each other before Will answered, "Just a friendly disagreement, nothing more."

"You call this a friendly disagreement?" Bevin's

eyes went to Patrick.

Patrick shuffled his foot. "Yeah, a real friendly disagreement."

Bertha went to Patrick to check his bruises while Prudence hovered near the young man. Gretchen inched over to stand at Benjamin's other side, a smug look on her face. To her chagrin Benjamin ignored her and gave his attention to that O'Dea woman.

Will was a sorry mess, but he had not taken the worst of it. Patrick looked to have two black eyes and a bloody nose. At least only one of Will's eyes seemed to have suffered from the altercation.

Benjamin started for the house with Bevin, stopped and turned back toward Asa. "I believe you'll agree, Asa, that Patrick has every right to order William from your property."

Asa rubbed his jaw with the barrel of his gun, his vision swinging between the young man and Will. Hell, he had always liked Will. "What say you, Patrick? Is that what you want?"

Benjamin gloated, assured that William had gone too far this time. At this rate it should not take long for the rest of the community to censure his stepbrother and he would be forced to leave, only this time forever. Then Benjamin would send Prudence back home and deal with Johnny. At last, then, he would finally be left alone without anyone's interference and could mold his bride-to-be into a proper farmer's wife.

Patrick looked from Will to Bevin to Benjamin and back again at Will. "There's no need for Will to leave. *Friends* often disagree with each other."

Will shot Benjamin a triumphant look and went over to Patrick. "What do you say that we go in and

224

get cleaned up?"

Astounded and strangely pleased, Bevin watched her brother and Will pass them and head toward the house, Prudence keeping pace close behind. Bevin looked up at Benjamin; his lips were clamped together.

Back in the kitchen the two men stripped off their shirts while Prudence put a pot on the stove to heat some water. Taking a clean dishrag off the cupboard, she poured the water into a bowl, dipped the rag into the basin and lathered it with the bar of lye soap on the drain board.

She passed Will and moved to Patrick's side. "Here, let me help you."

Bevin entered the back door as Prudence was ministering to Patrick. Neither Prudence nor Patrick looked up. They were oblivious to everyone but each other. Prudence had mentioned she thought Patrick handsome, but taking the initiative like she was doing, was something new for the retiring young woman.

Bevin smiled to herself. Prudence was coming out of her shell. The two were talking quietly together, smiling. Perhaps the fight had more far-reaching repercussions than anyone had suspected.

Then Bevin's attention caught on Will, naked to the waist. Visions of his total nakedness down at the creek, hot on hers boldly rose before her eyes. She snapped her vision away from him.

"Bevin, let me see," Will said, stopping her from forcing him from her mind.

"Leave her alone," Benjamin bellowed from behind Bevin. "This is all your doing."

"Stop it right now. I'll have no more of this arguing

225

under my roof," Bertha huffed from the doorway. "Let's see to all those bruises."

An uneasy silence fell over the kitchen once everyone was again seated around the table. Unable to tolerate the hostility between Will and Benjamin, Bertha suggested, "Gretchen, take Benjamin out and show him the new harness Asa bought."

"I don't think—"

"Nonsense, Benjamin," Gretchen said and pulled on his arm.

Benjamin asked, "Bevin, you want to come along? There's a lot you can learn about farm life from Gretchen."

"I'm a little sore. Another time." Bevin watched the pair saunter from the house. A feeling of relief similar to a burden being lifted from her shoulders over came Bevin. She put her hand to her temple.

"Girl, you look a little peaked. Why don't I take you to Asa's and my room so you can rest," Bertha suggested.

"Actually, if I wouldn't offend you, I would prefer to return to the farm."

"Don't bother us none at all. Asa, will you get Benjamin?"

"I'll take her home," Will offered.

"No!" All eyes turned on Bevin. "I mean, of course that would be fine with Prudence and I."

"Bevin, Patrick just asked me to take a walk with him. So if you do not mind, he will bring me back later," Prudence hesitantly said, wringing her hands. She leaned forward, a hopeful expression on her face.

"There a reason you don't want Will to take you?" Asa cocked a questioning brow.

Bevin was trapped. If she refused she would raise

questions in their minds. She didn't want these people voicing any concerns to Benjamin. She schooled her face.

"No, of course not."

along dusty & At last, she would let be alone with
While the buggie for de
be the tract

Chapter Twenty-three

Bevin struggled with herself as the buggy bumped and jarred over the dusty road on their way back to Benjamin's farm. Her cheek throbbed despite the cool cloths Bertha had instructed her to hold against it, and it was beginning to swell.

She was furious with Will for blacking both her brother's eyes and ruining their first Sunday social call. The entire town was sure to hear all about it, and she would have to live down all the gossip if she ever were going to become an accepted member of the community.

She pondered over the incredible order of events today. She had spoken to her brother for the first time in fifteen years; he had denied their kinship. She had become a woman in every sense of the word. Benjamin had agreed to give Johnny a chance to remain on the farm. Will Shoemaker and her brother had beaten each other into bloody pulps, and at the end of the fight her brother had, at last, acknowledged her as his sister. And once again she found herself alone with Will Shoemaker. Strangely enough, she felt more alive and vital than she had in years.

Bevin fixed her gaze away from Will. It was late afternoon. Benjamin, Prudence and Johnny would be along shortly. At least she would not be alone with Will too long.

The very thought of finding herself alone with Will again made her uneasy. It should not matter. Her plan to avoid him seemed so futile. How could she avoid him? They lived under the same roof. The only way for all of them to exist peacefully together would be for them to come to some kind of mutual agreement.

Hesitantly she reached out and squeezed his arm. The instant she touched him, her intention to hide behind the prim and proper exterior she had built around herself crumbled. Yet when she said, "Will?" his name came out stiffly.

Will pulled up on the reins and directed the buggy to the side of the road. He was not going to sit idly by and suffer another rude chastisement. "Yes?" came the arrogant reply.

The tone in his voice was enough to send her back to being the proper lady who had been the injured party. Only she no longer felt like the spinsterly lady who had left Boston only a few short weeks ago.

"I have been thinking about what happened between us," she said in a raspy voice.

He cleared his throat. "You've been on my mind a lot today too."

Bevin clasped her hands in her lap and dug her nails into her palms.

Will's first inclination after he discovered she was not going to attack him again for his impetuous act down by the creek had been to pull her into his arms. But her stiff posture warned him that what she was about to say was not the confession of love he realized he was hoping to hear.

Bevin forced down the lump of pain threatening to

block what she had to say. "I owe you an apology."

"An apology?"

"Yes, I want to apologize for saying that you took advantage of me earlier . . . down by the creek. I—"

"No need to apologize."

"Will, we had no right," she blurted out without prolonging the pretext.

"I know," he admitted, his heart sinking.

"I am promised to another man. I am going to marry Benjamin, and I shall be a good wife to him. I owe it to him."

The lady's mind was made up; Will could see it in the set of her mouth. His gaze lingered on her face. Perhaps he was hoping to find a glimmer of doubt. Her eyes were hooded, refusing to divulge the faintest hint of emotion. The only indication that something more, something hidden and secret, was going on in that beautiful head was her fingers, closed tightly into her palms, forming fists.

Will took her hands in his. He opened the fists. Quarter-moon indentations in red marked her palms. He ran his thumbs over the spots where she had practically scored the soft skin.

For the first time since he had left the farm a feeling of lonesomeness came over him. And he was jealous of Benjamin and all he had—namely Bevin. Swallowing the burgeoning desire to pull her to him, Will released her hands.

She was within inches of gaining her goal of marrying for security and having her brother and Johnny at her side. Will realized that he could not ask her to give up any portion of that.

Will took a deep breath and steeled himself for what he knew had to be done. "You'll make Benjamin a good wife. There never was any question of it. You're a perfectly matched pair."

Bevin sucked in a startled breath. She could not have stung any more than had he struck her. How foolish of her to have thought, even for an instant, that that conscience-lacking man sitting next to her could possibly have been anything but arrogant and insufferable.

"I am glad you have finally been able to recognize the errors of your actions. I hope I can feel confident that you will not forget yourself again."

His face tightened. "You needn't concern yourself."

"Good. Now I demand an explanation for your unacceptable actions toward my brother. I will not have you forcing my brother into a position of having to defend himself in a match of fisticuffs with you again."

Will almost could have laughed out loud at Bevin's return to the overstarched spinster soon-to-be married to his rigid stepbrother, but if truth be known he felt more like smashing his fist through the side of the buggy than laughing.

"Your brother and I were just straightening out a disagreement. You needn't worry about us punching it out again."

"I certainly hope not."

"Look, there is no reason for us to return to being adversaries."

A flicker of remorse grasped her. "No, of course not. I have to admit that you have been good to Johnny."

And I'm going to help you with your problems with your brother too.

"I do hope that you will reconsider remaining on the farm," she said, thinking that it was more important than ever that she and Benjamin share themselves to block out all visions of Will and her together.

"I think it might be best for all concerned if you and Benjamin resolved the issue of your inheritance and reached some type of satisfactory settlement so we all can live our lives."

With this last volley she had just put a symbolic knife through his gut!

He let out a string of vile curses, grabbed the buggy whip and snapped it over the horses' backs. The loud crack sent the animals lunging forward. "Don't worry, lady, I've no intention of upsetting the nice neat little package you have boxed your life in."

Patrick rushed back toward the kitchen, buttoning the last button on the fresh shirt he had put on, and stuffing the tails into his trousers. He knew that once Benjamin returned to the house with Gretchen and learned that Bevin had gone back to the farm alone with Will, Prudence would be whisked away. And he wanted to spend a little time alone with the shy beauty. He was used to the robust, neighboring farmers' daughters, and the sight of such a diminutive, delicate flower intrigued him.

Prudence looked up from her conversation with Asa and Bertha when Patrick entered the room.

"Are you ready to take that stroll?" he asked when he noticed her face light up.

"If you two do not mind," she questioned the Kruegers.

"Land sakes, why should we mind?" Bertha let out a hearty burst of laughter.

"Mind you, don't be wanderin' off too far afield," Asa instructed.

Bertha and Asa watched Patrick offer his arm, and the pair stroll from the house.

Bertha sighed. "Good Lord, it's been one of the most unusual Sabbaths we've had around these parts in years."

Asa shook his head in understanding. "Did you get a good look-see at our Gretchen on Benjamin's arm? Why I hain't never seen the girl glow for any young buck like that before in all my days. Pity the boy done gone and got himself hooked up with that city gal, not that I got anything against the likes of Bevin O'Dea. 'Cause I don't. Just that Benjamin's lettin' himself in for a peck of trouble, tryin' to teach her how things is done on a farm."

"Asa, if you and Benjamin hadn't been so unmindful all these years and so busy out in the fields, you'd both of noticed that Gretchen's only had eyes for Benjamin since she took to womanhood a few years back."

"That a fact." Asa rubbed his chin. "The girl ever give thought to mind of followin' in her ma's footsteps to get the man she wants?"

"Asa! I never thought you suspected," Bertha said, mortified.

"Think Adam ever suspected what Eve was up to either?" At her shocked expression, he laughed and added, "It wasn't the apple on the tree, you know, it was the pear on the ground that done 'em in."

Gretchen had led Benjamin into the very back of the tack room at the rear of the barn. While he admired the new harness and delighted in the feel, smell and craftsmanship of the smooth leather his back was turned toward her.

Gretchen pouted. The last four years, since her fourteenth birthday, she had been going over to the Straub farm, trying to get Benjamin to notice her. She had hung around after Straub's wife died, baking pies and helping out.

When the old lady passed away, she practically took over the duties of wife, cooking and cleaning, and even putting up the family garden. Still the man had not stopped to consider her more than the Krueger girl from the neighboring farm. Well, she was no longer a mere girl, and it was almost too late to prove it to Benjamin. Once he married he would be lost to her forever.

Her ma had given her an idea back in town a few days ago, and Gretchen was determined to put her ma's method of catching her pa to the test. She figured she had nothing to lose. Quickly, her fingers worked at the buttons at her bosom.

She left the top ones secure, so it would appeared that the buttons had worked themselves free. She untied the ribbons on her chemise, and rearranged her garments until she was sure Benjamin would get a tempting glimpse of her ample female offering. Just to make sure he did, she draped herself over the saddle on the sawhorse and waited.

Gretchen set her features in a mock frown and coughed.

Benjamin swung around and his eyes fastened on her exposed flesh.

She cocked a brow. "What do you think of them? You think you'd like to possess them?"

Benjamin appeared to be mesmerized, which caused Gretchen's nipples to darken and the centers to peak.

His Adam's apple bobbed. "Possess them?"

"Of course," she responded slyly. "There is nothing like the soft feel of them between your fingers, grasping them until they tighten, and you know you are in complete control."

He was a God-fearing man who believed in tradition and proper behavior, but this was the first time he had actually seen a woman's full breasts and he could feel his crotch beginning to swell. Before the growing discomfort in his trousers got the better of him, Benjamin rasped out, "What has gotten into you, Gretchen? Cover yourself!"

Feigning innocence, Gretchen painted a coy pout to her lips. Instead of immediately snapping her dress front closed, she moved over to stand in front of Benjamin. "What's wrong?"

"T-The way you talk. I'm shocked!"

Wide-eyed, she dropped her hands on her hips, opening her dress further and asked, "What's wrong with talking about the reins that go with Pa's new harness?"

His eyes glued on her chest, he said, "You were talking about your pa's harness?"

"Of course, what did you think we were discussing?" It was then she let her vision follow the course of his. "Oh, my goodness!"

As if in a panic, she swung her back on him, her fingers shaking while she tried—unsuccessfully—to retie the ribbons. "Oh, no, I can't get the ribbons tied," she sobbed, turned back to Benjamin, and raised pleading eyes to his bewildered face.

"Well, you can't remain like that."

"I can't very well go back in the house and ask Ma to help me," she wailed. "Why, she and Pa will think the worst."

And Bevin, what would his precious, innocent

235

Bevin think? Benjamin worried. "All right. Stand very still and I'll see what I can do."

While Benjamin's fingers worked the ribbons, Gretchen took in a deep breath and stuck out her chest. Her breasts brushed against the roughness of his hands, and the sudden intake of his breath gave her heart hope.

"The buttons. Help me with the buttons too."

Once Benjamin had repaired Gretchen's dress, he stepped back and stood studying her for a moment. He wondered how she had grown into a woman without his notice. She had always been the Kruegers' little girl. Before him did not stand a little girl any longer. Worry creased his forehead.

"I-I hope you don't think I was taking advantage of the accident to your dress. By the way, how could your dress come open like that?"

Gretchen schooled her features into innocent indignation. "How do I know how something like . . . like *that* could happen?"

"Sorry. I didn't mean to imply that you—"

"I sure hope not!"

Unformed words hung between them. Gretchen prayed that he was thinking about her as an adult woman now. She attempted to keep the uncurtained longing out of her eyes, but she knew it was there.

He broke the awkward silence. "Gretchen?"

"What, Benjamin?" she whispered.

"Can I ask a favor?"

She leaned forward, her heart slamming against her bosom. "Of course, Benjamin. You know you can always ask me anything. Anything at all."

"The parson's coming out to the farm Tuesday for supper, and I wonder if you would mind coming in the morning—if your folks'll let you get away—and

236

giving Bevin a hand. Prudence isn't much good, and I want Bevin to make a good impression on the man."

Gretchen's expression underwent a complete transformation from hopeful to disbelief to beet red with anger. It had worked for her ma. Either she was a complete goose or Benjamin, who had never had a girlfriend before becoming engaged to Bevin O'Dea, had a thicker skull than she thought possible.

"You stand there and stare at my—my bare bosom and don't tell me my dress has come open, and then have the nerve to ask me to help your intended make a good impression on the parson. I can't believe you. You must be blind," she hissed before she struggled to compose herself. "Oh! I'm sorry, Benjamin. Of course, I'll be over Tuesday," she cried, real tears streaming down her flushed cheeks. Stumbling over her own feet, Gretchen ran from the barn.

"Gretchen! Wait!" Benjamin yelled.

Left alone in the tack room, Benjamin scratched his head. Gretchen was acting awfully peculiar. And then it dawned on him; it must be her time of the month. He remembered his pa telling him how women got weird around the time of their miseries. There could be no other explanation for such behavior.

He had embarrassed Gretchen with his God-forbidden leering and he was remorseful; he never meant to cause his friends' daughter a moment's discomfort. Regardless of his self-chastisement, the glimpse of breast continued to haunt his mind, and he found himself wondering if his bride-to-be's endowments would be as inviting on their wedding night.

237

Chapter Twenty-four

Patrick directed Prudence out the yard and along the drive. The day was just beginning to cool as the sun rode lower in the sky and their shadows stretched out long before them. He was mindful to reduce the length of his stride to match her dainty steps. She looked like she would break if he attempted to steal a kiss like he often managed with the girls in town. Of course, he would never try anything with Prudence Truesdale; she was a real lady.

He stole a sideways glance at her. She wore lace and ruffles down the prettiest pink dress he had ever seen. Golden curls peeked out the edges of a matching bonnet. And he marveled again how tiny, yet perfectly curved she was.

"Tara told me that you work with my . . . ah—"

"With your sister." Prudence's pulse raced when she looked up into the male image of her idol. He was a very masculine version of Bevin O'Dea. His hair had some gold mixed in with the red, and his eyes were a shade or two lighter than Bevin's. He was big and muscled and bronzed from years under the sun. There was no mistaking they were siblings. Prudence had to keep herself from swooning, she was so overjoyed that he had asked her to stroll with him.

Prudence immediately fell in love.

"Yes, my sister," he repeated awkwardly, the pain evident in his voice.

"Bevin told me that you two are having a difficult time. I know it is not any of my business, but she really tried ever so hard to locate you, truly she did."

"Will Shoemaker said the same thing."

"Didn't Benjamin share any of her letters with you?" Prudence asked, surprised that Patrick would mention Will's name rather than Benjamin's.

"Benjamin mentioned it to Ma and Pa—the Kruegers—when he first received her letter, but we never discussed it at length." He did not tell Prudence that he had been livid at the time and refused to talk to Benjamin about Bevin, storming from the house.

"Why?" In her innocence Prudence never considered that it was a difficult subject for Patrick.

Color heightened on Patrick's cheeks over the probing question. "You know, I'd really rather talk about you."

Prudence tittered and blushed, and let all thoughts about Bevin drop from her mind. "There truly is not much to tell about me."

Relaxing once the conversation had shifted, Patrick patted the hand she had holding his arm. "Tara said you work harder than any of the other girls at the Society. She said you were dedicated and used to bring the children extra gifts. She really thinks you're tops."

Prudence tittered again and made a study of the ground before shyly raising her gaze. With Patrick she did not feel like another empty-headed debutante; she felt important. Both the O'Deas made her feel like her contribution mattered, and Patrick made her feel truly special as well. "Well, perhaps I am second, after Bevin."

"Golly, Miss Prudence, I don't think you're second after anyone."

The grays were lathered by the time Will pulled up to the house. Will expected Bevin to run from him the moment the buggy stopped. To his surprise she calmly turned toward him.

"I suppose you have just made some kind of point."

God, that woman could cut all the way through his gut! "Some king of point?" he repeated, astounded by the fact that any other female, no doubt, would have screamed all the way back, he had driven the horses so recklessly fast.

"I believe that is what I said. If you have nothing else to add I would appreciate your help from the carriage," she said to rile him. She silently reproached herself for her rashness as she watched his slim portion of reserve rapidly dissipate before her eyes.

He stomped around to the other side of the buggy, the words "if you have nothing else to add" assailing him like daggers. God help him, he did have something else to add. He reached up and closed his hands around her waist. Instead of setting her immediately down, he swung her around and let her slide slowly down along his body until her toes just barely touched the ground.

In no more than a whisper, he said, "I do have something else to add after all."

Bevin's head was spinning. She was a captive in the middle of an ironic folly. She was the central focus between two stepbrothers and she could not maintain control over her own reeling emotions as of late. Both men wanted her—for different reasons. She had to admit that she shared the guilt. She had not discouraged Will earlier, and she could not now.

Sensing what he intended, she softly took the bait, "What is it you have to add?"

"Just this," he groaned in a low, seductive murmur and kissed her.

The instant their lips met, Bevin surrendered despite all the fancy explanations and in-depth discussions she'd had with Will and herself.

Will savored the tender flesh, his tongue outlining her lips and coaxing entry to parry with a tongue that could be so sharp and cutting, and then so sweet, so inviting, so incredibly overpowering. All the while their joined mouths communicated in lengthy unspoken volumes, Will's hands glided up and down the small of Bevin's back.

Fires which devoured Bevin's thoughts to resist ignited everywhere Will's fingers touched, and she pressed herself against his hard strength.

Feebly, she pulled away. "Will, I don't think—"

"Don't think, Bevin, just let yourself feel," he breathed against her mouth. He was hoarse and breathing hard when he took her face between his hands and delved into those blue eyes. Longing reflected from the depths and a wild blaze of red tendrils cascaded through his fingers as he wound them in her hair.

Bevin rubbed her cheek against his palm. She flinched.

"The swelling is going down," he soothed, stroking the back of his hand along her left cheek. "Here is something to help it."

Tenderly, he kissed the bruise.

"It's said it is the best medicine for what ails the world," he added.

"Must have come from a vast field of experts," she concurred.

"Then let's see what else we can cure."

Bevin moaned and delighted in the pleasure of his touch, throwing back her head when his lips began to dot her neck with seducing kisses.

With bold precision, he swung her up into his arms and headed toward his room.

Nuzzling her neck, he lowered her to his bed. "I want . . . no . . . I need to make love to you."

Adept fingers worked the buttons down her dress while mesmerized, Bevin stared up into the face of the man she should not be with, the man she could not deny.

All the while he divested them of their clothing, Bevin's senses tensed. Nerve endings Bevin had not known existed came to life and cried out to be satiated.

"Oh, God, Bevin," Will mumbled, drinking in her beauty. He settled along her burning length and proceeded to pay homage to her flaming body.

Bevin whimpered as he touched her breasts. The twin peaks pointed toward him as if indicating a need of their own to be possessed and conquered. Will did not let the beckoning challenge go unheeded. His fingers splayed over and around the delicate flesh, taunting the darkening center circles. His lips and tongue nipped and suckled until Bevin squirmed and pressed her thighs together.

She wrapped her arms around his neck and dug her nails into his back, but the sweet torment continued. One hand left her beasts and glided through her heavily forested triangle to nudge her legs apart and slip past her dampened woman's lips.

He slid two fingers in and out of her, duplicating the mating rhythm. Building the intensity, he added pressure until she bucked wildly against his hand. She was panting with desire, past caring about anything but what he was doing to her, and still he wanted more from her. Unrelenting in his onslaught, he kept up the friction until he felt her explode against him.

"Will, please," she begged in a hot, molten voice.

Taking himself in hand, he positioned himself in between her thighs. Her juices glistened down her quivering flesh. He had all he could do to hold himself back from plunging into her and ending his own agony.

"You're ready for me," he rasped.

"Yes," she cried and reached out to pull him to her.

"No. Not yet. I want to make this special."

"For both of us," she whispered from deep in her throat.

He stared down into eyes heavy-lidded and glazing. She would not deny him, but he wanted more from her. He needed more than the knowledge that he could conquer her body. He needed more than a physical conquest of body over mind. He had to have her know him, so he would be indelibly etched in her heart and mind forever.

"Then take me in your hand. I want you to know what will be inside you . . . ah, good . . . that's right, close your fingers around me."

Bevin followed his instructions blindly for she had closed her eyes. The dreamy smile on her lips might have satisfied him with another woman, but not with this one.

"Open your eyes, Bevin. I want you to see what

you do to me."

Bevin's thick lashes fluttered and she focused on his arousal. He was magnificent. A deep urge claimed her sense of being. He throbbed in her hand, and she placed the other one around him to double the intense pleasure she derived from the velvety strength, the masculine power of him.

"What do you see?"

"You. Your beauty," came the moan in response.

"What do you feel?" he demanded between gasps.

"Life," she whispered. "Your life."

Her answer took him momentarily aback, then she squeezed him and another spasm threatened to engulf him before he was ready.

His breath coming faster now, he managed, "What do you want?"

"I want to join our lives."

He could not prolong their torturous suffering any longer. He mumbled something unintelligible as his lips captured hers at the same moment he drove deep inside her.

He filled her, she thought for a lucid moment. Fulfilled would be a better word, she decided before the surging intensity began building within her and she gave herself up to her body's all-consuming passions.

Bevin was still cocooned in that euphoric afterglow, lying quietly in Will's arms, her mind drifting in and out of reality when her thoughts began to clear. The world which had been tuned out and dissolved into mind-shattering sensations began to intrude upon her.

She became aware of the strangeness of the room; the plain-painted walls, the rough texture of the quilt and fading light, elongating unfamiliar shadows. The scent of their lovemaking surrounded her. Then the sounds of the retreating day became real, the clock ticking on the dresser, the birds outside, and the distant beating of hooves against the graveled drive.

The realization suddenly hit her, cold and hard.

Bevin jolted upright and stared at Will.

"Oh, my God, no. I have sinned again and now Benjamin is going to know," she cried and frantically began to collect her scattered clothes.

Will cursed. There was no mistaking the long-ago, familiar sounds of someone approaching the house. This was not how he wanted them to part: in a frenzied rush to hide the evidence of the time they had just spent together.

"Calm down, we have at least ten minutes before they get here."

"How do you know?" she cried, fumbling with her chemise.

Will danced into his trousers. "Because I used to time it as a kid. Had it down to a science."

"Why, so you could hide the evidence of whatever you had been doing?" she accused and fought with the buttons on her dress.

"Yes, if you must know. And I was pretty successful at it too."

Naked down to the waist, Will shoved her hands aside and continued closing her dress.

"You mean to tell me, you weren't *always* successful?" came the beleaguered cry.

"Almost always."

"Didn't anyone ever tell you that *almost always* does not count! Why, I probably had a better record when I was a child," she panted. Her survival instincts, honed sharp from the years she had lived on the streets as a child kept her from giving in to the urge to sit down and cry.

245

"Guess you must've."

Will had to stop and watch her bend over the small oval mirror on his dresser and fight to reshape her tangled tresses into some semblance of order.

Bevin caught sight of Will's reflection. My God, he was just standing there watching her!

"What are you doing?"

A lopsided grin spread over his mouth. "Watching you. You are most fetching."

"Please. Stop the flattery and help me. Benjamin can't find out. I can't lose him now!"

The second time today she had knifed him; once in the gut, and now through the heart. And here he was, despite everything, he was helping her frantic efforts to hide their lovemaking from her fiancé. If anything, he should be sabotaging her. But, no, not William Parrish Shoemaker, total sap; complete fool with sudden conscience par excellence. Oh, no. He was assisting her so she could belong to another man!

The clopping of hooves came to a halt out front and was replaced by the timbre of voices. Bevin sped up her efforts. Laughing, conversational voices drummed in her ears. Johnny's happy laugh, Prudence's titter, Patrick's slow drawl, and finally Benjamin's gruff voice attempting to disengage himself politely from the others so he could check on his bride-to-be.

His bride-to-be! That was her. And she stood in another man's bedroom. What had she done? And worse, why had she allowed things to get out of control . . . again? What was happening to her?

Oh, precious Lord! Bevin's mind spun. There was no more time. She could hear Benjamin's heavy footfalls coming up the steps.

It was now or never.

246

"Wait!" Will said. "Your top button is undone."

He tried to fasten it for her, but she batted his hand away.

"No! You have already done more than your share!"

She fled from the room and down the stairs, leaving Will to stare after her.

Hurrying down the hall, Bevin's fingers worked the last button into place. She had just passed the parlor and was nearing the kitchen when she ran headlong into Benjamin.

They both jumped back.

Their eyes locked on each other. Bevin held her breath as she watched Benjamin do an in-depth assessment of her. They had been caught: she and Will. She was sure of it by the intensity in Benjamin's eyes.

For the first time his eyes strayed down over her bosom. He had never let his gaze hesitate there before, at least when he knew she was aware of his actions. She swallowed hard and lowered her gaze, waiting for the proverbial other shoe to drop when she suddenly realized she wasn't wearing any.

Chapter Twenty-five

Benjamin forced his gaze away from Bevin's bosom. The glimpse he had gotten of Gretchen's well-endowed breasts earlier had made him painfully aware of what he had been righteously denying himself all these years. Forbidden desires entered his heart and a wave of guilt washed over him.

If he had not been fortunate to have had a thoughtful pa to instruct him in the dangers of self-induced release, he might have gone blind years ago. He had always been mindful not to touch himself too long when relieving himself. One's sight was too precious to chance the prospect of never seeing a field of corn ripen again. A thought hit him: there was only one blind man in town and he had been raised by a widowed mother.

He cleared his throat and looked around. The house was growing dim. That was when he remembered that as they had pulled into the drive the only lamp burning in the house was upstairs in William's room.

"Bevin, why is the house almost dark? And your hair, it is mussed up."

Subconscious reaction sent Bevin's hand to her hair. Survival instincts provided a level head. A quick mind supplied the answer. "I've been resting. I fear I must have fallen asleep. I did not feel well after sustaining a blow this afternoon during the fight between Will and Patrick."

Concern replaced question in Benjamin's eyes. "Of course, how thoughtless of me. Are you feeling better now? You do look a bit flushed."

Bevin placed a hand to her cheek. "Actually, I do feel a bit warm. I hope I'm not coming down with anything."

"Let me help you back to your room and then I'll get the house lit."

Benjamin took Bevin's arm and ushered her past Prudence and Johnny back toward the stairs. Bevin breathed a silent sigh of relief as she padded along beside Benjamin. He had not noticed that she was nearly two inches shorter than she normally was fully clothed. They had nearly reached the bottom of the stairs when Prudence's nervous titter stopped them.

"Why, Evvie, where are your shoes and stockings?" Prudence blundered.

Bevin had almost succeeded in getting away unquestioned when Prudence had to go and prove she had a terminal case of hoof 'n mouth disease! At that moment Bevin would have liked nothing better than to have called in a veterinarian and have Prudence put out of Bevin's misery.

Recanting her unkind thoughts about Prudence, Bevin said a silent prayer of thanks that Benjamin was looking down at her toes when Will descended the stairs, approaching them.

Bunched in his hands was one of her stockings!

Bevin swayed precariously, causing Benjamin and Prudence's attention to remain fixed on her. They rushed forward to stay her fall which allowed her the opportunity to wave Will off.

Will stuffed her stocking in his pocket and surged toward the star performer. Only Will had a different purpose in mind: at that moment he would have preferred to spirit her back to his room!

She had them all right where she wanted them. Spending time on the streets sure had not scarred Miss Bevin O'Dea; she was a lot stronger than she realized, and considerably more resourceful than anyone knew. Johnny looked frightened and confused. Prudence was her usual helpless self. Even rigid, single-minded Benjamin was fawning at Bevin's skirts. It was amazing, truly amazing!

"Evvie, are you ill?" Prudence cried, wringing her hands.

"I don't know. I felt a little dizzy for a moment."

"Will, go upstairs ahead of me and get the door," Benjamin directed. He carefully lifted her into his arms and carried her to the room she shared with Prudence.

Once she was settled in bed and everyone left her alone to rest, Bevin had the opportunity to reflect. Both men had held her in their arms today. Will's touch had fired her senses; Benjamin's touch elicited a sense of security, but had not made her burn. Now, more than ever, it was important that she discover if Benjamin could blot Will from her mind.

Troubling over the dramatic twists her life seemed to be taking, Bevin remained in bed all day Monday, not that she had had much time alone to consider her life. Prudence fluttered in and out, plumping her pillows, bringing soup, and insisting on reading to her. Johnny had cheerily told her all about the time he'd spent with Tara yesterday after she'd assured him she was feeling much better. Even Benjamin hovered over her between chores, raising her level of guilt.

Tuesday morning Bevin was the first up. This morning she would begin taking every opportunity to get close to Benjamin. It was a frosty morning and the house was chilled, signaling that soon fall would bow to winter. She laid a bed of dried corncobs from the wood box in the stove and lit it. Once the fire was blazing, she added four logs. Benjamin had set water out the night before for coffee, so she set the pot on the stove and busied herself readying a hearty breakfast.

"Morning," Benjamin said from the doorway.

Bevin had been leaning over picking potatoes out of the bin in the corner, and straightened up at the sound of his voice. "Good morning. I have almost got breakfast ready. From now on I'll get a good meal in you before you start to work every morning," she announced, beaming at his approving smile.

"You feeling better?"

"Perfect. Sit down and have a cup of coffee while I put the potatoes on."

Benjamin preferred to do the milking and set the cows out to pasture before breakfast, but he could not refuse her, she was so cheery. He sat down and took the cup from her hand. Their fingers touched, sending Benjamin's thoughts to the swell of her bosom and the rude sexual awakening he'd had Sunday.

He had thought of little else than women since he had glimpsed Gretchen's breasts. It was a wonder how he had so successfully substituted hard work all these years. With his bride-to-be in the next bedroom every night he could no longer submerge the thoughts.

He had even prayed to God that He would still such emotions. God had always shown him the way, and he relied on God's will. So it was that when he continued to conjure up the luscious visions, he decided that God must have sent him a sign that his feelings were no longer completely sinful; it was nearing time for him and his bride-to-be to serve the Lord by bringing a new life into the world. And he wanted sons.

Could it be coincidence or another sign that brought their hands together this morning? The thought sent Benjamin's mind thumping. He set the cup down so fast that he spilled the coffee.

"Here. I'll take care of it," Bevin said. She grabbed a dishrag and sopped up the spill. Then, to Benjamin's continuing confusion, she carefully ministered to his hands. Instead of withdrawing, he surprised her by taking her hand in his.

"Benjamin?" Bevin said his name softly. "I'm glad we're having this time alone together."

Benjamin's hands trembled as he rubbed his thumbs over her smooth skin. Bevin watched him, hoping she would feel something. Long seconds passed. The only thing she felt was shame for what she was doing. Seducing him was the only word for it. Seducing, like the women who took money for their favors.

Although her gaze never wavered, questions and guilt became her companions until Johnny joined them and Benjamin grudgingly took the boy along with him to tend the farm.

Will had appeared right after they left. Her nerves had assailed her that he would tweak his finger and she would go to him. He had remained distant and announced that he was going into town to give her a few days to think.

Bevin was sitting with her head on her arms at the table, trying to sort through her life for the fiftieth time when Gretchen hollered from the back door.

Bounding into the kitchen, she said, "One never would have reasoned that you'd be up yet, a fine, frail, city-woman such as yourself."

Bevin's head bobbed up. Her temples threatened to split. Gretchen's sarcasm was just what she needed!

"Gretchen, I am so delighted to see you too."

Gretchen had not expected the retort. She came up short. "Yes . . . ah . . . I promised Benjamin I would help out today."

"No doubt you have been quite used to helping out around here," Bevin said when Gretchen went directly to the curtained storage and pulled out a broom.

"I would do anything for Benjamin." Gretchen immediately slapped a hand over her mouth.

"I see."

The girl was in love with Benjamin! She was pretty enough in a sturdy way. Why hadn't Benjamin chosen her?

In stiff silence the two women went to work.

Together they rolled up the rugs, took them out into the yard and draped them over the fence. Gretchen beat each one as if they belonged to her. Bevin stood and watched for a moment, then returned to the house and swept the floors. By the time Gretchen called she was ready to bring in the first rug, Bevin had the floors mopped.

"Stop! No!" Bevin cried too late. Prudence had sleepily padded over her wet floor.

"What is all the shouting about?" Prudence rubbed her eyes. "How is one to get enough sleep around

253

here?"

Bevin had always been too tolerant of the girl, letting her start work after the other volunteers and not bringing her to task. She had no one to blame but herself.

Bevin dropped her sore, rough hands on her hips. "Today I guess you are not going *to get enough sleep*. I need your help around here. And from now on, as long as you remain here, you are going to start rising at a decent hour"—Bevin glanced at the clock on the mantle—"not at nine-thirty! I have been up since four."

Prudence's shoulders slumped. "All you have ever had to do was ask." She turned and fled toward their room.

"Prudence! Wait!" Prudence stopped and looked back. Her nose was red and her eyes runny. "I am sorry, Pru. I just want to make a good impression on the parson tonight and there is still so much to do." Bevin could have bitten her tongue.

To her surprise, Prudence said, "Evvie, I am the one who is sorry. I never realized that I was not being helpful. From now on, I am going to . . . to"—she splayed her fingers out—"work my fingers to the knuckles."

Prudence left Bevin with her mouth open and went, humming, to get dressed. She was never going to be a disappointment to Patrick. He had come calling last night and they had sat on the porch swing. He thought she was special and could do anything his sister could. And Prudence was going to start proving him right!

After an exchange of pleasantries with Gretchen, Prudence set to work. She was oblivious to Gretchen's slight. Bevin smiled wanly and deigned to ignore the girl's sharp tongue since she took pride in her work despite her feelings.

"I'll start with the sheets," Prudence announced.

Bevin's heart nearly stopped. "No!"

"Why not?" Prudence asked.

Bevin thought of the telltale signs left on Will's bedding. "Because we do not have time today. You can tear them down tomorrow."

"Benjamin has come to expect fresh sheets on Tuesdays," Gretchen put in.

"I am sure that if tonight goes well, Benjamin will not mind waiting one more day."

"I wouldn't be so sure," Gretchen snipped. "Of course, it is up to you what gets done today."

"Good. I'm glad we agree on that at least." Bevin had shown she had spine, but inside the fact that she was successfully hiding something that had no right happening in the first place greatly distressed her.

By late afternoon Bevin and Gretchen were working side by side, sharing anecdotes and laughter. Prudence's face was smudged and her fingernails caked with dirt. Bevin finished sectioning off hunks of bread dough, pushed each section through the hole made by her thumb and index finger and formed them into clover-shaped dinner rolls.

"If you'd like, I'll show you how to make German potato salad; it is one of Benjamin's favorites," said Gretchen.

Prudence massaged the small of her back. "I am truly glad you two are finally getting along so well," she said.

Bevin nearly dropped the pan of rolls. "Pru, why wouldn't Gretchen and I get along?"

Prudence shrugged. "I thought maybe it was because Gretchen is sweet on Benjamin and you are engaged to him."

"Prudence!" Bevin choked.

Gretchen froze.

"What is the matter? We all have eyes," Prudence said with all due innocence.

There was no use attempting to explain to Prudence that one did not always put voice to an opinion. "Prudence, I didn't finish dusting in the parlor. Would you mind finishing up for me?"

"You dusted everything in there. I saw you," Prudence complained.

"Prudence, I am sure I set the dust cloth down before I finished. At least go check. You know how important tonight is. And make sure the doilies are straight."

Bevin watched Prudence prance out of the kitchen. She set the pan down and turned to Gretchen.

Gretchen's eyes were wide. The color had drained from her face. Her lips were pinched.

"I apologize for Prudence. She does not always realize what she's saying. I'm sure she didn't mean anything by it."

"Oh, but she did." Bevin opened her mouth to protest, but Gretchen held up a hand. "I came over here this morning with a mind to show you up. Reasoned I'd show Benjamin that I'd make a better farmer's wife. Reckon I learned why Benjamin loves you instead. I've acted like a ninny all morning. You remained a lady and still worked as hard as me . . . harder. Ma said you was special. I should've known. Ma is always right. You are special. So, it's me who should apologize. S-Sorry."

Gretchen hung her head. Bevin's heart went out to the girl. Her conscience berating her that she was about to marry Benjamin when she didn't love him and Gretchen did, Bevin slipped her arm around Gretchen's shoulders and hugged the girl to her.

"There is nothing to be sorry for, unless it's my lack of culinary talents and I ruin the potato salad."

Thankful that Bevin did not insist on pursuing the painful subject of Benjamin, Gretchen brightened and reached for the bacon and vinegar. "Nonsense. You'll make Benjamin proud tonight."

"Would you like to stay for supper?"

Gretchen smiled weakly. "No."

Chapter Twenty-six

Bevin sat in front of the skirted dressing table putting the finishing touches to her hair when she heard the faint sounds of the parson's buggy turning up the drive. She smiled. She had ten minutes.

Bevin joined Benjamin on the porch as the parson was pulling up. Benjamin limply took her hand while they waited for the parson to alight. It was warm and rough with calluses, not like Will's which only hinted at hard work and had held her possessively. There was a chill in the air and dark clouds had been gathering all afternoon, portending the possibility of rain in the near future.

"Ah, Benjamin, Bevin, I hope I am not too early," the slender, aging parson announced and checked his fob watch.

"You are right on time as always, Gus."

The parson clasped his hands together. "Good. Good." The crack of a twig snapped the parson's attention to a big old tree next to the house. A freckle-faced boy leaned against the trunk, a stick in his hands. "Who do we have there? Come over here, boy."

Johnny shuffled onto the porch, all the while working the tight collar that Miss Bevin had made him wear. Taking her hand from Benjamin's, Miss Bevin pulled Johnny in front of her. Johnny smiled up at her.

"You limping, boy?" the parson asked.

"He's got a deformed foot," Benjamin said.

Bevin stiffened at Benjamin's unthinking comment. "He was born with a slight handicap, but he can do everything any other child can. This is Johnny Martin. He came out from Boston with me. Johnny, this is Parson Pryor."

The parson shook his finger at the boy. "Why didn't I see you in church last Sunday, young man?"

Johnny looked to Bevin, but Benjamin interceded gruffly, "Don't look to others to do your talking for you. Answer the parson, boy."

Johnny did not like Benjamin. He could not understand why Miss Bevin was going to marry that man. She had had a talk with him about being on his best behavior tonight, so Johnny fought down the urge to stick out his tongue at dumb old Benjamin Straub. "Benjamin let me tend the horses."

"Benjamin?"

"Johnny is going to be living with us," Bevin interjected. "So we are all on a first-name basis."

The parson shot Benjamin a questioning glance. At Benjamin's tightening mouth, Gus Pryor sagely decided to refrain from additional questions.

"I am happy we have another lad experienced with horses." Again he shook that bony finger in Johnny's face. "But I want to see you inside the church next Sunday, you hear?"

"Yes, sir."

The mention of horses claimed Johnny's interest and he walked alongside the parson telling the man all about learning to ride as they went into the parlor.

Prudence was curled up in the rocking chair.

Asleep. She had nodded off. She paled when Bevin awoke her and she hurried to straighten her appearance.

"Do forgive me, Parson Pryor. Housework can be truly tiring." Out of the corner of her eye, Prudence noticed Benjamin straighten the doily on the table near her chair. She had taken special pains to make sure they were in place earlier. Benjamin was so exacting that Prudence began to wonder what Bevin's life would be like after they were wed. Benjamin had not said one word of praise at their efforts either, and she had broken three nails too!

"Benjamin's mother and Mary Straub kept an immaculate house," the parson commented.

"I am sure Bevin will do equally as well once she's settled in," Benjamin said, causing Bevin to shoot him a look of disappointment that he seemed to find her efforts lacking after the way she had slaved all day.

The parson and Bevin sat on the divan, Prudence on the rocker with Benjamin across from them. Johnny perched on Benjamin's footstool, remaining quiet as instructed while the adults visited. Bevin enjoyed being around people and forgot all about supper until Benjamin cleared his throat and pointed out the time.

"My pa used to say that a farm run according to the clock was a farm run well."

The parson shifted in his seat. "Yes, well, everyone in the community can point to the Straub farm as the best-maintained one in the county."

While Benjamin swelled with pride, Bevin and Prudence excused themselves and went to the kitchen to fry the pork chops and set the food on the table.

"Johnny, why don't you go help out in the kitchen?" Benjamin suggested in a voice leaving no room for objections.

Johnny rolled his eyes and limped off.

Benjamin stared after the boy until he was sure he was out of earshot, then he scooted to the edge of his chair and leaned forward. "Before we sit down to supper, there is something I need to discuss with you in a professional capacity, Gus."

The parson uncrossed his legs and straightened. "Of course, you know the church and I have always been here for your family. What can I do for you, Benjamin?"

Benjamin took a buoying breath. "It is rather of a delicate nature."

"You know you can confide anything in me."

"It's about Bevin and me. What I mean is that I have been having f—forbidden thoughts lately and—"

The parson held up a stilling hand. "Say no more, son. I think the sooner you marry the girl, the better."

"We planned to talk to you about that after supper. But about these thoughts. It seems that Bevin may share them as well. I held her hand and she didn't pull away . . ."

The parson listened patiently to Benjamin's confession. He believed in the tenets of the church, but was a practical, realistic man. He never would have believed a healthy young man like Benjamin Straub would have hesitated when an opportunity presented itself; many of his congregation had to be watched very carefully when sparking, and not just a few had been led down the aisle after the fact. Benjamin Straub was most unusual among his peers; a man to be revered for his principles.

"Benjamin, I don't think the Lord is going to find fault with your thoughts or the decisions you make. You are human and about to marry the lady."

Benjamin's mind was greatly relieved by the time they went in to supper. Bevin had laid out a sumptuous spread. Benjamin was pleased. When she passed him the bowl of German potato salad his brows drew together.

"This looks like Gretchen's doing."

"She suggested it." Bevin believed in giving credit where credit was due.

"It would've been neighborly to ask her to stay for supper. She's same as family," Benjamin said.

Benjamin may have concluded that Bevin needed help today to pass the parson's inspection, but she was not lacking in the social graces. Silently fuming, she said, "I did invite Gretchen, but she declined."

"Strange. She's always stayed to take supper after coming over to help out before," Benjamin said with an edge to his voice.

"She said she had chores."

"Oh." Without further comment, Benjamin turned his full attention to eating.

Goodness gracious! Benjamin hadn't an inkling of the way Gretchen felt. Bevin looked around. At least Prudence had remained silent this time. Everyone was busy eating. Johnny had tucked his napkin under his chin. She nodded in his direction. The boy grinned, snatched the bit of linen from his neck, and spread it across his lap. Satisfied that the meal was progressing nicely after a questionable beginning, she dropped her eyes to her plate.

Once the parson had gobbled down the last pork chop, scraped the bowl clean of potato salad, and eaten a second helping of cobbler, Prudence offered to do the dishes while Bevin and Benjamin entertained their guest.

"Come on, Johnny, you can help me tonight," Prudence urged the boy who was trailing after Bevin toward the parlor.

"Aw, gosh, boys ain't supposed to do dishes."

"Aren't supposed to do dishes," Bevin corrected.

"See, Miss Prudence! Miss Bevin agrees with me."

"I do not think that is what Evvie meant," Prudence said.

"You don't know!"

The parson and Benjamin shot Bevin a look that warned they expected stern measures to be taken with the child.

Bevin swung around, grabbed Johnny by the arm and marched him toward the kitchen. "Yes, Miss Prudence does. And from now on you are to remember to treat all adults with respect!"

Johnny started. Miss Bevin never had talked that way to him before. He glanced back over his shoulder. It was that dumb old Benjamin Straub's fault. Just last Sunday he had bragged to Tara that he was luckier than she was because he got to stay with Miss Bevin. Now Johnny worried that the sourpuss farmer might make her mean like he was.

Bevin raised her hand to smooth Johnny's errant locks from his eyes and the boy flinched back as if he expected she might strike him. Bevin immediately bent down and took his hands in hers.

"Johnny, you know you should not talk back to people the way you did to Miss Prudence."

"I know. I won't do it never again."

"Good. And I also hope you know I would never raise a hand to you."

"What if he" — Johnny pointed in the direction of the parlor — "told you to?"

"Johnny, Benjamin would never harm you. What gives you the idea he would?" she troubled.

"He don't like me."

"Yes, he does. He is letting you become a part of our family."

"He's not nice like Will. Benjamin orders me

around and when I do what he says he yells at me 'cuz he says I didn't do it right. I don't like him!"

Bevin was startled at the child's force of words. And she had to admit there were sides to Benjamin's character that were rigid. *Rigid*, the very word Will had used to describe Benjamin. Why did Will Shoemaker have to constantly enter her mind, regardless of what she was doing. The thought made her stop and think a moment before answering.

"Johnny, Benjamin has to get used to us, just like we have some adjustments to make as well. Please give him a chance."

Johnny frowned. "Maybe."

"That's a start. Now apologize to Miss Prudence and help her clear the table."

Bevin waited until Johnny said he was sorry, then she joined Benjamin and the parson in the parlor.

"Did you get the boy straightened out?" Benjamin asked.

"He'll be fine now."

"I hope so. He needs to learn his place," he added and dismissed the topic. "Bevin, Gus and I were just discussing wedding dates. We decided on the second week in November."

"You decided?" *How could you leave me out of such an important decision?*

"Yes. It fits into our schedules nicely; it will give us several weeks to see if the boy will work out; you can get to know the people around these parts, and it should give you plenty of time to see to whatever else needs tending. And by then I'll have the farm readied for winter."

"You have thought of everything, it seems."

"Yes, you know I believe in order." He wore a self-pleased smile.

Security. Companionship. Compatibility. Those

were the things Benjamin represented. Someone to care for her and would provide a home. She was getting exactly what she had wanted, so why was it she felt so dispirited, and thoughts of Will kept surfacing. The word *compatibility* surfaced in her mind again, and she wondered why.

Before Bevin could respond, the parson rose. "I am so glad that is settled. I must be running along now. Thank you for supper. I hope we have the opportunity to spend another pleasant evening together again real soon."

"Y-Yes," Bevin said, feeling manipulated and wondering why she had not spoken up.

As they walked the parson to his buggy, Bevin felt an empty sensation in her heart. It was just a twinge and she quickly forced it from her mind.

Let Benjamin make love to you and erase all doubts. You are being silly to begin to question your decision now. You are within weeks of reaching your goal: Johnny, Patrick and a secure home. Do not be foolish. And do not even entertain the thought of throwing it all away. Besides, Will Shoemaker is not the kind of man you need.

She felt her arm grasped and squeezed rudely, calling an abrupt halt to her inner conversation.

"Bevin, aren't you going to say good night to the parson?" came Benjamin's gruff voice.

"What? Oh . . . yes . . . yes, of course. Do forgive me, I guess I was wool-gathering."

"About your upcoming wedding, I should think," the parson said indulgently.

"You are most perceptive. Good night, Parson Pryor." A brilliant smile hid the intimation of doubt nagging at her consciousness.

Despite the chill, Benjamin motioned to the porch swing. "Why don't we sit out here for a little while."

Bevin hugged her shawl around her. "It is a little

cold."

A twinkling smile curved the corners of his lips. Bevin swore he looked very much like a little boy with a secret he was bursting to share.

"M-Maybe we could help keep each other warm," he said.

His expression turned intense and Bevin wondered if holding her hand this morning had unleashed a stranger within the very reserved Benjamin Straub.

Remember, this is what you wanted.

"Bevin, is there something wrong?" He looked worried.

"No, let's go sit down." His face relaxed.

They had just settled onto the cushion when Prudence poked her head out the door. "What are you two doing out here? It is freezing."

Benjamin rose. Bevin pulled him back down. "We were enjoying the evening air."

Perhaps Prudence will join you and put an end to what you started.

"Well, I am heading off to bed. I shall tuck Johnny in for you so you will not have to worry about him."

"Thank you, Pru."

Yes, thank you, Prudence, for helping to seal my fate.

"Night," Prudence tittered and disappeared.

For more than fifteen minutes Bevin sat a respectable distance from Benjamin while he gently rocked the swing. When sounds no longer issued from inside the house, Benjamin spread his arm along the back of the swing.

"Why don't you move a little closer? You look like you are starting to turn blue."

You don't have to do this. Just get up and say you are tired. He will understand.

She slid over until their legs were touching. His arm hesitantly dropped around her shoulders. Her heart

266

began to rivet against her chest, not from excitement like it had with Will, but from a growing uneasiness that what she had started would come to pass.

"Thank you. I feel much better now."

"Yes, so do I. Bevin?"

"Yes?"

"May I kiss you?"

Will did not ask if he could kiss you.

Bevin turned her head and lifted her face. She closed her eyes and puckered her lips. She waited, hoping that the same passion would fill her breast as it had when Will kissed her.

Benjamin placed his hands on her shoulders and gazed into her face. It was an exquisite face. Her eyes were closed; she was ready for him. The escaping strands of red hair were aflame in the muted light streaming from the house. He looked forward to the time when he would see it hanging loose. He drew her to him.

Bevin felt unschooled lips press against hers. She waited to experience that special warmth. Nothing. She pressed herself to him as she had with Will. He tensed, then relaxed. Nothing. His heart pounded wildly against her; hers pumped without missing a regular beat. Nothing.

"Shh. Quiet boy. Come on."

Bevin and Benjamin broke apart at the intruding sound of a child's whisper. He snapped his arm from around Bevin's shoulders and edged away from her, embarrassed that they were not alone until he took in the whole scene of the boy.

"What the devil do you think you're doing heading into the house with that dog?" Benjamin growled with barely restrained ferocity.

Johnny froze in his tracks half inside the door, old Sourdough at his side, his fingers wound around a rope serving as a collar for the mangy animal. He slowly pivoted until he was looking into one of the maddest faces he had ever seen. Egad, he was in for it now!

Chapter Twenty-seven

After pawning his money clip and watch, Will took a room at Blain's Hotel in town. Had he been more than a moderate drinker, he would have taken to the bottle and obliterated his stepbrother's intended from his mind. But Will knew that would only put off his troubling thoughts, not lay them to rest.

Instead, he kept busy.

He visited Engle and Kelsick and ordered a new pair of boots. He checked with Bob Campbell to learn about the legalities associated with his inheritance if he chose to sell out to Benjamin as Bevin had suggested, and he stopped to visit the telegraph office and send off a wire to a friend and business partner outside of Denver in Black Hawk, Colorado Territory.

Bowling Green had grown since he had left; it was a city now. He passed many new faces on the streets. Despite the downpour, Will stopped to marvel at the fourth courthouse, built after its predecessor burned in '64. The third courthouse had been considered an ornament to the village. The new one was an even grander two-storied brick building.

Memories surrounded Will, and he picked up a stick and ran it along the iron fence surrounding the courthouse as he headed toward the mercantile to face old man Lutherby. It was time he made his peace with the haunting memory of Matthew Lutherby's drowning.

Oscar Lutherby fed the voracious potbelly stove another log. The splashing rain was keeping his customers away from the mercantile today. Not even the usuals who came to sit, chew fresh-cut plug tobacco, and ruminate had come in yet. At the clang of the bell above the door, Oscar looked up expectantly. The normal easy smile he greeted customers with immediately faded.

"What are you doing here?" Oscar barked.

"It's time we set the past aside," Will said, taking off his dripping hat and shrugging out of his coat.

"You might just as well put your coat back on, because I don't have anything I want to set aside."

Will ignored the man's frosty glare. He pulled up a chair by the stove and rubbed his hands together to warm them. It had been difficult enough to come here, and now that Will had he was not going to leave until he'd had his say.

"After Matthew drowned"—the older man gasped in a breath—"you refused to hear what happened," Will stated.

"I heard from the Frankfurt girl," Oscar sneered.

"Well, now you are going to hear the whole story."

"Like hell I am!"

Oscar swung around toward the back storage area. Will jumped from his chair and blocked the man's path. "You are going to sit and listen to me if I have to hogtie you," Will threatened.

If he were twenty-five years younger, Oscar would have accepted the challenge and gladly beaten Shoemaker to within a heartbeat of his life. His lips quivering with rage, his hands gripping the arms of the chair so tight the veins stood out between his knuckles, Oscar eased into the seat.

"You can talk until your voice fails you, but you'll never change how I feel about you."

"That may be. But I want you to listen without any interruptions until I'm through."

"Humph! Just get this over with. I got work that needs doing."

Will sighed at the close-minded man but deemed to tell the whole truth regardless of the sordid details. "That day there were four of us who decided to play hooky: your son, Ezra Parker, Lucy Frankfurt, and me. Three boys and one girl. Strange that no one ever questioned why no other girls went along, don't you think? I even followed her into the bushes as accused. But not because I was trying to steal a kiss as she swore. What Lucy didn't tell anybody was that she had just come out of the bushes with Matthew. He was the second boy to come out of the bushes with her that day, and I was last in line, because I lost the toss of a coin."

"I don't believe you!" Oscar bellowed in agony.

"Whether you admit it or not, you knew how Matthew and I were around girls. And most folks knew of the Frankfurt girl's reputation. The first boy, Ezra Parker, left because you know most folks don't swim. Matthew was sweating when he came out behind Lucy and announced he was going to jump in the pond to cool off. I begged him to wait until we all could swim together. He told me to go take my turn and then maybe we'd be able to convince her to swim naked with us.

"You see, Lucy was unbuttoning her dress and letting us have a feel. She especially liked your son and me, and told me to hurry after her and she'd lift her

271

skirts and allow me to touch her like she had let Matthew. Well, I followed her. I was kneeling over her when I heard a splash. Matthew hadn't waited. There were no cries for help or I would have left Lucy immediately.

"Whether you'll admit it or not you know how boys of fifteen are: Reckless and randy. I got what I went into the bushes with Lucy for, and when we came out and went to the edge of the pond to join Matthew, he was floating facedown. He must have hit his head on a rock."

Oscar's chest was heaving. "If what you say is true, why didn't the Parker boy come forward?"

"He had already left. Lucy and Parker started courting shortly afterward. He was crazy about her. So much so that he probably would've lied to protect her anyway. I heard they married and moved away."

Oscar's face began to crumble. He had heard the rumors, but refused to give them credence. "Why don't you leave? You've had your say."

"Yes, I have. And I can see that you know it's the truth."

"Goddamn it, yes, I know! Why'd you have to come back?" He began to sniffle. "All these years I've had my anger to keep me going after losing my only son. And now you barge your way in here and take that away from me." Tears surged down his cheeks, and he dropped his face in his hands and wept bitterly.

Will placed a comforting hand on the man's shoulder, and let him cry it out.

Once the wracking sobs slowed, Oscar raised haunted, swollen red eyes to Will. "Now, I've got nothing left."

"You've got friends, a fine business and a wife at home. And you no longer have to be weighted down by the hatred you've carried in your heart for all these years."

Will put on his coat and turned to leave, his step lighter, for he no longer was weighted down by the past either.

"Will, wait!" Will stopped to look back. "Put the closed sign in the window. Think I'll go home and spend the rest of the day with Sarah. And, Will, I—"

"It's okay, Oscar, we've both learned a lesson or two since my return."

Will was turning the sign in the window when Bertha and Gretchen entered and shook off their wet outerwear. "Will, what are you doing in here?" Bertha startled and glanced to Oscar.

Oscar stepped forward. "It's all right, Bertha. Will and I have reached an understanding."

"Glory be!"

"What can I do for you? I was just closing so I could spend the day with Sarah."

Bertha stood openmouthed. Oscar had been consumed by hatred for so long that he had neglected poor Sarah for years. "I'm glad you two finally put that terrible accident to rest. Gretchen, hurry and pick out that material I promised you so we can let Oscar close up."

"You drove into town in this weather just to pick up some material for Gretchen?" Will asked. "The roads are nothing but mud."

"God knows, with the terrible drought we've had, we bless the rain."

"Couldn't the material've waited?"

"Last time we was here, the day you arrived, we was supposed to get it. Didn't though. Gretchen's earned a new dress and I want her to have it in time for the Calico Ball Saturday night at the Watsons'. We're going to celebrate us a barn raising. You coming to the social?"

Will shrugged. He had moved into town to give Bevin time to think and put some distance between them. "Hadn't planned on it. Don't know that I'd fit in."

"Nonsense. Life is like a quilt, deary, ever'body's got their place. Think about it. Saturday'll be here before you know it."

"Johnny's place is with us tonight," Bevin insisted. "I think the spanking you gave him for trying to sneak Sourdough into the house was enough. He has learned his lesson." When Benjamin stood in front of her looking unconvinced and unmoved, Bevin continued. "Benjamin, please, it's Saturday. All your friends and neighbors will be at the Calico Ball. I want them to meet Johnny, and I want Johnny to have a chance to make friends. He has been confined to his room since Tuesday evening. Haven't you punished him enough?"

"After church tomorrow he can start rubbing the sprouts off the potatoes in the root cellar."

"I thought Sundays were reserved for necessary work. Johnny is only a boy."

"If he is going to stay, he's going to start learning that even boys carry responsibility on a farm."

"He should take responsibility, I agree. I have spoken with him; it won't happen again."

"If you are through with your entreaty, you and Prudence best finish up the supper boxes. And don't forget to put in the neckties you two made that match your dresses. And decorate the boxes up real fine. The money raised during the auction goes to help the church poor."

"Benjamin, please reconsider. Johnny is too frightened to stay alone tonight."

"I've got chores. I'll be in the barn with the mules."

Bevin glared at his retreating back. The man had completely ignored her. She had heard he couldn't be persuaded and Will was right. Well, she had no intention of allowing Benjamin to kiss her again before they were married. She would do her wifely duty as expected, but she no longer desired to try to find out if Benjamin could blot out Will's memory; she realized he couldn't.

Upset and disappointed, Bevin joined Prudence in the kitchen to finish preparing the box suppers. Prudence held up her gaily decorated package.

"What do you think? Should I tie another ribbon on it?"

"It looks simply grand. You did remember to insert the necktie you made."

"Oh, yes. Making those neckties from the strips we cut off to shorten those calico dresses you got at the mercantile was a truly superb idea. You are so clever." Prudence tittered. "I intend to make sure that Patrick knows which box is mine."

Bevin smiled. "You and Patrick have been keeping company every night since you met."

Worry creased her brow. "You do not mind, do you?"

"Pru, we have talked about Patrick every night after he's gone home and I have told you repeatedly how happy I am for you."

Prudence blushed and gave a nervous titter. "Can I help you pack your box? You haven't let me help as much as I'd like. Why, Wednesday morning you had the sheets stripped from the beds and in the wash before I got out of bed, and I rose at five-thirty. I want to feel useful."

Bevin maintained a straight face, thinking how she had slept little Tuesday night so she could change the sheets before anyone arose. Worrying about Johnny had made sleep quite impossible anyway.

"You can help. I need to talk to Johnny, so I would be most appreciative if you'd take complete responsibility for my box."

Prudence's face lit up and glowed. "Oh, thank you! As soon as I have your box wrapped I shall show it to Benjamin for you so he bids on the right one."

"No!"

"Why not? Do you not want to share supper with him?"

Prudence had set forth a question Bevin was not certain she could answer, for she was still angry with him. Not to alert Prudence to her state of confusion toward Benjamin, Bevin said, "Of course I want Benjamin to bid on my supper box. I simply want him to appreciate it; Benjamin values most the things he has to work for."

Bewildered, Prudence mumbled, "I suppose I understand."

Unable to share her concerns about Benjamin with Prudence, Bevin said, "Pru, I was merely teasing. Of course you should show my box to Benjamin."

Bevin lingered in the kitchen while Prudence set out the chicken and bread. When Prudence reached for the pickles Bevin excused herself to dress for tonight before she took Johnny his supper and explained he had to remain behind.

Will lay on the narrow bed in his hotel room, his arms folded behind his head, staring at the ceiling. He had been gone from the farm since Tuesday morning. Tonight was the Calico Ball Bertha had talked about. Should he go? Will braced up on an elbow to ponder his choices.

An hour later Will had checked out of the hotel, retrieved his horse from the livery, and was on his way back to the farm. Everything smelled so clean after a rain. A bird tweeted overhead. A bluebird. Bevin was his bluebird, he thought. No. She was going to become Benjamin's wife; a caged bird who would no longer be allowed to give voice to what was in her heart; a beautiful bird with her wings clipped to conform with Benjamin's ideals.

It was late afternoon by the time Will had stabled the horse and entered the house. There was no one around; they must have left already. Then he heard the pitiful, heart-wrenching sobs issuing from the attic room. Will took the stairs two at a time and burst through the door.

Johnny was huddled into a tight ball, cradling his pillow, and crying his eyes out. "What's going on?"

Through the blur of his tears, Johnny saw Will standing in the doorway. He bounded into Will's arms and hugged him, sobbing, "They wouldn't let me go to the social; they left me alone."

Will's heart ached for the little boy who tried so hard to act tough. He took out his handkerchief, held Johnny from him and advised, "Here, blow. After you've calmed down I want you to tell me why you didn't go with the others."

Johnny blew his nose and sat down on the bed. "I got in trouble." When Will joined him, but did not respond, Johnny decided he might as well get it over with. "I got caught trying to sneak Sourdough in the house while Miss Bevin and that dumb old Benjamin were kissing on the porch swing. . . ."

All the while Johnny explained how he'd been punished, the fact that Benjamin had been kissing Bevin kept reverberating in Will's mind.

". . . and that's why I didn't get to go tonight."

"You were crying as if you were scared of something," Will observed, forcing his attention back to the boy.

A sheepish grin came over Johnny, then he sobered. "Might as well tell you. Just promise you won't laugh."

"I promise."

"I was ascared. Always been ascared when left alone. Probably 'cuz my ma ran off and left me when I was three and I was so ascared, I didn't know what to do." His eyes wide, he asked, "Will you stay here with me tonight?"

"I won't stay here with you"—Johnny's shoulders drooped—"but I'll take you to the social with me."

"What about Benjamin?" Johnny worried.

"I'll handle Benjamin. Get ready. We'll be leaving soon."

Johnny jumped off the bed and tore his bedclothes off as Will headed toward his room to freshen up and put on a string tie. Will had passed the doorway, when Johnny's call stopped him.

"Will, they're havin' a box supper. Miss Bevin told me."

Will returned to the doorway of Johnny's room. "Yeah?"

"She said that all the ladies made neckties to match their dresses and put the ties in with their suppers. She showed me the ties she and Miss Prudence made. The men bid on the boxes and get to eat with the lady who has the dress that matches the necktie inside."

"So?"

"I know what Miss Bevin's wearing tonight."

"Oh."

"You want to eat with her, don't you?"

The kid's perception nearly knocked Will off his feet. Were his feelings for Bevin O'Dea becoming that obvious?

"Don't worry, I ain't gonna tell no one you might be sweet on her," Johnny said, making Will wonder if the kid wasn't actually a midget dressed like a boy, he sounded so mature.

"You sure you're a kid?"

Johnny crinkled up his nose. "Huh?"

"Never mind. What if I might be interested," Will said cautiously. "Did you see what her supper box looks like?"

"No, but I know where Miss Bevin keeps the left-over scraps of material and wrappings. How hard could it be to make up a necktie and stick it in one of them supper boxes?"

"I don't know how to sew."

"Don't worry. You should see the ones Miss Bevin and Miss Prudence made."

The kid really was a hoodlum in miniature! If Johnny hadn't come under Bevin O'Dea's influence he probably would have become a brilliant criminal mind someday! Will laughed at the absurdity, moved to Johnny's side, and tousled his hair. "Runt, I think this time I have to admit I like your way of thinking."

Chapter Twenty-eight

When they arrived at the Watsons', Prudence scrambled from the buggy and immediately rushed off to locate Patrick. The social had already begun. The sun was low in a brilliant orange sunset. Bevin marveled at all the activity going on around her.

Children crouched over three scattered mud puddles, dropping pebbles into the miniponds and squealing over the ripples. One group of younger children was engaged in a game of ring-around-the-rosy; another group was engrossed in drop-the-handkerchief. It made Bevin all the more unhappy that Johnny could not be here to join in.

"Here, Bevin,"—Benjamin intruded into her thoughts and handed her the supper boxes—"you are supposed to take these inside and set them on the table with the rest."

Bevin nodded, took both boxes, and went into the barn.

"Over thar, deary, stow them suppers with the rest." An old woman who resembled a stewed prune, she had so many wrinkles, pointed with her cane. "Then you come on back here and join us."

"Thank you for the invitation, but my fiancé is waiting for me outside the door."

"Ahh, so you're the one who Benjamin's gonna steal a march with."

"I beg your pardon?"

"Marry, honey girl, marry. You may fancy clingin' on the boy. But you're gonna learn that he's busy with some of the members of the Sons of Hermann passin' a jug." At Bevin's blank expression, the woman clarified, "The boy didn't tell you he belongs to a lodge. It's important to Benjamin. Never misses a meetin'. But back to the social. Us woman band together 'til it's time to auction off supper. Food always brings a man runnin'; you remember that and you won't go wrong, you hear? Name's Bessie Ryker. Ever'body calls me Aunt Bessie whether kin or no."

"I'm Bevin O'Dea."

The other women, sitting stoically in a semicircle around the commanding presence of Aunt Bessie, nodded. Bevin smiled, then took the boxes over to the rest. She set them down and strolled back toward the women. Bevin was sure if she could win over Aunt Bessie she would be accepted by the other women, three of whom had already snubbed her in the mercantile.

She noticed Benjamin upend a jug and pass it to a long-necked, long-armed man. He was surrounded by six men and seemed to be openly sharing in a companionable conversation, something he had not participated in with her. She took a deep breath and went over to the women determined to win them over.

Bevin stood on the fringes of the group listening to screaming children running wild. The women talked about a new concept in stores: Montgomery Ward had opened a mail order house in '72 and offered seventy-two shirt buttons for thirty cents. Bevin tried to appear interested, but she was not a seamstress and could have cared less.

For over an hour she stood listening to fruit canning

and drying, candle-making, washing, ironing, knitting, gardening and housework. When she tried to introduce the topics of literature, the country's affairs and fashion, she received blank stares. Only Aunt Bessie bothered to respond to any of her remarks.

"Pshaw, deary, if you fancy belongin' in this neck of the woods, you best be reminded that any city-bred girl who deems herself better than her equals hain't goin' to gain respect."

"Right good words to heed," another seconded.

"Mind you, get yourself in the grange if you need somethin' 'cept the farm and Benjamin to keep you content. 'Course, once the babies start comin', you'll have plenty to fill your days."

Bevin smiled weakly. "Yes, I suppose I shall."

Bevin was saved from further advice on being a proper farmer's wife by Parson Pryor. The man was followed by the horde of revelers toward the supper boxes.

Bevin noticed Prudence and Patrick stroll in hand in hand. Their open display of affection surprised her. The way Benjamin acted Bevin expected them to be condemned. No one seemed to notice.

Young and old crowded around the table.

"Wait, here's another supper box," a voice in the back called out. The box was passed up front and set with the rest.

Bevin's attention caught at the barn door. Will Shoemaker was standing in the back. Her breath came out in a gasp. Johnny was sitting atop Will's shoulders, as big as you please! Benjamin was going to be furious! She forced her attention to the parson, who had lifted the first box over his head.

"Folks, this pretty pink box is chockful of goodies; it weighs enough to use as a doorstop," Gus Pryor boomed out to roars of laugher.

The men shoved in closer while the women and girls

stood at one side waiting for their boxes to be bought.

"Who wants to start the bidding?"

"Two bits."

"Come now, good people, remember this is for charity."

The pink box went for one dollar. A hardy farm boy stepped up and was joined by a giggling girl Bevin guessed to be about sixteen. He opened the box and the girl removed the necktie and tied it around his neck. Cheers rose as they moved off and the next box went on display.

Bevin fidgeted while a dozen boxes were claimed. The bidding was lively for Prudence's overdecorated one, and Patrick managed to outbid another young man by a penny.

Bevin's box went on the block, and she held her breath fearing Johnny might have seen her box and told Will which one was hers, and he would liven the bidding against Benjamin. To her horror, Will moved next to Benjamin as he stepped forward.

The parson smiled widely. "There's only four left. So if you haven't got yours you'd best dig into your pockets if you hope to eat tonight. Who'll start the bidding on this appetizing bow?"

"One dollar," Will bid.

Benjamin scowled. "Dollar ten."

"One fifty."

"Two dollars," Ben growled.

"Three," came Will's unperturbed response.

"Three ten," Ben huffed.

"There gold in this little box, boys?" the parson attempted to lighten the darkening atmosphere.

"Must be red-gold," yelled one of the old codgers, leaning heavily on a cane.

All eyes fell on Bevin's mass of curls.

The barn strained with laughter, and Benjamin's face

turned bloodred. Bevin was mortified. She placed her palms on her flaming cheeks. She had hoped to be accepted by the community, instead she was a spectacle and undoubtedly would be the subject of juicy gossip for at least a week. When Benjamin discovered Johnny's presence there was no telling what he would do; he was already so angry. And despite everything, Bevin's eyes continued to stray to Will.

"Will, I believe it's your turn. You want to up the ante?"

More laughter.

Will camly pulled the bills from his pocket and thumbed through them. "I'll go for another buck."

"How 'bout you, Benjamin? You willing to untie the knotted strings around your purse?"

Benjamin glowered. The other boxes had been auctioned for half what he had already bid. "What you doing here?" he sneered at Will.

"Bertha invited me."

Silently, Benjamin cursed Bertha's big mouth. He could not lose face by being outbid by his stepbrother.

Parson Pryor shrugged. "Going for four dollars, once . . . twice . . ."

"Five dollars," Benjamin ground out.

All eyes turned to Will.

Will held up his palms. "I concede defeat."

"You did this on purpose, didn't you?" Benjamin spat while the parson yelled out "sold. Come 'n fetch your prize."

Benjamin hated parting with that much money for his own food, but he had a principle to uphold. He claimed the box and Bevin. He was leading her through the crowd, stopping to talk and introduce Bevin, stoically accepting pats on the back, and good-natured ribbing when the parson's voice stopped him.

"Benjamin, hold up there."

Benjamin turned toward the table. There was a buzz of whispers humming through the front of the crowd. Something was amiss.

"What is it, Gus?

"Seems we've got another box up here—"

"I'm not in the market for another."

No one laughed at Benjamin's debut at humor. His face turned serious. "Come on, Bevin, let's get whatever is going on straightened out so we can get to eating supper."

Benjamin pushed back through the throng, Bevin following him to where the parson stood.

Benjamin glared at Will, who was standing next to the parson, an open supper box in his hand. "What is it?"

"Benjamin, there seems to be a problem here," Gus Pryor offered.

"So, what is it?"

A sickly pallor to his face, the parson pulled the necktie out of Will's box and held it up. "This."

Shock claimed Bevin's face.

Benjamin smoldered.

Will grinned.

"Don't rightly understand it, but the box Will just bought has got a necktie in it that matches yours."

Benjamin swung on Bevin. "How can this be?"

Bevin shook her head. "I don't understand it. Benjamin, you know we only brought two boxes. Patrick claimed one and you the other."

Benjamin detested being the center of attention. A man should only get public recognition three times in his life: once at birth, when he married, and when he died.

"I have a solution," Will offered easily.

Benjamin's teeth clenched. He suspected that whatever William was about to suggest, he was not going to

285

like it.

"What do you have in mind, Will?" Parson Pryor asked as all ears turned to hear the proposed solution.

"Since no other lady has stepped forward with a dress matching my necktie, it looks as if Benjamin and I are both going to be forced to share the attentions of the lady wearing the dress that matches our ties."

"Sounds fair enough," said the parson quickly. He had no other idea how to solve the problem. They had been living under the same roof, so sharing another meal should cause no harm. "Is it all right with you, Bevin?"

Bevin looked from Benjamin to Will. Then out of the corner of her eye she saw Johnny; the little imp was grinning from dimple to dimple. He and Will were responsible for her predicament; she was sure of it.

Benjamin followed Bevin's line of vision and spotted Johnny. Benjamin no longer wondered how there came to be two neckties alike. That boy was nothing but trouble. At that moment Benjamin decided he would ignore this incident. But the smart-mouthed boy had sealed his own fate. No argument on earth could convince Benjamin to allow that boy to remain on the farm now. When Prudence Truesdale left to return to Boston, he would announce that Johnny's trial period was over and he was not staying.

"Folks are waiting," urged the parson, anxious to be done with the whole business.

"If Benjamin approves, it is all right with me," Bevin said.

"Hurry up and put the necktie on him so we can go eat," Benjamin snarled. "Might as well go collect the boy, too, since he's responsible for this fiasco." He swung on his heel, not waiting to watch Bevin slip that damned strip of cloth over William's head.

"Hain't never seen nothin' like it in all my days." Aunt

Bessie chuckled, enjoying the spectacle. "Why, this is better'n the last minstral show that came through Old Mizzou."

"Okay now, that's that," the parson announced, drawing attention back to the auction. "We got two more boxes up here, so let's have your attention. There are two anxious young ladies waiting to be claimed."

Benjamin led the way to a far corner of the barn. His face flamed, he was so angry. He glared at the three of them, then his expression softened toward Bevin. He knew in his heart her only crime in all this was she would try to protect that cripple.

"Why don't we all sit down? I'm sure everyone is as hungry as I am," Bevin said. She folded her legs beneath her and laid out the two box suppers as the others joined her.

All began to eat in strained silence.

"You cook this?" Benjamin grumbled, waving a chicken leg which resembled leather. The thought that he had paid five dollars for nothing more than chicken jerky made him choke.

"Prudence has been wanting to be useful, so I had her take responsibility for the boxes," Bevin admitted.

"Didn't know she disliked you enough to try to poison you, did you, Ben?" Will joked.

"From the looks of your box, seems she dislikes you as well," Benjamin retorted.

"Looks like she must have made your tie too." Will laughed, staring at the sorry length of fabric.

Benjamin fingered the pathetic tie. He looked to Bevin. She was trying to hold back a grin which heightened his rancor. He believed in dressing well for these socials. Then his gaze caught at Will's tie. "I wouldn't laugh so hard if I were you. Your tie looks as if it were stitched by someone with two left hands."

"I'd say we're pretty evenly matched," Will offered,

hoping to disarm some of Benjamin's anger.

"Except Bevin is my bride-to-be," Benjamin crowed, pleased that he had been able to best his stepbrother.

Bevin held back a smile at the competition between the two men until Benjamin reminded Will that she was engaged to him. She hoped Patrick was being more tolerant of Prudence's efforts. Johnny then caught her attention. He hid his eyes. "Johnny, I want you to look at me and explain what part you played in the two boxes."

Johnny looked up, his expression tight. Dumb old Benjamin knew he had a hand in it, and he was not supposed to be here tonight. "I'm sorry, Miss Bevin. It was all my fault. I wanted to come tonight so I made up a story to Will. I done it all. Please don't be mad at me," he begged. His chin was now quivering.

"Is that true, Will?" Bevin asked.

Will looked into those blue eyes; disbelief was mirrored there. He could not allow the kid to shoulder all the blame, and he did not want Benjamin to take his wrath out on the boy. "The runt—"

"His name is Johnny," Benjamin intruded dryly.

"Johnny's trying to protect me. He was in bed when I returned to the farm. When I learned that he had been left alone, I had no intention of doing the same thing. Over the poor kid's protests, I insisted he accompany me. That isolated farmhouse is no place to leave a little boy all by himself."

Bevin could have relaxed if it had not been for the matching supper boxes. "And whose idea was it to cause Benjamin and I such embarrassment with the neckties?"

"Guilty on that count too," Will said as Johnny was opening his mouth to confess. "I thought it would be a right good joke. Remember when I used to play pranks on you when we were youngsters, Ben?"

Benjamin surveyed the boy's face. He appeared to be innocent, although Benjamin did not believe it for an instant. Keeping to his earlier decision not to pursue the incident, he said, "Maybe the boy didn't have a hand in it, maybe he did, but he should've known better than to allow you to bring him here."

"Chrissake, Ben, he's only a boy. You have punished him enough already. Why don't you just chalk up another black mark on my record so we can get on with enjoying this social?"

"Humph!" Benjamin ripped a slice of bread apart and gnawed on it as if it were raw meat.

They had just finished the rest of their supper in tension-filled silence when the fiddler and squeeze box player started warming up.

"All youse paired up with matching duds out to the dance floor," hollered the fiddle player. "It's time we liven things up a bit."

Bevin watched couples pour out to the center of the barn ready to kick up their heels. Now what was she going to do?

"Ready?" Benjamin and Will said in unison.

Bevin knew she should take Benjamin's hands, but a voice inside her that had been growing stronger held her back. She looked at both expectant faces until Johnny said, "Miss Bevin, I know how to settle which one you dance with first."

"There needs to be no settling," Benjamin snapped. "She's my bride-to-be."

Will had a lopsided grin on his lips when he said, "But the rules of the Calico Ball are that the lady dances first with the gentleman who is wearing the necktie that matches her dress."

"That disqualifies you, William, since you have never been a gentleman," Benjamin retorted.

"Please!" Bevin exasperated. "Let's hear Johnny out."

All eyes turned to the boy. "Why don't you draw straws?"

"No!" Benjamin snapped.

"Seems fair enough to me," Will said.

Bevin sighed. "Benjamin, it is only a dance."

"Oh, all right." Benjamin had no other choice, he could see that.

As Johnny turned his back and arranged two straws from the floor he thought of the shell game he used to play on the streets. If Will was half as smart as Johnny knew he was, there would be no contest. He turned back toward the adults and held out his fist, two lengths of straw peeking out. "Shortest one loses," he announced.

Johnny held out the straws toward Will. Their gazes met for an instant, long enough for Johnny to blink his left eye. Will pulled out the left straw. Johnny then offered the other to Benjamin.

"Looks like the first dance is mine, Ben," Will announced.

He helped Bevin to her feet and ushered her out onto the floor. A waltz was struck up, and Benjamin glowered as his stepbrother gathered Bevin into his arms. Somehow he'd just been had, but he couldn't quite figure out how.

Johnny scampered away to join a group of children about his own age before Benjamin could accuse him.

Benjamin gained his feet and leaned against an upright, his arms folded across his chest, rage in his heart as he watched the pair glide gracefully about the floor. And the worst part about it all was that they seemed to be totally enjoying themselves before the eyes of his friends and neighbors!

Chapter Twenty-nine

Mentally, Bevin began marking off the days on the calendar. Three more weeks. Three more weeks before she became Mrs. Benjamin Straub. Three more weeks in which to change her mind. It was long after midnight and still Bevin could not sleep. Three more weeks.

She rose quietly, so as not to awaken Prudence, and moved to lean against the windowsill. The sky was cluttered with stars. Pity wishing on a star was for children, since she needed help with her dilemma.

She had worked so hard and long to achieve her goal in life, and now in three more weeks that goal would be reached. So why wasn't she overjoyed and filled with jubilation?

A replay of her life since her arrival in Bowling Green marched before her eyes. Will Shoemaker was irrevocably entwined in each scene. He had spent hours talking to her brother, sharing common experiences and feelings until Patrick agreed to give her a chance. Will had tempered Benjamin's anger, and interceded on Johnny's behalf. Poor Johnny, the child seemed to have a way of getting into trouble regardless of what he did.

She had been fully prepared to defend Johnny when

they returned from the Calico Ball last week; she had overheard Johnny thanking Will for covering for him at the social. To her utter surprise, Benjamin behaved totally out of character: he merely added to Johnny's chores, making no further mention of the incident with the neckties or Johnny disobeying his directives. Therein lay the problem: Benjamin was not everything she had always dreamed of, but he was an enterprising man, independent and proud. He was respected in the community and devoted to his farm. And he was making every effort to accept Johnny.

"Evvie?" Prudence stretched and sat up against the pillows. "What are you doing out of bed? It is nearly two A.M."

Bevin swung around. "I was just thinking."

"About Benjamin or Will?"

"I don't know what you mean," Bevin protested.

Prudence rubbed her eyes and yawned. "Evvie, I know most people think I am a total scatterbrain. And in many ways I suppose I am. People often ignore my presence, thinking I am oblivious to what is happening. But I am not. I listen, and I have eyes."

"You are not a scatterbrain."

"No, I am not. Patrick has helped show me I have worth. Of course, you have always made me feel important too. It is just that with Patrick, well, he—"

"I know, Pru. I know. Being part of a pair is a very special thing."

"Then isn't it truly difficult for you?"

"Me?"

"Yes. There seems to be some sort of a triangle going on among you, Benjamin and Will. You are in the center between those two men, Evvie. It is unnatural. Benjamin seems to be going out of his way to be more tolerant than he was when we first arrived. And Will has won over Patrick and Johnny. He is always around."

"Will does live here too."

"Evvie, even I can see the man is in love with you, even if you cannot and he will not admit it."

"That's nonsense. I'm going to marry Benjamin."

"Are you so sure that is what you still want?"

"It's late. We have to rise early, so I'm going back to bed." Bevin got into bed and pulled the sheet up to her neck.

"Evvie, tonight Benjamin goes to the Sons of Hermann lodge meeting. Those Germans sure do stick together. It is the one night he stays out late even though he gets up before light the next morning."

"Yes?" Bevin said, trying to follow Prudence's train of thought.

"Patrick has invited me to go for a drive, and Johnny asked if it would be all right for him to spend time with Tara. Bertha said it was fine with her as long as you approved. Patrick and I shall drop him off. We shall all be gone."

"Why are you telling me? I shall be fine alone."

"You will not be alone. Will will be here. It will give you time to straighten things out with him."

How can you straighten things out with Will when you, yourself, are not sure what needs to be straightened out?

"Go to sleep, Pru, we have ironing and walls to scrub tomorrow."

Bevin had hoped the backbreaking chores would get easier. She wondered how Gretchen had managed them by herself. Even with Prudence's help, Bevin was worn through by evening. Perhaps what Benjamin's neighbors said was true: she was city-bred and cut from different cloth. And she was not even certain she cared anymore what they thought as she set up the ironing board Benjamin had fashioned for her.

She wiped the sweat from her forehead with her shirtsleeve while she waited for the iron to heat on the stove. The iron weighed eight pounds, she shuddered as she started in on the chore. Each time she used it her arm ached all the next day. Finally she came to the last shirt. She ran the iron over the fabric, smoothing and turning as she pressed it. She was finishing up the back when Prudence yelped and there was a loud crash.

Bevin ran into the parlor. Prudence was sitting in the middle of shattered pieces of Benjamin's favorite lamp around her.

"Oh, Evvie, I am sorry. I was just trying to clean the shade."

Bevin shook her head and helped Prudence to her feet. "Are you all right?"

She held out her index finger. "Just a little cut. Evvie?"

"What?"

"What is that smell? It smells like something is burning."

"Oh, no!" Bevin ran back to the kitchen and snatched the iron off the center of Benjamin's shirt. She held it up. A perfect black imprint adorned the white fabric.

"Oh, my." Prudence slapped a hand to her mouth. "Isn't that the shirt Benjamin wears to his lodge meeting every week?"

Bevin sighed. "It was."

"It is so cool outside that if he does not notice the scorched spot when he puts it on, he probably won't notice it either because he will keep his jacket on."

Bevin sighed. "Prudence, I must be losing my mind, because you are starting to make sense."

By the time Benjamin trudged into the kitchen it was dark outside. He shrugged off his work shirt and washed up. Bevin hung in the rear and handed him a towel.

"Thank you," Benjamin said.

When he dried his arms and hands, Bevin held out the scorched shirt, careful to keep the black spot hidden. "Let me help you."

Benjamin smiled warmly. "You remembered which shirt I wear to my lodge meetings."

"Yes," Bevin said feebly. What had gotten into her? She would never get away with it. "Let me help you with your jacket too."

"Are you trying to rush me out of the house without supper?"

"Supper? Oh, yes. Supper."

The evening meal was a stressful affair. Prudence tittered at the least little thing. Johnny had to be warned three times not to talk unless spoken to. Only Will kept a straight face, but he kept glancing at Bevin, a twinkle in his eyes.

Benjamin rose and Bevin popped up behind him. She grabbed his coat. "Here."

"Thank you. You are becoming more and more like a farmer's wife each day."

Prudence and Johnny broke into rolling laughter.

"What is so humorous?" Benjamin demanded.

Prudence immediately sobered and Bevin interceded. "They were laughing about Johnny's efforts to hold on to one of the hogs."

Benjamin saw no humor in the topic. "You mind how you treat our mortgage raisers," he advised.

"Mortgage raisers?"

"Benjamin's talking about the hogs. Breeding and selling them is the best way to make a quick profit and get rid of the mortgage," Will explained.

"Reckon you won't be bothering the sows. The Jersey's about to birth," Benjamin said, breaking an unwritten code not to talk about such topics in mixed company.

Johnny suppressed a giggle at the shirt when Benjamin turned his back and put on his coat. "T-he, t-he, I won't bother the old sow none."

"Just see that you don't, boy." He turned to Bevin. "I put the socks out that need darning. It'll give you something to do so you don't get too lonely tonight. I left an example of the way Gretchen mends. That's the way I like them done."

"You need not worry, Evvie won't be alone," Prudence piped up when she noticed Bevin's expression of disbelief. She shot a conspiring glance at Will, then quickly signaled Johnny to hold his tongue.

Benjamin was secretly glad he would not have to miss another lodge meeting. He had remained at the farm the first two weeks after Bevin's arrival. At last his life was beginning to return to normal.

Will watched Bevin walk Benjamin out the back door. He turned his attention to Prudence. Prudence had come to him earlier and announced that she was taking Johnny with her when Patrick came for her tonight. The young woman had tittered as was usual, but beneath the nervous giggle Will detected that she was sending him a subtle message he did not miss. Tonight he would have time to be alone with Bevin.

Prudence rose and said, "Come along, Johnny, you need to get ready to go. Patrick will be here soon, and we do not want to keep him waiting."

Johnny lagged behind as Prudence hurried toward her bedroom. "Just want to thank you again for taking the blame at that dumb old social. And I wanted to know something."

When the kid stood there, shuffling his built-up shoe, Will said, "Ask away, runt."

"Well, ah, I was wondering, ah . . . oh, hell, I want to know why you ain't gonna marry Miss Bevin instead of dumb old Benjamin."

"Johnny!" Bevin snapped, returning to the kitchen. "If you don't want to be sent to bed instead of visiting Tara, you best hurry along. And I had better never hear you talk like that again, young man."

"Wait, runt, I'll walk down the hall with you." Will grinned at Bevin. She turned away and began clearing the table.

Will dropped a hand on the kid's thin shoulder as they climbed the stairs. "Guess I oughtn't've said what I did to Miss Bevin."

"There's nothing wrong with speaking your mind, runt."

Johnny stopped and looked up at Will. "Then why you letting Miss Bevin marry someone else?"

"That's a good question."

"Well?"

"You aren't going to let a man off the hook, are you?"

"I'd rather have you for a pa."

Will's breath caught at the kid's statement. He had stayed away from children since the drowning. Now that all the painful guilt feelings had finally been laid to rest, Johnny's comment had a particular impact on him. He tousled the boy's hair.

"You sure like to do that, don't you?"

"Yeah, guess I do."

"What about what I said?"

"Runt, if I ever do have a family, I'd like to have a son just like you."

Johnny brightened. "Then marry Miss Bevin."

"Miss Bevin has other ideas, runt. You better hurry before Patrick arrives," Will suggested in an attempt to change topics.

"Will, if you can't be my pa, would you at least teach me how to make a corncob pipe like you told me you used to make when you was a kid?"

Will laughed. "You don't forget a thing, do you?"

"Nope!"

Prudence called for the boy to hurry, saving Will the necessity of a reply. Stuffing his hands in his pockets, Will ambled to his room with another thought added to the ones already weighing on him.

When Patrick pulled up, Bevin spoke with him briefly, then saw Prudence and Johnny off. Her heart swelled that Patrick's animosity had all but disappeared, and she credited it to Prudence's influence, denying Will's efforts. First opportunity available she planned to spend some time alone with her brother. They had so much to learn about each other's lives. She hugged her shawl around her and went back into the house.

You are alone in the house with Will. If you want to marry Benjamin, you best go to your room and avoid Will.

She ignored her inner voice and laid a fire in the fireplace. She was fanning it in an attempt to ignite a blaze when Will's voice from behind her caused her to start.

"Need some help?"

Bevin turned to gaze up into those warm brown eyes. She felt heat flood her face. She wished she could blame it on the fire, but fact was a flame had not flared in the fireplace; it had sparked inside her.

"Thank you, but I can manage."

Will took a step forward and lifted a handful of socks Benjamin had left for her to darn. "Like you have been managing your life lately?"

Bevin's gaze caught at the socks. She thought of Benjamin's instructions, and how in love with Benjamin Gretchen was. Another wave of guilt washed over her. She fought to force it down, but it lodged in her throat, refusing to be denied.

"I just need time to adjust," she defended herself.

298

"To adjust to Gretchen's ways, the way Benjamin expects you to? Gretchen is a farmer's daughter. She grew up here."

"And because I didn't, I can't be expected to make a life here for myself?" she cried.

"Gretchen has always looked forward to marrying someone like Benjamin, and she will be content living *this* kind of life."

He shook the socks at her.

"Will you be content year after year bending to Benjamin's dictates, discussing quilting bees, putting up your garden's crop and deferring topics such as your country's affairs to the men? These women don't ride horses, swim, or receive recognition from their husbands for all their hard work because these men have little skill in expressing gratitude. It's their way of life. Benjamin defines himself by his farm."

"It is a wholesome way of life."

"Bevin, there is nothing wrong with the way Benjamin lives if that is what you want from life as well. Is that really the kind of life you want to tie yourself to?" When she did not answer, he continued. "You grew up on the streets in a big city. You have always made your own decisions. You are a bright lady. Benjamin views mental ability as a useless abstract next to physical ability. Are you willing to give up everything you've strived for to sit home in a rocking chair and darn socks while your husband attends his lodge meetings?"

In the next instant Will had tossed the socks aside and was kneeling before Bevin, holding her at shoulder length from him, searching her face. "Are you?"

Bevin's heart was smashing against her chest. Tension squeezed inside her breast. Tears filled her eyes and threatened to spill over her lids, revealing how close to the truth Will had come. He had not said anything she had not been thinking and troubling over.

Will pulled her into his embrace. He stroked her hair and held her against his hard chest. He could feel her despair in the tension of her body. His heart was so full of her.

"Are you, Bevin?" he murmured.

A gasp escaped her. "I don't know."

Chapter Thirty

The kindling in the fireplace smoldered, then flared. The dry wood crackled and sparked, causing Bevin and Will to break apart. Will set two small limbs and a large log in the fire and turned back to Bevin, who was sitting on her haunches staring at the flames in despair.

"Come and sit on the divan," Will said softly and helped her to her feet.

Bevin remained quiet as she allowed herself to be settled next to Will. She was mulling over everything he had said. For long moments no one said a word until Bevin finally broke the silence, reaching for the pile of socks. "I best get busy. Benjamin will want his socks finished by the time he gets home."

Will grabbed the socks and tossed them on the rocker. "To hell with them. Bevin, there are things we have to talk about."

Emotion threatened to sweep her features. She looked at him, trying to contain the myriad of bottled-up feelings. Garnering her strength, she said, "I don't know what you mean."

Will was not going to let her hide behind that façade she presented to the world. He intended to break through her inner reserves this time, not only her physical reserves. He needed to know what was in that well-guarded heart of hers.

"Like hell you don't!"

Bevin shook her head from side to side in desperation to sever further discussion of the topic she knew he was about to broach. "Will, please. I am going to marry Benjamin in three weeks. We don't have the right to be sitting here like this, much less . . ." Her voice trailed off.

"Much less what, Bevin?" he probed, not about to let the subject die.

Bevin was battling to stem the tide stirring within her. She jumped to her feet. Will was right behind her. He placed his hands on her shoulders and pulled her back against him. His breath was warm and moist on her neck, and sent shivers down her back.

"Bevin," he whispered in her ear. "We can't put it off any longer. You know it and I know it. You may try to deny your feelings to me and the world, but you can't deny them to yourself."

Bevin turned in his embrace and lifted her face toward his. Tears sat perched on the edge of her lower lids ready to give her away. She struggled to present a serene appearance. But Will was right, she could no longer deny what others around her saw so clearly.

"Will, what about Benjamin?"

"What about us?" he murmured.

"I have given Benjamin my word. I owe him so much. If it weren't for Benjamin I may never have found my brother. And Benjamin has offered Johnny a home. That child has never known a real home in his life."

"So you are going to sacrifice yourself, is that what you are going to do?"

"But my word—"

"What about your love? You have never once mentioned the word love in relation to Benjamin."

"But I owe—"

"No! We aren't talking about what you owe or your word or your principles or goals, or any of those fancy titles you use to pent up your emotions. We are talking about love, what is in your heart, what you feel."

His eyes grew in intensity as he delved into hers. He was breathing fast, short, shallow breaths. Her own breath was coming shorter now too. She felt dizzy. He was battering at her defenses, unrelenting in his onslaught.

"Can't you let it be?"

"No. And I am not going to let up until you admit the truth. Tell me you love Benjamin with all your heart and I'll leave you alone; I'll go tonight."

Bevin dropped her gaze.

"You can't say it, can you?" His tone softened. "You can't say you love Benjamin because you don't. You don't love him."

She felt ill. "No."

Will had known the answer before she voiced it, but nonetheless, her response sped up his pulse. Never before had he wanted a woman the way he wanted this one. He had had her as a man has a woman, but this was different. The nesting instinct was claiming him.

"Bevin—"

"Will, please, can't we just drop it? Let's not pursue something that can only hurt others, because I won't ruin Johnny's chance for a normal life, and I can't lose my brother again, because I . . ." Her voice trailed off.

He grabbed her arms, his resolve refusing to allow him to let her slip away this time. "Because you are in love with me?"

303

Bevin's chin was trembling and she stared up at the ceiling, wishing she had never met Will Shoemaker.

Silly goose, you can't wish the man away. It is time you face what you have been refusing to acknowledge.

She leveled her gaze with his. She saw warmth, desire and hope in his eyes.

She let out a cry of anguish.

"Bevin, you are only compromising yourself if you refuse to face the truth. Face it before it's too late. If you don't, you'll be forced to live with it the rest of your life.

"You can't run from your feelings. I know. I left the farm because I couldn't face all the hurt and pain I had growing up. I denied my feelings and thought that by leaving . . . no, running away . . . I could put the past behind me and start fresh. But you can't run away from yourself. No matter where you go, your past goes with you. All the feelings you think you have set aside are still there. And until you face them, you will never lay them to rest.

"Bevin, when I got Benjamin's letter I thought about tearing it up. But I realized I had to come back. I had to face Oscar Lutherby. I'm not saying it was easy, because it wasn't. It was one of the most painful things I have ever done, but I forced myself to accept my past. Lutherby and I worked through all the hatred and pain. And coming back here has given me a different perspective of Benjamin's father and my childhood. Now I don't have to keep running or denying anything. Bevin, you don't have to any longer either."

"I am not denying anything."

"Aren't you? What about Benjamin? Is it fair to him? And Gretchen? She loves Benjamin the way a wife should; the way he deserves to be loved. Aren't you denying yourself the chance to know love? If you marry Benjamin, won't you be denying him the same chance?"

Bevin slammed her hands over her ears. "Stop it! Stop it!"

"What's the matter, don't you want to hear the truth? Can't you face it? Bevin, open your eyes . . . and your heart before it's too late."

Bevin looked into his face. He was so earnest, so sincere and open she wanted to scream he was right. The words would not come. She shook her head.

"Don't you understand, I can't!"

"No! You won't." He dropped his arms to his sides in defeat. "Oh, God, I can't force you to change your mind. Just remember, there is nothing noble about self-sacrifice; it has many victims and no real victors. While I was in town I checked on a fair price for my half of the farm. Never intended to stay here. I'll be gone before the wedding."

He turned away from her and headed toward his room, shaking his head.

Bevin stood, pinned to the spot, reaching out a trembling hand, unable to speak. Once he was out of sight, she sank to the floor. She gathered the pile of socks around her. For the longest time she stared blankly at them. If she didn't go to Will he would soon walk out of her life. She picked up a sock and studied the hole in the heel. The torn threads seemed to be a perfect representation of her life.

Once Prudence and Patrick had dropped Johnny off at the Kruegers' farm, they continued along the road leading north from town. They passed by another farm, then drove through the thinning forest as night

305

engulfed them. A deer darted out in front of the buggy. Patrick pulled up on the reins and stopped the buggy off the road under a hickory tree. He reached for the rifle he kept nearby whenever he went out at night.

Through the moonlight, he set a bead on the animal which had stopped a short distance from them.

Prudence stood up and cried, "Oh, no! You must not harm it! Why look at those soulful eyes."

"You are so softhearted, Miss Prudence." Patrick returned the rifle to its resting place.

Relieved that he was not going to kill such a beautiful creature, Prudence settled a little closer next to him on the seat. "Thank you for not shooting it. I just could not endure the pain it would suffer." She dropped her eyes to her hands folded in her lap for a moment before she added, "Bevin calls me Pru. I—I would really like it if you would call me Pru."

"I would rather call you Prudy girl."

"I would like that very much."

His heart swelled. She was so special, and Patrick found himself with the need to protect her and take care of her. "Prudy girl, would you think me too bold if I asked if I could put my arm around you?"

Prudence's pulse tapped against her throat double time. "N-no."

Patrick slipped his arm around her shoulders. They sat rigidly still for a minute. Prudence held her breath; Patrick fought to control his.

Lord in heaven, he wanted to kiss her. He wondered whether she would recoil in horror if he tried. He had determined to go slow, but his body ached. A question suddenly came to mind. She was such a pretty little thing that surely she must have a beau back in Boston. A streak of unaccounted-for jealousy reared its head and he had to know for sure if he had any competition.

"You probably have lots of friends back in Boston."

"Evvie is my best friend."

Frustration grasped him. "No . . . ah . . . I mean men friends."

"I have a few friends who are men . . . boys, truly," she responded, thinking how Patrick was a grown man.

"Aw, Prudy girl, that's not what I mean. I mean do you have any beaux?"

"Oh, my, no."

"I'm glad," he blurted out.

"You are?"

"Yes. If you wouldn't object I'd like to call on you."

She turned wide eyes to him. "You have been calling on me . . . every night."

"What I mean is come courting. Formally, of course."

"Formally?"

"Only if you don't object," he repeated. He was starting to sweat. He had never declared such intentions before, and she was proving difficult. He knew she was not being coy; she was too innocent. But he had never been serious before, and having to speak the words was tough on a farm boy trying to court a special city-girl like Prudence.

"I do not object at all, truly," she interrupted with a nervous titter.

"You don't?"

She tittered again. "You sound surprised. Why would I not want you to court me?"

"Aw, gosh, Prudy girl, I'm just a helper on somebody else's land. I don't got nothing to offer a fine lady such as you. Although someday I aim to get me a plot

307

of land of my own. I got lots of plans."

"I am sure you do. And you will have the best farm in the whole state someday."

Patrick sat up straighter. "You really think so?"

"Truly, I do."

"Golly, you really have faith in me, don't you?"

"You should not sound so surprised. What girl would not have faith in such a strong man like you?"

"Then you wouldn't mind if I've got some real serious sparking in mind in regards to you?"

Prudence's heart threatened to leap out of her throat. She suddenly realized that this gorgeous, genuine man was truly interested in courting her!

He pulled her closer to him. Prudence turned to look at him. Moonlight glistened gold across his face and lit his features. He had a wonderful profile, so masculine, and his arm was muscled with incredible strength.

She wished he would look at her, although she knew she would truly melt if he did. She had never been adventurous. But Patrick was serious. He said so. Prudence took a buoying breath. She was about to take a big chance, and do something she had never dreamed she was possible of doing before.

She lifted her face and closed her eyes.

"Patrick?"

His name on her lips sounded like the strings of a fiddle. He turned in her direction and nearly flew out of the seat, he was so startled.

She sat next to him with her face lifted in his direction, her eyes tightly squeezed shut, and her lips puckered.

Chapter Thirty-one

Bevin was sitting in the corner of the divan, her legs curled beneath her, resting her head on her arm when she heard the familiar crunch of gravel beneath hooves coming up the drive. Benjamin was home from his lodge meeting. She glanced at the pile of socks on the floor. She had not started darning them, and she did not even care. She was exhausted, drained from her encounter with Will. Everything he said had been barraging her for hours.

"Bevin," Benjamin shouted as he bounded through the kitchen door.

There was a harsh sound of anger to his raised voice. It was out of character for him to raise his voice toward her. Then it dawned on her: he had taken off his coat during the meeting.

Bevin looked up as Benjamin stormed into the parlor. His cheeks were red. She wondered whether his color was from the cold ride home or anger. He was not smiling. His features were set in stone.

Without a word he removed his coat and pivoted around. "Would you like to explain this?"

Bevin swallowed. Her reserves were gone. She wiped a few strands of hair back off her forehead. She rose, rubbing the small of her back and stared back at Benjamin.

"No, I would not."

Benjamin's mouth tightened. "Well, I am afraid you are going to have to."

Bevin gave a puff of impatience. "It was an accident."

"I certainly hope one of you did not do it on purpose!"

"One of us?"

"You or that prissy city-girl, who has never done an honest day's work in her life."

Bevin's face was starting to heat up and she wondered if it looked as hot as his. "For your information, Prudence works very hard. But I was the one who scorched your shirt."

"How could you do a thing like that?" he blustered. "And worse, how could you let me wear the damned thing?"

"It was an accident," she answered indignantly. "I thought you would keep your coat on since it was so cool out tonight."

She watched him slap a hand to his mouth and his cheeks bulge as if he were trying to exhale and his hand was in the way. When he finally took his hand away, he said, "Why didn't you tell me what happened?"

"You always wear that shirt. What was it you called it when you gave it to me? Oh, yes, your lodge shirt. You are so set in your ways that I hoped to get by with it and then go into town and see if I could get you another one."

Benjamin had stiffened when she said he was set in his ways. Of course, he was. Life was supposed to be predictable. That's what made it comfortable. But when she had added that she planned to replace the shirt, he relaxed.

"I reckon you meant well. Just don't ever up and do anything like that again."

Bevin clasped her hands in front of her and kept her back straight. "You needn't worry, I shan't."

She was almost out of the room when that grating voice hailed her back.

"Bevin, my socks? You haven't touched them. And my lamp, what's happened to my lamp?"

Her voice icy, she said, "I was too tired to get to your socks. And as for your lamp, that is how your shirt got scorched. Prudence had an accident and I rushed in to her aid. Now, I am going to bed. Good night, Benjamin." She turned and left him with his mouth agape.

Will had been lying on his bed, unable to sleep, listening to the angry exchange. Bevin O'Dea seemed to be regarnering some of the backbone she had displayed when he'd first met the lady. The irony of it made him smile. That wasn't going to set well with Benjamin at all. Perhaps he should hang around until they were actually wed.

Benjamin was gathering up his socks as Will joined him. "Hear your lodge meeting didn't go so well."

Benjamin looked up and scowled. "My relationship with my bride-to-be is none of your business. What are you doing up?"

Will took a seat and crossed his legs. "Wanted to talk to you about selling my half of the farm."

Benjamin immediately forgot about the socks. He settled across from William. "So, you have finally realized that there's no place for you here."

311

"Let's just say I've finally come to terms with my past. I hope you can come to terms with yours."

Benjamin fumed inside. "There's nothing I'd change. I'm satisfied with mine."

"Pity. Hoped you'd realized how set in your ways you are and decided to loosen up a bit."

Benjamin's scowl deepened. Bevin had used the very same words to describe him earlier. The notion that they might have been discussing him disturbed him, and he wondered what else they might have been discussing.

"How much?" Benjamin ground out.

"I'd say you have a long way to go before you could be considered halfway reasonable."

For the second time tonight Benjamin's face flamed. "No! How much for your half?"

Unaffected by Benjamin's display of temper, Will shrugged. "Thought you could use a little advice, is all."

"Damn it! I'm not interested in your advice. Name your price so we can get this over with."

Will removed the paper the lawyer had prepared for him and handed it to Benjamin. "Bob Campbell said it's a fair price."

Benjamin studied the document, then handed it back. "You know damn well the farm wouldn't bring that much on the open market."

"You might as well calm down, Ben. That's the price."

"I won't pay it!"

"Then, until I can find someone who might be interested, guess we'll have to put up with each other a little longer."

"That's blackmail, you son of a bitch!"

Will's easy expression hardened into granite, and

he rose to stand over Benjamin. In a harsh tone, Will snarled, "I don't give a damn what you call me, but don't you ever make that kind of reference to my mother again. I won't let it pass next time."

Benjamin immediately realized his error. "Didn't mean anything toward Mary. You know I liked her."

"That's the price. Take it or leave it."

Will left Benjamin with something else to think about.

Bevin was sleeping fitfully when Prudence floated into the room, humming to herself. Bevin rose up on an elbow and looked at the clock. It was after two A.M. She watched Prudence dance through her nightly ablutions.

"You must have had a nice time tonight. Did you get Johnny tucked in?"

Prudence swung around and lit the lamp. "I am sorry, Evvie. I did not mean to awaken you. The Kruegers invited Johnny to visit for a few days. I said he could stay until after church Sunday. He was wearing his good clothes, and the Kruegers said he could wear the extra pair of overalls they bought Tara. I do hope it is all right with you. Johnny and Tara are such fast friends that—"

"Pru, you do not have to explain. It's fine with me."

Prudence put her hand over her heart and exhaled a long breath. "Thank goodness." Then she smiled and her face glowed. "Oh, Evvie, I had a truly wonderful time tonight."

"I am so happy for you," Bevin replied, thinking about her own evening.

"How was your evening with Will?" Prudence

asked.

Bevin put on a brave smile. She had hoped Prudence would not ask. "We have an understanding."

"Then you are not going to marry Benjamin?" Prudence blurted out.

"Of course I am going to marry Benjamin."

Bevin spoke with such conviction that Prudence took a step backward. "I am sorry, Evvie. I did not mean anything to im—"

Again, Bevin interrupted the girl. "Pru, tell me about your evening."

The dreamy glow came back to Prudence's face. "Patrick kissed me." She tittered. "It was truly so wonderful."

Bevin propped herself up against her pillow. "It sounds serious."

"It is. Patrick asked if he could formally court me."

A troubled expression came to Bevin's countenance. "Pru, you know Patrick is a farmer. He has no recollection of city life. Farmers can be pretty set in their ways. Listening to Patrick talk this past week, I do not think he would embrace any other kind of life."

"Oh, no. Someday he is going to have the best farm in the whole state of Missouri."

"Prudence, your family is expecting you to return home soon."

"You only use my given name when I have done something wrong. Evvie, we have done nothing wrong. My family expects me to marry. That, I intend to do."

Dread replaced Bevin's troubled expression. "Patrick has not asked you to marry him, has he?"

"Not yet, but I truly believe he is going to. And I intend to say yes when he does," Prudence said

314

proudly, then dropped her eyes.

"Perhaps you should reconsider. You know nothing about farm life. You have always lived in luxury. Your family will never approve."

Prudence would not look at her friend. She had always taken Bevin's advice. Bevin was her idol. But this time Prudence had made up her own mind. She loved Patrick and was not going to be deterred by anyone.

"Evvie, please understand," Prudence begged. "My family has always controlled my life. I have been told when to rise, when to go to bed, when and what to eat, how much, with whom; I have been told what I can say and what I cannot; whom I may befriend and whom I may not. Even permission to go on this trip with you was granted only after a lengthy discussion. Every aspect of my life, up until now, has been decided for me. This time it does not matter whether my family approves or not."

"Perhaps you should at least consider all the ramifications first."

Prudence swallowed down the remainder of her entreaty. She desperately wanted Bevin's blessing, her understanding and support. Prudence's thoughts shifted to how she had always tried to be like Bevin. Bevin made her own choices and clung to them. Prudence licked her lips. She was going to remain true to the choice she had made. She forced her gaze level with Bevin's.

"I have already considered all the *ramifications*. I love Patrick, truly I do."

Bevin was growing weary. "But you have only known him for such a short time."

"The length of time does not matter. I know all I need to know; I know what is in his heart."

Bevin squeezed her eyes shut and pinched the bridge of her nose. This conversation was leading nowhere. Prudence was quite determined. Bevin considered conceding defeat, but she had a responsibility to uphold. She had promised to watch out for the girl.

"I promised your parents that I—"

"I am releasing you from your promise. Tomorrow morning I shall go into town and send my family a telegram informing them that I intend to control my own life."

"What if Patrick does not ask you to marry him? Then what are you going to do?"

"He will," Prudence stated flatly.

Prudence went over and perched on the edge of the bed. She reached out and placed a hand on Bevin's arm.

"I thought you would be happy for us," Prudence cried. "Patrick is your brother. I thought you would love him as much as I do, you have searched for him for so long."

Bevin released a breath. "Oh, Pru, I do love Patrick. I am just concerned for your happiness. Patrick has been an angry young man for a long time. You can't be sure whether that anger will come back."

Prudence brightened at once and let their prior conversation melt from her mind. "If that truly is all that is bothering you, you need not worry a second longer."

"I suppose it wouldn't do me any good anyway." Bevin conceded defeat, shaking her head. "I simply pray you are making the right decision."

"I am. Patrick is not angry at all anymore. We've talked about his childhood. He said he was furious at first when he discovered you were coming here, but he has spent hours with Will."

"With Will?" There it was again: Will's name. Why did he have to keep intruding into every facet of her life!

"Oh, my, yes. Will made it a point to go to the Kruegers' farm and pay a call on Patrick. Will spent hours and hours convincing Patrick how hard you tried to find him. Will even shared his own childhood with Patrick and forced him to come to terms with his feelings . . ."

As Bevin listened, she could not help but be struck by what Prudence said. Will had wanted Bevin to come to terms with her feelings as well. Was she ever going to be able to put Will from her mind? She shifted her attention back to Prudence.

". . . Will has done so much. I do not know how Patrick and I will ever be able to thank him."

"I am certain you have given it consideration."

Prudence's eyes rounded. "Oh, my. I hope you do not think I have been trying to convince you to change your mind about Benjamin because Patrick and I owe Will our gratitude."

Why did the conversation have to continue to focus on Will? In an effort to lay to rest once and for all, all ideas Prudence had harbored concerning her future, Bevin sternly said, "I have no intention of ever changing my mind. Benjamin meets my requirements most satisfactorily."

Before Prudence could stop to consider weighing the gravity of her response, she burst out, "Unlike you, I, at least, intend to marry the man I love."

Chapter Thirty-two

During the next week Bevin saw little of Benjamin. He was out doing chores long before she arose, then spent the rest of his time getting ready for the fair to be held in St. Louis. To add to the tension, Benjamin had gotten a lower price than he had expected for his new corn and was in a constant foul mood lately.

"Forty cents a bushel!" he'd grumbled. "How am I expected to buy William out if that's all I get for my labor?"

Bevin's breath caught when she heard that Will had actually approached Benjamin about selling. She had not expected Will to go through with it so soon, and it bothered her.

Her wedding date was creeping up, and the closer it came, the more unsure she felt. Benjamin had enticed the Kruegers into keeping Johnny until the fair was over, which seemed to Bevin he was merely getting the boy out of his way. Will continually turned up wherever Bevin seemed to be with that I-warned-you expression on his face.

Prudence had sent the telegram to her family and had been ordered home immediately; she tore it up. Bevin had worried about the growing closeness between her brother and Prudence, but watching them together evening after evening gradually proved that what they had was very special indeed. All their billing and cooing only served to cause Bevin to reflect on her own engagement and life until she decided she needed more time to think about it.

It seemed that no matter when Bevin attempted to talk to Benjamin about postponing their wedding, she was thwarted by one excuse after another. And to make matters worse, the one day Benjamin had come back to the house for the noonday meal, Gretchen was sitting in the kitchen darning his socks. He had given Bevin an accusatory look, eaten in silence, and returned to work.

After Benjamin was gone, Bevin turned to Gretchen. "I know we didn't talk much about it a couple of weeks ago, but you really do love Benjamin, don't you?"

Startled by Bevin's candid remark, Gretchen pricked her finger with the darning needle. "Ouch!" She sucked on the bleeding finger. "He is going to marry you," Gretchen finally said, hoping the awkward moment would pass.

"I was suppose to mend those socks a week ago. Here you sit happily doing it. Gretchen, every stitch you take demonstrates it's done with love. Why, look at the extra pains you've taken to keep house for Benjamin since his father died."

"Ma just taught me well."

"Gretchen, please, let's be honest with each other."

Gretchen set the sock she'd been working on aside. "All right, I fancy since you have a mind to we might just as well get it all out into the open."

"May I ask you a difficult question?"

"Reckon you might just as well."

"Why didn't Benjamin ask you to marry him?"

"He's always thought of me as his friends' child," she answered dejectedly.

"Would you like to be considered more?"

Gretchen looked suspicious. "What does it matter? He is going to marry you in two weeks."

"I have a confession to make, if you promise to keep it between us."

Gretchen scooted forward in her chair, her face expectant and hopeful. "I promise."

"I care a great deal about Benjamin."

Gretchen's face fell. "Oh."

"Gretchen, I want Benjamin to be happy." Bevin's resurgence of nerve failed her. She had no right to raise Gretchen's hopes, since she had not reached a final decision yet. So she said, "I would deem it an honor if you would agree to be part of our wedding party."

Tears filled Gretchen's eyes. She tried to blink them back. "Of course, I'd be obliged to."

"Thank you."

"I fancy I must be heading back. I got to help Ma out. She's baking her favorite pies to enter in the fair."

Bevin watched the girl hurry from the house and down the drive. Silently, Bevin berated herself. She had almost confided in the girl her uncertainty about going through with the wedding. If she did indeed have a change of heart, she owed it to Benjamin to speak with him first.

Could she throw all her carefully executed plans away?

Since the night Will had tried to force her to face her feelings, and Prudence had made that telling remark that at least she was marrying someone she loved, Bevin had been tortured by her conscience.

Bevin went into the parlor and paced back and forth. There was no easy decision. Whatever she decided to do someone would be hurt. But the longer she resided here, the further convinced she was that she needed more time to sort through the mire.

By suppertime, Bevin was not sure whether she should cheer that Prudence had already left with Patrick for the evening, and Will had announced he had business in town, or whether her nerves would get the best of her.

Right on time, Benjamin came into the kitchen and washed up. Supper was on the table. He sat down without formality and began to eat.

Bevin hardly touched a bite. She waited until Benjamin sopped up the last of the gravy with his bread. He ate it, then leaned back in his chair.

"Good meal."

"I'm glad you enjoyed it."

He grabbed a toothpick from the holder and stuck it between his teeth. "Yes, well, I'd best be getting back out to the barn. I aim to take a prize for my mules this year."

He stood up.

"Benjamin, could we talk first?"

"You know the fair starts the end of the week. Can't it keep?"

"No, it can't." Bevin frowned at how easy he set aside her needs for his own without first bothering to find out the merit of her request.

Benjamin lifted a brow and sat back down. "I always try to tote fair. What is it?"

Bevin rather would have had this conversation in the parlor, but while she had his attention she must not waste precious time. She tented her fingers to keep from fidgeting. What was wrong with her? She had always spoken her mind.

"Benjamin, we have exchanged letters and I thought our goals were similar. I came to Bowling Green to marry you and be reunited with my brother—"

Benjamin frowned. "Don't beat around the bush, Bevin. What are you trying to say?"

"If you will give me a chance, I'm coming to the point of our conversation. We have not spent much time getting to know each other, and I believe we both have adjustments to make; therefore, I think it would be in our best interests if we postpone the wedding."

He leaped to his feet; his face a mass of tense muscles. "What?"

"We should post—"

"It's William, isn't it! He has been talking against me and put doubt in your head, hasn't he?"

"No," she cried.

He plunked back down on the chair and slammed his fists on the table. "Why then?"

"You are raising your voice to me again."

Benjamin softened. "I'm sorry, Bevin. I don't usually react this way. You see, this is quite a shock. I know I'm not much with words, but from the first moment I laid eyes on you, even before, I have loved you and known you were the one I have waited for all my life.

"We've had a lot of outside distractions. My stepbrother hasn't made it any easier. The boy you brought along with you, I've accepted." The thought about how he had even gone into town and started the paperwork to adopt the child when he had made up his mind to send Johnny away, flashed through

322

Benjamin's mind. "I admit it was hard, but I'm letting the boy stay for your sake. I thought that would make you happy."

"It does."

"And your friend, Prudence, I took her under my roof so you'd have her with you until we marry. I even saw to it that Gretchen came over to help you adjust. And I know the community will accept you as soon as you're my wife; they just need a little time." He ran his fingers through his hair. "With me, you'll have everything you wrote in your letters that is important to you: security, a home, a family. I know the farm demands a lot of my time, but you knew that before you came out here. It's hard work. It's worth it, because we are building something to leave to our children. Bevin, what more can I do?"

His declaration made her feel loathsome. "I don't know."

"Then think about it before we postpone our wedding. I'm sure you will realize that you're just a little nervous. I know if you think about it, you'll be just as sure as I am that our marriage is the right thing."

Bevin opened her mouth, but Benjamin held up a hand to stop her. "No, don't say any more now. After the fair is over we'll work this all out, you'll see."

Once Benjamin had left, Bevin rested her head on her hands. Benjamin loved her. She had begun their conversation to give herself more time to work through her feelings. Benjamin's declaration had merely served to further complicate her life. He had presented such convincing arguments to go ahead with the wedding.

Two men love you. You never thought much about love before, did you? You have said it is not for you. Now you are going to have to face up to it. You are going to have to decide what is most important, and you do not have a lot of time to do it in, so you best get busy.

Her head was hammering so loudly she did not hear the carriage pull up out front. Bevin was clearing the supper dishes away when pounding at the front door broke her concentration.

"Anybody home in there?" came the annoyed voice.

Bevin wiped her hands on her apron and hurried to the door. Aunt Bessie stood on the porch, leaning heavily on her cane.

"Aunt Bessie, what are you doing here? I—I mean I am happy you have stopped by."

She shook her cane at Bevin. "Where you been? I been pounding for a coon's age."

"I was in the back of the house."

"You gonna leave an old lady standin' out here, or you goin' to invite me in, deary?"

"Please, do come in. I'm afraid Benjamin is busy in the barn getting ready for the fair in Saint Louis—"

"Cain't reason why the boy insists on going to that tower of evil for the fair yearly."

"I can go call him."

"I did not come here to talk to Benjamin. I came to talk to you."

Once they settled in the parlor and Aunt Bessie turned down Bevin's offer of coffee and cornstarch cake, Bevin underwent the old woman's scrutiny as long as she could stand it.

"You said you came to speak with me?"

"You surely are a well-composed young lady, although purely a mite more meat wouldn't hurt you none. Most 'round these parts are a sturdy lot."

"Aunt Bessie, I do not mean to be rude, but I am

certain you did not come out to discuss my anatomy."

Aunt Bessie waved her off. "Pshaw, of course not. I didn't get all gussied up just to come calling neither."

"Then why did you come?"

"I swar, you're a gutsy little thing, you are. Came to fetch you so you can go with me to the local Patrons of Husbandry get-together. It'll show the rest of them old biddies that you're one of us."

"Patrons of Husbandry?"

"Hain't Benjamin told you nothin'? The grange. We're gettin' organized to band together so no one puts it to the farmers anymore."

Bevin's head had been spinning before the dear old soul showed up. She was not sure she was up to going through another evening trying to convince the women of the community to accept her. And she wasn't even sure she cared whether they did or not.

"Quit sittin' there like a bump on a horse's rump. Go tell Benjamin you're steppin' out tonight, get rid of that apron and grab your coat."

"I'm not—"

"Don't go givin' me no backtalk, deary. I won't take no for an answer. Folks need a better look-see at you. Now, hurry yourself along. You don't want to keep an old lady waitin' for you. I'm not gettin' no younger, you know."

There was no arguing with Aunt Bessie. Bevin went out to the barn to inform Benjamin. He was currying one of his mules. He looked up as she approached.

"I'm glad you came out to join me," he said with a hopeful smile. "Does it mean that our talk earlier helped you to realize what we have?"

Bevin ignored his question. "Benjamin, Aunt Bessie is in the house. She's invited me to attend the Patrons of Husbandry meeting in town with her. I tried to beg off, but she would not hear of it."

"Glad she thought to take you under her wing. It'll be a good opportunity for you to feel more a part of folks' lives in these parts. Aunt Bessie'll see to that. People listen when she talks."

"Yes. I noticed that at the Calico Ball. She is quite a character."

"She's kind of an institution around here. Comes from one of Bowling Green's first families."

"Benjamin, I am not sure I should go tonight."

"Nonsense. Going out tonight should help you make the right decision."

Chapter Thirty-three

Bevin sat on the hard chair at the meeting for what seemed like an eternity. The room was filled with women who had come to hear Miss Carrie Hull, the niece of Oliver Kelley, an organizer of the national movement. Bevin felt stifled in the stuffy atmosphere. She did not pretend to understand all the issues the eloquent speaker addressed. Nor did she share the rousing enthusiasm over issues such as mutual insurance rates and cooperative banking, since she doubted a man like Benjamin would readily allow her to share in those matters anyway.

Once the meeting was over, Bevin again felt she had been up for inspection and found little common ground with the farmers' wives. They sat around discussing their preserves, quilts and handicrafts which they were entering in the fair.

Bevin climbed into the buggy next to Aunt Bessie and waited patiently for the woman to speak first as they headed back toward the farm in the dim glow of moonlight. It was cold and Bevin gratefully accepted sharing the use of the woman's wool lap robe.

"You didn't say much tonight, deary," Aunt Bessie reproved. "You're goin' to have to learn to speak up a mite or folks won't never come to know you."

Bevin sighed. "I don't know much about farming, and I have nothing to enter in the fair, so I thought it wiser to listen and learn."

Aunt Bessie snapped the reins over the horse's rump. "Git up, there." She took her attention off the road and turned to Bevin. "Mind you, I understand. It's most natural not to speak your piece if you got nothin' to add, but you got to take up some womanly pastimes if you ever hope to feel to home here."

Bevin's jaw tightened. She knew Aunt Bessie meant well, but Bevin was growing weary of everyone telling her she had to change. Why couldn't people accept her the way she did others?

"Why are you going to so much trouble for me?" Bevin questioned.

" 'Cause I heard you got spunk. I figgered any little girl who could get Benjamin Straub to the altar had to have a lot of grit. Gretchen Krueger's tried hard enough all these years and it hain't got her nowhere. 'Course a body knows that you cain't go chasin' after a man 'cause it's the man what likes to do the chasin'. Just like when my dear departed husband Walter and I was sparkin'. . . ."

Bevin listened to the old woman reminisce. Aunt Bessie was so caught up in her past that she did not see the craggy rock in the road. The buggy hit it with a thud. The wheel broke, tipping the buggy and sending the two women into the dust. To Bevin's surprise, Aunt Bessie grabbed her cane and was the first one to her feet.

"You hurt, deary?"

"No, how about you?" Bevin moved to check the old woman, but she batted Bevin's hand away.

"Hain't nothin' wrong with me that paying closer mind to the road wouldn't of cured."

328

"Why don't you stay here with the wagon, and I shall walk back to town for help."

"You expect me to roost here while you go fetch the fellers from town?"

"Yes, I do," Bevin said with authority in her voice. "And I do not want any backtalk from you."

Aunt Bessie rolled her eyes. "Well now, Walter, do you hear the girl?" She let out a hardy laugh. "I'm indebted to you, deary. Have to admit I daren't try to trail along with you. I'd only slow you down."

Aunt Bessie waved her cane in the direction of town. "Hurry along now."

Bevin hesitated. "You will be all right until I return, won't you?"

"I hain't scairt. Just don't be dawdling."

"I won't," Bevin promised, gave the woman a hug and hurried back in the direction from which they had come.

"Keep to the middle of the road!" Aunt Bessie called out.

As Bevin headed back to town, she figured they could not have gone much more than a mile or two before the accident. Night engulfed her and she realized she was all alone in the middle of nowhere. The night sounds grew eerier; bushes took on lurking shapes, and Bevin began to imagine unspeakable horrors.

She picked up her pace.

You are a city-girl. What are you doing out here? You are used to walking with an escort along streets at night lit by lamps. Is this the type of thing you want to get used to?

Bevin was never so happy when she heard a faint whistle coupled with the snort of a horse.

Her heart began to pound and she ran toward the sounds, waving. "Thank goodness. Hello! Hello! We

329

need help!"

The dark, shadowy figure headed toward her at a fast clip. Bevin stopped to catch her breath. When he reached her, he asked, "What's wrong?"

Bevin's head snapped up. "Will?"

"Were you expecting someone else?"

Bevin clenched her hands. He was the last person she needed to see tonight. "Hoping would be a much more appropriate term, I believe."

Will dismounted and stood, staring down at Bevin. He could make out the outline of her silhouette. Her features were shadowed, but he imagined her snapping blue eyes, full lips and the inviting freckles across her upturned nose.

"Never imagined I'd see you out on the road late at night. You decide to walk out on Benjamin after finally coming to your senses and telling him you changed your mind?"

"Why did you have to happen along?" she said.

"I was headed back to the farm. But, of course, if you'd prefer, I'll get back on my horse and leave, so you can wait until someone else rides by or you make it back to town on foot."

"Nothing would suit me better," she snapped out, then silently berated herself.

"Never let it be said I didn't try to oblige a lady," he said with an easy smile he did not feel.

To her utter dismay, Will swung up into the saddle and wheeled his horse around. He looked back over his shoulder at her and tipped his hat. "Miss O'Dea."

Swallowing her pride, Bevin called out, "Will, we need your help."

Will pulled up on the reins. "Who is *we?*" he asked suspiciously.

"What does it matter? You can't leave us out here

alone at night."

Benjamin would not have allowed Bevin to walk into town alone . . . unless he had been hurt. "Is he hurt?"

"He?"

"Benjamin."

"I was with Aunt Bessie, if you must know before you force yourself to help us. And no, she was not hurt. We were just shaken up a bit when the wheel on her buggy broke."

Will had always liked the old gal. She was one of the few folks who had taken his side as a boy. "Chrissake, why didn't you say it was Aunt Bessie?"

"You did not give me the opportunity," she said. "Oh! What do you think you're doing?" she cried as he grabbed her around the waist and lifted her up in front of him.

"Would you rather run along behind me?"

Bevin tried to wiggle away from his hard length warming her back. Aunt Bessie was sure to disapprove of her sitting so close to Will Shoemaker.

"If you don't stop wiggling and sit still we might not make it back to the buggy for some time. You're giving me ideas."

"I would never give you such salacious ideas!" Bevin stiffened, although she could not deny the visions of them entering her head despite her efforts to suppress them.

"What is the cliché? Like minds think alike, or something like that. You thinking what I'm thinking?"

"I would never!" she protested, knowing the untruth of it.

" 'Fraid you already have. Or shall I say, we already have . . . more than think," he muttered to himself.

"Quit trying to be so cavalier and let's get back to Aunt Bessie. She must be terrified by now, out there all alone."

Will gave a laugh and nudged at the horse's flanks. "You obviously don't know much about Aunt Bessie. That old lady could scare the scalp off an Indian."

Aunt Bessie was sitting comfortably, puffing on a corncob pipe when Bevin and Will rode up. Bevin looked horrified. Will smirked.

"Aunt Bessie!" Bevin gasped and forgot all about the words she had exchanged with Will a few moments ago.

The old woman settled an annoyed gaze on the pair. "What's all the fuss and fume over? Cain't a body even take pleasure in a little smoke without the leaves turnin' their backs up to pray?"

Aunt Bessie tapped the ashes into the ground and smothered them with dirt before tucking the pipe away in her reticule. "Didn't expect you back so soon."

"I guess not," Bevin answered.

"Look, deary, at my age hain't much else I cain get away with."

Will moved to Bevin's side. Unconsciously, he draped an arm around Bevin's shoulders. "Don't worry, Bevin isn't going to tattle on you, Aunt Bessie."

Aunt Bessie was a wise old woman who did not miss much. "Fancy I should be thanking you. Instead, I'll continue to roost here while you two ride back yonder and send help out to me."

Bevin disengaged herself and knelt down to Aunt Bessie. "I'll stay with you," she announced, glaring up at Will.

332

"Won't hear of it. From what these old eyes see there's a few things you two got to work out away from the Straub farm." She pushed Bevin away from her. "Now, get you two so I can enjoy a few more puffs on my pipe before help arrives."

Bevin gained her feet while Will knelt down and kissed the old lady on the cheek. "You always were my champion."

"Don't you try sweet talkin' me, you young whippersnapper. Take the girl and be gone with you before I'm forced to remember who she's promised to."

Thoroughly confused, Bevin shook her head. "I don't understand."

"If you really don't, I think it is time you do before it's too late. You two got a private place to talk it out?"

"I'll find a place," Will said.

"Send some food back too. I feel like an old greedy gut."

"Will do."

"Good pun. Always liked them, you know." She laughed, then crinkled up her forehead. "Mind you take that little girl to my place and wait until I get there," the old woman directed.

Will gave Aunt Bessie a conspiratorial smile. "I'll follow your instructions to the letter, Aunt Bessie. Anything else?"

"Yes, don't tucker an old lady out with any more talkin'." Aunt Bessie dismissed them with a flip of the wrist and pulled out her pipe.

As Will escorted her to his horse, Bevin was astounded. She would never have believed that Aunt Bessie would bless, much less condone, her riding off with Will Shoemaker when in two weeks she was going to become Mrs. Benjamin Straub.

Will helped her up into the saddle and settled behind her. "We'll send someone right back for you."

The old woman was nodding and puffing on her pipe as they rode back toward town in silence.

She knows, you goose. Aunt Bessie knows there is something between you and Will. You are going to have to admit it to yourself. If she knows how many others do you think suspect? No wonder you're still an outsider. Think they'll ever accept knowing you are in love with one man, yet married another? You can set it straight tonight.

"You are being awfully quiet," Will said, cutting off Bevin's inner voice.

"I was just thinking."

"About what?"

"Aunt Bessie. I can't believe she sent me off with you. I thought she was a close friend of Benjamin's."

"She is. She also befriended me. She's a pretty perceptive old lady. She and her late husband had to fight against disapproving in-laws before they got married, so I guess one could say she has her own way of looking at things."

"Yes, so it appears."

"Why does that surprise you?"

"She is so respected in the community."

"Respect doesn't mean you always have to agree."

"Conform would be a better word."

Will laughed. "Aunt Bessie does . . . in her own way."

"Smoking a pipe's her own way, I suppose."

"You're finally coming to understand."

Bevin remained silent. She did not understand at all. It was not her place to try. She liked Aunt Bessie regardless of the old woman's vices.

They rode on without another word. The chill of the night turned cold and Will nudged the horse into a faster clip.

"You're being awfully quiet. You thinking again?" he asked.

"Yes."

It was a faraway reply, which caused Will to say, "Must be something terribly important. You sound as if you are far from here."

"Not so awfully far. And yes, I suppose it is important. Very."

"Oh? And just what were you thinking this time?"

"Something Benjamin said earlier."

Will let out a disgruntled sigh. "Benjamin, of course, I should've known."

Before he could stop himself, Will asked, "What about Benjamin?"

"He said that my going out tonight should help me make the right decision about my future with him."

Will's glum thoughts brightened. He was taking Bevin to Aunt Bessie's with the sole intention of convincing her to do just that.

Chapter Thirty-four

Bevin chose to remain in the background while Will got the livery owner out of bed, and sent him to Aunt Bessie's aid with a rented buggy. Bevin felt like a thief stealing into town, and was grateful that most of the inhabitants had gone home already. A man stumbled past her, and she pulled her cloak up around her head.

"I've got Aunt Bessie's rescue party on the way. Ready?" Bevin jumped at the sound of Will's voice.

It seemed to take an eternity to reach Aunt Bessie's place, although the delightful plain plank house was not far out of town. Will went inside and lit a lamp. Holding it, he came out to the porch.

There was a hint of amusement to his voice when he said, "You coming inside, or do you intend to stand in the yard until Aunt Bessie and her escort arrive?"

There would be too many questions if the livery man saw her at Aunt Bessie's. Bevin pushed past Will and sat down on the divan in the tidy little front room. She should have insisted he take her home.

That was not an option. How would she ever explain leaving with Aunt Bessie and returning with Will? Benjamin would be furious.

"I shouldn't be here," she said quietly when Will settled down on the other end of the divan.

"Suppose not. We could be here alone for hours. Why did you agree to come?"

"I'm not sure."

"Maybe it's our last chance for you to make that right decision tonight that you told me about earlier."

Bevin dropped her head into her hands. "My life was so simple until you barged into it. I knew exactly what I wanted and how I was going to spend the rest of my life. Now I—"

Will edged closer to Bevin. "Now you're no longer sure that the kind of life Benjamin will provide is what you want. You have learned that you have needs Benjamin can't meet."

He was forcing her to come to grips with her emotions. She could not fight it. "Yes, if you must hear me say it. Yes. I am helplessly drawn to you, but I can't simply dismiss Benjamin."

Will snorted. "Can't or won't? Bevin, you can't have it both ways."

"Are you asking me to chose between you two?"

She startled him with her question. He had been thinking a lot about Bevin and settling down, but he had not mentioned anything permanent. He had never proposed before; never even came close. He studied her. He was not sure what he saw in her eyes.

She was outspoken.

Any home they'd have would undoubtedly become a haven for homeless miniature hoodlums.

The longer he looked at her face he realized there was no doubt in his mind he could spend the rest of his life with this obstinate, wonderful woman. All he had to do was convince her to come to him without guarantees of the nice little life Benjamin offered.

He moved over until he was right next to her. This was a major step for him. He took her hand in his. "Yes, I guess I am."

Bevin's heart pounded. "Are you asking me to give up security with Benjamin for a questionable future with you?"

Why did she have to dwell on that damned word, *security?* A surge of impending disappointment gripped him. But he could not tell her about the telegram he had sent to Black Hawk. Not yet. He had not received an answer.

"I guess my future at this point is questionable. If you marry me you will have to share that future, whatever it may be."

"You are asking me to marry you?"

"If you want, I'll get down on bended knee."

"I have others to consider."

"Bevin, it's time you think about yourself first for once." He had been tempted to tell her he would happily accept Johnny, but he had to hear she would come to him without strings.

"No one can make you feel the way I do." He kissed her palm, the inside of her wrist. "Your heart knows it."

Bevin opened her mouth to protest; he kissed her protest away.

"Don't try to deny it," he whispered.

She threw her head back as his lips ignited a trail of fire down her neck. Not waiting for consent, he unbuttoned the front of her dress. His mouth moved back to her lips and buried his tongue inside her, while he slipped a hand inside her dress and caressed her rounded flesh.

An instant later, Bevin found herself sitting on Will's lap, his hand riding up her thigh. She could feel his arousal pressing against her bottom. Moistness surged from that intimate place, and she squirmed as his fingers touched her there. He slid inside her, cupping her mound with his palm and began to simulate a lover's rhythm.

On the edge of losing control, Bevin plucked at Will's trousers. Unable to release him, she began to stroke the straining bulge.

Will groaned. He caught her hand with his. "God, woman, you're incredible. I want you so bad I hurt."

"Then let me ease your pain," she purred.

He grinned at her. "Say yes to my proposal and I'll let you ease my pain twice a day for the rest of our lives."

His comment brought Bevin back to her senses. She shuddered. She had been about to give herself to him in the front room of Aunt Bessie's home. What kind of a woman was she? she wondered. She was engaged to one man, about to be married, and still she could not deny another man.

Will could see the hesitance in her face and sought to dispel it. "Bevin, I love you. Let me take you away from here. We'll make a new start, and you can even take the runt with us," he offered despite an earlier decision to wait until she accepted him.

Will's disclosure and willingness to include Johnny in their lives caused a floodgate within her to disintegrate and tears poured from her eyes.

"You would do that for me?" she sniffled.

He cupped her face, wiping away the tears with his thumbs. "I'd do anything for you."

"Then give me a little more time . . . please."

He tensed. Disappointment and fear that her insecurity would cause her to procrastinate until it was too late for them made his answer come out more harshly than intended. "You don't have much time."

"A few days. That's all I ask. A few more days," she pleaded.

His senses were raw. He had hoped she would make the right choice tonight, so they could tell Benjamin and be done with the unpleasantness Will knew would follow. "Why can't you answer me now?"

She in turn ran trembling fingers along his jaw. "I must have time to put everything in order in my mind and talk with Patrick. I love you for helping him accept me. Now that we are reunited I can't just announce that I am leaving again without first talking to him."

Will's heart hammered at his throat. "Then you have decided to come with me?"

She refused to answer. Not yet. Not until she had given Benjamin the courtesy he deserved of being told she could no longer marry him; she owed Benjamin that much.

Bevin pressed herself against Will's chest and whispered, "Hold me. I need you to hold me."

His hands shaking as if he were a young man with his first love, Will held her away from him while he reworked the buttons back into place and straightened her skirts. He then gathered her into his arms. "I'll hold you for the rest of your life if you'll let me."

God, he wanted to make love to her. He held her

to him, restraining himself. He unpinned her hair and wound a hand in the silken red strands, pressing her head against his chest. "All right, Bevin, I won't press you until after the fair; you'll have the time you need."

Will held Bevin, rocking her, until she slumped in his arms. She was asleep. He cradled his chin in her hair. She was an impossible, obstinate, wonderful woman. He was still holding her when Aunt Bessie, followed by the livery man burst through the door.

Aunt Bessie took one look at the pair on her divan and came up short. Clem Harris ran into the back of her. Aunt Bessie swung on him, using her superior height and girth to shield the couple from the town gossip.

She shook her cane. "Why, Clem Harris, I never thought you, of all people, would try to take liberties with an old lady who is all alone in this world."

Stunned, Clem backed out the door. "Now, Aunt Bessie, don't go building up such a head of steam. You know it was an accident, pure and simple."

"Clem Harris, don't you ever be tryin' to push your way into my front room again when I'm alone, or I'll march right on over to your little woman and tell her 'bout what you tried, you hear?"

Clem cursed Will Shoemaker under his breath for getting him out of a warm bed to help the old lady, only to be rewarded for his generosity with the end of a cane.

"Mind you, you best have my buggy back bright and early tomorrow mornin'."

"Yes, ma'am." Clem bobbed and scrambled out to his wagon.

Aunt Bessie stood on the porch and watched the

341

lanky man drive away before she went back inside.

Bevin and Will had broken apart. Bevin was sitting on the edge of the divan frantically repinning her mussed hair back into a knot. Aunt Bessie's gaze went to Will. He looked as if he had eaten her pet goldfish.

"Got to take a load off these old feet," Aunt Bessie said. She settled her large frame in an overstuffed chair and leaned her hands on her cane.

"Harris gone?" Will asked.

"Yeah! Clem left here with his tail between his legs. I wouldn't be worryin' about that one." She dismissed the topic with a shrug. "Well, you two finally reach an understandin'?"

Will cast Bevin a lopsided grin. "Not yet. But I'd say we're close."

Bevin sputtered, "I—I fell asleep." She leaped to her feet and nearly knocked over the fishbowl. "Sorry. I must be getting back to the farm before Benjamin comes looking for me."

"My, but you're one of the most confoundin' girls I've ever known in all my born days. Hain't you made up your mind yet?"

"Please, I must go."

Aunt Bessie threw up her hands. "A body's got to do what a body's got to do. Cain't escort you back, though. Won't be gettin' my buggy back till mornin'. You'd be best to stay here and go out to the farm with me tomorrow. Less questions than if Will takes you back at this hour."

Bevin glanced at the clock on the mantel. It was nearly three A.M. Benjamin would be rising soon. He could be up waiting for her. She could not let him find out about her and Will that way. She had to be the one to tell him. Her gaze trailed to Will. The way his smile widened she knew it would not bother him a hairpin's width if Benjamin saw them together.

"All right, I'll stay," Bevin announced.

"Good." Aunt Bessie pointed a gnarled finger at Will. "You get on out of here. Us ladies need our beauty sleep."

Will rose and kissed the old lady on the cheek. "Aunt Bessie, you are beautiful no matter how much sleep you get."

Will took a step toward Bevin.

Aunt Bessie pounded her cane on the floor. "I'll have none of that in my presence, young man. Now be gone with you, you flatterer, while my motherly instincts are workin'."

Once Will was gone, Bevin's attention snapped to Aunt Bessie. Bevin stared at the old lady. Although Bevin's mother was dead, Bevin felt a strong bond between herself and Aunt Bessie.

"Let's us not waste what's left of the night sittin' here. Follow me and I'll show you where you'll be restin' your head."

Bevin trailed the old dear. "You know, Aunt Bessie, my mother died before she could step foot in this country. She and my father dreamed of giving Patrick and me a good home. While we were on the ship coming to America, she used to sit me down and tell me about all the wonderful things we would have someday. I haven't had anyone to confide my dreams to since the sickness took her.

"For the first time since she died I feel that I have someone I can openly talk to like my own mother. You are an incredible lady." A sob broke from Bevin and she rushed to the old woman and hugged her.

"Thank you for caring, Aunt Bessie."

"Aw, child," Aunt Bessie wrapped her arms around Bevin, "Will and you are like my own. His ma was worked to the bone and didn't have much time for the boy when he was growin' up, so Bertha Krueger and I looked after him. He's the son my Walter and I never had. So it stands to measure that anyone he cares about would be like a daughter in this house. But after gettin' to know you, you're as dear as my own blood regardless of what you decide."

For the remainder of the night Bevin poured out her life's story to the old woman. She told of her dreams and fears, her feelings for Will, and her sense of duty toward Benjamin. She described Johnny and the hardships the child had endured. Aunt Bessie knew about Patrick and added to Bevin's understanding of her brother.

As the first rays of light came in through the curtained windows, Aunt Bessie said, "Well, will you just look. It's gettin' light and we hain't slept a wink yet. I cain't have you goin' back to the farm with dark circles under them blue eyes, and you need your rest. When you wake up we'll get us a hearty breakfast. By that time Clem should've returned my buggy and I can get you back to the farm. Get to bed now."

After Aunt Bessie left Bevin slipped into the cotton nightgown provided for her. She climbed under the covers, lay her head on the pillow, and closed her eyes. A smile hovered about her lips. It had been a night of tears and joy, of a bond forged and a decision made.

Bevin had just fallen asleep when heavy footfalls beating on the porch floorboards, and pounding on the door accompanied by the sounds of rain falling startled her awake.

"Aunt Bessie!" Benjamin beat against the door, his heart filled with worry and dread. "Aunt Bessie, let me in! I've got to see you . . . now!"

Chapter Thirty-five

Aunt Bessie gave a start when she opened the door and Benjamin shouldered past her. It was not like the boy to be so rude. His face was full of concern and worry, and he was wringing his hands. "Benjamin Straub, I hain't seen you display so much gumption since you was a boy and your pa seen to it that you hardened up."

He ignored her comment and shook off his soggy coat. "Damned rain was falling so hard when I started out that I nearly got bogged down in the mud."

She pounded her cane on the floor. "Watch your tongue, boy. You know better than to swar at the elements lest the storm hears you and retaliates."

Benjamin clenched his fists. "I didn't come here to talk about old wives' tales. Bevin's missing. She didn't come home last night."

There was a frantic tone to the boy's voice. Aunt Bessie rubbed her chin. "Lord save us all, you really got a hankerin' for the girl, don't you?"

Bevin had tiptoed to the doorway and stood hidden, dreading the answer. She had not given thought that the undemonstrative man could be so totally smitten with her that he would openly admit it to another person. He had declared his feelings to her, but this was more than she had suspected. Aunt Bessie's gaze shifted to her. Bevin brought her finger to her lips. She had to hear Benjamin's reply.

"She's going to become my wife," he cried.

"Boy, you sound to be in anguish. Why cain't you admit you upped and fell in love?"

Benjamin splayed his fingers through his hair. "If you must hear it before you answer my questions, yes, I love Bevin. Now, what happened last night? Why didn't she come home? Where is she? She's not hurt, is she?"

Bevin's hand flew to her throat. She had not considered this complication of Benjamin declaring his love for her in front of others before she could talk with him. She froze, holding her breath, until Aunt Bessie cleared her throat. When the old lady said, "Put your mind to rest, boy, she's fast asleep in my spare room," Bevin turned and fled to her bed. She pulled the covers up around her neck and listened.

With her cane Aunt Bessie blocked Benjamin's attempts to see for himself. "Take yourself back home. I'll bring her out later when it dries out a bit."

"Why didn't you bring her home last night?" Benjamin demanded, frustrated that he was being kept from making sure Bevin was all right.

Once Aunt Bessie set Benjamin's mind to rest and sent him back to his farm, she joined Bevin. She laid a comforting hand on Bevin's arm.

"Now, honey girl, seems my well-meanin' has made life a mite more complicated for you. Whatever the outcome, deary, mind you that it takes life to love. . . ."

* * *

347

Pleading a headache, Bevin took to her room, avoiding both men after she had returned to the farm. She forced herself to listen to Prudence's details of her courtship with Patrick. They seemed to be such a happy couple. She was glad Prudence and Patrick had found each other.

Prudence stopped fluttering about the room and climbed on the edge of Bevin's bed. She folded her legs beneath her skirt and leaned toward Bevin. "Oh Evvie, I know I said some dreadful things against Benjamin earlier." She hesitated and took a deep breath. "But I want to tell you that now I am so happy we are going to be living so close to one another."

Prudence did not notice Bevin's face fall. She had jumped back up and was twirling around with her hands clasped together. "Patrick has asked me to marry him! Evvie, we are going to be sisters and neighbors!" she squealed.

"I am so happy for you and Patrick, Pru." Bevin opened her arms and Prudence rushed forward. The two women hugged and cried. Prudence cried with joy; Bevin cried over the sad recognition that she would not be remaining close to them after all.

Prudence broke away and wiped her eyes. "It is truly going to be grand! I must hurry. I am going to meet Patrick soon." Prudence flounced from the room, and Bevin collapsed back against her pillows.

You are creating your own problems. You have already made your decision. You are not going to lose your brother again if you do not marry Benjamin. Tell Benjamin and get it over with; it is that simple, you silly goose.

A knock at the door ended her inner musings. Benjamin came in carrying a tray. "Brought you some soup."

348

"Oh, no," she moaned. Benjamin was the last person she expected to see.

"I know Prudence made it, but actually it's pretty tasty."

She sighed. He misunderstood. "Thank you for your thoughtfulness."

He set the tray in front of her and turned to leave. Bevin garnered her courage and set the tray aside. The tension of knowing what she had to do was too much; she had to get it over with.

"Benjamin, we need to talk."

"We will, Bevin, but right now you need your rest after the accident last night, and I'm off to Saint Louis with my mules. Intend to win first prize, you know. We'll spend time together on the way back from the fair. William is the only one I could get to bring you and Johnny downriver day after tomorrow when you're feeling better. Then we'll celebrate my winning you and at the fair."

Bevin's heart threatened to sink over being privy to this new, gentler side of Benjamin, and knowing that he loved her the way he did and she could not return that love.

"Couldn't Johnny and I go with Patrick and Prudence?" she asked, hoping to avoid Will while she finished sorting through everything.

"I wish," he mumbled. "No, they're going tomorrow morning with the Kruegers and there's no more room or I wouldn't leave you here. They're going to drop Johnny off on their way. I don't want you to stay alone." He was tempted to remain on the farm, but he was so sure he would win this year that despite burgeoning fears he had to go.

With Will.

He leaned over as if he were going to kiss her, but

withdrew at the last moment.

Bevin's heart did sink as she watched him leave.

Attempting to appear as cheery as possible, Bevin rose early to see Prudence off and greet the Kruegers when they arrived with Johnny. Johnny looked happier than she'd seen him for some time. So when he begged to be allowed to go with Tara and the Kruegers, Bevin relented after they assured her they would be able to squeeze him in.

"Won't that leave you alone here with Will Shoemaker?" Gretchen asked from her seat in the wagon wedged behind Prudence and Patrick.

"Ah, no, not actually," Bevin said awkwardly.

"Then what actually?" Gretchen pressed.

"Gretchen! I'm sure Bevin has made proper arrangements," Bertha broke in.

Bertha's intrusion gave Bevin the moment she needed to think of a plausible explanation. "Aunt Bessie will be out later; she promised to show me how to tat."

"If you pick up Aunt Bessie's skill, I'll bet at next year's fair, you'll take first prize for your handmade lace," Bertha commented.

"You can show me how to tat when we return," gushed Prudence, who had not given thought that Bevin would be alone with Will.

"Yes, I shall do that," Bevin said weakly and changed topics. "I shall see you all at the fair."

Silently questioning her own motives for remaining behind, Bevin waved as the wagon rumbled out the drive. She had troubled all last night what she should do after learning Benjamin loved her so deeply. She did not want to hurt the man. So why had she declined when she had the opportunity to avoid Will by going to the fair with the Kruegers?

When she stepped into the kitchen Will was sitting at the table, sipping a cup of coffee. "So, Aunt Bessie will be out later?"

Bevin sat down across the table from Will and poured herself a warming cup of coffee. "You heard."

"Yes."

"You were spying on us," she accused.

"No, just watching to see if you would decide to go with the Kruegers or stay with me." He reached out his hand and laid it over hers. "I'm glad you chose to remain," he said softly.

His thumbs rubbed over her knuckles; his touch was mesmerizing. All self-doubt Bevin'd had about the fib she told the Kruegers to stay on the farm with Will faded and she let her dilemma slip from her mind.

"I am too."

He squeezed her hand. There was a silent understanding between them. She glanced into brown eyes that radiated knowledge of the decision unspoken of between them. Without a word he knew she had chosen him. Their souls had forged a lasting bond.

"Patrick asked Prudence to marry him," she said, breaking the tension.

"They seem very much in love."

"Her parents do not seem to think so. Their wire demanded she return to Boston. Prudence tore it up. I am not sure how they will react when they receive her latest telegram, announcing her plans to be married soon."

"They will have to learn to accept it if they want to continue to have a good relationship with their daughter; she seems pretty determined."

"Yes, she told me how happy she and Patrick are that they're going to be neighbors with Benjamin and me."

A curtain dropped over his eyes and he withdrew his hand. "I guess I'd best get the chores done. Ezra Bruener's boy's going to come out and look after the farm while we're all at the fair."

Bevin rose and set her cup on the counter. "There's not a lot to do in the house. I'll help you."

Will gulped down the rest of his coffee. "Farm work's hard. It makes you old before your time. I'd prefer it if you stayed inside."

"I am not a delicate flower. I am a strong woman, Will. I'm used to hard work."

Will snorted. "Perhaps it would do you good to get a further taste of the backbreaking work required on a farm."

He set his cup next to hers and she touched his arm. "Helping you today is not going to be part of my decision. Please, do not try to sway me. You promised to give me a few days."

When he looked down at the tight set to her jaw, he wanted to whisk her away. "Bevin, I have every intention of trying to sway you, as you put it. Although I believe you have already made your decision. You just haven't got the nerve up to stop this madness."

Although she protested, she knew what he'd said was so. Nonetheless, Benjamin had the right to be told first. She picked up the milking pail. "Hadn't we better get started? Benjamin usually has the cows milked hours ago."

The day had been filled with a growing tension between them. Bevin felt it in Will's voice, his actions, the distance he kept trying to erase between them. After supper Will built a fire in the fireplace and an uneasy silence settled over them as Bevin curled up to read, and Will sat across from her staring openly.

"Why are you staring at me?" she finally asked when she could stand it no more.

"Just wondering if it is as hard for you as it is for me to sit in the same room together without touching?"

She dropped her eyes to the book in her lap before she leveled her gaze even with his again. She took a deep breath. "I guess there is no use trying to endure the strain until I can speak with Benjamin."

Will inched to the edge of his seat. "Meaning?"

"I think you know what I mean," she said in a mere whisper.

"I hope that I do. I would like to hear you say it, though."

Bevin sighed. She had known in her heart this morning when she'd allowed Johnny to go with the Kruegers that this would happen. She had wanted to be alone with Will. No, needed to be. And she was going to give him her answer.

"When I told you I needed time, I had already made up my mind. I know Benjamin has a tendency to be unyielding and rigid in his thinking, but he is a good man—"

"Bevin, don't—"

"No," she interrupted, "let me finish what I have to say."

There was trepidation in his eyes when she set the book aside.

"As I was saying, Benjamin is a good man. He helped me locate my brother and offered to take

Johnny into his home. It is all I could have ever hoped for," she paused to take a breath before continuing, "before I met you.

"At first you were an annoyance, and then I got to know you and realized that we share many things in common: the pain of our childhoods, values, love of Johnny. You went out of your way to help Patrick understand and accept our separation, and you even stepped aside for your stepbrother when you discovered Benjamin and I were to be married.

"I've watched you day after day. Johnny loves you, and even asked if you could be his father. I've tried to deny my feelings, but I can't. I do love you, and, after I talk to Benjamin, I plan to spend the rest of my life with you."

To Bevin's horror, Will sat in his chair and scratched his head. "Jesus," he puffed out.

"What's wrong? You haven't changed your mind, have you?"

"No, it's just that no woman has ever accepted my proposal before."

Bevin frowned before she realized he was teasing her. She arched a brow. "Oh? And just how many women have you proposed to before?"

"Let me see," he said and paused to look up at the ceiling as if he were doing a mental accounting.

Bevin sucked in her cheeks and watched him. His playfulness was something she would always love about the man, for it set aside thoughts of the unpleasantness that the upcoming days would hold.

"Must have been a vast number."

He looked at her with a boyish smile. "A good round figure, yes."

"Oh?" She tried to sound annoyed, but the word came out in more of a giggle.

"I didn't know you knew," he said.

"What?" she asked, confused. Then she realized what he meant: zero.

He was trying to keep a straight face. She threw fisted hands on her hips.

"William Parrish Shoemaker, if you do not come over here this very moment, I am just liable to change my mind."

Will was out of his seat and next to Bevin in a flash. He gave her a big bear hug. "Oh, no, you're not. I've never had to work so hard in my life to get such an obstinate, opinionated woman to marry me. And if you think I have any intention of letting you go now, you had better get it right out of your mind."

Bevin drew back. "Obstinate? Opinionated?"

He grinned. "And one hell of a fighter too."

Bevin opened her mouth to retort, but Will lay claim to her lips in a wet, searing kiss. When they finally came up for air, Bevin panted, "What are you waiting for?"

"Huh?"

"Why, Will Shoemaker, I never thought of you as slow. Aren't you going to spirit me off to your room?"

A pleased smile swept his face. His woman would never be cold and unresponsive like some he'd heard complain of their wives. An instant later his smile of pleasure was replaced by a sly grin.

"I thought maybe this time you were going to *spirit me* away."

"The way you're just sitting there, I might have to."

He opened his arms. "I'm all yours."

She kissed him. It was a teasing peck. "Not yet, but you will be soon."

Chapter Thirty-six

Will's heart was overflowing with love now that Bevin had made a declaration of her intentions. He jumped to his feet and lifted her high into his arms.

"You missed your chance to spirit me off to your room. Guess I'll have to take the initiative."

Bevin was so caught up in the monumental joy of sharing her feelings with Will that the nagging thoughts about Benjamin slid from her mind. She looped her arms around Will's neck and leaned her head against his chest. She could hear his heart racing.

Will bounded up the stairs.

"Be careful," Bevin squealed when he nearly tripped.

"Don't worry, nothing is going to keep me from showing you how happy you have made me."

They reached his room and he nudged the door open with his foot. He strode directly to the bed and set her down on the worn quilt. "I hope you realize that you won't be going anywhere for some time."

Bevin gazed up at him. Although the room was nearly dark, there was anticipation in the eyes that gazed back at her. He broke their line of vision and lit the lantern on the dresser.

"What are you doing?" she asked.

Holding the lantern, he moved back toward her. Her color had heightened on her cheeks and blotched her neck. "I want to know that I am giving you pleasure while we make love, and I want you to see the immense joy you give me. Does it disturb you?"

"No, I suppose not. This won't be the first time I have seen you."

He sent her a warm smile and wordlessly began to remove his clothing. Her eyes never wavered from him as he divested himself of his attire. In all his splendid male glory, he moved to her and kneeled down.

His fingers moved nimbly over her clothes until Bevin's naked flesh glowed in the lantern light. He joined her on the bed and rubbed his open palms over her heated body.

"Bevin—"

She pressed fingers to his lips. "Let's not talk just now,"— she murmured.

"Mmmm."

He removed the pins from her hair and spread it out on the pillow, delighting in the red silk of the curling strands. Bevin reached up and pulled him down to her.

Taking the lead, she kissed him. Her tongue inched his lips apart and twined with his. Will pressed tight against her and thrust his hips to hers, all the while scooping up a handful of soft breast.

Bevin's breath came in shallow pants as he increased the intensity of his exploration. An urgent desire grew in her breast, entrancing every nerve ending within her. She moaned softly and twisted so his fingers would not be hampered.

With unending gentleness he delved and probed

357

every curve, every peak, every valley. He enticed and teased, pleasured and demanded until Bevin thought she would explode. A rainbow of colors shot before her closed lids as her world became replete with love for this man. In turn she paid homage to his body with her own exploration, opening her eyes to watch the expression on his face as her fingers spread fire over him.

His eyes closed and she could see and feel him tense when she applied pressure to those most sensitive areas. After luxurious moments, he opened his heavy-lidded eyes and pulled her down to him.

An instant later he had rolled her onto her back. He ran a hand along her inner thigh and felt her arousal. "You are ready for me. Open wide for me, Bevin," he whispered in a husky voice.

Bevin reached for him and guided him deep within her.

She pulsed her muscles around him, drawing him in deeper.

He surged, lengthening within the tight fit of her and began to move rhythmically.

The sensations were profound as he immersed himself further and further into her with strokes so crushing that wave after wave of shimmering bursts orbited around her until powerful spasms grasped her. She cried out as she felt him pour himself into her before he collapsed with a groan.

When Bevin awoke she was snuggled against warm, naked flesh. She opened her eyes to come face to furred chest. She nuzzled her cheek against him. His masculine scent surrounded her and she was reminded of their lovemaking last night.

Will stirred and wrapped his arms around her. "Good morning."

She lifted her face to his. "Good morning."

Will gave her a lingering kiss, then rose. She sat up, but he plumped the pillows behind her and settled her back against them.

"You just stay put. I'm going to bring you breakfast in bed this morning."

"But I should get up so we can get started for Saint Louis."

Will's face fell. "I thought we'd forgo the fair and spend the time alone together."

"Benjamin's expecting us."

Will frowned and put on his clothes. "Bevin, I think we should wait until he gets back and then tell him together."

"No."

He perched on the edge of the bed and searched her eyes. "Why not?"

"Because he loves me, Will," she said softly, a hint of agony in her voice. "I thought my marriage to Benjamin was going to be one of mutual need and would be built on a foundation of consideration and respect. But he told me he loves me, and then I overheard him admit it to Aunt Bessie."

Will took a deep breath. "We have to tell him."

"I don't want to hurt him."

"You'll hurt him more if you continue to let him think you are going to marry him."

Bevin studied the ceiling. When she leveled her gaze with Will's, her face was full of anguish. "Perhaps I shouldn't go to the fair. I wouldn't want to ruin it for him." She hesitated, her eyes pleading with Will to understand. "I must be the one to tell Benjamin. And I owe it to him to tell him alone."

Will embraced her. Although he did not want her to shoulder the burden alone, he had too much respect for her. So he acceded to her wishes in spite of the feeling that it could only cause more pain.

The rest of the day they picnicked in a secluded spot away from reality and the boy hired to tend the farm while everyone was to be at the fair. Late in the afternoon, Will drove Bevin over to Aunt Bessie's place, since Bevin seemed to need another woman to talk to and Aunt Bessie was a good soul who could be trusted. He dropped her off and went into town to check on whether he had received an answer to the telegram he had sent to Black Hawk yet.

It was nearing dark when he picked Bevin up. "Have a good visit with the old girl?" he asked as they headed toward the farm.

"Aunt Bessie is wise beyond her years. She suggested I direct Benjamin's attention toward Gretchen where it belonged in the first place. She thinks I have made the right decision," Bevin added.

"Of course, so do I," Will said playfully and ducked when she teasingly tried to box his arm.

"I made her promise not to say anything; I expect the same from you."

"As long as you don't wait too long, you have my word."

Benjamin paced back and forth in front of his mules' stalls. The judging was about to begin and all he could think of was that he was here in St. Louis and his precious Bevin was alone back at the farm with his stepbrother. Johnny was supposed to have remained with Bevin, and when the boy showed up with the Kruegers Benjamin had nearly headed for home. He chided himself for being so foolish to leave Bevin at the farm while William was there despite the Kruegers' assurances that Aunt Bessie was going out to be with Bevin.

"Benjamin, come on, your mules are up next," Gretchen cried, running up behind Benjamin. When he turned to face her, she sobered. "What's the matter? You look like you did that time your favorite mule took sick."

Benjamin looked at the girl. Concern set her features. "You haven't seen Bevin, have you? She should have been here by now."

She set a comforting hand on his arm. "Stop fretting. She and Will were probably just delayed."

"That's what I'm worried about," he mumbled and let Gretchen lead him toward the judging.

Once the judging got underway, Benjamin forced his concern for his bride-to-be out of his mind.

Gretchen held tight to Benjamin's arm as, one by one, the entries were inspected. Although he tried to keep his attention directed toward the animals, Benjamin's consciousness caught at the ample breast pressed into his arm.

When he'd glimpsed Gretchen's bosom in the barn at the Kruegers' farm he had thought of Bevin. This time he discovered that it was Gretchen holding him enthralled by her woman's endowments and enthusiasm over all the hard work he had put in to readying his mules for the fair.

He was starting to sweat as it came down to three mules, but not over the contest. He was ashamed that visions of Gretchen's breasts kept entering his mind.

"Oh, Benjamin," Gretchen cried and threw her arms around his neck, driving both breasts into his chest. "You won. You took first place."

Without warning, she kissed him.

Benjamin felt a foreign sensation slide down his spine. Quickly he held her from him. Her face was guileless and held only adoration which confused him. He had never thought of her as anyone other than his friends' daughter before.

"Benjamin, you won. I knew you raised the best mules in the state," she gushed. When he did not move, she urged, "Go collect your ribbon."

Benjamin snapped his head to chase away such sinful thoughts and stepped up to receive his accolades. Afterward he returned to Gretchen and was immediately surrounded by the Kruegers and a host of well-wishers.

Benjamin was still basking in the warmth of victory when Prudence strolled up to him with Patrick and the children. Patrick congratulated Benjamin, and the men began a serious discussion of the farm implements and animals they had viewed.

Bertha tried to lead Prudence toward the baked goods, but Prudence would have none of it. She had worried all the way to St. Louis about leaving Bevin alone with Will Shoemaker, and Bevin had not arrived yet.

"Benjamin," Prudence said, interrupting. "I thought Bevin would be here by now."

Gretchen glowered at the birdlike young woman. Why did she have to remind him of the Irish woman?

"So did I," Benjamin said.

"Don't go worryin' about them none. Any number of things could've delayed them," Bertha interceded.

Benjamin had a faraway look in his eyes when he said, "Yes, any number of things."

"Perhaps we should send a telegram to the parson in Bowling Green and ask him to ride out to the farm and check," Prudence suggested.

Benjamin shot her an incredulous look. The last thing he needed would be for Parson Pryor to ride out to the farm and unearth the impropriety that Aunt Bessie might not be there and his bride-to-be was alone in the house with William Shoemaker, known ladies man.

Gretchen did not miss the tightening of Benjamin's jaw. She thought Bevin O'Dea a fool to jeopardize Benjamin's love. "There's no need to involve the parson," Gretchen offered.

"We'll be heading home tomorrow morning. No point fretting over something that probably's got a reasonable explanation," Patrick said, defending his sister.

"Patrick's right," added Asa. "Lets us mosey on over and take a look see at the rest of the livestock."

"I got my preserves entered," Bertha said. "And I expect to win first prize this year. So us ladies'll leave you men to the animals."

Benjamin watched the women and children weave their way through the throngs of people. In years past Benjamin took much pleasure from attending the fair, but not this year. Even winning with his mules did not excite him, and he had no desire to wait until tomorrow to head back to the farm.

"You comin', Benjamin?" Asa asked.

"No, I think I'd best head on home. You fellers mind bringing the mules back for me?"

Asa and Patrick looked at each other, and then at Benjamin. Asa patted Benjamin on the shoulder. "Glad to do it for you, Benjamin, if goin' home today is something you fancy you must do. But I don't

363

rightly think you got anything to worry about."

Benjamin ignored Asa's last comment. "Mind if I take one of your horses? You can hitch one of my mules to your wagon."

Asa shrugged. "Suit yourself."

"I'm indebted to you, Asa."

Patrick scratched his head as he watched Benjamin hurry off. "Don't know why he had to rush on back to the farm like he's doing. He shouldn't have nothing to be afraid of."

Asa lifted a brow. "That's most likely 'cause you don't know Will Shoemaker the way Benjamin does."

Chapter Thirty-seven

Benjamin drove the Kruegers' draft horse without his usual regard for the work animal. If there was one thing a farmer believed in, it was taking care of his work animals. Despite guilt, Benjamin stopped only long enough to water the horse, not even stopping to sleep.

All during the trip his mind shifted between disturbing pictures of William leading his precious Bevin astray to chastising himself for having such absurd visions, since he hoped in his heart that Bevin would never let a man like William influence her; Bevin was much too strong a lady for that.

The sun had set by the time Benjamin reached Pike County. He was careful to avoid Bowling Green; he did not want folks to think he was sneaking back to check on his bride-to-be. He was angry with himself since that was exactly what he was doing, and the very idea of having to creep up to his own farm infuriated him.

Benjamin pulled up on the reins a safe distance from the farmhouse when he noticed the warm yellow light glowing from the downstairs windows. Something in the back of his mind warned him to wait instead of riding in, despite a lifelong belief in adhering to a strict moral code of honesty and openness. He dismounted, tied the animal to a nearby shrub and moved stealthily toward the house until he reached the perfect vantage point from which to survey the goings-on unobserved. He pulled his heavy work coat up around his neck and waited.

Bevin finished the supper dishes, folded the dish towel and hung it on the rack. Will sat at the kitchen table, idly toying with a salt shaker until Bevin finished the chores. She took a chair at the table. Mounding the spilled salt, she pinched up some and threw it over her shoulder.

"Didn't know you were superstitious."

"I'm not actually, but I suppose it doesn't hurt to get all the help I can."

"I would've helped you with the dishes," he said, reaching out across the table to take her hand. He turned her palm up and rubbed his thumb along it. "I don't want those hands to get all rough and red."

Bevin smiled at him. "I've enjoyed being with you these last few days. It has been like having a home of our own."

Will had not received an answer to his telegram yet, so he could not assure her she would have a home of her own. "I'll always take care of you," he said. Then he turned serious. "Have you decided what you're going to say to Benjamin when he returns?"

Bevin pulled her hand back and clasped it with her other one over her mouth while she took a deep breath. "Can't we just pretend there is just us tonight?" she said in a pleading voice.

"If that's what you want."

"Thank you, Will."

"Sure." He flashed his eyebrows at her to lighten the mood. "Would you like to go out and sit on the swing and do a little sparking before it gets too cold?"

Bevin sent him one of her warmest smiles and tilted her head. "I'll get my shawl."

Benjamin's attention perked up when he saw William walk out onto the porch. Benjamin had been berating himself for a fool to be worrying when Bevin came out of the house and sat on the porch swing. Benjamin's breath caught and his eyes narrowed when Will settled next to her, ringing his arm around her shoulders. His blood pumping furiously through his veins, Benjamin crept closer until he was within earshot.

Will rocked his foot back and forth swaying the swing gently. "When I decided to accept my inheritance I never dreamed I'd end up meeting anyone like you."

Bevin recalled their first encounter with a grin. "I thought you were the rudest man alive."

"And I thought you were a sourpuss."

They laughed together in an easy camaraderie.

Bevin brushed back a lock of his hair that had fallen over his forehead. "I was."

"Never. You were and are a beautiful woman who would have grown old before your time on this farm."

A sad smile held her lips. "I like the farm."

"Yeah, there's nothing like slopping hogs, milking cows and cleaning out barn stalls to give one an appreciation for farm life."

"It's not all backbreaking work," she protested.

"No? You sure couldn't tell it by Benjamin."

Her face fell. "Please, let's not talk about Benjamin tonight."

367

"Okay." He hugged her and gave the swing a push with his heel, sending it swaying at a precarious angle.

They laughed congenially together.

Benjamin burned as he saw William nuzzle her neck; she did not try to discourage the man. He clenched his fists, blaming William's influence; William was turning Bevin against him. Benjamin held himself back until William turned Bevin's face to his and kissed her, his lips lingering on hers. Unable to control his fury any longer, Benjamin bounded from his hiding place and up onto the porch.

At the sudden rustle of shrubbery and pounding footfalls, Bevin and Will broke apart.

"Benjamin?" Bevin squeaked, horrified. She jumped to her feet and smoothed her aqua, ruffled silk.

Will stood up by Bevin's side. "What are you doing here?"

Benjamin's face flamed. "Don't you think I should be the one to ask the questions?" His eyes slid over the fancy dress Bevin was wearing. "What happened to the clothes I bought for you?"

All color drained from her face and a deep shame squeezed her heart. "I—"

"You don't owe him an explanation of what you choose to wear," Will said.

"You keep out of this," Benjamin hissed. His adrenaline was pumping and he itched to send William sprawling in the dirt.

The burgeoning tension threatened to overcome Bevin. She did not want this to happen, and she cursed herself for being so weak in spirit not to have told Benjamin before he found out this way.

" 'Fraid I can't do that, Benjamin," Will returned

darkly.

Bevin turned pleading eyes to Will before settling her vision on Benjamin. "Benjamin, we need to talk," she said softly and dropped her vision.

The harsh lines around Benjamin's mouth softened when he looked at Bevin. God help him, despite the full impact of what they had done, he still wanted that woman. "Go inside, Bevin."

"But Benja—"

"I said, go inside." His voice contained no rebuke, only disappointment. "Looks like this is between William and me after all."

Bevin stifled a cry and looked to Will. They exchanged guilty glances, then with a nod Will seemed to be attempting to reassure her. She looked at Benjamin. His stance was tense with leashed violence straining just beneath the surface of his being. She had never seen him display such emotion before, never thought him capable of it.

"Benjamin, please," she begged, fearing a confrontation between the two half siblings. "I am as much a part of this as Will."

Benjamin squeezed his eyes shut and shook his head before collapsing on the swing and dropping his head into the hands. "Why you, Bevin?" he groaned hoarsely.

Bevin reached out trembling fingers and placed them on Benjamin's shoulder. Her voice quivered with great emotion. "Oh, Dear Lord, I am so sorry. I never meant to hurt you."

Benjamin threw off her hand. His eyes were overly bright, his color high. "I can't talk to you right now. Go inside."

Bevin ached with shame and misery that she had not spoken with Benjamin first. She was not sorry for falling in love with Will, but she had never meant to cause Benjamin so much pain.

She stood in her place not certain what to do until Will urged quietly, "I think it would be a good idea if you left us alone."

Bevin covered her mouth, shook her head, and fled into the house.

Once the two men stood alone on the porch, Will faced Benjamin directly. "It wasn't Bevin's fault."

Benjamin got to his feet and glared into William's face. "I never thought it'd be her doing. I told you to keep away from her. But you had to go after her, didn't you?"

Will sighed. "That wasn't exactly the way it happened."

Benjamin would hear none of it. He cut off William's attempts at an explanation and poured out all the venom stored in his gut since they were children. Despite all the accusations and name-calling, Benjamin felt a portion of the responsibility bordered on his shoulders for this triangle.

Bevin was a city-girl, and Benjamin had expected her to behave as if she had lived her entire life on a farm. He had known she was having a difficult time being accepted by the closed attitudes of the community, and he should have made it easier for her. Silently he berated himself for not recognizing that Bevin had needed more support until she adjusted.

Benjamin could rationalize Bevin's behavior; she was only a mere, weak female who could not help herself and needed the influence of a strong male. But that did not excuse William's actions.

"My pa put a roof over your head, and even though you ran off I did the right thing by letting you know he had left you half the farm. Trying to take away my bride-to-be is how you repay me. . . ."

If their confrontation had not involved Bevin, Will would not have stood for Benjamin's tirade. But Will could not help but feel sympathy for his half brother. Bevin was a treasure for whom Will would give his life. So he let Benjamin vent all the anger and hurt that had festered for all these years.

Will listened without comment until Benjamin was through, then Will said, "Benjamin, I love Bevin. I didn't intend for it to happen. Even thought about getting back on the train when I learned she was your intended."

"Damn it, why didn't you!"

"Thought I could handle it, since Bevin and I had only shared a few pleasant conversations. If you'll remember, I tried to warn you that you couldn't treat her like one of your farm animals. She is a warm, loving woman and deserves someone who'll treasure her."

"And I suppose you think you're that someone?" Benjamin hissed.

"Yes, I do," Will said in a calm voice.

"Bevin is going to marry me!" Benjamin raised his voice. "I want you out of my house!"

Will squared his jaw. "I can see there is no use trying to reason with you now. Just remember, this is half my house, and unless Bevin asks me to leave, I'm not going anywhere without her."

"We'll just see about that!" Benjamin shoved past Will. He stopped at the door and ground out, "I planted some apple trees a few years back. They need to be picked during the next few days. Got to get them boxed up and ready to take into town to be shipped up north to the Dakotas. Since you own half the farm, you can take responsibility for seeing that

371

they get on the train. The boy can help you."

Benjamin slammed the door behind him without waiting for a reply.

Will rubbed his jaw. He knew Benjamin wanted him and Johnny away from the farm, so Benjamin would have an open field with Bevin. Bevin had wanted to speak to Benjamin alone. Will let out a puff of exasperation and sat down heavily on the swing. After mulling it over until he could see his breath, he figured he owed her that much. Although he did not like the feeling that somehow he was abandoning her to shoulder all the responsibility.

Bevin was lying across her bed when Benjamin rapped softly on the door and asked permission to enter. Quickly, she wiped away her tears and regained control. She moved over to the chair and sat with her back erect. "Come in."

Benjamin stood stiffly inside the door. His face was strained, his lips tight. "I was worried when you didn't show up at the fair. So I hurried back in case you needed me."

Bevin had expected him to rant at her. It would have been easier if he had accused her of breaking her promise. Then she could have apologized and explained. But he was acting as if nothing had happened. She struggled for the right words; nothing came to mind.

Shaking her head, she finally said, "Benjamin, we must talk." There was no easy way to say what had to be said.

Benjamin ran his fingers over his face and threw up his hand. "There's nothing to talk about."

Bevin took a deep breath. "What about Will and me? You saw us sitting together on the swing. You have to know that it wasn't all innocent. We shouldn't

372

have been there. We had no right."

Benjamin looked into that lovely face, those open blue eyes. He had always lived by principles, and this time when he should stand by those principles he found he could not turn from this woman. Despite the gnawing anger, the residue of betrayal that would haunt him, Benjamin garnered the courage to say, "I-I don't blame you."

"How can you not blame me?"

Not entirely sure he believed it himself, he said, "It wasn't your fault."

"Benjamin, I care for you. You are a good man. But Will is not all to blame. I am equally responsible."

Benjamin shook his head, refusing to listen to her defend his stepbrother. "No more. I don't want to hear any more of that kind of talk. We'll put this . . . this mistake behind us and pretend it never happened."

Bevin heaved a sigh. "But it did happen, Benjamin."

"It doesn't matter. The wedding will go on as scheduled." She started to protest again, but he held up a stilling hand. "No. You don't have to say another word. As far as I'm concerned, it's all settled," he said and turned from her before she could stop him.

After Benjamin had left, Bevin slumped in the chair. She felt totally drained. Nothing had been resolved. Benjamin had refused to listen. She should have insisted that he hear her out. She had not. Everything was more complicated than ever, and she was right in the middle of it.

Chapter Thirty-eight

Bevin put on a cheerful face when the others returned from the fair and filed into the parlor to enjoy some refreshments and share the latest gossip Benjamin missed by leaving early. Bertha was jubilant that her preserves had taken second place. Bubbling with enthusiasm over all the displays, Prudence sat next to Patrick. Johnny handed over Benjamin's first-place ribbon and rushed out of the house with Tara to be with Sourdough.

"You didn't tell me your mule won first prize," Bevin said without looking directly at Benjamin.

Gretchen watched the strained interactions between Benjamin and Bevin, and she wondered if anyone else noticed the change between them. Nor did she miss Will's absence.

"What happened to you, Evvie? We thought you and Will would meet us in St. Louis," Prudence probed, ignoring a warning look from Patrick.

Gretchen moved to the edge of her seat; Prudence had given voice to the question boiling in her throat.

"We . . . I—" Bevin began.

Benjamin intercepted Prudence's question. "Will discovered that the apples couldn't wait to be picked or we wouldn't be able to get them shipped up north

374

in time. Bevin stayed here and kept Aunt Bessie company since the old girl can't make the trip any longer."

Prudence's eyes grew wide with excitement. "Did she teach you how to tat?" She clasped her hands together. "Oh, won't you teach me? I saw the most lovely samples at the fair, and I am truly dying to learn."

Bevin shifted uneasily before she answered, "I am still learning. It takes time, Pru."

Bertha sent Bevin a queer look. "Of course it does." She jumped to her feet. "Come along, Asa, it's purt near time we got on home. We got chores to get back to. Bruener's boy couldn't've seen to it all, what with two farms to tend."

Bevin saw the Kruegers off with a grateful sigh that no one had seen fit to ask more than a passing question about her absence. Benjamin took Johnny to the barn with him, leaving Bevin alone to walk back to the house with Prudence.

"Evvie, Patrick and I have decided to ask Parson Pryor if he'll marry us next week. I know it is rather close to your own wedding, so I told Patrick I would ask you if you would mind or not."

"Are you sure you shouldn't try to reconcile with your parents again first?"

Prudence took on an unbending pose. "I am sure."

Bevin gave Prudence a sad smile. "Since your mind is made up, of course I don't mind. You can even wear the wedding dress I brought with me from Boston."

"But you will need it for your wedding. You would not want Benjamin to see me wearing it so soon before you are to be married." A troubled expression captured Prudence's normally animated face. She stopped, causing Bevin to stop beside her, and searched Bevin's face. "Is there something going on between you and Benjamin that you have not told me?"

Bevin sighed. "Why don't we go inside?"

Her brow dropped into a worried line as Prudence followed Bevin into the kitchen. Bevin started wiping down the drain board to keep busy while Prudence took a seat at the table and fidgeted with her fingers.

"Well? Are you going to tell me what is going on? I am going to be family soon."

Bevin dried her hands on the dish towel and joined Prudence.

Bevin tried to think of a tactful way to inform Prudence, but decided she might as well get it out into the open. "Benjamin came home early from the fair and caught Will and me on the porch swing together."

Prudence looked as if she were going to cry. "Oh, Evvie, I knew it! I told Patrick something like this was bound to happen when you remained behind with Will. Does Benjamin still want to marry you, Evvie? We are going to be neighbors, sisters, aren't we?" implored Prudence, beside herself now that her fears had been realized.

"Prudence, please, stop and calm down."

"What did Benjamin do?"

Bevin shrugged. "Nothing, really. He wouldn't hear an explanation. He wants to pretend that nothing happened and go ahead with the wedding."

"Thank God," breathed Prudence, slapping a hand to her heart. "Everything will be all right after all. Nothing has changed then." She looked hopeful.

Bevin shook her head. "No, Prudence, everything has changed. I am not going to marry Benjamin."

"I thought you said he still plans to go ahead with the wedding."

"He does. But I intend to talk to him after supper tonight, so I would appreciate it if you would take Johnny upstairs."

"What about Johnny? He thinks he is going to get to stay on the farm."

"Will and I are going to adopt him."

"Then will you be remaining in Bowling Green?"

"I don't know. We haven't discussed where we are going to live yet."

"But all your plans . . . we all were going to be so happy together. Oh, Evvie, how could you?" Prudence cried and ran from the room.

"Prudence," Bevin called after the girl.

Prudence ignored Bevin's plea and ran to her room.

"Where'd Miss Prudence go all upset?" asked Johnny, coming in with an armful of wood for the stove. "What's wrong with her? I thought she was all happy since she caught your brother."

"Prudence is upset because she hoped we would be neighbors."

Johnny dumped the wood in the box. A suspicious twist to his face, he moved closer to Bevin. "Ain't we?"

Bevin pulled the boy over to her and gave him a hug. She had not meant to have this conversation with the boy now, but nothing seemed to be happening in an ordered manner any longer. She took a breath. "Johnny, we won't be remaining on the farm after all."

"I knew it! That dumb, old Benjamin Straub don't want me. I knew he wouldn't let me stay. I knew it!" he cried and rushed off before Bevin could stop him and explain.

"Johnny, wait!"

The front door slammed.

Bevin ran after the boy, but by the time she reached the porch she only caught a glimpse of his shirttails as he disappeared down the drive. She sat heavily onto the swing. Each time she had attempted to explain about her love for Will she had been thwarted.

She pondered everything over for a long time. Perhaps she was being foolish to give up a secure life with Benjamin; practically everyone but Aunt Bessie seemed to think so. Oh, why did she have to fall in love with Will and complicate her life so!

"I finished the chores early so we could spend some time together," Benjamin said, startling Bevin out of her troubling thoughts.

Bevin's head snapped up. Benjamin was standing over her. He was all cleaned up and holding a few sprigs of flowers in his hand. "May I join you?"

Bevin nodded and he handed her the flowers as he sat down.

Last night Benjamin had remained awake, mulling everything over in his head. His thoughts had shifted from strangling Will and tossing Bevin and that brat out to keeping to what he had said to Bevin that it was all Will's fault.

After he had thought it through, he realized that he could never completely forgive the pair, but he had a position in the community to maintain and would not be put up to ridicule before his neighbors

378

and be told he should have known better than to try to marry an outsider. No, he'd decided, he and Bevin would make the best of their life together as his father had done with Will's mother.

"Thought you'd like the flowers," he said awkwardly.

"Yes, thank you. It was thoughtful of you. But, Benjamin, we can't act as if last night never happened because it did, and I must speak to you."

"I know. I was furious last night, but I've had time to think about it, and I have not changed my mind. We will still be married on schedule."

"I don't think you understand—"

"Yes, I do. Will swept you off your feet like he has so many impressionable young girls in the past. You didn't know what kind of man he is." She opened her mouth, but he shook his head. "No, let me finish. From your letters, I think I know what is important to you. You want to be near your brother. I can offer you that. You want security, companionship and a family. I can offer you those things, and I am willing to set aside the mistake you made, and as I said last night, we'll try to pretend it never happened."

Will had rounded the corner of the house and stood listening to the conversation as long as he could without comment.

"Benjamin," he said, stepping onto the porch, "Bevin and I did not make a mistake."

"Will, please," Bevin pleaded, beside herself with the agony of it all. "Benjamin and I must finish this conversation."

"I'm afraid I can't leave you alone to face this. I never should have agreed to go to the apple orchard."

Will boldly took up a position on the other side of

379

Bevin, leaving her sandwiched in between the two men.

Dread filled her so full that it threatened to cut off her voice.

Benjamin balled his fists, incensed. William's presence brought all the old hatreds to the surface. Without thinking it through, Benjamin jeered, "I'll pay the price you want for your half of the farm. But I want you off this land . . . now!"

"I accept your offer, but I am not leaving without Bevin. Whether you want to face it or not, Bevin and I are in love. I didn't start out to make it happen, but it did. I am sorry if I hurt you; I never meant to when I decided to return. I thought maybe we could put the past behind us. But, fact is, Bevin and I fell in love with each other, Benjamin."

Benjamin flew to his feet and swung around facing William. Benjamin's face turned ugly and he fought to temper the urge of erupting violence. "How do you think you are going to support a woman like Bevin?" he practically yelled.

"We'll work it out," Will said calmly, ignoring the challenge in Benjamin's voice.

"Bevin" — Benjamin swung on her out of desperation — "what about your promise to me? You owe me!"

"Oh, God, Benjamin, please don't do this," she begged. "Please don't let this come between what is left of the relationship between you and Will. Please, Benjamin, please."

Benjamin was yelling at the top of his lungs now. "My *stepbrother* and I have no relationship! And I am not doing anything! I am gone from the farm for a few days and return to find my bride-to-be in another man's arms, and you ask me not to mention your promise!"

"You can talk to me any way you want, but I won't have you yelling at Bevin that way," Will warned.

"I'll yell at her the way she deserves for betraying me. Did you bed Will too?" Benjamin accused wildly, losing control. "Did you?" he hollered. "Did you?"

At Benjamin's escalating accusations, Will took a swing at Benjamin. The two men tousled and rolled off the porch, punching and pummeling each other in the dirt.

"I should've done this to you a long time ago," Benjamin grunted and jabbed Will in the gut. "You woman-stealing bastard!"

"Oof!" Will grunted from the blow, then landed one in return. "You don't know how to treat a woman."

They fought on.

"You're so cold you probably couldn't have kept Bevin if you had married her," Will growled, his anger speaking.

Benjamin landed a blow to Will's eye. "That ought to keep your eye from roving for a while," Benjamin panted. "You'll never be true to her."

Not able to stand it any longer, Bevin tried to pull them apart only to be thrown backward into the dust. She regained her feet just as Prudence stepped out onto the porch. "Oh, my, whatever is happening out here, Evvie?"

"Get back to your room," Bevin ordered, sending Prudence scurrying for cover as the men continued to grapple.

Bevin was beside herself and frantic that they were fighting over her. And guilt assailed her for her part in destroying what little kinship the two men had left. Finally, when it seemed as if neither man would concede defeat and put a stop to such madness, Bevin ran into the parlor and grabbed the shotgun Benjamin kept over the mantel, remembering how Asa had stopped the fight between Will and Patrick. She grabbed a cartridge and she loaded it in the chamber.

She ran back out onto the porch and fired off a blast; it knocked her off her feet. Using the gun as a cane, she got up and straightened her dress.

"Stop it! Stop it! I won't stand out here and watch you two beat each other senseless because of me! Dear God, I wish I had never met either one of you," Bevin screamed, dropped the gun and ran into the house.

The gun had momentarily stopped the two men.

Will stood panting. "You had enough?"

"Not until you can no longer stand, you whoring bastard!" Benjamin lunged and rained blows to Will's body. Will broke free and charged Benjamin, tumbling him backward into a bush.

Johnny was out of breath running toward the house, when he suddenly stopped. To the side of the house was a huge bush shuddering, its leaves shaking like a tornado had it under siege. He did not know what to think until his eyes caught at the blur of booted feet wildly flailing out from underneath the shrub. Then he realized that Will and Benjamin were fighting.

Bevin pulled the lace curtains back and peered out in hopes that the two men had ceased their battle; she caught sight of Johnny. She rushed out to shield the child from such violence.

"Come inside with me, quickly," she ordered

382

Johnny.

"But the old sow," he protested. "She's trying to have her babies and seems to be having a tough time of it. You gotta come help her."

Despite his overwhelming anger, Benjamin heard the boy. He gave Will a hard shove and jumped to his feet to grab Johnny by the shoulders. "What you talking about, boy?"

"The sow. She don't seem to be able to birth her babies."

Nothing was as important to Benjamin as his farm, so he turned hate-filled eyes on Will, who was brushing himself off. "I'm not done with you. We'll continue this later."

Benjamin clasped his hand around Johnny's arm and dragged him toward the pigpen. Bevin ran behind them with Will bringing up the rear.

She was frantic that Benjamin had lost complete control of his senses and might take his anger out on the boy. Trying to catch up to the pair, she pleaded, "What are you doing with Johnny? Please, Benjamin, he's just a boy."

Chapter Thirty-nine

Despite Bevin's pleas, Benjamin marched Johnny into the barn, grabbed a lantern and was entering the pigpen by the time she caught up with them. Benjamin had been like a madman a few moments ago and now he was bending over the sow, gently stroking the animal which seemed to be having trouble giving birth.

In awe at the sudden change in Benjamin's demeanor, Bevin stopped and listened to him croon to the beleaguered hog. In the next instant Benjamin pulled Johnny down beside him.

She took a step forward prepared to shield the boy if necessary, but Will grasped her arm and pulled her back. "Shh," Will whispered, "Benjamin may need Johnny's help to pull pigs if the old sow can't birth them herself."

"Pull pigs?"

"Johnny's hands are small and he'll be able to reach into the birth canal and help pull the pigs out if the sow can't manage by herself."

Bevin watched the unfolding scene, amazed that Johnny, a city boy, seemed to understand what was needed and followed Benjamin's instructions without question.

The sow lay there grunting as the small boy reached up to his elbow in the birth canal and pulled the piglets out. It was as if the animal understood she was being helped, for the off-white sow did not squeal as the child worked.

Bevin could not deny that Benjamin and the boy seemed to be working quietly and efficiently together. The domesticity of the scene distressed her. Watching the pair together appear like a father and son sharing part of the farm duties had been what she had desperately hoped for when they'd first arrived.

"I think that's the last one," Benjamin finally said to Johnny. "You did good, boy. I'm proud of you. Now, you best get to the house and get washed up."

Johnny turned wide, questing eyes to Benjamin. "Then you ain't gonna kick me out no more?"

"I was never going to kick you out, boy. You did a man's work tonight. I'm beholden to you."

Johnny's face glowed and all thoughts of getting even with the farmer vanished. Johnny puffed out his chest as he got to his feet. His arms were bloody, as were his shirt and pants.

Bevin had tears streaming down her cheeks at Johnny's triumph. She clasped her fingers over her lips to keep them from quivering.

Will patted the boy on the back as he limped past him. "You've really proved yourself."

Johnny stopped and looked up at Will. "Benjamin said I done a man's work, guess that means I can act like one now."

Bevin swelled with pride over Johnny's statement, but there was something about the implication that warned Will to be wary. Will stared at Johnny until the boy went inside the house, then knelt down beside Benjamin.

385

"Let me help you get the piglets into the barn; it's going to be cold tonight."

Benjamin's expression of benevolence disappeared and was replaced by a hard line. He glanced at Bevin before he turned back to Will. "Can't afford any more of your kind of help."

Will got to his feet beside Bevin. "Suit yourself."

Bevin flinched at Benjamin's remark.

"Benjamin, I am so sorry," she said. "At least, please, don't let this destroy the relationship you have with the boy. You made him feel needed tonight, and I am so grateful."

Benjamin glared at her. "I've seen your kind of gratitude."

"Benjamin, please."

"I want you all off my land," Benjamin spat.

"It's only half yours. Just as soon as you pay me for my half we'll have enough money and be happy to leave," Will returned darkly.

Benjamin's icy pose remained glacial. "Supper's late. I'll be in shortly and I expect to have food on my table at mealtime as long as you continue to reside under my roof."

After the burgeoning tension of the last few days, Prudence decided to forgo any further attempts to talk some sense into Bevin this morning. She pretended sleep while Bevin washed, dressed and quietly left the room they shared.

Prudence waited five minutes once Bevin was gone, then stretched and selected one of her prettiest violet print dresses. She had not seen Patrick since they returned from the fair, and she was anxious to seek his counsel about Bevin when he arrived to take her for a drive today as he had promised. She was certain her Patrick would know a way to convince his sister how important it was for them to stay close.

Prudence remained sequestered until she heard the familiar clopping of hooves coming up the drive. She flew down the stairs and hopped into the buggy before Patrick had a chance to get out and talk to anyone.

"Ready to go?" she asked as Patrick adjusted a blanket over her lap to keep her warm against the cooling weather, signaling winter's onset.

"What's your all-fired rush?" Patrick asked, unaccustomed to pulling away without stopping to talk. "It's not polite to head out without first paying my respects."

"They know we are going. Please, Patrick, I am truly anxious to be away this morning."

Patrick tipped his head at the urgency in her voice. "Is there something I need to know?"

"My stomach is a little torpid this morning, I shall be fine."

"Benjamin probably has some stomach bitters inside. Maybe we should get you some before we go."

"No. I shall feel better once I am away from here. Drive to our favorite place under that big tree, so we can talk."

Patrick sent her a confused look, but snapped the reins over the horse's rump.

Prudence could hardly remain patient, her stomach was churning so. In silence, they drove out the drive, past the fields and out into the countryside amidst the thinning forest lands.

Patrick pulled off the road and turned to Prudence. "It's still a mite cool. Would you rather stay in the buggy?"

Prudence blushed. "I am quite warm sitting next to

you, truly I am. Why not spread the blanket under the tree away from the road?"

Patrick brightened. He liked the idea of being shielded from the road. He could steal a few kisses and even if anyone passed by, they would not be detected. He leaned over the seat, scooped up another blanket and hopped from the buggy. "You can wrap up in this if you get cold."

They settled next to each other and Prudence fidgeted with her fingers, trying to select the most tactful way to inform Patrick about his sister. She loved them both so dearly that she did not want to cause a schism in their newly mended relationship.

"What's bothering you? You don't seem to be yourself this morning, Prudy girl."

Prudence threw herself into his arms. Hysterically, the words rushed from her lips. "Oh, Patrick, Bevin says she is not going to marry Benjamin. What are we going to do? We are going to be a family. Bevin is going to be my sister. What are we going to do? We cannot let her marry Will and move away."

He wrinkled his brow. "What are you saying?"

"Bevin says she is not going to marry Benjamin. She is going to marry Will and probably leave Bowling Green."

To Prudence's chagrin a wide smile broke out on Patrick's face. "Well, I'll be. I'm happy for them."

Horror shrank Prudence's irises. "How can you be happy?" she cried.

"Because I'm glad my sister has found love like I have instead of settling for anything less, that's why. It would be sad if Bevin could not share with another person what you and I share, don't you think?"

Prudence's face underwent a transformation from angry frustration to a dawning understanding. She dropped her eyes, pinched her lips and returned her gaze to Patrick. "I never thought of it in that light before." She gave him a warm smile. "I knew talking to you was the right thing to do. You are so wise. I truly would not want Bevin to have anything less than we have."

Patrick could not help himself; he cupped her precious face and drew her mouth to his. "I love you, my Prudy girl," he whispered against her lips.

"I like it when you call me that."

They kissed long and hard; a wet, demanding kiss which urged further exploration and ignited a yearning torment between them.

Prudence pressed herself against Patrick. She splayed her fingers through his red-blond hair. Excitement and passion built in her breast. "Bevin said she did not mind if we are married right away."

Patrick searched her face. He swallowed hard. She was driving him beyond endurance to resist keeping his hands from her. With great effort he withdrew his arms from encircling her.

Prudence inhaled and took his hands. Coyly, she said, "I do not want you to take your hands away. I—I want you t—to touch me."

She looked so innocent, so doll-like that Patrick was not sure how to react.

When he did not do anything, Prudence said, "You do not want to t—touch me?"

"Oh, yes, I do, Prudy girl. But I would never dishonor you before we're married."

"I am sure it is all right, since we are going to be wed soon. It is not as if we were not promised to each other," she ventured.

Patrick's breath was ragged when he took Prudence back into his arms. "Oh, Prudy girl," he said softly. He tightened his arms around her and began pressing kisses over her face and down her throat. "I think I'm just about the luckiest man alive to be marrying you."

She tittered. "And I am truly the luckiest girl."

Patrick's hand slipped down to her well-rounded breast, and she pressed it against his palm. He could feel the nipple harden and pinched it ever so lightly.

Prudence had never experienced such fiery sensations before and grew bolder. "Why don't you unbutton my dress?"

Patrick held her from him. "You sure?"

Straightening her back, Prudence raised her chin. "Yes."

He kissed her, a long, passion-flooding kiss, then lowered her back against the blanket. He was about to claim this beautiful girl as his own. With trembling fingers he released her from her bodice and took her breasts in his hands.

"A—Am I—I beautiful to you?" she stammered when he seemed to be doing little more than staring at her bosom.

"Oh, God, yes." He bent his head and suckled like a greedy babe, all the while bunching the soft mounds so he could take more into his mouth.

Prudence squirmed at the heat between her thighs. Although she had learned last year how men and women mated, she had not imagined the feelings that accompanied it. Straining against him, she raised her slippered foot and ran it along his calf.

His hand immediately slid down over her flat belly that would someday shelter their unborn children, and he prayed she would be fruitful and they would have a large family, since he had grown up feeling so lonely.

His hand gathered up her skirts and snaked up her thigh. "I am going to work so hard for you and our family," he whispered.

Prudence was moaning and could hardly endure the anticipation of him touching her there. "Untie the band at my waist," she directed.

Patrick worked diligently, but the stubborn knot would not give. He sat back, looking a little sheepish. "I can't get it undone."

"I'll take care of it while you take care of your clothes," she suggested, appearing just as sheepish.

Patrick did not waste time. He divested himself of his trousers, shirt and light jacket in record time, and then sat back on his haunches to watch Prudence slip from her gown and underthings.

"Golly, these lacy things sure are pretty." He paused, then gasped at the first glimpse of milk-white skin.

She stopped. "What is wrong?"

"Oh, Prudy girl, nothing's wrong. You are just about the most beautiful thing I've ever seen. Even prettier than a newborn mule."

She crinkled her forehead, but continued to peel the last of the layers of clothing away. Patrick had such a way with words.

When she sat naked in front of him, he groaned with delight. He was so excited that he quickly launched himself into her arms, knocking them both back against the blanket.

They hit with a dull thud.

"Oh, my," Prudence squealed.

He rose up on his elbows. "I didn't hurt you did I?"

"Truly, no," she enthused. "What are we supposed to do next?"

"Let's try this," he rasped, incredulous at the love he felt. He had touched girls before, but never had the experience *touched* him so deeply, so profoundly.

His fingers glided along her heated flesh and

stroked the lightly furred triangle at the top of her legs.

Prudence was near exploding already. "Am I supposed to do the same thing to you?"

"Would you?"

"Silly, I want to," she gurgled and touched him tentatively.

Patrick groaned at the sweet torture. When he got together with his friends, they never spoke of their conquests as returning in kind what they did. Patrick silently blessed his good fortune to have this girl as his future wife, and vowed to cherish her always.

Unable to go slowly any longer, his hands were suddenly all over her in a heated rush. He probed and dipped, delved and explored until both were panting and gasping, and clawing at each other.

"Are you ready?" he asked, positioning himself over her.

Prudence giggled and pulled him down onto her. She was so caught up in her body's sensations that she did not feel the first hint of pain when he entered her and rode her to exhaustion.

Afterward Patrick pulled the extra blanket up around them and held her in his arms.

"Oh, Prudy girl, you'll never be sorry you chose to marry me. I promise you won't."

She nestled closer to his muscled length. "I have never doubted that since I met you. Since we *know each other so well now,* do you think we should go visit the parson and set our wedding date today?"

"The sooner the better."

Chapter Forty

Johnny was still feeling important when Benjamin told him he could take over responsibility for slopping the hogs. He whistled all the way out to the barn and picked up the pail containing the bran, barley and skimmed milk soaked up into the grain he watched Benjamin ready the day before. He entered the pigpen and tried to imitate the way he had heard Benjamin call the hogs.

"Woo-ee . . . woo-ee . . . woo-ee . . . pig, pig, pig," he sang out and slopped the mixture into the trough.

While the hogs pushed to guzzle up the food, Johnny gathered up the corncobs that the hogs had cleaned off. He had the routine down pretty good now. He dropped the cobs into the empty pail. As soon as they dried, he would take them into the kitchen for kindling to start the cookstove.

"Good piggies," he crooned when the food was almost gone. "That's good, eat it all up so you get nice and fat."

Benjamin was coming out of the barn just as Johnny finished his chore. The boy was feeling pretty confident as he approached Benjamin. "Since I helped birth the pigs, you think I could have one for my own?"

393

Benjamin tried to keep the bitterness out of his voice when he said, "Hogs are food, not pets; besides, at four months the males that aren't used for breeding are castrated and as soon as they're fatted up enough I slaughter them."

Disappointment dropped in Johnny's eyes, but he was an inquisitive child and soon asked, "What's cast-castigated mean?"

If he had not been filled with so much anger, Benjamin might have smiled at the boy's choice of words. "Plain and simple, it means I cut their balls off and toss them to the dog."

Johnny grabbed his crouch. "Oh."

Without another word, Benjamin started toward the house. Johnny decided to make one last plea, since he had gotten attached to the piglet with the crooked corkscrew tail.

"Couldn't you let me have one, just once?" he pleaded.

Benjamin frowned. He knew better than what he was about to say, but resentment and animosity continued to gnaw at him since Bevin had broken their engagement. "No. Bevin is taking you away, so you won't be here to tend it if I did give you one."

"She wouldn't do that!" Johnny screamed. He dropped the pail, spilling the corncobs, and scrambled toward the house to confront Miss Bevin.

Bevin and Will were sitting on the porch swing as Johnny rounded the corner. He bounded up the steps and stood glaring at the pair, his little hands clenched on his hips.

"Johnny," she said, "I saw you out at the pigpen a little while ago and you did a good job."

Johnny did not swell with pride. "That was before," he hissed.

Will could not help but notice the runt's rigid stance, and his lower lip jetted out into an angry pout. "Before what, runt?"

"Before she," he pointed an accusing, stubby finger, "decided I ain't gonna get to stay on the farm."

"Who told you that?" Will asked.

Bevin's face fell. "I am afraid I did."

"So did Benjamin," Johnny added.

She got up and tried to gather Johnny to her, but he swung out of her reach. "I thought you wanted me," he accused, trying valiantly not to cry.

Bevin kneeled down despite the distance Johnny insisted on keeping from her.

"I do want you." She glanced back at Will, who had leaned forward with his hands clasped. "We both do."

"But Benjamin said you are going to take me away."

"Benjamin," she groaned. Benjamin had been unforgiving, and her heart ached that he had not been able to put aside his feelings toward her where Johnny was concerned.

"Johnny, do you remember several days ago when I first tried to explain why Prudence was upset and you ran off before I had the chance?"

Suspicion settled on the child's brows. "Yeah."

"Well, Prudence was upset because I told her that I am not going to marry Benjamin after all. That means I will not be living here with him."

Question replaced the boy's cynicism. Although he had made peace with Benjamin, Johnny was secretly glad Miss Bevin was not going to marry him; Johnny had always known she deserved better. Now maybe she would wait for him to grow up. "Then where will you be living?"

Bevin looked to Will and back to Johnny. "I am not sure yet."

Will got up and pulled Bevin to her feet next to him. He circled his arm around her shoulders. "Johnny, you and Bevin are going to be living with me."

Johnny's face began to sparkle. "Me too?"

"Yes, runt, you too," Will said. "Bevin is going to marry me because we love each other. And we want to adopt you for our very own."

"Really?" he asked, not quite able to believe that he was truly wanted by the very people he loved most in his life. If Miss Bevin was not going to wait for him, at least she picked right this time, he decided.

"Yes, really," Bevin confirmed. When he seemed awfully quiet, she asked. "You do want to be part of our family, don't you?"

"Yeah." He shrugged and looked down at the ground for a moment before he raised his eyes to Miss Bevin. "It's just that I was beginning to get used to it here."

Children possessed such openness it never ceased to amaze Bevin. "Johnny, I'm sorry you are being uprooted again. I know you have come to think of the farm as your home, and it's the first real home you have ever known, but once we settle in our own home you'll love that too because you are going to be our very own little man."

He mulled it all over. It would be hard to leave the farm and Tara, but he finally had a family of his own . . . just like Crissy. A sadness came over him at the thought of the little sister he had lost, but it quickly faded. With Miss Bevin and Will as his folks maybe he would get to see Crissy again someday. He was so pleased that he'd come up with such a grown-up realization that he said, "I am a little man, ain't I?"

Bevin's eyes glistened with tears of joy. "You certainly are."

Johnny seemed to grow six inches when he darted off the porch and headed down the drive before Bevin could give him a big hug.

"Where are you going?" Bevin called out at his sudden departure.

"To tell Tara that I am luckier than her. Boy, is she gonna be jealous!" he shouted and skipped away in spite of his handicap.

Bevin hugged Will and they laughed over Johnny's childlike exuberance. They broke apart when they caught sight of Benjamin. His face was sour, his lips set in a hard line.

"Pity adults aren't as resilient as children," Will said, shaking his head.

"Or as forgiving," Bevin seconded sadly.

Benjamin stopped in front of the pair. The sight of them sickened him, and he vowed that as soon as he got the rest of the apple crop in he was going to town and see the lawyer and get them the hell out from under his roof.

"You coming out to the orchard and help me finish getting in the crop, so I can pay you off and be rid of you?"

Will was not going to let Benjamin's continued bitterness toward them rile him. He flashed his brows and cast Benjamin a grin. "Well, since you put it that way, how can I refuse?"

Johnny was out of breath and panting hard by the time he reached the Kruegers' farm. Tara was hanging from the fence, her long braids dangling to the ground.

"Hiya, Johnny," she sang out.

He stopped in front of her and bent over so he could view the world from her angle. "Gosh, don't the blood all go to your head and addle your brain?"

"I don't think so," she answered and swung down. "You wanna go get some of Bertha's fresh-baked cookies, then climb up on the chicken coop? It really makes the chickens squawk." She giggled.

"Sure," he said and followed her toward the house. "Howse come you don't call her ma?"

"I dunno. Guess 'cause she ain't."

"Don't she want you to?"

"She says I will when I'm ready. Guess I just ain't ready yet. Why you asking?"

They went into the kitchen through the back door.

A wide smile split Johnny's face. " 'Cause I'm gonna have a ma of my own."

"Hello, Johnny." Bertha stood at the work counter cleaning up the flour she spilled baking earlier. "What's this about you goin' to have your own ma?"

"Yes, ma'am, I am."

Gretchen joined them and set the clothes basket on the table. She gave the boy a cordial greeting and began folding the linens.

"Johnny was tellin' us that he's goin' to have a ma of his own, Gretchen," Bertha announced as Asa came in to swell the numbers crowding the cheery, fragrant kitchen.

"Is that so," Asa said. He shrugged off his work jacket. He took up a place around the table and proceeded to light up his pipe. He took three good puffs off the homemade pipe before asking, "Who's goin' to be the lucky lady, boy?"

"Miss Bevin." Johnny beamed. "They're gonna

'dopt me all legal and everything."

"Golly, then you'll get to stay, that's great!" Tara said. She snitched a couple of cookies off the cooling rack and handed one to Johnny.

Johnny bit into the crisp cookie. "Mmm, this is good, ma'am." With his mouth full he added, "But I ain't gonna be stayin'."

"Where you gonna be, then?" Tara's expression changed to a frown.

"Miss Bevin and Will don't know where they're gonna live yet, so I don't know."

Gretchen only had been half listening to the conversation while she worked until the boy said Will's name; her interest immediately was captured. "Don't you mean Benjamin?" Troubled eyes turned to her father. "Benjamin'd never leave his farm, would he, Pa?"

"Benjamin loves his place," Asa said between puffs.

All eyes swung to Johnny. He finished off the cookie before he said in all innocence, "I ain't talking about Benjamin. Will's gonna be my pa."

"Will?" Bertha questioned. She had noticed how ill at ease Bevin and Benjamin had been when they'd returned from the fair to drop Johnny off, so it was not a complete surprise to her.

"Yeah! Ain't it great?" Johnny gushed. "Miss Bevin ain't gonna marry Benjamin; she's gonna marry Will and they're gonna be my folks."

Tara opened her mouth to speak, but Gretchen interceded. "Benjamin really isn't going to marry Bevin?"

Johnny pulled a face. "That's what I said."

Gretchen's heart started to soar. Her Benjamin was not going to be married after all. Perhaps she still had a chance with the only man she had ever cared about.

Bertha noticed the quickening of Gretchen's breathing. The girl's eyes were suddenly very bright. Bertha furrowed her brow; she prayed Gretchen was not getting her hopes up in vain. "When did all this happen?" Bertha prodded.

"Couple of days ago, I guess. Dunno for sure. Miss Prudence was pretty upset."

"If Prudence knew, why didn't Patrick tell us?" Bertha wondered out loud.

"Maybe the boy thought we should hear it from the parties involved." Asa supplied the logical answer. "You know how closed-mouthed Patrick always has been."

Gretchen left three pillow cases folded crookedly, she was so excited. "You really think it's true?"

Bertha let out a breath. "S'pose there's one way to find out for sure . . . once the chores are done, that is."

"Tara, I'll let you have the doll you've been eyeing on my dresser if you finish folding clothes for me," Gretchen blurted out.

"It's a deal!" Tara shoved the rest of the cookie in her mouth. She wiped her palms on her overalls and snatched the pillow case out of Gretchen's hands before she could change her mind. "Come on, Johnny. We'll get done sooner if you help."

"Okay," he ground out.

Gretchen ripped off her apron and hurriedly smoothed her hair back. "Do I look all right, Ma?"

Bertha smiled at her only child. "You look like a young lady with her hopes up a mite high."

"Oh, no, not this time. If I get a second chance I'm not goin' to waste it by sittin' back and not fightin' for what I want. And I don't care what I have to do," she announced, past caring how it sounded.

Asa laughed despite Bertha's sharp look in Gretchen's direction. "You get more like your ma every day, girl."

"Asa!" Gretchen heard her ma bellow as she rushed from the house.

Bertha looked to Asa. "Ain't you goin' to help your daughter?"

Asa winked at his wife. He went to the back door and hollered, "I'll help you hitch the buggy, it's faster."

Gretchen tore down the drive, laying the whip to the horse. Her heart beat doubly fast and her breath came in ragged gasps as she drove along the road connecting the two farms. She was about to get a second chance with the man she loved, and she was not going to miss out this time if she could help it!

Chapter Forty-one

The sun was low in the sky, illuminating the apple orchard with a golden hue when Gretchen nearly passed by without noticing that Benjamin was out there alone loading the last basket of fruit into the wagon. Out of the corner of her eye she caught sight of Will's retreating back heading toward the house. She thought of driving to the farm and asking Bevin if what Johnny had told them was true, but she did not want to waste precious time. If Benjamin was hurting, it was important that she console him right away.

She pulled up on the reins and stopped a short distance from where Benjamin was working. She wanted to say the right thing, so she waited to approach him until she had formulated the best way to draw him out so he would open up to her without directly asking him.

A secret smile hovered about her lips when she had settled on a method of approach. She hobbled the horse and walked through the orchard swinging her arms. "Hello, Benjamin."

"Gretchen," he grunted without looking directly at her.

She was not going to let him dismiss her! "I was

returning from an errand for Ma and saw you out here all alone. So I thought I'd stop and see how you've been since Pa told me you missed the Sons of Hermann meeting. Pa said you hardly ever missed a meeting."

"Been busy" came the gruff reply. He immediately went back to work and ignored her.

"I hear Prudence and Patrick are going to be married next week."

"So I hear tell."

She pinched her lips. He was not cooperating at all! "Kinda close to your wedding, don't you think?" she blurted out.

Benjamin blanched and Gretchen was immediately sorry she had caused him pain, although his reaction told her what she had come to learn.

"Something wrong?" she asked innocently.

Benjamin's head started to pound and he swung around to give her a good tongue-lashing on the virtues of minding her own business.

He stopped in his tracks.

Gretchen was standing in front of him, her chest thrust out and the top of her dress unbuttoned . . . again.

His eyes fastened on her bosom.

"Something wrong?" she repeated and leaned forward a tad more.

N—No," he stammered. "I mean, yes, just-about-everything-in-my-life-right-now."

She sent him a big, concerned smile and rocked back and forth on her heels, which caused her breasts to sway beneath the dress.

"Is there anything I can do? Golly, I'd do just about anything for you."

The first time he got a glimpse of Gretchen's full,

mature breasts Benjamin had realized that she was no longer the child he had thought her. He had considered it and finally decided it must have been an accident at the time, but now he was no longer sure.

He ran his hand over his face.

"Your top is unbuttoned."

"I know."

"Then you'd best see to it before folks get the wrong impression of you," he advised.

Her eyes wide, she worked the buttons. "I wouldn't want that."

Benjamin exhaled. "I know."

She swallowed hard. Now was her chance to bring Bevin into the conversation again and pray he'd take the bait. "I want to be a girl you'd choose."

"Humph! 'Fraid I didn't do such a good job choosing."

Gretchen waited, hoping he would broach the topic of Bevin so she could console him.

Benjamin waited, hoping she would quit peering so deeply into his eyes and talk about something, anything, other than that scheming woman he had thought was so pure.

She just stood there. He was defeated. Oh, hell, he might just as well get it out into the open, he decided. Folks were going to find out soon enough anyhow.

"Gretchen, you might as well hear it from me now as from the gossips later. Bevin isn't going to marry me. She jilted me for the likes of William Shoemaker," he said with the jagged edge of bitterness to his voice.

Gretchen stepped forward and placed a hand on his arm. "Benjamin, Bevin is a fool to ever give up someone like you."

404

Strangely enough Gretchen's empathy, along with giving voice to his feelings, was cathartic. He had held it inside for too long, and then suddenly he had someone to unburden himself to. Although he could never forgive Bevin and William for what they had done to him, sharing the shame of rejection with his neighbor was not as difficult as he had feared.

Over Benjamin's virulent objections, Bevin went ahead with planning Prudence's wedding reception at the farmhouse. Guilt continued to weigh heavily on her in the face of Benjamin's constant condemnations and scorching scowls. She had hoped that time would provide a salve for his pain and they could come to terms and be civil to one another, but she was not going to forgo celebrating the wedding at the farm due to Benjamin's venom.

Bertha came over daily to help with the baking while Prudence cleaned or spent time away from the house with Patrick, and Bevin altered her own wedding gown to fit Prudence's smaller frame. Johnny threw himself into the chores around the farm, and Will sagely went to town each day.

Will had not received a reply to the telegram he had sent off to Black Hawk, so he could not tell Bevin his plans. Instead, he ran errands and remained at the saloon until suppertime, sidestepping the townsfolks' questions about his future plans until Benjamin decided to make the announcement of his broken engagement; Will owed Benjamin that much, although he often questioned himself why since Benjamin continued to be so intolerably bitter.

Benjamin took to remaining out in his barn until the scourge he'd brought under his roof retired for the night. He felt displaced by that fallen woman, a stranger who had misrepresented herself and then showed up on his doorstep with a castoff on top of it!

He was sitting crosslegged in the hayloft, chewing on a length of straw, contemplating the ramifications of his conversation with Gretchen when childish giggles wafted through the clear, cool dusk. Benjamin crawled to the door and peered out, craning his ear to listen so he could overhear their conversation.

Johnny and Tara were sitting in the corncrib. Benjamin could see the boy clearly. He stared at the child with growing irritation over the castoff's actions.

"Just watch, Tara, and you'll see how it's done. Then maybe I'll let you make one of your own."

Tara put her elbows on her knees and gave Johnny her rapt attention.

"First, you cut off a section of the cob, then dig out the middle." He demonstrated his skill as he explained. "See how I left lots in the bottom for a base?"

"Yeah."

Johnny pointed. "Hand me that sharp stick next to you . . . thanks." He poked a hole at the side of the cob and blew through it. "Now give me that reed. Quit horsing around with it and give it to me." He snatched the hollow stem out of her hand. "All you gotta do now it stick it in the hole like this and it's all done. See? Ain't it a great pipe?"

"I guess so. Benjamin's sure gonna be mad when he finds out you stole some tobacco from that tin by his favorite parlor chair."

He waved her off and stuffed the tobacco in the pipe. "Benjamin'll never know. I crushed up some dried leaves and mixed them in at the bottom so his tin still looks full."

406

"You sure we should be doing this?" she asked as he struck a match and puffed on the pipestem until the tobacco smoldered and filled the air with a sweet fragrance.

He let out a choking cough.

She slapped him on the back, all the while suppressing a giggle.

Holding the pipe away from his lips the way he'd seen Asa Krueger do, Johnny said, "Why not? After all I told you how Miss Bevin said I'm a man now."

"Thought you told me she said you were her 'little man'?" she taunted.

Johnny gave over a huff. "She only used the word 'little' 'cause I ain't reached my full height yet."

"And you're never going to reach it at that rate, boy," Benjamin said, standing over the two children.

Johnny choked again and his eyes snapped up. Benjamin was glowering at him. Johnny tried to hide the pipe behind his back, but Benjamin yanked it out of his hand.

Tara immediately scrambled away, but as Johnny tried to follow her hasty retreat, Benjamin grabbed him by the seat of the pants.

"I'm going to learn you not to steal, then I'm going to learn you not to smoke," Benjamin sneered.

"No, don't," Johnny screamed. He tried to struggle free, Benjamin held fast.

Ignoring the boy's pleas, Benjamin hauled the little devil toward the woodshed while he took off his belt.

Bevin bolted out the back door of the house with Tara right behind her. She lifted her skirts and ran toward the corncrib. Her heart drummed when she caught sight of Benjamin dragging the fighting child toward the woodshed. She wished Will were here instead of in town and at the same time was glad he was gone, for she knew Will would surely thrash Benjamin. Although she had to admit that at the moment she too would like to be the one to thrash Benjamin.

"Stop it, Benjamin. Don't you harm that boy!" she hollered.

Benjamin halted, gave her a scathing look, and rounded the corner to the woodshed.

Panting, she was right on his heels. "What do you think you're doing? I demand you release that child at once. Do you hear me, at once!"

Benjamin's hand tightened on his belt. "I'm going to learn this one what happens to boys who steal and go behind folks' backs to smoke."

Bevin feared that in Benjamin's state of mind he would not listen to reason, so she picked up an ax which was laying nearby. Benjamin had raised his hand and now lowered it.

She held the ax menacingly. "Put the belt down, Benjamin, or I swear I shall use this to defend Johnny if I must. Then you better explain yourself."

Benjamin grudgingly released the boy and Johnny scrambled behind Bevin's skirts to join Tara. In a sneering voice, Benjamin explained what he'd seen and overheard.

"I'll handle Johnny's punishment," she said when he'd finished.

"Harumph! My pa knew how to raise a no-account; you could take a few lessons before that one grows up to be like William."

Bevin gathered herself up to her full height. "Perhaps if your father had had a gentler hand, you might have learned compassion and forgiveness.

And, for your information, I truly hope Johnny matures to be *exactly* like Will . . . no thanks to you *or* to your father's methods."

"Yeah, Will told me how he made pipes as a kid," Johnny added and stuck his tongue out at Benjamin. "I'm gonna tell on you when Will gets back."

"No, you-are-not. I am handling this." She pulled Johnny around the front of her by the ear and started for the house. "I shall deal with you inside." She stopped and said to Tara, "You better run on home, Tara."

"Yes, ma'am."

Bevin watched Tara scamper away before she turned her attention back to Benjamin. Glaring at the man, she said, "Don't you ever even think of laying a hand on my child again."

"Then you and that *lover* of yours had better take him and get out of my house soon!"

Bevin stung under the truth of his accusation, and she tried not to show it by a display of temper. "As soon as it *is* your house, we shall be delighted to live elsewhere."

Benjamin ground his teeth until that fallen woman disappeared inside the house with that brat. As he swung around to return to the barn, he smoldered with malevolence and swore to head into town tomorrow and hurry up that lawyer before he lost hold of the fragile thread maintaining his last measure of control.

Long after she had punished Johnny and sent him his room, Bevin stood in the empty bedroom staring out the window toward the lighted barn. She shifted her gaze to the star-speckled sky. This farm was to

409

have been her home and now she could hardly wait until Patrick's wedding was over and they could leave this lovely setting.

She sighed and moved away from the window. Grateful that Prudence and Will were out and Benjamin had remained in the barn, she slipped into her nightgown and climbed into bed. She laid her head on the pillow.

She was no longer filled with the slightest hint of remorse or assailed with guilt. She had made the right decision. Tonight had proved that beyond doubt. She had forestalled Will's efforts to set a wedding date out of deference to Benjamin's wounded pride. Benjamin had shown that had been a mistake. As she drifted off to sleep she determined to speak with Will first thing in the morning.

Chapter Forty-two

The morning of Prudence and Patrick's wedding dawned to a brilliant blue sky. Bluebirds sat on the limbs outside Will's room chirping their most gay songs. Will opened the window to listen, thinking about his own *bluebird*.

By the time he went downstairs, the house was a beehive of activity. The food was already set out for the day of celebrating; furniture had been pushed along the walls and handmade decorations adorned the parlor and dining room.

Will peered into parlor. Prudence was all aflutter, giving Bevin fits as she tried to finish a last repair to the girl's gown.

Leaning against the doorframe, Will said, "Patrick's a lucky man."

Prudence tittered.

"Hold still, Pru, or you'll rip another seam and be running down here again, and I'll never get the parlor readied." Bevin finished her handiwork, directed Prudence upstairs, and then went to greet Will. "Good morning," she said and reached up on tiptoes to give him a peck on the cheek.

He drew her in close and nibbled on her neck. "Mmmm, good morning, my beautiful bluebird."

"Bluebird?"

"From the first moment we set foot on Missouri soil, you have reminded me of the state bird with those gorgeous blue eyes of yours. I was afraid Benjamin would clip your wings, but no more. Now you are going to become my bluebird," he crooned and tried to kiss her again, but she pulled out of his embrace.

Her face serious, she said, "Speaking of Benjamin, I must tell you we had a slight confrontation last night over Johnny. But it was resolved without difficulty," she added in a rush when she noticed his face turn dark.

"What happened?" he demanded.

"Please, before you get upset, sit down."

Will settled down on a chair, every muscle tense.

"Benjamin caught Johnny smoking a corncob pipe he'd made and filled with Benjamin's favorite tobacco."

Will's scowl changed to a lopsided grin.

"Before you condone what Johnny did, I think you should know he stole the tobacco and replaced it with crushed leaves so Benjamin would not find out until after we had left the farm."

To Bevin's dismay, Will broke out laughing.

"What is so amusing? Johnny should know better," she insisted.

"I know he should. It is just that I did the very same thing when I was a boy. And I remember telling the runt about it on the train. Funny," he mused for a moment, "I knew he'd get into trouble when all of us were congratulating him for being a man. And men smoke, you know."

"Johnny did deserve to be punished for what he did."

Will's easy smile vanished. "Benjamin didn't touch

the runt, did he?"

"No, thank heaven. But he was dragging Johnny out behind the woodshed when I stopped him."

His face thoughtful now, Will said, "I see. Looks like Ben and I need to have a talk."

Bevin was afraid of that when she'd decided that she'd best inform Will of the incident before he heard it from someone else.

"Please, let it drop. I stopped Benjamin and punished Johnny myself. And you did threaten the very same thing on the train, I recollect."

Bevin and Will were locked in each other's gaze when Prudence's call ended the tension. "Bevin, will you come help me with my hair, then I shall be ready to go to the church."

"Will, please say you won't do anything rash."

"Quit worrying and go help Prudence."

Bevin breathed a sigh of relief. "Thank you. Will you call Johnny in and help him dress while I see to Prudence? We must be prepared to leave in half an hour."

The churchyard was filled with milling clusters of folks, dressed up in their Sunday best, waiting for the arrival of the bride before they filed into the church for the ceremony. All headed inside when they saw the bride arrive.

Settled in the pew, Bevin looked around. It was painfully obvious that Benjamin was absent. The music began and Bevin shifted her attention to the pageantry of her younger brother's wedding.

Tears flowed freely down her cheeks at the beauty of the ceremony. Patrick. Prudence. Her lovely gown. Their abiding love so evident in the glow of their youthful faces.

413

Afterward everyone retired to Benjamin's farm-house. The tidy little house was full of guests who overflowed out into the yard, all intent on celebrating the nuptials and feasting on the sumptuous spread set out.

Bevin was aided by Bertha and Gretchen, refilling the punch bowl and the platters. Gretchen waited until Bevin was alone in the kitchen and then approached her.

"Bevin, Ma said to ask if Johnny can sleep over with Tara tonight."

"Of course he can. I'd like him to spend time with her before we leave," Bevin said and went back to work.

"Can I talk to you a minute?"

Bevin looked up from mixing up another bowl of potato salad. "Of course, you know you can, any time."

Gretchen hesitated, then took a deep breath. "It's about Benjamin."

Bevin set the spoon aside. "I see by your expression that you know."

"People are talking about him not being here to-day, but yes, he told me down at the orchard."

"You really love him, don't you," Bevin said candidly.

"Yes, I do. He's always thought of me as a little girl though."

"Perhaps now is the time to let him know you aren't. You were the best choice for Benjamin all along. I hope he comes to realize that."

"Thanks, Bevin. So do I."

"I fear there isn't much I can do to talk to Benjamin. He has not forgiven Will and me, and I'm not sure he ever will."

"Maybe in time." Gretchen had hoped Bevin would

be able to somehow convince Benjamin that she was right for him, but the girl was not daunted that she would have to do her own convincing.

"We'd best get this food out to the table before we run out," suggested Bevin, lifting a bowl filled to capacity with salad.

Bevin was clearing away the empty bowls from the table when Aunt Bessie came up behind her and beat her cane against the ground.

"Deary, where's that Straub boy? Ever'body's been wondering. I think it's high time you told 'em. It's better'n letting the gossips get hold of it, don't you think? You know how stories grow like grainy mushrooms."

"I suppose you're right."

" 'Course I'm right. There'd be less fuss and fume. You run along and find Will and tell 'em together. I'll tend the horde and supervise the gifts."

Bevin took her apron off and found Will standing with her brother and Prudence. Oh, Dear Lord, she detested having to make such an announcement on her brother's wedding day. Easing her trepidation, Patrick also recommended she take advantage of the gathering to make the announcement since Benjamin had not seen fit to inform folks himself.

They waited until everyone was gathered out in the yard, their plates piled high with food. Will took Bevin's hand and led her toward the porch steps. She could hear the buzzing whispers of shock.

Standing by Will's side, Bevin took advantage of his strength as she prepared to face Benjamin's neighbors. Before Will began he offered a toast to the newlyweds. Then all conversations ceased and they waited.

"As I'm sure you are all aware, Benjamin is not in attendance today . . ." Will held their attention as he explained the situation in such a way as to allow everyone to save face. With finesse he detailed how Benjamin and Bevin had realized someone from his community would make the best choice for a wife. It was then that Will and Bevin discovered how much alike their lives had been and with Benjamin's blessing decided to marry and adopt Johnny.

The day was exhausting by the time the last guest congratulated the newlyweds and left after agreeing that Benjamin had come to the right conclusion to look for a wife within his own community — no offense meant, of course.

Standing alone in the yard with the wedded pair, Bevin said, "You never have told me what your plans are."

"You have been rather busy these last couple of weeks," Patrick said.

Bevin kissed Patrick on the cheek. "I know, and I am sorry we haven't had more time together."

"I understand. And Bevin, I'm glad you are going to marry Will."

Tears brimmed her eyelids. "Thank you. But you still haven't told me your plans."

"We are taking the train back to Boston so Patrick can meet my parents," Prudence announced. "Then we'll return and set up housekeeping on the farm Clyde Hubbard has agreed to rent us."

Wide-eyed, Bevin said, "I'm glad you're going to Boston to meet Pru's parents."

Patrick pulled his bride to him. "It was Will's idea. He said it would be a shame to just write them off. Thinks they will have a change of heart when they meet me."

Bevin hugged them both. "I know they will."

From the porch, Will hollered. "You two best get a move on if we're going to get you to the hotel in town much past dark. You'll want to get plenty of sleep since the train's going to be pulling out bright and early tomorrow morning."

Linking their arms and laughing at the silly notion of sleeping tonight, they headed to the house to change.

Heading back from town after bidding good-bye to Patrick and Prudence, Bevin snuggled closer to Will in the buggy. She was filled with a sweet sadness. She had been reunited with Patrick for such a short time and now he was gone. She reminded herself that this time he was not lost, and now she had a special sister-in-law as well.

They traveled in silence until they turned up the drive and noticed the lights burning in the house.

"Benjamin has returned," Bevin said.

"Yes, and I have a few things to set straight with him."

"Oh, Will, can't we let it be for now. I don't want you two clashing again."

"Don't worry I'm not going to start a fistfight."

"It's not you starting a fight I'm worried about."

"Quit fretting. After I drop you off I want your word you'll go to your room and leave Benjamin and me to settle things." When she did not answer, he urged, "Bevin, your word?"

She let out a sigh. "Oh, all right."

Will dropped her off at the front door and then got the horse put up in its stall before he entered the house and headed directly to the parlor where Benjamin sat before a fire he had built in the fireplace, staring intently at the flames.

"Benjamin," Will said, "I think it's about time we talk."

Benjamin swung his head around and looked up with blazing eyes. He tried to shoulder past Will, but Will blocked his exit.

"You missed the wedding. Everyone was asking after you."

"Yeah? And what did you do, tell them why I wasn't there?"

"Told them you changed your mind about Bevin and had business in town."

"If you're waiting for me to thank you, you can go straight to hell."

"I'd just like to talk to you, but if you insist we can finish this once and for all outside."

Benjamin returned to his chair and sat down. "I've nothing to say to you."

Will took a seat across from Benjamin. "Then you can just listen. Whether you want to accept it or not I didn't come back to steal your intended. It just happened. Bevin's not a farm girl and she would have had a dickens of a time adjusting to your way of life. Her attempts drew us closer since we shared a similar childhood."

"So? What do you have to say that hasn't already been said?" Benjamin ground out.

"You are one hardheaded son of a bitch. Hell, I can see this was a mistake."

"Yeah," Benjamin sneered, "a big mistake."

Will rose with the knowledge that he had attempted a reconciliation and no longer owed Benjamin the least consideration in the future. "Just don't ever try to discipline Johnny again, hear?"

Will was to the doorway when he decided to add, "If you weren't so damned blind you'd realize that Gretchen Krueger probably would have been the best choice for you all along. The poor girl is crazy over you."

Benjamin gave Will a strange look. "While I was in town today I learned your money'll be ready tomorrow afternoon. I want you all out of here right after I hand it to you."

"My pleasure, you ignorant fool." Will started up the stairs, then halted and returned to the parlor. "Pity you're so filled with hatred because it's your loss."

"Some loss, bastard," Benjamin jeered.

A long time after he sat alone in the parlor, Benjamin digested everything he'd talked about with William. Despite the way William had informed the community of his rejection by Bevin so he had saved face, Benjamin could not bring himself to forgive the pair. The most startling thing William had said had to do with Gretchen.

Although he wasn't sure he would ever be able to totally trust again, Benjamin had been giving quite a bit of thought to Gretchen since they'd talked out in the orchard. He had finally realized she was no longer a child but a most fetching young woman. Her empathy and caring had caused him to think of her in still another light, and she took on an additional dimension in his life.

Gretchen was not an outsider but an accepted member of the community. She had grown up on a farm and knew what to expect. She would be content with the same kind of life he loved. Suddenly, as if it just hit him, he realized he never had farther to look for a wife than the next farm.

Chapter Forty-three

Bevin was grateful Benjamin had already finished his morning chores and left for town by the time she entered the kitchen. She warmed her hands over the stove, then stoked it up again in preparation for cooking Will a hearty breakfast. She had just tossed in three more corncobs, visualizing each as a pipe, when a strong arm suddenly snaked around her waist and pulled her backward.

"Morning, bluebird." Will nuzzled her neck.

Bevin pivoted around to face him and gave him a peck on the cheek.

"Is that all I get?"

"From a bird, yes."

He grinned. "Then by all means, let's dispense with ever calling you anything in reference to fowl again. How about cuddle bear?"

She wrinkled her nose. "Cuddle bear?"

"Yeah. While we finally have some time alone before Johnny and Benjamin return I thought we might think about cuddling up together. What do you say?"

"You are hopeless," she said and immediately kissed him.

"Not entirely." All amusement left his face and was replaced by a seriousness she did not glimpse very often.

"Is there something wrong?"

The grin returned. "Not unless you have decided against getting married."

She sighed and put a hand to her chin. "Well, let me see."

"Don't even think you're going to have a chance to change your mind, lady. Because I've been thinking it's about time we quit putting it off."

"Yes, I agree."

"I want to start taking care of you and Johnny. And whether Benjamin brings the money back from town or not, since Patrick and Prudence are married and gone, and you gave them the celebration you wanted, I don't think we should remain here any longer."

"You're right. I have been thinking along those lines as well. By staying here all we do is keep reopening Benjamin's wounds. I had hoped he might come around, but it doesn't appear that he's even inclined to make an effort."

"Sometimes families work out their troubles and sometimes they don't."

"I know," she answered, thinking about her own brother.

"As soon as Johnny returns I'm going into town and see about the arrangements for our wedding. How does that sound?"

She gave him a squeezing hug. "Sounds terrific."

"That is if you don't put me out of commission with your exuberance."

"What's the matter? I thought you wanted a cuddle bear," she teased.

"I did and do." He swooped her up into his arms. "Let's try this again upstairs."

421

Will carried Bevin to his room and set her on the bed.

"I've been dreaming of this . . . of being here with you like this since the last time we were together, Bevin," he murmured, changing the mood.

Bevin stared up into that handsome face. She was lost in the depth of those brown eyes. The intensity of his gaze undressed her without touching her. She raised her arms to him.

"No, not yet. Let me stand here and watch you take your hair down for me. Take it down for me one pin at a time, my love."

Without blinking her eyes from his mesmerizing gaze, Bevin sat up and began to remove the hairpins. One by one she slid the pins holding the mass of red curls in place. The silken strands tumbled over her shoulders and over her back, and Will bent over her and let the threads cascade through his fingers. He nuzzled his cheek against her hair, inhaling the fresh soapy fragrance.

He stood back and Bevin rested against her elbows. "I love the silky feel of your hair."

She felt the need for him to uncoil inside her. She was ready for him, for his arms, his lips, his body. "Come join me, Will."

Instead of joining her, Will dragged a chair over near the bed and sat down. "I want to watch you undress for me. I want to feast on the beauty of your body; I want to savor the anticipation. Then I am going to peel my clothes off layer by layer for you."

Bevin's breathing increased and her fingers hesitantly went to the buttons on her collar.

"You are a beautiful woman, Bevin. You are going to be my wife, we will often see each. I love you," he whispered.

As Bevin stripped off her dress and chemise she heard Will's encouraging words, "so lovely, so soft, so exquisite," urge her to continue the arousing mating ritual she was performing. All thought of modesty fled under the heat surrounding her, and she removed her underdrawers and stockings slowly, languidly, until she stood before him unclothed, unashamed.

"Come here," he moaned in a growl. When she moved to stand directly in front of him he swiveled her around and lightly kissed the indentations at the top of her buttocks.

"What are you doing?" she startled.

He moved her around to face him, his hands cupping her buttocks now. He kissed the triangle at the top of her thighs. "I want to brand every inch of you as mine for all time."

Her breasts peaked. "Then you had better start right now."

Will pulled her down on his lap and proceeded to suckle and nip at the pointy tips. Her body's senses were afire and she squirmed shamelessly against his arousal.

He got up with her in his arms. "Now it's your turn to lay back, relax and watch me," he whispered hoarsely.

"Mmmm." She nodded.

To her delight he stripped off his shirt and trousers with great pomp. Each movement displayed a ripple of muscle beneath his bronzed skin. He was a prime example of the male of the species, and her breath caught when he moved toward her in all his masculinity.

He folded his frame on the edge of the bed and touched her chin tenderly. "We belong together," he said and stretched out next to her. "We always have."

His hand stroked her heated flesh; his fingers igniting a blazing passion between them. She arched into him as he traced a path down the indentation of her backbone to squeeze her rounded bottom and pull her against his maleness.

"Oh, God," he groaned, rubbing himself along her moistened lips. His hands roved freely over the peaks and valleys of her skin, learning every pleasure point and each sensitive spot.

Desire and lust spiraled and throbbed through her entire being. Still lying on their sides, she put one leg over him. Encircling fingers of fire around his shaft, she guided him into her.

Primitive movements built within them until Will grabbed her shoulders and rolled her onto her back without removing himself. He moved in and out with long, slow strokes. All the while he kneaded her breasts and twirled the hard nipples between his fingers.

"Will," she cried, craving that sweet release. "I can't wait any longer."

He pulled out until he was poised at her honeyed entrance. "But I'm not through yet."

His face held the fire of love when she opened her eyes. "As long as you stay inside me I won't complain."

In a flash she grabbed him at the small of the back and pulled him back into her.

He gyrated his hips and she met every movement with building urgency. There was nothing taboo between them. Nothing one would not do for the other as they greedily explored a variety of positions, thrilling, feasting, savoring and filling themselves of each other until need replaced all other thought.

Coherence fled to be replaced by sensations so acute, torture so exquisite, pleasure so intense that they were consumed by insatiable hungers. Ravenous for that consummate release, they were enslaved by voracious agony as the friction built until Bevin cried out, rocking furiously against him. Will gave three more hard thrusts and surged into her, his seed coming in spurts.

"Oh, Bevin," he panted, collapsing on top of her to kiss her drenched face. "I love you."

Her woman's muscles throbbing around him, she returned his kiss. "And I love you."

For an hour they lay side by side, their glistening bodies slick from their lovemaking. A cool breeze from the open window danced across them, causing goosebumps to raise down Bevin's legs.

"You're cold," Will observed and rubbed her thigh. "Why don't you let me warm you back up?"

Bevin giggled and fluttered her lids closed as his fingers played sweet chords over her eager body again. She was edging near that mindless void of sensation when a horse whinnied outside. She bolted upright.

"What was that?"

Will sat back. "I'd say we have about five minutes left before company knocks at the door."

Bevin swung a pillow at him and laughed. "You really have it down pat, don't you?"

Stepping into his trousers, he replied, "I was right before, wasn't I?"

Bevin got dressed and hurried downstairs and out onto the porch.

"Johnny, what are you doing on that horse?" Bevin waved to the child riding up the drive.

He halted the horse at the base of the porch and

slid off the animal's back. "Gretchen let me ride it home. She said she'd come over later to get it." He giggled. "I really think she just wants to come over so she has an excuse to see Benjamin."

Bevin ignored the child's keen observation. "Did you have a good visit with Tara?"

"Guess so. She's real jealous though."

"Why?"

" 'Cause I get to be your kid." He yawned.

"Tara has a good home too. Now I think it's time you go inside and get cleaned up. An early supper and bedtime is in order. You've had a pretty busy day, young man.

"I am kinda tired. But what about the horse?"

Will was coming out of the house and said, "I'll take care of it." He took the reins. "Want anything while I'm in town, Bevin?"

"No, just hurry back."

"Will you bring me some hard rock candy?"

"Sure, runt."

" 'Bye," Johnny said, then scampered into the house.

Bevin walked arm in arm with Will to the barn while he put one horse in a stall and saddled another one. He gave her a big kiss before mounting up.

"Will, I'd like to be married by a priest if one is available."

"If there is one in town, we'll be married by him. If not we'll find one."

She reached up and he leaned down to share another warm kiss before he left her to head toward town.

Bevin watched him ride out the drive, then returned to the house. She got Johnny fed, readied his bath and tucked him into bed before settling down in he parlor to read. She heard a buggy pass the front of the house. It had to be Benjamin returning. There was no one to rush out with a warm greeting for Benjamin, and despite his meanness as of late, Bevin felt a twinge of pity for the man.

She had just returned her attention to her book when the back door slammed and Benjamin stomped into the parlor.

"Where's William?" he demanded.

Bevin's head snapped up. Benjamin stood framed in the doorway, a lantern in his hand, glaring at her. She set the book aside. "He went to town."

"Damn it!" He slammed the lantern down on a nearby table, cracking its base. Undetected, kerosene was forming a puddle around the broken lantern as the flame burned lower, heating the base.

"You should be more careful," Bevin advised. "You might have broken something."

"This is my house and I'll do as I please. Why the hell did William have to go to town now when he knew I went to get his damned money so all of you can get out of my house!"

Bevin was not going to allow a display of temper to cause her to meekly go to her room. "There's some leftover biscuits and ham. If you'd like I'll warm them up for you. You must be hungry."

"I don't want anything from you. I'd rather you left me some peace and quiet in my own house." He immediately turned his back on her.

"Very well." Bevin rose stiffly, raised her chin, and went upstairs to her room.

Benjamin stood in the parlor and cursed his luck. The air hinted of the odor of kerosene, but Benjamin was in no mood to heed his senses. His stomach grumbled and he headed for the kitchen to fix him-

self some supper, ignoring the telltale signs of leaking
kerosene and the precarious tilting of the top of the
lantern as the bottom heated up.

Chapter Forty-four

The sun was sinking behind the hills to the west by the time Will reached Bowling Green and made his way to the telegraph office. It was near closing time as he approached the building. Will tried to turn the knob and open the door. It was locked. He peered in through the window and saw the clerk inside straightening the counter. He tapped on the glass to draw the man's attention.

The clerk looked up and pointed toward the closed sign, deigning to ignore Will. Will was not going to be put off; he pounded against the door, bringing the scowling clerk.

Cracking the door open just enough to peer out, the clerk frowned. "Don't you read? I'm closed."

"It'll only take you a minute to check whether there's a telegram for me from Black Hawk, Mr. Brennan."

The pudgy man's scowl deepened with resignation. "You always was the determined one, Will."

"Just check."

Brennan shook his head and let Will in. At his desk, he shuffled through the stack of telegraph messages he'd received earlier. Stopping at the second to the last one, he read it before looking up. "You expectin' an answer from one Simeon Dudley out of Black Hawk, Colorado Territory?"

Will ripped the message out of the nosy man's hand. "Yeah. Thanks, Mr. Brennan. This is what I've been waiting for." Will smiled. Now he'd have the funds to ensure Bevin and his future and could reclaim his money clip and watch.

"I expect Benjamin's gonna be right glad that that Dudley fella's sending you the money to join him, seein' as how Benjamin decided not to wed that fancy lady and to hear tell it, now she's linked up with you."

Will glared at the man, causing him to shrink in his shoes. "That fancy lady is going to be my wife, and I suggest you don't forget it, or I might not be so sociable next time."

"Sure, Will. Sorry. No harm done." Brennan followed Will to the door. The instant Will was outside the office the man turned the lock and pulled down the shades.

If the news hadn't been what Will was hoping for, he might not have been so tolerant of the man. But Will was feeling that all was right with the world. He reread the telegram, stuffed it in his pocket and headed toward the mercantile to buy Johnny the rock candy he'd promised the boy before he reclaimed his money clip and watch and then made one last stop at the courthouse to check on the procedure necessary for him and Bevin to adopt Johnny.

Entering the kitchen, Benjamin was still fuming after his conversation with Bevin. He threw together a couple slices of ham and bread and trudged out to the barn where he could still feel at home. The moon

430

illuminated his way, allowing him to forgo a trip back into the parlor for the lantern he had brought in from the barn. Anxious to be out of the house until that fallen woman and her lover were gone, Benjamin decided to stay out there until William returned and he could pay him off and be done with them.

Bevin drifted off to sleep, only to awake choking from a heavy smoke billowing under her door.

"My God!" She rushed to the door and swung it open. Black smoke as thick as soup surrounded her. She slammed the door and screamed, "Johnny! Johnny!"

"Help!" came the hysterical, high-pitched voice filled with terror. "Help me! I can't get out! Help me!"

Her chest heaving with an intense, overpowering fear, Bevin gasped in a breath and ran out into the hall but she could not reach the boy's room. Flames were licking through the floorboards all around her.

She ran back to her room. Quickly she dipped a hankie in the water pitcher and covered her mouth. Her first inclination was to open a window but she knew the air would only draw the fire.

In a frantic effort to comfort the child, she called out, "Johnny, it's going to be okay. Dip one of your hankies into the water pitcher on your dresser and lie down on the floor near your window, but don't open it. Can you do that for me?"

"Yes," came the choking reply.

"Good, now cover your mouth and breathe through the hankie. I'll get to you as soon as I can."

Unable to wait any longer, Bevin managed to es-

cape down the stairs and ran from the house screaming.

Smoke billowed into the sky and ashes drifted onto
her head like snowflakes as she scrambled toward the
barn.

"Benjamin!" she choked. "Benjamin! The house.
Your house is on fire! Help me! You have to help me
get Johnny out!"

She threw open the barn door screaming.

Benjamin caught her up in his arms. "What?" His
vision caught at the skyline glowing above his house.
"My God!"

"Johnny. He's in the house. You've got to help me
get him out."

Digging his fingers into her shoulders, Benjamin
directed, "Take the horse and ride to the Kruegers for
help." When she just stood there, he gave her a
shove. "Get going!"

"But Johnny?"

"Damn it, get going!"

Benjamin grabbed a bucket and ran toward the
house. He yanked open the door and smoke rushed
out. Filling his lungs with air, he entered the house
in an effort to get to the boy before it was too late.

Bevin watched Benjamin's heroic efforts as if in a
trance until reality brought her out of her daze. With
superhuman strength, she mounted a horse and
spurred it toward the Kruegers. She had barely
ridden out of the drive when Asa and Gretchen met
her.

"Fire!" she screamed.

"We was on our way in from the fields and saw it.
Come on, let's get a bucket brigade going," Asa ordered.

Within minutes the three of them were passing

buckets of water from the pump to douse the flames. Benjamin came out of the house empty-handed, his face smudged, his clothes singed.

Bevin let out a bloodcurdling scream. "Johnny!"

Asa caught her and held her back, finally having to shake her. "Get hold of yourself, girl. We'll get the youngun. The fire hain't reached upstairs yet."

Bevin fought to maintain her sanity when the little boy appeared at the window framed in the angry red glow of the flames shooting up behind the other side of the house. "Get down and breathe through your hankie," she screeched.

Despite her desperate efforts, Johnny broke the glass. He was hysterically crying, beyond heeding advice, as Will rode into the yard.

Bevin had all she could do not to desert her post with the buckets and rush into his arms. She passed her sloshing burden to Asa and shouted, "Will, Johnny's inside!"

Will raced onto the porch as Benjamin was coming out for the fourth time. Benjamin grabbed Will. "You can't get to the boy. I've tried, damn it! I've tried everything I can think of."

All animosity was set aside between the two stepbrothers. Will patted Benjamin on the back. "I know."

Not wasting time on talk, Benjamin turned to Gretchen, "Gretchen, go to the barn and get the old blanket hanging behind the door in the tack room. Hurry!"

Gretchen did not question Benjamin, she lifted her skirts and sprinted to the barn and back.

"Bevin, bring that bucket of water here . . . now!"

Will immediately caught on. "You'll never get the boy out through those flames."

"I have to try."

Will blocked the door as behind him the roar of the fire intensified. "You're not going in there."

"Get out of my way!"

"No!"

A beam crashed, sending sparks flying. The men jumped out of the way just in time. Will turned his back on Benjamin to intercept Gretchen just long enough for Benjamin to pick up a flowerpot and smash it over Will's head. As Will fell to the ground, Benjamin said, "It's my house and my responsibility." He looked up at Gretchen. "Give me the blanket and help Bevin get William out of the way."

Benjamin grabbed the blanket out of Gretchen's hands before she could react. He slit a hole in it and draped it over his head. As the women dragged Will off the porch, while Asa flung a shower of water at the flames, Benjamin poured another bucket of water over himself.

An instant later Benjamin was climbing up the old gnarled tree to the left of the porch. He kicked the shards of glass remaining from the bedroom window in, and through the choking smoke disappeared inside the house as other neighbors summoned by Bertha joined in the effort to combat the growing fire.

It seemed like hours before Benjamin reappeared on the limb, coughing. Carrying the limp form of the boy slung over his shoulder, Benjamin managed to shimmy down the tree.

"Oh, God, no!" Bevin screamed. Will had just come around and tried to stop her, but she broke free of him and raced to where Benjamin was laying the deathly still boy on the ground away from the house.

Will caught back up with her and held her, fearing the worst. Johnny's face was ashen in color against the raging firelight and he was not moving. Benjamin

434

loosened the boy's collar and slapped his face.

"Stop it!" Bevin screamed, hysterical. She wrenched out of Will's embrace and pushed Benjamin out of the way. "I'll take care of him," she sobbed and cradled his little body in her arms.

Benjamin got to his feet, glanced at Will, and shrugged before running to join in the efforts to save his house.

"Benjamin," Bevin called out. "Thank you for bringing Johnny out. We'll always be grateful."

He stopped and looked back over his shoulder. Emotionlessly, he said "then leave my house" before he turned away again.

Bevin lifted her gaze to Will, anguish in her face. "You better go help Benjamin. There is nothing you can do here."

Will reached out, then withdrew and grabbed a bucket.

Bevin sat on the cold ground, held the boy tight against her bosom, and prayed as the frantic actions of those around her took on a surreal quality. Somehow it seemed that the fire signified her life; it became symbolic of her careful design, her goals. All her nice, neat little plans, too, had gone up in smoke. Then her mind shifted to thoughts of the Phoenix, and she prayed.

More folks arrived with buckets and shovels and set about dousing the blaze. She caught sight of Will taking a bucket and leaping onto the porch.

"No!" Bevin screamed. "Don't go in there, you'll be killed."

Her heart in her throat, she watched him ignore her and dash into the house time and time again. Each time he returned to the porch, he was choking and gasping for breath. Benjamin brought Will a

435

bucket and seconds later they both disappeared inside.

The two men came out carrying Benjamin's favorite chair. Will's shirttails suddenly flared.

"Gretchen, quick, over here with that bucket," Benjamin hollered.

"Gretchen, get over here . . . now," her father called out from the front of the brigade.

The girl did not hesitate, she immediately ran to Benjamin. He yanked the pail out of her hands and sloshed the water on Will.

"Girl, quit standing around and get back to work!" Asa hollered.

Gretchen looked to Benjamin. He gave her the hint of a smile. Grabbing her hand, he said, "Come on, together I think we still might be able to salvage part of the house."

Will ignored the burning pain in his back and joined the others battling the blaze.

Continuing to hug Johnny's face against her bosom, Bevin cried inside that it had taken a tragedy for the two stepbrothers to set aside their animosities and work together, if even for a short while. As she rocked back and forth, a muffled choking issued from Johnny. Holding back a sob she held him from her.

"Oh, God, you're alive. You're going to be all right," she cried and hugged the child to her. She caught sight of Will and joyously sang out, "Johnny's going to be okay; he's coming around."

Miss Bevin was hanging onto him so tight she was going to squeeze the life out of him, Johnny thought, trying to pull away and gasping for breath. Pushing with all his strength, he finally managed to break her hold.

"Johnny, I was so afraid you weren't going to wake

up; you inhaled so much smoke." She sniffled. "Thank God, you're going to be all right." She wiped back her tears.

She tried to hug him again, but he cocked his head back and with eyes wide, said, "If you don't quit huggin' on me, I am gonna croak, 'cause you're cuttin' off my air with all that mushy stuff."

Through her misty eyes, Bevin once again thought of the Phoenix and how it had risen through the ashes. She said a prayer of thanks as Will joined them on the ground and they all hugged. Surely, Benjamin would forgive them now and they could begin mending the rift and be a real family. No sooner had the thought entered her mind than Benjamin's grating question assaulted her ears.

"What did you hope to gain by trying to burn down my house?"

Bevin's head snapped up. Benjamin stood over them, his shirt singed, his face smudged, his expression tightly fixed on her. Behind him, the house smoldered with wisps of smoke drifting up into the black night.

Will opened his mouth to reply, but Bevin interceded. "No, please let me answer."

She climbed to her feet. "I did not attempt to burn down your home. Johnny and I could have been killed in that dreadful fire. It started downstairs."

"How do I know that?" Benjamin sneered.

Will was not about to remain on the sidelines any longer. "Because that was where we were battling the blaze. In the parlor to be exact."

Gretchen came up behind Benjamin and without a word began spreading salve over his burned palms and bandaging his hands. While Benjamin absently allowed the girl to minister to him he thought back to the lantern he had brought in from the barn and the memory of knocking it over, and he grudgingly had to admit he was at fault.

Bevin was furious that Benjamin could think her capable of such treachery and gave him a thorough scolding, ending with, "And if you weren't so blinded by the anger in your heart, you could see how much you're loved." Her gaze shot directly to Gretchen.

Benjamin followed her line of vision. Then he silently studied Bevin as she helped the boy up.

Gretchen shifted uneasily and stammered, "Ma said to tell you all you can stay at our place tonight."

"Thank you. Come on, Will, I need to see to the burns you sustained helping your stepbrother save his house, and we need to get Johnny in bed."

As they walked toward the Kruegers' wagon, Bevin could not help but consider all that they had overcome in such a short period of time. Surely once they moved from the farm the adversity they had endured would be behind them. Nothing else could possibly be put in their way to test their love.

Chapter Forty-five

Will and Bevin remained at the Kruegers' overnight, turning down an offer to stay longer. Early in the morning they said their good-byes to the kind farm family and a tearful Tara, gathered up Johnny, and headed for a hotel in town. In the borrowed wagon, they traveled slowly over the rutted road.

"Gretchen and I spent some time talking after she returned last night," Bevin said. She waited for Will to display some interest.

He did not respond.

She forged ahead. "Benjamin seems to have finally noticed Gretchen. She's pretty excited. Although he hasn't declared his feelings, she mentioned that he said he had to bring me out from back East to finally realize he never should have considered an outsider." At that Will squeezed her hand. "Gretchen said Benjamin asked if he would be welcomed if in the future he might call on her. I hope he does decide to call on her; she would be so good for him."

"Only someone with your soft heart could be so forgiving," Will grunted.

"Bearing grudges serves no purpose. I asked Gretchen if she thinks he'll ever be able to forgive us. She said that Benjamin is still filled with a lot of anger. Although she hopes someday he may be able to set aside his bitterness so we can become family."

Will shook his head, rolling his eyes. "Despite everything, you'd really like that, wouldn't you?"

"After growing up alone, being part of a family is important to me."

"You have Patrick and Prudence now."

The thought warmed her heart. "Yes, and I would like to add Benjamin too. But the most important thing is for us"—she motioned to Will and Johnny—"to be a family and have a permanent home someday."

Doubting the possibility of Benjamin ever coming around, Will brightened at the change of subjects. "That, my love, you will be happy to learn, I have already taken care of."

"You have? When? How? Where?"

Will pulled her close to him on the wagon box. "While I was in town yesterday I received an answer to a telegram I had sent my partner in Black Hawk, just outside Denver."

"I didn't know you had a partner."

He winked. "There is a lot we have to learn about each other, love. But in answer to your question, Simeon Dudley and I were working a mine together in Black Hawk when I got the letter about my inheritance. When I learned I would be in need of a home, I sent him a wire. I didn't want to say anything until I knew for sure I would have a home to take you to, and I finally got the confirmation."

"How long ago did you send the telegram?"

"A couple of weeks."

"You were that sure I would give up the security Benjamin offered?" she puzzled, since she had not been as confident as he had.

He stopped the wagon and looked into her eyes. "I

440

never doubted you'd find your security in our love."

"William Parrish Shoemaker, you are a pretty smart man."

He snapped the reins over the horse's rump, jerking the wagon into motion again. "I picked you, didn't I?"

She cuddled into the crook of his arm. "Are you so sure you did the picking?"

There was no need for a response.

"Will, for the first time in my life I don't care whether I have a roof over my head or not as long we're all together."

"I'm happy to hear it, but we are the proud owners of a roomy house and yard in Black Hawk, Colorado Territory, not to mention the fact that you are going to be the wife of half owner of the now very profitable Golden Spur mine; seems Simeon hit a vein while I've been away. We won't have to worry about running out of money."

Johnny let out an audible gasp.

Will leaned back and ruffled Johnny's hair. "I also stopped by the courthouse and got the paperwork started to adopt you, runt." He turned from Johnny back to Bevin. "When we leave Bowling Green we'll be a real family. Married with a kid and home to go to."

Johnny perked up. "Do you think we can ever go back and visit Crissy?"

Emotion threatened to overcome Bevin. She knew it took a lot of courage for Johnny to mention the little sister he loved so dearly. "Of course, we can."

"First trip back this way we'll make a stop in Ashland, runt," Will seconded.

"Really? And you think Benjamin would let me have Sourdough?" Johnny asked, excited and expectant.

"We couldn't leave Sourdough behind." They hit a rut, refocusing Will's attention on the road. He smiled inside. A month ago he had been drifting through life, now he was about to have a wife, a kid and a dog.

It was a good feeling.

Once they were settled in adjoining rooms at the Kentuckian Hotel, they went out to fetch Aunt Bessie. In an intimate ceremony before the priest Bevin had requested, Aunt Bessie, Johnny and a few witnesses already on hand, Will and Bevin were married. After a wedding luncheon at the hotel restaurant, they returned Aunt Bessie to her house.

They had one more important thing to do today.

In spite of the chill in the air they glowed as they mounted the steps to the courthouse late in the afternoon to appear before the judge in order to finalize Johnny's adoption papers.

Bevin presented the papers to the haggard-faced man sitting on the bench and stepped back. Her heart pounded with anticipation. Another few minutes and her life's circle would be complete. Will. Patrick. Johnny. A home. She could barely breathe as the judge perused the papers and picked up his pen.

To her utter dismay, the juror set the pen down without signing the documents. "Is this the same boy Benjamin Straub came to see me about adopting?"

Bevin was beginning to tremble, sensing her world was about to break apart yet another time. Benjamin had mentioned nothing to her about seeing the judge.

Will squeezed her hand. "Johnny has been living at Mr. Straub's farm, your honor."

"Then this is the boy for whom Mr. Straub picked up papers nearly two weeks ago." The judge looked directly at Johnny, who had taken up residence behind Bevin's skirts. Frowning, the man said, "Once Mr. Straub reurns the signed documents, this child legally will be required to reside at the farm with Mr. Straub who will be the child's legal parent."

"No!" Bevin and Johnny cried in unison.

Frightened that the man would take him away from Miss Bevin and Will, Johnny scurried as fast as his foot would allow from the room.

"I'll get him," Will offered and followed, hot on the boy's heels.

Frantic and fighting to regain the composure of an informed Children's Aid Society worker, Bevin stepped up closer to the judge. "Since Mr. Straub has not yet returned the papers, can't you simply sign the ones we've presented to the court today? It is obvious the boy is in our custody, not with Benjamin Straub. Surely you can see the child has developed a strong bond with Mr. Shoemaker and myself, and therefore should be allowed to remain as a part of our family."

Uneasily, the juror cleared his throat before pounding the gavel with finality. "I am sorry. There is nothing further I can do. Since neither of you is known to this court, it remains Mr. Straub's decision. Until he informs this court of his intentions, I am afraid you will be forced to take the matter up with the man himself. This court stands in adjournment."

His black robe billowing out behind him, the man swept from the room, leaving Bevin in tears. She was numbed by the knowledge that Benjamin's bitterness could very well stand in the way of keeping Johnny.

A damper had fallen over their wedding night despite Bevin's attempts to appear cheerful and reassure Johnny everything would be straightened out in the morning. She had been tense during their lovemaking and Will swore to ride out and see Benjamin first thing the next morning.

A light mist fell on Will as he rode the white horse he had rented at the livery toward the farm. Bevin had insisted she accompany him. He knew she would not be pleased to learn he had not awakened her before he left after insisting she go to Johnny when a nightmare caused the boy to cry out in the night.

The charred shell of the once tidy farmhouse came into view as Will prodded the slow horse up the drive. Against the cold, gray morning, the sad structure looked vacant and seemed almost haunted by better days. A light echoed from the barn and Will headed toward it.

"What are you doing back here?" Benjamin snapped. His heavy work jacket was pulled up around his neck and he held a pail filled with slop for the hogs.

Will dismounted and faced Benjamin. "It seems we have unfinished business."

Benjamin glowered. "Farm's not worth as much today as it was yesterday, if that's why you came."

"Can we go inside and discuss it?"

"I'm living in the barn until I can restore the house."

"Then it wasn't a total loss."

Benjamin stiffened. "If you're looking for gratitude, don't bother to follow me inside."

They walked in silent reflection. It was warm in the tack room where Benjamin kept a potbelly stove to ward off the chill during the winter months he spent in his special room. Will shrugged out of his jacket and warmed his hands. Benjamin did not remove his. Instead, he withdrew a stack of bills from an envelope on a table near the sawhorse.

Holding out the money, Benjamin said harshly, "Say what you came to say, I've got work to do."

Will took the bills and absently counted them. Half the amount they had agreed upon was there. "Gener-

444

ous to a fault," he mumbled.

"It's what your half of the farm's worth the way the house is now."

Will thrust the money back into Benjamin's hand. "You can keep the money. You'll need it to rebuild."

Benjamin looked suspicious. "Half the farm's yours, and you already took my woman: What else do you want from me?"

Will held up two fingers, replying, "Two things."

Will was not surprised when he sighted Bevin and Johnny heading toward him in the Kruegers' wagon as he rode back in the direction of town. The sun had broken through and made Bevin's red hair seem as if it were on fire. Much like her temper, no doubt, when she had awakened and discovered he had gone to see Benjamin without her.

As he neared them, Will could see Johnny's little face. It was gaunt and dark circles ringed eyes red from crying. Although Will had known it before, there was no mistaking that Johnny really was just a frightened little boy underneath that hoodlum-in-miniature exterior.

"Mr. Shoemaker," Bevin hissed as he rode up alongside the wagon. "How dare you sneak out on us like that!"

Will held back a grin. "Actually, it wasn't easy what with you leaving the adjoining door open and being such a light sleeper. I had to tiptoe out with my shoes in hand and then—"

"Will you stop trying to keep us in suspense, and explain what happened between you and Benjamin?" she demanded.

"God, I love it when your face matches your hair."

445

"Will!"

He flashed his brows. "Okay. Okay. I love it any time."

In a huff, she snapped, "If you don't tell me immediately I'm going to drive on to the farm and ask Benjamin personally!"

"Somehow I don't believe Benjamin is ready to be receptive to any overtures yet."

She narrowed her eyes and snapped the reins over the horse.

"Wait!" Will called out. "You win. You won! We all won!"

Bevin pulled back hard on the reins. "We did?"

Johnny whooped, "Hooray! I knew you'd best old Benjamin. I knew it all along."

Will tied the horse to the back of the wagon and climbed onto the seat with Bevin and the child. "I didn't best Benjamin, runt. We came to a mutual agreement."

Will turned and whistled, then waited. Moments later Sourdough broke from the bushes, wagging a singed tail. Johnny jumped down and ran to the old dog, ringing his little arms around the mutt's neck.

Bevin cried with joy and Will shrugged. "Benjamin and I made a deal. I relinquished all claim to my half of the farm and he relinquished all claim to Johnny and Sourdough."

Raining kisses over his face, Bevin cried, "I love you!"

"Then perhaps you have to admit that some childish fantasies do come true."

Bevin looked puzzled.

"Remember back on the train coming here when you said that you didn't believe in tall, dark, handsome knights on white chargers saving the day?"

She hesitated before answering "Yes."

446

"Well, if you'll look at my horse, you'll see its white. And you can't possibly contest the fact that I am tall, dark and handsome."

She fought to suppress a wide grin. "I suppose that's true. I can't."

He withdrew a set of papers from his pocket and waved them in the air. "With mighty skill I slayed the dragon and saved the day," he boasted.

"You slayed the dragon with paper?"

He showed her the signature giving them Johnny. "The pen is mightier than the sword, it's said."

She could not help herself, a giggle burst from her lips and she hugged him. "Oh, Will, I never doubted you would convince Benjamin to let us keep Johnny . . . and Sourdough."

Will laughed. "That's why you were heading out to Benjamin's farm with such determination in your eyes, right?"

After a day of making arrangements to leave for their new home and celebrating all over again, Will and Bevin were standing in their hotel room, Will pressing a lingering kiss to Bevin's lips until the door crashed open and in marched Johnny.

Will frowned down at the persistent boy. His brow arched and he had to laugh. "I guess the first order of business when we get to our new home will be to install a good-size lock on the bedroom door."

"I learned to pick locks a long time ago," Johnny crowed, unimpressed.

"Not the one I'm going to get."

Bevin grinned up at Will, loving him with all her heart. But when he left her side, took Johnny's hand and started for the door, confusion dropped over her.

"Where are you going?" she asked.

Will winked. "Don't move a muscle, I'll be right back."

He turned back to Johnny and tightened his hold on the recalcitrant boy. "Now, you and I, young man, are going to have milk and cookies in the restaurant downstairs. Then the first lesson you are going to learn is the importance of never disturbing your ma and pa when they are about to take a nap."

The eight-year-old screwed up his face and slapped his free balled fist on his hip. "I ain't no halfwit, you know. I lived on them streets long enough to know what you got on your minds."

"Good." Will chuckled at the boy's apparent perception. "In that case, runt, here's a quarter." Will dug into his pocket and tossed the coin to Johnny. "Get your own milk and cookies."

Johnny was speechless when Will gently shoved him from the room and closed the door in his face.

Bevin watched, hiding a smile, as Will dragged a chair over to the door and propped it under the doorknob. He turned to her with a wide grin on his face.

"Just a little insurance, I suppose," she said.

Moving to rejoin his bride, Will said, "No, my dear wife, a lot of insurance. There'll be no further interruptions while we go to work and try to make another urchin to keep that one company when we want to nap."

Bevin could not help herself, a giggle erupted from deep within her throat, and she circled his neck.

"I'm going to love the notion you have of *work*."

"In that case, what are we waiting for?"